The Legacy of the Talents

The Legacy of the Talents

GILL KNOX

Matador
9 Priory Business Park,
Wistow Road
Kibworth Beauchamp
Leicester LE8 0RX, UK
Tel: (+44) 116 279 2299
Fax: (+44) 116 279 2277
Email: books@troubador.co.uk
Web: www.troubador.co.uk/matador

ISBN 978 1848766 068

British Library Cataloguing in Publication Data.
A catalogue record for this book is available from the British Library.

Typeset in 11pt Palatino by Troubador Publishing Ltd, Leicester, UK

Matador is an imprint of Troubador Publishing Ltd

Printed in Great Britain by the MPG Books Group, Bodmin and King's Lynn

To Brian, with love.

"For the kingdom of heaven is as a man travelling into a far country, who called his own servants, and delivered unto them his goods. And unto one he gave five talents, to another two, and to another one; to every man according to his several ability; and straightway took his journey."

Chapter 25 v. 14-15 King James Version of the Bible

PART ONE

Spring 1986

"So there you are, gentlemen, the prize is Blayborough House!" Mr. Paul Winstanley leant back in his leather upholstered chair and smiled smugly at his two clients. His junior partner, John Bates, likewise peered across the table feeling somewhat jolly at the thought of the fat fee which would result from this particular will – the charges would be on-going and rather juicy.

Charles, the eldest brother, was the first to recover his composure. His handsome face broke into a wry grin. Ralph, however, only felt a sense of foreboding and requested that Mr. Winstanley, of Parker, Jones and Winstanley, Solicitors and Commissioners of Oaths, should repeat the terms of the will again.

"Certainly," was the reply, as indeed anything which lengthened the interview and so upped the fees that would be recoverable from the estate of the late Sir John Augustus Pearson-Cooper was to be agreed. Mr. Winstanley had at one time wondered about installing in his office a machine akin to a taxi meter, but rejected the idea in favour of the vaguer accumulation of time equals money; such an equation seemed to bring him almost limitless income.

"The first part of the will does not particularly concern you, so I will not go through that again. The second part is all about who will inherit Blayborough House and its 20,000 acres with ten tenanted farms, home farm cottages, shooting rights and fishing rights etc. etc. What I would describe as a remarkably self-sufficient estate by all accounts."

Mr. Winstanley paused there to observe the two brothers. Charles Pearson-Cooper was now looking totally composed, there was not flutter in this manner, no pounding of his chest could be seen under his hand-tailored shirt; Ralph Pearson-Cooper was visibly sweating – his hair-line, even in its receded position, was quite damp and there was a definite motion and movement under his C & A shirt.

"Then the will is perfectly clear – 'to all my sons I leave £100,000' – in a sort of biblical fashion but more even and fairer…"

Charles interrupted, quoting from the Bible the parable of the talents, to which John Bates added, "St. Matthew, Chapter 25," when he had finished. With a smile, Bates knowingly continued, more for Ralph's benefit than the others, "The advantage of an Eton education!"

"Yes, quite," Mr. Winstanley, educated in a minor public school, was somewhat sensitive about those so-called advantages and indeed was rather inclined to halt the ever upward march of John Bates to prove his point. Talents – God given – were the new order of the day. The old boy network was not going to pull weight in his practice, not while he did not have a network worth pulling weight with! "Let's get back to the will. To the sons, there are cheques waiting. You have two years to create wealth with it. In two years' time, supported with account books, bank books, all certified etc. etc. – all conditions are written down and I will give you a copy – the one who has created the most money wins Blayborough House! The losers have to return the money, plus interest, to the winning brother. Incidentally, there are provisions within the will for the continual upkeep of the estate – I won't bore you with those details but suffice to say that everything will be in apple pie order for the winner!"

Ralph and Charles took stock of each other. This was the first time that they had met and each disapproved of the other. Ralph immediately disliked the way that Charles was so composed, as if such a will was normal everyday procedure. Also, if truth was known, he was uneasy about the whole business – surely, he privately reckoned, any man who can look so cool, when faced with a competition to make as much money as possible in two years and so gain nothing short of a stately home, must be nearly halfway to the winning post already. Charles, for his part, considered Ralph to be both odious and common.

"What about my other brother, James?" enquired Charles, after taking his half closed eyes off Ralph and focusing them on Mr. Winstanley. "Or more to the point, where is James?"

"We have his last known address in Australia and we will send him the details but the cheque, of course, will be left in a British bank for the conditions do stipulate that the wealth has to be accumulated in Britain and the £100,000 must remain in Britain at all times."

"Tell me again what happens if you come second…" began Ralph nervously.

"Don't you mean third?" smirked Charles.

"I was thinking about you!" retorted Ralph but without much conviction.

"Gentlemen, please, don't resort to nastiness," pleaded Mr. Winstanley. "If you come second or third," and he paused whilst glancing at both of the clients, "then you forfeit not only the original £100,000 but also the compounded accrued interest!"

This time, even Charles began to look just a shade uneasy!

* * *

As Ralph and Mr. Winstanley both left the room – one in search of port and glasses, the other in pursuit of the gents – John Bates sidled up to Charles.

"Strange thing, this will of your father's."

"Bloody stupid!"

"Of course for a man in your position…" began Bates suggestively.

"Yes, I know what you are trying to say – winning should not be a problem but…"

"But why should you have to put yourself through hoops? Is that what you're thinking?" John Bates wet his lips a little, allowing the words to linger in the air. He stared at his compatriot, his fellow Old Etonian, "Hoops are for performing animals, for the Ralphs and Jameses of this world…"

"What I need," began Charles, raising his profile so that he could stare down at the slimy Bates, "is someone who will remove the hoops!"

* * *

Winstanley returned, clutching a decanter of port and five glasses. Ralph, composure nearly regained, followed closely behind. Winstanley poured out the port which he retained for just such occasions as this. He passed a full glass to each of the men present and clutched two glasses himself.

"Raise your glasses, gentlemen – I'm raising two,

one on behalf of James – and the toast is 'the winner'."

"To the winner," murmured Ralph, John Bates and Winstanley – twice. Charles smiled in acknowledgement – no point, he thought, in toasting himself!

* * *

Paul Winstanley showed Ralph to the door. They went through the general office, where typists sat shuffling papers as soon as they heard the firm steps of the senior partner coming down the corridor, to the large front door. The Georgian wooden structure kept the masses firmly at bay – as did the fees – and Ralph shook hands with Winstanley before returning to find his car.

He took the parking ticket, carefully placed under his wiper, to be a bad omen.

* * *

Bates picked up the large envelope with the Australian address on. "Australia is a long way away," he purred.

"An extra hoop away," agreed Charles.

Bates pressed the intercom button and spoke into it.

"Mary, there is a letter here for Australia."

"Australia?" she queried, as if it was another planet and not just the other side of the world.

"Yes, dear, Australia."

"But how many stamps shall I put on?"

"Just one first class stamp will do – they are in the Commonwealth, after all!" John Bates glanced up at Charles and smiled. He switched the intercom off.

"That should delay things a bit! Just a tiny gesture to demonstrate how useful I could be to you…"

* * *

Ralph drove slowly back to the engineering factory in Leeds. He needed time to think – basically, to think about the unfairness of it all. Here he was, thirty-five years old, having led an upright life but blessed by the Almighty with both a father and father-in-law who produced odd wills. Ralph's father's will was not such a shock – not in that sense – due to the fact that he did not know this Sir John Augustus Pearson-Cooper at all. Ralph had never clapped an eye on his father in his whole life. So he was not exactly expecting to hear that he had inherited a fortune after he had been informed that his father had died.

Then Ralph thought about his father-in-law's will. Ezra had died two years ago and left his daughter Amelia, Ralph's wife, fifty-one per cent of the shares of the firm, the Wilkinson Engineering Works; forty-nine per cent of the shares were left in an employee share scheme; and zero per cent went to Ralph, in spite of the fact that he had worked in the company all his life and was married to Amelia. Why had this happened? Ralph knew why! It was all a plot by the solicitors – Spencer and Spencer – who handled the Wilkinson's legal affairs, it was a plot to get their own back on Ralph and make sure that he did not profit from his marriage. It was a plot to do him out of his rightful money.

Ralph yanked his car into gear and sped off from yet another set of lights. Yes, he thought to himself, I was diddled out of Ezra's money just because Amelia chose to marry me and not marry into that wretched solicitor family. Diddled because she turned down John Spencer of Spencer and Spencer, Solicitors. Diddled because the Spencer family saw the Wilkinson Engineering Works as a wealthy company and wanted their son to have a part of it. And Ralph tried to put his car into an imaginary sixth gear, grating the gearbox in the process, "Employee share scheme! Huh! A scheme which I can't join! Spencer and Spencer made sure of that in the will. John Spencer – I thwarted you and married your girl!" And Ralph put his foot down on the pedal to give the car some extra oomph, only succeeding in causing it to make weird noises. "Then you thwarted me and made sure I didn't get the business."

Ralph had another bash at sixth gear and failed again. Then, as he drove along in fifth, he mused about how Amelia was quite flattered by the fifty-one per cent shareholding and the power it gave her.

* * *

Charles plonked himself in the leather armchair. "What ever happened to the right of primogeniture?" he muttered as he took another swig of the port. "I'm the oldest. I should have Blayborough House – with its cottages, acreage and money." Mr. Winstanley removed the port decanter from the reach of his client.

"What did the old fool think he was doing?"

"Hardly an old fool, Charles!" reproached Mr. Winstanley.

Charles sneered in reply and reached for where he thought the port was.

"You are driving, aren't you?" reproved the solicitor.

"I need comfort!" scowled Charles but he accepted the need to halt his drinking and instead launched further into the issue of the rights of the firstborn.

"Your father did not die intestate; and in any case, if he had done, think of the taxes you would have had to pay – so that issue does not come into it," advised the solicitor.

"I believe in the right of primogeniture!" stated Charles.

"All firstborn sons usually do!" smiled Mr. Winstanley indulgently. "But such a thing was more suited to feudal times, not to today's modern world."

"You can't get anything much more feudal than the Blayborough estate."

Mr. Winstanley nodded his head in agreement. The door opened and Paul Winstanley's up and coming junior star entered. Mr. Winstanley decided that he had had enough for today and wanted to return home to his garden. He rose and strode out of the room, managing to whisper to John Bates on the way.

"He's slightly pickled – been at my port – and somewhat melancholy," he murmured, "so I'll leave him to you." With that, he left the office, thinking to himself that Bates did have some uses.

Charles gestured to the seat next to him. "Sit yourself down here, John." John did as he was told, eager to be of help for helpfulness was seen as an investment to John Bates. "Oh, and by the way, thanks for slowing that letter up."

"Not at all – like I said, it was a small token…"

Charles smiled in acknowledgement and then continued on the theme that had been troubling him previously.

"Do you know what?" asked Charles.

John confessed that he did not.

"I am the only one out of the three of us to have lived in Blayborough House. Just think of that!"

John leant back in his chair and let the port inside Charles talk.

"It was my tiny feet that pottered along the corridors – not theirs! Ralph never set foot inside the house – not one foot!" There was a pause.

"I used to ride my toy tractor up and down the corridors – again and again – and do you know what father said? Do you know?"

"No," answered John.

"He turned to my mother and said that one day I'll be riding a real tractor around the Blayborough estate. Around the estate, mark you! When I was five, he was thinking of leaving it all to me, so what possessed him to change his mind? What did I do wrong? Heavens above, I even look like him – which is more than you can say of that idiot!" shouted Charles, gesticulating towards the door.

"Ralph, do you mean?" inquired John, for he could think of another idiot who had just left through that doorway.

"Of course I mean Ralph!" Charles drew himself up to his full height, straightening his back, "Blayborough House is mine – I'll be damned if I am going to let either of them get their hands on it. It's mine by right!"

Determination was by now etched on to Charles' face. His lips had set into a hardened line and his eyes glared. His handsomeness had reduced; his hard and arrogant featured face had increased in intensity. John Bates saw his chance, his main chance.

"Then you will have to win the house back."

"Luck – Lady Luck – is that how I've got to do it, with the help of that fickle woman."

Bates smiled slightly. "Come, come, now, Mr Pearson-Cooper – you did not get to where you are now with just the help of Lady Luck or with hard work…" He let the words linger.

Charles turned his eyes towards Bates, lifting his head in that superior fashion that always got him what he wanted from his fag at Eton.

"Yes?" inquired Charles, unwilling to reveal more than just a flicker of interest lest he was being led up the wrong path.

"Successful outcomes are not just the result of luck and work."

"And?" Charles lifted one eyebrow, urging Bates to continue.

Now it was time for Bates to sweat – he was not used to dealing with someone who was the master of the superior position and he was somewhat unsure of how to approach the next stage. Suffice to say, he knew that he was on the right track with what he was starting to suggest and he wanted to make sure that he, Bates, shared the track with Charles.

"And," began Bates, "life is a question of manipulating situations."

"You always were a dung beetle Bates!" and with that Charles turned away disdainfully.

Beads of sweat started to become visible on the solicitor's forehead. He had gone too far, he knew it. It had happened before, not with Pearson-Cooper, for Bates was more than a year junior to him at Eton, but with someone else when he was a teenager and Bates recognised the signs. That time it was the finding out that some chap's father was not who he purported to be – a little elementary blackmail in order to get Maths prep. done for the rest of term was what Bates had attempted. The plan had backfired and Bates felt the nervousness in his stomach now, as he did then, in his third year at Eton College. After that, Bates developed the technique of being extraordinarily helpful in order to further his advancement – so helpful, that the recipients of such favours were obliged to return the gesture; a return that John Bates made sure was hundredfold.

"But I suppose dung beetles have their usefulness!" volunteered Charles.

The sweat started to evaporate on Bates' face.

"They remove human dirt…" agreed Bates.

* * *

Ralph continued on the road back to the engineering works in Leeds. The cheque was still in his breast pocket and indeed he had given little thought to what he was going to do with it. The competition, if that was what it was, was perfectly clear. Use the £100,000 and show how you have used it and the one who makes the most with that money gains the Blayborough Estate; lose, and the money plus interest has to be returned.

The traffic lights turned from green to amber and Ralph slowed down. The oncoming red light afforded him time to think. Life was complicated enough running the Wilkinson works, without having to think of ways of creating a fortune. He could do without this extra little problem. His eyes lighted on a branch of the local building society and he put two and two together and came up with £100,000 plus interest in five years' time.

He pulled into the nearest car park and wandered over to the building society. He had not chosen it for any other reason than it was the nearest one to the car park and the one that he had spotted.

He waited patiently in the queue. The other customers were obviously quite well-heeled – this was a prosperous area and wealth was cunningly concealed behind high hedges and long driveways. He himself lived in not quite as good an area as this – middle-class but not moneyed class as this so certainly was. The lady just behind him was impeccably coiffured, she carried her dog under one arm whilst the other arm juggled with a multiplicity of account books. Ralph was impressed and secretly congratulated himself on having found such a good home for his cheque.

"Next please."

Ralph trotted obediently over to the vacant desk.

"I want to open an account please," he said and handed over the cheque.

The cashier did not bat an eyelid when she saw the amount – she just informed him that he would have to open two accounts. Large sums of money meant nothing to her in this area.

She advised him on the type of account which was to be one of those which tied the money up for a few years, removal of a penny resulting in immediate loss of the top rate of interest and Ralph duly began to inform her of his name and address.

"Pearson-Cooper?" she asked.

"Yes, that's right," he confirmed.

"That's funny – my mum works for a Charles Pearson-Cooper," she commented, showing quite a large flicker of interest. "That's a coincidence, isn't it?"

"Yes, he will be…" began Ralph.

"I bet you wish you were related to him!"

Ralph decided not to admit to anything – ignorance can be rewarded by knowledge.

"My mum says that he's rolling in it!"

"Does she?" Ralph smiled for he was growing somewhat interested in this brother of his. All these years they had lived within twenty miles of each other and had never known of each other's existence and in just one day, he had both met this Charles Pearson-Cooper and a whole family of his admirers!

"She told me that he told her – if you follow me?"

Ralph assured her that he did.

"That today he expected to hear that he had inherited the Blayborough Estate and…"

"There's more?" asked Ralph.

"Yes," confided the cashier, "he asked my mum if she would like to work for the family at Blayborough House. My mum is over the moon, as you can imagine. I mean, we'd all give our eye's teeth to work there, I mean, I bet you wish you weren't born on the other side of the tracks!" She meant quite a lot, this cashier, but at that precise moment, to Ralph she meant someone that he wished to throttle!

Ralph started to go red – anger and fury bubbled up inside him. The audacity of the man and to think that he, Ralph, had been thinking of giving up Blayborough without a fight.

"I'll put that money on instant access, please!" was the best that he could say and even those words jerked out in deep set annoyance. "I need to invest it, to double and triple it, in better places than here!"

The cashier threw the original forms into the bin and reached for another.

They continued the job of form filling in silence.

When the books were duly entered, Ralph announced to the startled cashier, "And you can tell your mother that Blayborough House is no more his than mine or James'."

The cashier opened her mouth in astonishment. The lady with the blue-coloured rinse, who had been gazing out of the window, spun round so swiftly that she dropped all her building society books and her dog.

"And, what's more, when I get it, I shall not be employing servants – your mother, yourself or anyone else for that matter!"

Ralph stormed out of the door, leaving it ajar for the Pekinese to escape into the traffic.

"Cleo, come here, come here!" cried the blue-rinsed matron.

"Was it something I said?" muttered the cashier.

The manager strolled in from his office, ready to point the accusing finger.

Ralph stormed back to his car, oblivious to the mess he had left behind.

* * *

Charles was helped into his Jaguar Sovereign by his poodle of a solicitor. Well, that is how Charles saw him but in reality, John Bates was more of a rottweiler in poodle's clothing.

"Are you sure you can manage?" simpered Bates, for the last thing that he wanted was for his recently found benefactor to get himself squashed under a lorry.

"Of course, this car can drive itself!"

"It certainly is very beautiful, like a large silky cat." John admired its sleek black lines.

"It purrs too, listen." Charles switched the engine on. It did indeed purr.

"I expect you'd like one of these," suggested Charles.

John smiled in agreement; he knew he'd get one of these and Charles Pearson-Cooper was going to provide the means. They would work together, thought Bates, only Charles Pearson-Cooper would not know that, he would think that Bates was working for him, until it was too late. Then the cat would show its claws... and he, John Bates, would be the one to slink off into the sunset in a Jaguar.

"I'll be in touch," smiled Bates, whilst patting the big cat goodbye for the moment...

* * *

Meanwhile, at the Charles Pearson-Cooper household, his wife, Fiona, could be heard complaining.

"Really, Mrs Armitage, if you are hoping to follow us to Blayborough House then you had better get your dusting improved!"

"I'm sorry, Mrs Pearson-Cooper but it is this polish – can't I use spray instead of a tin, like I do at home?"

Fiona, pouring scorn on that suggestion, said that spray polish may be alright for MFI furniture but not for hers, and certainly not for when they moved to Blayborough.

* * *

With his money safely invested, Ralph made himself confront another problem. Should he tell his wife about the money or not? He had told her that his father had died – but his father, dead or alive was a subject of total indifference to Amelia. She had long since ceased to be interested in the Pearson-Cooper family tree.

Ralph decided to keep the little matter of the money secret. If he did, in two years' time, prove the successful one of the brothers then Amelia would be surprised and delighted with the present. If, as could be the case, he was not successful then Amelia would be none the wiser. He could keep his self-esteem intact. If he informed Amelia of the competition then her hopes and expectations would be raised. She would expect him to win. She would leave him if he did not.

So Ralph reasoned that secrecy was the best policy.

* * *

The Jaguar pulled itself effortlessly into the drive and drew to a relaxed halt outside the doric portico that graced the front door. Charles alighted and walked slowly towards the waiting Fiona.

"Darling, welcome home!" she murmured, as if he had been away for years. "Or should I say welcome to our old home!"

Charles grimaced internally.

"Tell me all about it!" The two of them walked arm in arm up the steps into the hall. In front of them the staircase swept upwards to the five bedrooms on the first floor; the attic rooms were reached via a staircase from the kitchen.

Charles followed his wife into the morning room

and settled himself down in the sumptuous armchair. She poured him a whisky. He still had not spoken.

"Well, then?" she prompted.

"Father had obviously gone senile…" began Charles.

"Good God, you don't mean to say he left it all to that little floozy at the Nag's Head do you? The one with the ginger hair and overgrown cleavage?" cried Fiona.

"No, no," Charles shook his head.

"Then you must mean the nurse who used to come and cut his toenails," suggested Fiona.

"No!" shouted Charles. "how do you know about those two anyway? If I hadn't seen him for forty-odd years, how come you know all about his sex life?"

"I was brought up to keep a strict tab on one's fortune. Sir John was our fortune – even though he refused to see any of us!" She could see that her husband, who was leaning forward in his armchair, was looking slightly bemused. "My masseuse at the health club, his sister is the nurse who used to cut the old boy's toenails and the barmaid at the Nag's Head – the floozy, remember – is our milkman's much shared ex-wife!"

Now it was Charles' turn to stutter, "Good God!"

"Well, then?" Fiona prompted again.

"He's set a sort of competition…" began Charles, at a loss to explain the whys and wherefores of this complicated will that his father had devised.

"A competition? Then the old fool must have gone senile!"

"I think you're probably right there, Fiona," agreed Charles.

"And, pray, what is the prize?" inquired his wife.

"The Blayborough Estate!"

Fiona sat down on the coffee table, something which, had the boys done it, would have brought immediate retribution.

"Good grief!" She was visibly shocked and her aristocratic features paled. "And the questions, what are the stupid questions?"

"There are no questions, Fiona."

"Then how do you win the wretched prize, if there are no questions?" she was becoming angered.

Charles reached into his pocket and pulled out an envelope. He handed it to her.

Five minutes later, Fiona cast the envelope and its contents to one side.

"So I have to live in this tiny house for another two years?"

Charles did not say a word. Fiona had set him his task.

* * *

Ralph pulled his Sierra into his allotted car-parking spot. The neatly painted sign informed everyone that this place was reserved for the managing director. That was fine as far as things went, but the space next door to his sported a sign indicating that that section was for the chairman's car, and Ralph was pleased to note that the chairman was not in for his wife's Rover was not parked there.

Ralph wandered in and received the acknowledgements of his staff. The building was old and signified that better times had existed for the company. The paintwork on the walls had yellowed with age and the offices spoke of the austerity of the thirties. When other companies were refurbishing, the Wilkinson

Engineering Works did not. Just quite what happened to the money which accrued during the war and whilst demand was high for their products in the fifties, Ralph did not know. By the time he joined the firm in 1973, the sun was already starting to slip towards the west.

Ezra Wilkinson told Ralph that he saw great promise in him and indeed Ralph remembered quite clearly at his interview that Ezra was particularly impressed with his B.Sc. in engineering. This worried Ralph at the time, largely because he was not very impressed with it himself. The degree had taken a year longer than the four years it should have done, due to failing the exams in the first year, and when eventually Ralph passed his finals, he was awarded an ordinary and not an honours degree. It took Ralph a couple of years in employment to work out just why he got the job.

"Mr. Pearson-Cooper, I think we have a problem on our hands," stated Jenny, his secretary. Ralph looked around his office and considered to himself that the whole place was a problem.

"What is it, Jenny, not that wretched machine broken again?"

"No, no – and oh, I'm sorry, I forgot, my deepest sympathies about your father…" She put on her special meek look.

"Thanks," acknowledged Ralph, for this was the first time that he had been in the office for four days. It was not that he needed time at home to recover after hearing about his father, it was just that any excuse not to turn up was a good idea.

"What's happened now?"

"We've lost Johnson and Hawkins Ltd."

"How do you mean, lost them?" Ralph was starting

to get worried. He knew what lost meant but thought that he had better confirm that his worst fears were justified.

"To our competitors – they have taken their business elsewhere!"

"Do you know what this means?" It was a rhetorical question and Jenny just nodded. "It means that nearly a quarter of our business has just gone down the swanney."

Jenny nodded again – what could she say? she wondered to herself.

"Why? Why?" Ralph just could not believe it. He stabbed his pencil into the desk until it broke and then snapped it in half.

"There," he declared, "that's what our business is worth today!"

"We've not lost half!" Jenny protested. "Only a quarter!"

"A quarter, a half, what does it matter? Who's to say that there won't be other firms following suit. Did they say why? Did they give some excuse?"

"No."

"Then what happened?"

Jenny sat down on the chair opposite her boss and told him exactly what occurred.

"On Friday, after you had gone home," began Jenny. Ralph winced – he had left early on Friday, feeling low, and had gone down to the golf club.

"Yes, go on."

"Their purchasing department phoned to say that they had been reviewing their buying policies and unfortunately regretted to inform us that they would no longer be using us as suppliers."

"And that was it?"

"Yes."

"Why didn't you get in touch? You could have rung me at home and I would have tried to do something about it."

Jenny looked a little uneasy; she realised that perhaps she should have done more, shown more initiative. "I thought that you probably had gone to have a round of golf so I rang your golf club and they said that you had had to return home. They told me that they had passed on a message to you about your father."

"So?"

"Well, I thought you might be grieving…" suggested Jenny.

"Not half as much as I am about losing our major client!"

"I'm sorry," apologised his secretary, "but I thought, well, you know, it being your father who had died and all that, that I shouldn't disturb you."

"Oh, you weren't to know. My father had become a sort of recluse – he never wanted to see his children – in fact it is perhaps as well that they did not ask me to identify the body. I wouldn't have known him from Adam. Apparently a nurse found him slumped in the library."

"At Blayborough House?" inquired Jenny.

"Yes, and don't ask me what the house is like inside because I haven't a clue!"

"And who inherits?"

"Oh, you know, death duties and all that, trusts and things – complicated," he glossed over it all. "Not yours truly, if that is what you're wondering! Yours truly has to continue slogging away at his late father-in-law's wretched engineering works. Not for me the luxury of dying in the library of some stately home. Mine is a living death!"

"Oh, come on now, Ralph." She touched his arm, trying to comfort him. "Things aren't so bad."

"They are and now I'll have to get in touch with Johnson and Hawkins."

"Do you want their managing director?"

"I suppose so."

Ten minutes later and Ralph was trying to illicit information from the MD of Johnson and Hawkins.

"Look, it is quite simple, I told my purchasing department to examine everything – absolutely everything – that they bought. Right down to the coffee for the canteen. We got other companies to quote and then compared."

"And how did we compare?" asked Ralph, fearing the worse.

"Not so good – your prices were ten per cent higher than the highest quote we received and a full twenty-nine percent higher than the company we have asked to supply us now."

"But why didn't you ask us to see if we could do it cheaper?"

"Well," began the managing director of Johnson and Hawkins, "it is a question of quality…"

"Quality?"

"Look, I'll be frank – you know that this company has been buying from you for decades but the quality had gone down hill recently. I've got to watch costs and it is no use if we have to reject some of your stuff because it is just slightly off centre… I think it's your machines, they're past it…"

"Well, thanks anyway."

"Take my advice – renew them. That's what we did – and that's how we found out that your products are just not up to scratch."

"Yeah, thanks…" mumbled Ralph. Renewal of machinery was expensive. It should have been done years ago – when Ezra was in charge – he reflected.

* * *

An hour later saw Ralph returning to his house in the suburbs of Leeds. The suburbs bored him to tears and he did muse that perhaps this was because he came from landed stock! However, he concluded, as his car inched forward in the traffic jam, as his father had made his fortune in industry and then bought Blayborough, the countryside connection was a little tenuous. His house was quite large by suburban standards and they now had only a small mortgage on it. Not that that meant they were well off, for three children at private school saw much of their money off.

"Don't ask me how today was – it was bad!"

Amelia just shrugged her shoulders. She had wondered if Sir John's death might have produced something but she did not ask. She poured him a sherry and had one herself.

"What's gone wrong?" she inquired, choosing to ignore the fact that he had suggested that he did not want to talk about it.

"We've lost Johnson and Hawkins, that's what's gone wrong!"

Amelia sneered, "That wasn't very clever of you. How did you manage that?"

"Manage it?" stuttered Ralph.

"Well, you are supposed to be the managing director, so obviously it is your job to manage!"

"Very funny! They found cheaper and better elsewhere."

Amelia chose to ignore that and instead launched her attack from another angle, "Johnson and Hawkins was the first company that Daddy supplied. They had been with us for decades. Daddy knew Mr. Johnson personally. What did you do?"

"Mr. Johnson has been dead for these past eight years! I did not do anything!"

"Then you should have done something! That's the trouble with you – you vacillate, you don't take action when you should do. Managing director – you can't manage to save your life!"

"Well, your father obviously did not take that view, or else he would not have made me managing director in the first place."

Amelia sneered and then stated, "He only made you MD because you were married to me," and she paused before adding, "then he obviously regretted your elevation and decided to even things in his will."

Ralph drunk all his sherry in one go and made for the kitchen door. "Well then, Madam Chairman, I think you had better come down and earn your keep – before there isn't any keep to earn!" It was a threat that Ralph was quite sure she would not take up. Relations between them had been strained ever since Ezra left fifty-one percent of the company to Amelia.

"But of course, you are too busy helping out at the local Oxfam shop to find out what running a real business in the real world is like. Wilkinson Engineering is not like an overgrown charity shop, full of twee assistants working for nothing, selling garments given for nothing!"

"Yes, I know, that is why I'll be down there tomorrow at nine!"

* * *

Ralph and Amelia's three boys spent the evening wanting various types of assistance with their homework. All three of them attended the most expensive day school in the area and were being coached in preparation for a minor public school, the common entrance exam and boarding school life. Amelia was desperate for them to succeed in the system, go on to Cambridge or Oxford and then who knows? Ralph knew. He knew that they could not afford to send them away to school unless they gained a scholarship, which they would not. He knew that they could barely afford to send them to the top day schools in the area. As the family income was never increasing in real terms, Ralph was trying to drop the jaundiced view he held of the state comprehensives; as he went past their modern cement facades in afternoons and saw the children escaping to their various homes, he even attempted to ignore the fact that they looked such a mess. Clothes and appearances are not important, he told himself, results are. Yet, what are the results? Were there any results coming from these egalitarian buildings worth regarding as important?

Ralph had tried to shield his wife from these thoughts. To her, the boys were on their way to the greater glories of public school life, as befitted the grandsons of Ezra Wilkinson. To her, the Wilkinson Engineering Works had provided the daughter with the best that money can buy so why should it not continue to do the same for the grandchildren?

"William, dear," she was oft heard to murmur, "you'll never pass if you don't put your back into it!"

Sometimes Ralph hoped that his eldest would fail so miserably that he would be sent by his mother to the local school in disgrace. Then he would not have to go through the humiliation of explaining to his wife that there was just no way the family income could sustain one boy, let alone three, at public school, minor or major.

So, as father helped son with his maths, the prospect of Amelia Pearson-Cooper, Chairman, taking up residence in the Wilkinson Engineering Works and actually finding out what was going on, did not generate much enthusiasm in Ralph's breast. It generated fear.

Later that evening, as wife and husband lay side by side in their marital bed, Amelia posed the question that had fluttered inside her head all day.

"Well then?" she began.

"Well what?"

"Did he leave you anything?"

"Not a penny!" answered Ralph, which was quite true, he had not been left a penny…

Amelia sat bolt upright in bed. She pulled the cord, which switched on the light above them. Ralph blinked as he stared up at the light bulb dangling in a lacy shade.

"You are telling me that you, the youngest son of a millionaire, a man who made such a fortune out of scrap, surplus and then art dealing and associated wheeling, that you, you… not a thing?"

The light was bright and Ralph was reminded of the World War Two films when the Gestapo interrogated prisoners. Amelia, once roused, was quite a formidable creature and she could have easily found a place in such headquarters in Nazi Germany. Ralph tried to smile – he could do nothing else.

"Why are you smiling?"

"I'm not quite sure," he said, "but I think it is because I never realised before that you were expecting to get something from him. I always thought it was my manly body which sent you into shivers of ecstasy, not my father's money!"

Amelia's hair – benefiting from regular treatment at a top Leeds salon – was blonde and curly. At night time she pinned it back so that it would not tangle in her sleep. This contributed to her austere and angry look. Her nostrils flared slightly as she drew in a breath. Her large and still pert bosoms heaved in anger. Yet it was a hidden and controlled anger. Hers was the temper which executed itself in sarcasm, not shouting.

"The only manly thing about you was your father's wealth," she began.

Ralph rolled over and feigned sleep. He did not want to hear anymore. Suffice to say that it was enough that she was going to the works tomorrow – to inspect his chains, he wondered, or to cut him loose and free him from the bondage that being the managing director of a failing engineering works had become? Time would tell. Maybe that £100,000 tucked away would be the cutting tools that he needed.

* * *

The breakfast room in the Charles and Fiona Pearson-Cooper household was taking on the shape of a boardroom. Mrs Armitage was busy clearing the pots away in the kitchen. Fiona had rung her up that morning at seven-thirty to arrange her early start. Charles had been awakened at seven, so that he could wash, shower and breakfast before the arrival of Mrs Armitage. Fiona took the chair at the head of the table. Charles, looking resplendent in his suit, silk tie and silk shirt, sat next to her. The positioning was not lost on him but power was not weaved by seating arrangements, not in Charles' experience, so it did not worry him in the slightest that he had been downgraded to a seat away from the top.

It was the second week of the summer term, so their two sons and two daughters were safely ensconced in their respective educational establishments. The boys were at Eton, following in father's footsteps, the youngest daughter was at Cheltenham Ladies' College, following mother's footsteps and the eldest daughter was at Cambridge, following her don's footsteps into bed.

A folder full of empty paper and a pen had been placed on the breakfast table. Charles wondered how long this home board meeting was due to go on for, as he had real board meetings of his own to attend.

"I have been thinking," Fiona said, and she smiled. Fiona had three types of smiles: one that she reserved for those rare sensual moments, a second for those even rarer occasions when she found something amusing and a third which Charles had privately labelled as her Mr. Sardonicus smile. It was this third type that spread over her face that morning. Charles wished himself in the boardroom of the Westover Group fending off impending takeovers, numerous predators and a dozen strikes – anything other than sit here in the breakfast room with his wife's smile.

"Oh, yes?" Charles inspected his fingernails for imaginary dirt.

"Yes!" she replied determinably.

She paused until Charles realised that she was waiting for him and left his fingers alone.

"We shall obtain the Blayborough Estate only if we run this five year competition as one would run a business."

Now it was Charles' turn to smile. "As you have never run a business, you had better leave it all up to me!"

"Would that I could!"

"What do you mean by that?"

"Quite simply, if I let you run it and win the estate, who's to say what will happen then? You might turn around and leave me – and as I could not prove that I had done anything to win the prize, the judge would rule that I was not entitled to a penny from it!"

"You'd have this house."

Fiona glanced around and snorted, "My dear, you seem to forget, before I married you, I was the daughter of a lord. We had a family seat!"

"Which the National Trust is now sitting in!" It was Charles' turn to smile sardonically. His wife's impoverished aristocratic background had been a continual source of amusement to him and annoyance to her. Fiona chose to ignore the jibe about her family's failing fortunes – death duties and overspending had dealt deadly blows to her family in the past.

"I shall help you to get Blayborough Estate and we

shall live there as is our right!" She was quite emphatic about it all.

"Well, I'm sorry but you will have to adjourn this meeting until another time because I have a real meeting to attend. This house may not be grand enough for you, but at the moment it is all you've got and so if you will excuse me, I must go out to work to maintain it!"

Fiona was not so easily dismissed.

"While you are away, I'm going to write down all your connections, directorships etc. that I know about, so that we have an agenda to go on and information to use to make our fortune and put those other two out of the running! If you would be so good as to list all the things about yourself that I don't know about, it will greatly assist me."

* * *

That morning, John Bates made a detour to Companies House. The few friends that he had often referred to him behind his back as a devious little toad; those he crossed were apt to refer to him as a snake in the grass. John saw himself more as a crocodile – for he possessed a lovely smile and ate lesser mortals for dinner.

* * *

Later that week, Charles attended the board meeting of the Westbury Group – it was a stormy affair. The chairman was not really up to managing the large concern that the Westbury Group had become. He had a small company mentality and objected to the young whippersnappers who now sat on his board; he would often fall into periods of musing when he recollected those days in the past when he controlled the company totally and a board meeting consisted of him dictating to his secretary. How much easier things had been then!

"Mr. Chairman, I beg you to consider our shareholders!" began one irate director, who had a particularly large holding in the company.

"The shareholders don't consider us – we're just something they buy for a quick profit!"

"But can't you see, with all these freehold premises, low gearing and our wide diversification of interests, we're ripe for a takeover!"

The chairman, Angus McNeil, snorted, "So, what do you suggest – sell our freeholds, borrow money we don't need and strip our assets? Don't talk stupid! I am not going to agree to alter the whole strategy of the company just to please a few shareholders! Years of careful planning went into building this business – yes, years and most of them while you lot were in your nappies!"

"May I suggest that we turn the problem on its head," began Charles, deciding to ignore his chairman's remarks. Charles was fifty-three and considered that he could pull weight on the board, bridging the gap between the two age groups.

"Problem, what problem?" thundered the chairman in his deep Scottish brogue.

Charles smiled in answer. "We should sell our freeholds to a holding company and then rent them back. With the money achieved, we can buy out other firms that are either complimentary or are our competitors. So instead of being takeover material, we will be doing the taking over!"

"And run foul of the Monopolies and Mergers

Commission!" roared Angus; save me from this new breed of capitalist, he thought. He then added ruefully to himself, if only Marie and I hadn't been tempted into going public, I wouldn't have been pushed into all this hassle.

"Would you like us to look into it?" simpered Roland Peterson from the firm of brokers to the Westbury Group PLC. The scenario passed quickly through his mind as he thought of the accolade he would achieve when he reported back to his partners – at last they would be gaining even greater fees from the Westbury Group; takeover battles did wonders for a stock broking firm's balance sheet!

"We will arrange to have your properties revalued with a view to selling on the freeholds – you will be pleasantly surprised," murmured Atkins, the senior partner in the accountancy firm that audited the Group's accounts. There were a lot of properties for their associate firm of surveyors to value; such monies that would result from this little escapade, Atkins could hardly imagine.

"Well, if I am going to be so pleasantly surprised, why wasn't this done before?"

"Mr. Chairman, if I can be so bold as to remind you – the idea of assets being revalued without a subsequent sale of them is so that it can appear on the balance sheet and cause a rise in the share price. This in turn makes us interesting to other companies. They start sniffing around. Is that what you want?" inquired Charles.

Angus did not want that. He did not want a takeover that would result in him losing his position as chairman and being put out to grass, even if he had a golden goodbye or whatever! What he would do with his life if he was not running his company, as he still regarded his position in spite of only owning thirty-five percent of the shares, he did not know.

"And if assets are not revalued then predators notice it, realise that we are sitting on a fortune and start buying our shares and that in turn makes us interesting to even more companies!" suggested Angus, feeling that this was a distinctly no win situation.

"However," continued the accountant, ignoring the chairman's remarks, "if we do as Mr. Pearson-Cooper has suggested, and place the assets in a holding company, we would have more money in the bank. It would be the subsidiary company which was asset rich – Westbury would have money in the bank and be on better footing to stalk other firms. I could arrange to have the revaluations done discreetly."

"If you like, I'll make enquiries about other companies that could be possibilities…" suggested the broker, Roland Peterson.

Charles smiled sweetly. This could be very interesting, especially when one had £100,000 that needed multiplying. What a good job that he and the dear broker had been such good chums at Cambridge.

* * *

John Bates managed to get one lead in Companies House that he could use. He drove back to the office and gave short shrift to the ethics of the next course of action he was going to indulge in. When needs must, the devil drives!

* * *

Amelia dropped the children off at school and then did her shopping at Morrisons. After a spot of lunch, she drove straight to the factory. Though she had announced to her husband last night that she intended to be at the works at nine o'clock, the reality was that she could not just drop everything she had planned for the next day. When she had said nine o'clock, she was not talking literally. Ralph was not sure what she had in mind, so he arrived at quarter to nine and sorted the mail into two piles: one for public gaze, meaning Amelia, and the other for his eyes only; these letters were filed under S for 'Secret' and 'Stuffed Away'. The S file was quite a large file, it was a file that one opened when one had achieved a stiffened resolve.

Ralph, having mooched around for a while, left for an early lunch. As he turned left out of the car park and into the adjoining road, Amelia drove in. She was pleased to see that her husband was not there. Where he exactly was, she did not know. Her Rover fitted into the chairman's allotted space with extra room to spare – the car parking lines were painted with Ezra's elderly Rolls in mind.

Amelia walked straight into the works. She had expected to hear the hum of machinery, the whirl of the metal parts, the drone of the plates. Instead, Radio One blared out.

"What has happened?" she inquired in her very best tones. Her accent cut no ice with the workforce.

"Good morning, Miss Amelia," greeted one of the elderly foremen, "I hope that you and the children are well?"

"We're fine, thank you," acknowledged Amelia,

slightly flattered to be referred to by her maiden tag, even though her maidenhood had flowered and bloomed a while since.

"Are you looking for your husband?" asked another.

"No, I am not," she answered and pulled herself to her full height, smiled her best sickly smile and informed the assembled workforce of ten that as chairman she was intending to take a more active interest in the company. "And that is why I am here now, and will be every day from now on."

John Forbes put down his copy of the *Sun* and regarded this woman with new interest. She did not scare him with her designer clothes and cut-glass accent – he gave her a fortnight before she returned to her tennis parties and voluntary work. She would find the Wilkinson Engineering Works just as boring as her husband did, he thought, and picked up the newspaper again.

"No work?" inquired Amelia.

"Lunch break – statutory hour off," replied Forbes whilst taking his eyes of the nearly nude woman for the few seconds it took him to answer.

"Then I'll disturb you no longer." And Amelia walked away. Forbes nudged the chap next to him and made some risqué comparison between the newspaper nude and their Madam Chairman. Laughter ensued, the cause of it Amelia could guess.

* * *

Charles made a mental note to invite Roland Peterson from Westbury's brokers to dinner very soon. After all, he could not gather important information without first indulging in little social pleasantries. He would get

Fiona to make contact with Roland's French wife – that way it would seem more natural.

The Westbury Group's headquarters were in Doncaster. The A1 is an admirably awkward road but Charles spun his Jaguar into automatic and went zooming up to the leafy plains of the Vale of York as best as he could in the circumstances. He cursed the tractors, the milk tankers and other assorted vehicles that caused him to slow down. He spurned the fast food cafés which plied their wares. He cocked two fingers up at the reps cars as he overtook them.

He turned into the slip road that led off the dual carriageway. Left at the crossroads and then first right up a small track. There were no lights on yet in the cottage but a 2CV was parked outside. Charles drove his Jaguar around the back, out of the way.

The rear door opened before he even had the chance to alight.

"Darling, you made it!" a woman's voice cried.

Charles smiled broadly at the thought of the delights to come. No doubt Fiona would have described her as a bit of a floozy…

* * *

Amelia settled herself down at the vacant desk. She was not quite sure what to do next but thought that she ought to be seen doing something, if she was going to make her point. She went to a filing cabinet and took out the large file on Johnson and Hawkins. She knew that if she laid it on the desk, she could pretend to view it and at the same time work out some sort of strategy. Ralph's secretary was supposed to be busy typing away in the adjoining room. This gave Amelia the opportunity to pretend to survey the contents of the file and think.

She could tell that something was very wrong with the factory. She could not quite put a finger on it but assessed it vaguely as a general lack of hum; the typewriting, for example, was intermittent and punctuated with gales of laughter. The noise from the machines, which she could remember hearing so vividly in her youth, was subdued, as if only some had been switched on. She presumed that to be the case, for without the Johnson and Hawkins order, there was a considerably reduced workload. She then turned her attention to the file laid out on her desk. There were a series of letters complaining about quality. There was a letter querying the price. There was a letter from the managing director of Johnson and Hawkins suggesting a meeting to discuss various points concerning the orders. Amelia closed the file.

* * *

Fiona spent the afternoon at the beauty parlour. At least, beauty parlour was how she described it when mentioning it to her friends. She waxed lyrical about its treatment rooms; she described to others how wonderful it was; she drooled over its prices – for prices were, to Fiona, an indicator of quality. Yet she never revealed just where it was; "Trade secret," she would murmur to any inquiring friends. "After all, I can't have everyone beating a path to its door and giving me competition in the good looks stakes!"

The salon was in Bradford – this could in itself have accounted for the secrecy. Finding it involved driving through the centre and then into the myriad of back streets. The trip seemed always to initially remind her of the holiday she had taken when she was ten. Her father had taken her and the rest of the family to the hill stations in India he had frequented in his youth. Even in the fading days of the Raj, these resorts seemed magical and of a different world.

The visit to the beauty parlour in Bradford took on the same sense of adventure. A visit to the unknown: the babble of foreign voices, the pyjamas, the smell of curry, the dirt and the endless numbers of tiny children. No, she thought to herself, as her car took her round endless streets of terraced houses occupied by numerous families, it was not at all like the hill stations where they had holidayed. The hill stations represented the halcyon moments of pure air, dances, star-lit nights and warm days; the only locals seen were servants. This city spoke only of the Asian exotica represented in the squalid cities on the plains below, where they had been forced to spend the first night of the trip.

The frontage of the salon was rather smart. A receptionist sat behind a desk with the appointment book in front of her, an external telephone to the right and an internal telephone to the left. She recognised Fiona immediately.

"Mrs Anderson, do sit down," she spoke with a slight Pakistani accent and beckoned with be-ringed fingers to the row of empty chairs. Fiona did as she was bid. Anderson was her mother's maiden name, so Fiona Pearson-Cooper and the name Anderson were not too distantly related.

The receptionist then picked up the internal phone and dialled a number.

"Mrs Anderson is here, Mr. Page."

She put the phone down and, on instructions from Mr. Page, she told Fiona to go straight down to the usual room. Fiona, feeling slightly flushed, walked slowly to the treatment room. Mr. Page, a West Indian, opened the door and smiled at his client.

* * *

At two o'clock, Ralph returned form his lunch to find his wife poking around amongst the files. He was glad to note that she had not reached the latter part of the alphabet, however his pleasure was short-lived for he noticed that she was stuck amongst the Js.

"Hello, hard at it?"

"I don't know," she replied.

"Well, if you don't know, then I'm sure that I don't!"

Pleasantries over, Amelia sat herself back down on the seat she had been occupying for the past two hours. Ralph ran his fingers through his curly hair, something he always did when he was nervous. He felt a little worried now, for there was an air of trepidation floating around the office. His secretary had greeted him with rolling eyes when he entered the outer office. He now plonked himself in to the visitor's chair, sitting opposite his wife, and wished himself back in the pub.

"Something is wrong here, Ralph, what is it?"

Ralph acknowledged that to be a good question. He had often asked himself the same query. He detested the factory so much that he was scared to reply to his own question. He was not too keen to reply to his wife's selfsame ponder. He shrugged his stocky shoulders.

Amelia repeated the question.

"What is wrong here?"

Ralph took a deep breath and attempted to explain.

"Our customer base has eroded over the years. A fall in orders has meant that we could not re-invest in better equipment, and if we could not re-invest then our products were not as good as our competitors'. It has been happening all over the country, haven't you heard?"

"I don't care about elsewhere, all I want to know is how the hell did you let it happen here?"

"It was happening when your father was alive – he just kept it hidden. It just accelerated over the last year. How can we compete against the Koreans? They have new machinery and cheap labour; we have old machines and expensive labour. This factory is slowly dying."

"But I own fifty-one percent of it!" Amelia spluttered. "What are you going to do about it?"

"And I own nothing, so why should I do anything about it?"

* * *

Fiona laid down on the couch and felt the warm oil trickle down her back. Her body quickened in anticipation. Then his dark hands massaged her shoulders, rubbing all those tensions away.

"I forgot to tell you," Mr. Page began, "I'm buying a house."

"How lovely!" Fiona gasped as he pummelled a particularly knotty bit of muscle. "Is it new?"

"Not even built. I've put a reservation on the plot – a deposit that guarantees the price. Guess what?"

Fiona said she could not possibly guess.

"It is already worth two thousand pounds more and they haven't even laid a brick!"

Fiona started to grow ever so slightly interested in this. Money was something quite close to her heart, especially as she came from a rather impoverished aristocratic background – so Charles kept telling her anyway.

"Why is that?" she managed to say, in spite of his hands advancing downwards.

"You must know – house inflation!"

She did know, of course, but she had not realised that it had reached the lower orders yet. Nor had she realised that once reaching them, they would react like true capitalists and enjoy their assets appreciating.

Mr. Page's hands left her back and began on her thighs.

"So you put a deposit down, secure the house, and even though your house has not been built, it is going up in value?" She had to have her facts totally correct.

"Yes, you know – they then release details of the second phase, which really is just another word for the next lot of houses, which cost a few thousand pounds more than the previous. If you get in at the beginning, you get the pick of the cheapest."

This had possibilities. Fiona had just enough time to make a mental note to tell Charles all about it before Mr. Page removed the white towel covering her delicate backside and joined her on the couch for a spot of quick relief.

* * *

Ralph and Amelia went home separately, at different times and in different cars. Amelia had to go in the middle of the afternoon to do the school run, after which the boys settled down to their usual routine of television and a snack.

When his wife left at just after three, Ralph knew that he could relax for the rest of the afternoon. He shut the outer door that led to the office, where his secretary sat engrossed in a magazine. He pulled the blind down so that the internal window, which had given Ezra a private view of his workers busy creating products, was obscured. The workers were not working anyway, and one's employees idling around is never a pretty sight – especially when one is trying to avoid facing up to that situation.

The *Daily Mail* would have made interesting reading to Ralph, if he had not already read it during his two hour lunch break. There were only the sports pages left. Sport was not something that titillated him at all, so these pages were usually left unread. Today, depression and Amelia drove him to the back of the newspaper, on account of the fact there was nothing else for him to do.

There were two whole pages listing the races at Goodwood and Beverley. His eyes ran over the list of runners. Their names were weird – it was probably because there were so many horses trotting around that they had had to use odd types of names and had run out of the normal ones, pondered Ralph.

Then he gave a glance over the list of jockeys. Some jockeys seemed to win more often than others. What if I put a bet on the jockey and not the horse? Ralph thought. He was so terribly bored that doing anything that involved a moment of excitement was worth it. The trouble was, as he acknowledged quite freely to himself, he had not got a clue about betting.

He gave a sniff and looked at the list of runners. There's a horse that sounds like a goer – 'Count me in' noted Ralph; yet the journalist wrote that he had not disgraced himself in April when he came fifth

Heaven knows, thought Ralph when he read the remarks. I'm no elitist but anything other than first is bound to be a disgrace – the whole object of the exercise is winning! Count me in can count himself out! Ralph concluded that backing the jockey was the best and surest way to win.

He studied the jockey form and decided to back the jockey who had won the most races. All he had to do now was to find out where he was racing. A quick perusal found that the jockey would be at Goodwood storming towards the finishing line just a short while after 4.10.

The next task was to remove £100 from the building society. Ralph inspected his new building society books, nicely full of money.

"Damn," he muttered out loud, "the cheque won't have cleared. Oh well, it will just have to be the petty cash!"

The betting shop was quite near to the factory. It was exceptionally uninviting from the outside. It was smoke filled and grubby inside. Ralph made his way to the counter, noticing that at least two of the clients were his workers. This did momentarily trouble him – what were they doing here when they should be making money for the Wilkinson Engineering Works, replacing the cash he had borrowed from the petty cash?

"Afternoon, Mr. Pearson-Cooper."

"Tom, Jack," acknowledged their boss.

"Having a bit of a flutter?" they asked.

"Yes, thought I'd put it down on the favourite in the 4.10 – favourite horse, winning jockey."

"Never make your fortune by backing the favourite!"

Ralph was forced to agree with that statement. The word fortune also brought the question of his so-called inheritance back into focus. Apart from the occasional bit of betting – which, if he did not win this afternoon, would be a short lived bout – just what was he going to do with the money?

If he had been the entrepreneurial sort, he would have been making his fortune without the prompting of this legacy. His brother Charles seemed a totally different type to him. Ralph, who was starting to take to this betting lark, wagered that Charles had already put a dozen money making ideas into practice. He was quite convinced that Charles did not have an ailing engineering works around his neck, a wife who suddenly had the itch to investigate the works' ailments and a complete vacuum of successful ideas.

He considered that what he really needed was a drop of luck. If only Lady Luck would ride the horse, flick the switch that would make the steed gallop to the winning post. Even if the horse was marked as the favourite, Ralph still thought that he would win something.

The commentary announced that they were off and all the odds and sods collected in the betting shop turned their attention to the television set. Some of them sucked on cigarettes, others clutched their slips, Ralph just propped himself up on the counter feeling ever so slightly sick.

The television commentator added to the excitement of the whole proceedings by getting himself worked up. It did not seem to matter one jot who was in the lead, the voice seemed thrill on whoever was the present leader. Ralph kept hearing the name of his horse, as he now regarded it, again and again.

"It's Instantly Wonderful in the lead. Coming to the last furlong, Instantly Wonderful is going to do it; it's Instantly Wonderful, followed closely by Jingle Jake and Lord Pandy. Jingle Jake is coming fast and closing the gap. Can Instantly Wonderful make it? She's pulling ahead, Instantly Wonderful is pulling well ahead of Jingle Jake, who seems to be running out of steam and has slipped into third place, behind Lord Pandy. It's Instantly Wonderful heading towards the winning post, Instantly Wonderful has done it. Second, Lord Pandy, third Jingle Jake."

Ralph felt instantly wonderful; he felt successful for the first time in years; he felt he had turned a corner. Ralph felt like a winner.

* * *

Fiona arrived home later that day feeling exhilarated. Her body had been first rested and then served. The cost had seen her personal bank account £120 lighter. It was money well spent. She looked forward to June, when she was due for her next service. Mr. Page did her proud.

Charles had not yet returned to the humble family seat. This was not at all unusual, Fiona was well used to him coming in at odd hours of the day and night. A small glass of wine rounded off her day. She shut her eyes and slowly sipped the contents. If only, she thought to herself, we were living in Blayborough House, then my happiness would be complete.

The remembrance of Blayborough temporarily interrupted her daydreaming. Pushing the pulsating Mr. Page to the back of her mind, she switched back to the money languishing in an envelope on the side board. What was it that Mr. Page had said – reservation of plots, profits before a brick had been laid? As there was still no sign of the returning husband, Fiona took herself off to Leeds, where she knew that there was an enormous housing development going on. There she considered that it would be possible to find the likes of Barratt, Wimpey and so on. She shuddered a little at the thought – was Blayborough House really worth tarnishing her day by visiting a vast housing estate for the middle and lower middle-class masses?

As she approached the area, carefully following the signs attached to the lamp post and left by the builders to aid the plebs to their new residences, she spotted the flags. There had been a time when she had a fancy for a flag pole in their acre paddock that fronted their house. Seeing the builders' flags, fluttering so proudly and so commonly, she fancied a front garden flag pole no longer.

The show house was particularly easy to find – it was not only signposted quite brazenly but was the only house to have a garage that sported a weather cock! The garage also had patio doors, which caused an involuntary shudder to go down Fiona's spine. French windows, garden doors – those were the type of rear external doors that she was used to. Patio doors were not something found in real Georgian houses.

However, if it was a real Georgian house of enormous proportions that one hankered after, then one just had to appreciate that the masses like their patio doors. Even if, as Fiona noted when she tripped around the show house, the patio was no more than a few paving slabs!

The sales executive, as he was called, was most helpful. This was probably because his meagre salary was supplemented by commission gained on selling houses. He was a little bemused by the rather aristocratic lady that was showing such interest in the development, but privately concluded that perhaps she was on her uppers.

"We are now onto our second phase."

"What happened to the first phase?" interrupted Fiona.

"Completely sold out – everyone reserved plots within two days of opening the books."

"Goodness!" Fiona exclaimed, and then thought to herself that this was better than she had hoped it would be.

"There was even a fight between two chaps just here – right where you are standing – over the last plot."

"Here?"

"Right under your feet – they rolled around on the carpet and one of them slugged the other in the eye just where your feet are now!"

Fiona was impressed.

"And which one of them got the plot?"

"Neither of them!" He smiled in the way that sales executives do when they are making money hand over fist. "While they were busy knocking the hell out of each other, I sold it to someone else!"

"Amazing!" Fiona's eyes grew large in wonderment at the thought of how that £100,000 invested in building plots would very soon multiply. She added "What I'm interested in is your early reservation scheme."

The sales executive (he was just a plain salesman until he had his job title upgraded when the building company decided to improve their image) handed her the details.

"We are taking reservations on our second phase as from tomorrow!" he announced, using his persuasive vocal tones to such effect that a slight feeling of panic was generated in Fiona's recently massaged breasts. "So I suggest you look around now and make your decision tonight."

Fiona plodded through the garage to the room entitled utility – it looked a little pokey compared to what she was used to, and she presumed that it was the room that combined the flower room, boot room and wash kitchen found in her present abode. The kitchen was the next on the list and by now Fiona was getting a little more used to the scale of the place. She did notice that the room, although small, looked more up to date than her own, but the chef she hired seemed to manage to conjure the occasional dinner party nosh quite easily, so it could not be too old-fashioned.

The dining room was tiny, and the room called the lounge was not much bigger. After inspecting the bedrooms and the various bathrooms, Fiona left clutching the particulars of the estate. The sales executive had only just time to acknowledge her departure – there were three other families clamouring to look round.

The rest of the estate – and in particular the

designated second phase – was very muddy, so Fiona refrained from inspecting that too closely. Instead she headed for home. She knew if she stayed around there for much longer, she would get an attack of claustrophobia.

* * *

Ralph replaced the borrowed stake money and then deposited his winnings in his newly favoured building society. He decided that he would open a third account for the profits to be put in. Full of zest after his success, he returned home to face Amelia.

She was not full of zest, as he half expected that she would not be, and she was barely talking. When she did eventually open her mouth, the words Daddy and disappointment seemed to figure largely.

After the children were safely tucked up in bed, the two of them sat down to thrash it out.

"Let's be honest with each other," was how she began. This was her well known euphemism for Ralph to admit his failings and for her to admit her compassion when faced with his failings. It was a well tried formula but this time Ralph was not going to use it the way she wanted him to.

Ralph began: "I shall repeat again what I said before: the products are too expensive; the machinery is too old and is now becoming inaccurate. Our customers are going elsewhere and if they are not going elsewhere it is because they are in the same situation as we are and have probably already gone bust."

"But why? I just don't understand how you let this happen."

A look of anger began to envelope Ralph's face: "Don't you realise? This was already beginning to happen in a small way when I joined the firm. It just accelerated in the last couple of years."

"Well, the firm was thriving once, when I was little and before – I know it was, once." Ralph noted that the word once had been spoken. Once, the firm was thriving… Ralph concluded that his dear wife was hiding something…

"It was thriving – before the war and during the war. Then your father lived off the fat of the land. I reckon that you all just got used to the rich lifestyle and were reluctant to give it up. When he should have been using the profit to buy new machinery, he was using the money to get you a horse, or to take your mother on a cruise! So tell me, what could I do to stop the rot?"

Amelia did not answer.

"Well, then, know-it-all, what special skills could I produce that would cause the slump to turn tail? How was I to tell the boss to stop playing at being a rich man with the firm's money and spend it on boring old machines."

Still there was no reply.

"There he would be, at the year end, working out how much extra he could pay himself in director's fees! Money that should have been put to better use. Money that should have gone on the firm, the golden goose that was laying the golden eggs!

Well, Mrs High and Mighty know-it-all, what would you have done if you had been married to the daughter of the boss? If you had seen your father-in-law squandering the wealth that was to keep your wife in future days to the manner to which she had become accustomed." Ralph was growing out of breath with all the shouting. His wife was not answering any of his accusations.

"Answer me!" he demanded. Emboldened by his win on the horses, he felt he could now face anything, even the truth about his unenviable position at the Wilkinson Engineering Works, even the truth about the enigma which surrounded his appointment in the first place.

"What was I supposed to do about it all?"

Amelia looked him straight in the eye.

"You were supposed to persuade your father to invest his money in the firm."

It was a bald statement of false presumptions.

"Persuade my father…" began Ralph, incredulously.

"Yes."

"But," he stammered, the wind taken completely out of his sails.

"Yes, I know," agreed Amelia. "You see, when you answered the advertisement to the job, Daddy was overjoyed…"

Amelia began to describe the day when her father had opened the letters form the various applicants to the position he had advertised.

"What I need is someone with a bit of talent – someone who could get the firm back on its feet," Ezra said with a sniff as yet another letter from a hopeful was cast aside.

His wife, whose spending habits were ingrained and quite legendary in her own circle, agreed wholeheartedly.

"Look at this one here – Ralph Pearson-Cooper. Taken a darn long time just to get a degree and at the end of it, only an ordinary one. Someone like that will have the business skills of a Siberian peasant!" He handed the application form to his wife, who scanned her eyes across it before returning to her piece of gateau.

"I've heard of that name,"she commented through a mouthful of coffee gateau.

"What, Pearson-Cooper?"

"Yes – isn't Pearson-Cooper the name of that millionaire who owns the Blayborough Estate?"

Ezra picked up the application form again and this time studied it with more interest. "You could be right – hey, perhaps this Ralph is his son?"

"Perhaps," agreed Mrs Wilkinson.

"They say that he has diverse business interests… that he likes to invest in local firms… that he is a supporter of the medium-sized business man…" and Ezra fumbled with his spectacles while considering this.

"A finger in every pie…" added Mary Wilkinson, licking the coffee cream off her own fingers.

"I think I'll make a few enquiries."

Ezra's idea of making a few enquiries consisted of a telephone call to the registrar at the university where Ralph studied. A return phone call later confirmed the paternal connections of Ralph.

The interview that came about later that week was short and very sweet. This had been Ralph's first interview and he was pleased at how easy it had seemed to get a job. The title of executive manager was very grand and the salary was impressive too. Unfortunately, Ralph was not so impressive in his position but that did not worry Ezra too much.

"And how is your father these days?" was quite a common enquiry in the early days.

Ralph did not want to admit to his boss that his

father had disowned his wife and three sons. What boss wanted to hear about the family problems of the Pearson-Coopers? So, instead of the truth, Ralph would murmur such things as "Fine, just a little touch of gout!" or "Abroad at the moment – cruising around the Bahamas!" Both of those facts he gleaned from the gossip column of the *Daily Mail*.

After a few months in employment, Ezra Wilkinson announced to his executive manager that it was Wilkinson Engineering Works' year end.

Ralph's heart gave a little flutter; this must be dividend and bonus time. At twenty-four and with very little real experience in the capitalist world, he presumed that four months employment qualified him for a bonus if the year end had been reached. Ezra was not one to hand out bonuses willy-nilly – because most of the money earned throughout the year had already been spent in a willy-nilly fashion by himself and his family. However, this year he had reserved a decent amount for a bonus for his executive manager.

Along with the bonus came a statement of future intentions. It was very wordy and spoke of hopes and thoughts, of commitments and futures. It did not speak directly of investment but the words were there, hidden in the typewritten document. Mary Wilkinson had composed this piece of writing. There were to be four copies. One for the bank – to keep the overdraft afloat and to accompany the accounts when they were ready; one for Ezra to keep, so that his ideas would not get lost among the mists of time and in the delights of money spent; one for the new executive manager – who was suitably impressed, for his course in engineering had not touched on the wonderments of management and money, so it was all new stuff to him; and one for Sir John Augustus Pearson-Cooper.

"I thought that you might like to give this to your father the next time you see him," suggested Ezra. "After all, I understand that he often invests in private companies."

Did he? wondered Ralph to himself, wishing that he knew a little bit more about his father than Nigel Dempster of the *Daily Mail* did.

"Thank you, I'm sure he'll be most interested!" And Ralph took the broadsheet from Ezra's outstretched hand.

"So are you and Amelia going out anywhere this weekend?"

"A meal, I think," answered Ralph, who was amused by Ezra's constant interest in both his father and his relationship with Amelia.

"Wonderful!" he declared before adding, "You know, Mrs Wilkinson – Mary – and I think that you make a lovely couple." After uttering that statement, Ezra smiled benignly. It was all very encouraging for Ralph, who found Amelia quite attractive. Amelia found him quite attractive too – better, she declared, than her previous boyfriend, who was the son of the family solicitor. Amelia and Ralph were getting to know each other very well, very well indeed.

* * *

The following month, Ezra had a draft copy of the previous year's accounts. It was not good reading. Through the window of his office, he could see the car of his executive manager arriving. For five months Ralph Pearson-Cooper had been in his employ and the

Pearson-Cooper family fortune had not found its way to the Wilkinson Engineering Works. Time was getting very short. When Ralph entered the office, Ezra decided to up the stakes.

"Would you like to ask him to look around the factory?"

"Who?" asked Ralph, a little bemused.

"Your father – I have a particular investment scheme that might interest him."

Ralph mumbled something in reply and made off to the shop floor, where work was in progress and conversation impossible above the noise of the machinery.

Thankfully, for Ralph's sake, the announcement of the impending pregnancy of Amelia Wilkinson, the rushed marriage and hasty settlement of a deposit on a house for the prospective parents, halted further requests.

Amelia was married in white and her side of the church was full to overflowing. Her father had wanted to do her proud and spend a fortune – an amount he hoped to get back from the match between his daughter and the Pearson-Cooper family. The lack of relatives on the groom's side was explained away by the haste of the rushed wedding.

It was while his daughter and new son-in-law were away on their honeymoon that Ezra found out what Ralph could not bring himself to tell him – Sir John Augustus Pearson-Cooper did not have anything to do with any of his off-springs.

"So you see," said Amelia, "Daddy was quite disappointed in you but he never wanted you to know it."

"I always wondered why he kept mentioning my father and then when we came back from the honeymoon, he never mentioned him again!"

"Daddy had his pride!"

"You're telling me that I got the job on the strength of my father's money…"

"And," interrupted Amelia, "I got the shares, and you got none, on the strength of my father's disappointment over the money!"

They smiled at each other for the first time in ages but it was a wry sort of smile that each gave to the other.

* * *

Later that afternoon, after a very busy day at the salon, Mr. Page made an appointment at his private doctor for a renewal of his prescription. There was no brass plate, announcing the name of the doctor, fastened to the gate post. There was no aura of pretend exclusivity in the waiting room. It was dingy in this particular doctor's abode.

Mr. Page settled himself down in the waiting room and picked up a copy of *Yorkshire Life*. It was not his normal reading material. Indeed, a glance around the room would show that it was not the type of magazine that any of the other occupants would skim through.

An article on Skipton did not interest him for he never went out of the boundaries of cities; market towns spelt boredom to him. He flicked over the page on society weddings. He was just about to dismiss the profile on a successful business man when a photograph caught his eye. He scrutinised it closely. The caption was quite clear: 'Mrs Fiona Pearson-Cooper at home with her husband Charles.' The article detailed the affluent lifestyle of the Pearson-Cooper family, his business interests, her aristocratic background…

Well, well, Mrs Fiona Anderson… he thought to himself.

He ran his tongue over his lips. The thoughts that were running through his head were already giving him a high. He laughed out loud, shaking his head and shouting to the others, "Fiona Anderson, your number's up!" The doctor ran out from the kitchen, which doubled up as his surgery. He handed a piece of paper to Mr Page and urged him to depart quickly, before his shouting alerted anyone outside.

* * *

When Fiona returned clutching her little bits of sales literature, Charles was already back. He too looked contented – it had been a good day for both of them.

She spread the information out on the occasional table.

"You must be joking!" Charles exclaimed.

"Not for us dear, not for us to live in!"

Fiona picked up the sheet that explained the advantages of reserving a plot – the fixed price, the opportunity of choosing the site you prefer, etc. etc.

"You put a small deposit down and begin the legal work. This commits them to the price completely – they can't back out."

"And nor can we!" interrupted Charles.

"Oh, but we can! You see, demand is so high for these properties that we can sell the property onto someone else before the building is finished and before we even complete with the builders. We can sell it for a large profit."

Charles smiled. His heart, which was conveniently positioned under his wallet, began to warm.

"A deposit of £250…"

"And a profit of £2,000!" added Fiona. "Think about it: we could do it up and down the country; with different builders; sometimes in your name and sometimes in mine!"

Charles considered the plan in its simplistic form. It was good – quite a nice little earner. It would do for starters!

* * *

John Bates left the office a little after six, as he always did. His brief was company law and in his own domain, his bulging filing cabinet even impressed Mr. Winstanley.

Mr. Winstanley would not have been quite so impressed with the contents of the locked filing cabinet, where the information that John Bates had gleamed from Companies House was now placed.

"For the future," was how Bates saw it as he slipped the piece of paper, full of neat handwriting, in the file marked C. Pearson-Cooper.

PART TWO

Autumn 1986

"How's the arm, mate?" Tom cried across the road.

"Still a bit crook!" came the reply.

Tom wandered over to see his friend and give his opinion on the arm.

"You want to go and see the doctor about that," he advised, "looks as if it's going to turn nasty."

Tom and Henry sauntered off together to grab a couple of middies – it was Spring in Perth now and the temperature was pleasant and warm. Over beer, the two of them chatted about the old times, pausing to look out over the Swan River to watch the yachtsmen heading towards Fremantle.

"You seen anything of old Jimmy lately?" inquired Henry.

"Last I heard of him, he was heading out toward Wolf Creek but that was six months ago or more."

"Must have made it then – wonder where he went to then?"

"Search me – why the interest?" Tom turned to his friend, shielding his eyes from the sun.

"Oh, no reason – just that there's a letter for him from England."

Henry took another swig of his beer and, as it was his shout, ordered another round.

"This letter – important, is it?" Tom continued when they had received their order.

"Meg reckons it could be – got some pommie solicitors' names on the front," answered Henry. "Mind you, can't be that important – there's a great big beaut of a rubber stamp on it announcing a surcharge but no one asked me for any money. Not that I'd have paid up! You'd think that they would have got the postage right – Poms think themselves so bloody clever but when it comes to it, they can't even get the right number of stamps on a letter!"

The two of them laughed and made arrangements to meet with their wives the following week to make a foursome.

"Went to a great seafood restaurant in James Street – how about us all going there?"

"Sure thing," agreed Tom, "and if I hear anything about Jimmy's whereabouts, I'll tell you then."

* * *

Fiona reached into her handbag and fished out the keys. She quickly found the one she wanted – it was new and fitted the lock on the study door. Once open, Fiona went in and locked the door behind her. The study was now out of bounds to Mrs Armitage. It was the only room in the house that Fiona had to clean herself – hence the reason it was the only dusty room in the house.

Seating herself at the desk especially bought for the purpose, she reached into the filing drawer and took out a file bulging with sales literature, half finished legalities between builders, herself and others. There were building plots reserved in the name of Fiona Pearson-Cooper all over the South East; then there were those in the name of Charles Pearson-Cooper largely around the Devon area; some were in the name of Fiona Anne Cooper (these were in and around London) and others in the name of Charles John Pearson (again, around London with a few in the South East, one even next door to a certain Fiona Anne Cooper!). The addresses were interesting too and were varied, making use of the Pearson-Cooper home in Yorkshire, the Pearson-Cooper pied-a-terre in London and a couple of company flats that Charles had occasional use of and that went with two of his directorships.

Fiona scanned through the mail she had picked off the mat that morning. Some of it was redirected from their various addresses and bore the franking of Barratt and of Beazer; there were two letters from Parker, Jones and Winstanley – missives from John Bates, no doubt, she thought.

Fiona relaxed in the bosun's chair and rested her fingertips together. It had been four months since they had started this little caper together and already they were much richer. She did wonder if the new furniture that they had to buy in order to equip the study properly for the task in hand would fit well in Blayborough House. They would probably have to sell the reproduction desk and chair and invest in antique. Repro might appear a trifle incongruous, it looked alright in a neo-georgian setting but a real Georgian place needed real Georgian furniture. The desk and chair would have to go, she concluded. She slit open the letter from the solicitors, thinking as she did about how all this would not have been possible without the cooperation of John Bates. It was his idea to use different addresses and alter their names slightly – after all, there is a limit to just how may building plots one family would want to reserve!

She opened the letter out and read its contents:

Dear Charles and Fiona,

I have been giving some thought as to how you can

use the present situation to better advantage. If you have a spare hour in the next few days, I would be glad to explain it to you.

Kind regards
John Bates

What a nice man! thought Fiona. And so helpful!

* * *

Ralph was waiting for the doors of the betting shop to open. He wanted to put an accumulator on before racing began in the afternoon. He had won quite a decent amount since he started. He studied the form and consulted *Racing Life* like an expert. He had even begun to form a couple of friendships with other chaps in similar positions, swopping tips and so on.

There was one bloke he often chatted to while he was waiting for a race to go under the starter's orders. Pat O'Reilly and Ralph were of a similar ilk – both of them could not be described as successes but nor could they be thought of as failures. Both had found themselves a niche in society, but if an outsider examined them the conclusion would be reached that they had achieved that position through false pretences.

Councillor Pat O'Reilly was the third son of an Irish Roman Catholic family. The two eldest boys had both entered the priesthood but such celibacy was not for the likes of Pat. He was rakish in an amateur sort of way and charmed the ladies – but to be precise, the ladies he was able to charm were the ones who inhabited the council offices, the secretaries and typists; fellow councillors also fell under his spell – his Irish brogue won them over to his Socialist cause even if his espousing of that cause was a little faulty at times; the ordinary housewives turned out in their hundreds to cast their crosses in his favour; the ladies who were past that certain age or who possessed a more sceptical and cynical nature, were, like the men, unimpressed by this soft-talking Irishman. They saw behind his spaniel eyes and noticed the lack of intellect. However, he did have an eye for the horses and he was amusing, so Ralph and Pat struck up a sort of friendship that Ralph could not have formed with any other punter who inhabited the betting shop.

"Whatever you do, don't back the favourite!" advised Pat to the waiting Ralph.

"Why's that?"

"It's not rained in days – he likes soft going!"

Ralph nodded and said he was not going to put a bet on him anyway. He showed him the accumulator he had worked out.

"You'll never win anything with that one!"

"Blake's Risen Now? He's a cert!" stated Ralph.

"He's no such thing – on my mother's grave, I'll swear he won't make it past the first bend; why, he's as blind as a bat!" Then Pat murmured, "But strictly between you and me, if you're dead set on it, we'll have a little side bet, just you and I."

They shook on the deal. Just then, the doors opened and they both strode in.

Ralph placed the £1,000 cash alongside his list and gave it to the bookie. He backed them all to win.

If they did win, Ralph thought, both Charles and the elusive James could start to kiss Blayborough House goodbye.

* * *

The restaurant was a BYOG, so Tom and Henry got stocked up with some good Aussie wine and brought it in with them. It was a bit of a nuisance in these Bring Your Own Grog places if you ran out of the stuff halfway though the meal, but most of the locals brought more than enough. What was often amusing was to see the system explained to any of the tourists that Perth attracted – Bring Your Own Grogg was always difficult to describe to someone who had just arrived from Singapore and was passing through, doing Western Australia as a stopover on the way to Sydney.

The two couples sat down and Meg took the letter out from her bag. The words James Pearson-Cooper, c/o Mr. and Mrs H. Baker and their address were carefully typed on the front of the envelope.

"Lord knows why it came to our house – I mean, I know he stayed with us for a while when he first came over to Oz but that was donkey's years ago!" Meg commented.

"How old was he then?" asked Tom, who, like Meg and Henry, was well into his sixties.

"Eighteen and just left Eton."

"Eton?" queried Tom.

"Yeah, Eton – you know, that poofter boarding school. You must of heard of it!" stated Meg.

Tom shook his head.

"Anyway," continued Meg, ignoring Tom's lack of knowledge, "he came over here in a cloud of mystery, like he had done something he shouldn't have!"

"But they let him in, so it couldn't have been

something too bad!" put in Doris. Meg agreed with Tom's wife and they went on to discuss just where Jimmy could be.

"Gone walkabout, as usual, without a care in the world I've no doubt. I reckon he's got some Abo Sheila he visits, or maybe a whole string of them! I mean, he's forty now and you just wouldn't believe it to look at him. Strides around like a man half his age!"

"You're right there, mate – never seen a bloke work as hard as him. Most of the men I know take at least a few sickies off when the weather's hot and they want to get a bit of swimming in, but not Jim. Never known him to take a sickie in his life!"

"Yeah, but then he saves them up and goes on walkabouts every couple of years. Then you don't see him for months on end."

"Meg's right, Tom, I mean how long's he been gone this time? Six months, seven?" Henry asked.

"Last saw him in December '85 when we took that vacation on Rottnest Island – he was just wheeling his bike on the ferry to the island as we were driving to go home. We waved but he didn't spot us."

They then started to discuss the virtues of the 'Quokka Arms' on Rottnest Island until Meg just happened to glance up at the entrance to the restaurant.

"Jimmy," she cried out, "over here."

* * *

Charles parked his Jaguar in the visitor's car park. He went over to Fiona's side and opened the door for her. As she swung herself out, he admired her legs – not bad for a woman of fifty he thought! The two of them strode into the offices of Parker, Jones and Winstanley, through the original Georgian wooden door ("not a patch on the one at Blayborough House!" whispered Charles into Fiona's ear) and into the waiting room.

"Tell Mr. Bates that the Pearson-Coopers are here," announced Charles to the receptionist. She looked up at the haughty couple and smiled at them.

"Mr. Bates said that you were to be shown in just as soon as you arrived," she stated and then rose with the purpose of taking them through to Bates' inner sanctum.

They followed her tripping steps. Fiona could not help smiling – indeed she often found herself smiling these days, there was so much to amuse and entertain her that she could not stop her glad feelings from expressing themselves all over her face. It gave her an attractive appearance which even Charles, to his amazement, found stimulating. Altogether, the two of them were enjoying a sort of renaissance in their relationship, a blooming of togetherness – a rosy feeling that did not preclude Mr. Page and the floozy occupant of a certain cottage, of course.

"Fiona, dear," murmured Bates, rising from his desk as they entered and giving Fiona a kiss on the cheek. "Charles – do sit down both of you!" John Bates was at his simpering best now. Fiona and Charles did not realise, for they were used to talking to people who acted in this sycophantic manner.

"Fiona, has anyone told you how young you look lately!" and he beamed his most patronising smile in her direction.

Fiona did not tell him that a certain Mr. Page had told her that only the other day, she instead merely smiled even more.

"You mentioned that you wanted to tell us something," prompted Charles.

"Just a little thing that you might not have thought of – just wondered if you wanted to know, that's all," began Bates. He was warming the bait, sticking on the open worm for the couple sitting in front of him to bite into.

"Well, you've been so helpful," Charles replied by way of an answer.

"That's what I'm here for," answered Bates, "that's my job!"

Both Fiona and Charles liked the notion of the ever-faithful servant, it appealed to their latent feudal urges.

"You're so kind!" Fiona said in her best patronising tones – the same tone she used to Mrs. Armitage when she had an old dress she could not possibly wear any longer ("I could not even be seen dead in it, it is terribly infra dig now, but it will do marvellously for you, I'm sure!").

John Bates gritted his teeth and ignored her tone and snooty look. "What I have been thinking is this – you have lots of plots going through the pipeline now, but the trouble is that the idea is alright in itself but is limited."

"Limited?" queried Fiona, for the whole thing had been her idea and she had been rather pleased with its success.

"Yes, limited in its scope. What you want to do is raise some loans on the back of them. Get some extra money in to invest in other money making ideas."

Charles perked up a bit at this.

"But won't we need some valuations – the bank will want to see proof of ownership."

Fiona then added her bit, "And that will be a little bit difficult, considering that they are not all strictly in our names!"

Both Charles and Fiona raised their eyebrows expectantly, waiting to see if their learned friend would provide an answer to that little poser.

"Valuations can be arranged – after all, do you know of a valuer who checks who actually owns the particular piece of property or land he is valuing? No, indeed, he does not check anything, he just presumes, especially when someone like myself instructs him to value the plots. Of course, they will be valued on the basis of full ownership… I shall make that quite clear."

Fiona glanced at Charles and then they both nodded in agreement. Life was so wonderful these days!

* * *

Jimmy sat down in the spare seat next to the two couples.

"Where you bin, mate?" inquired Tom, "we've missed you."

"That's nice," said James Pearson-Cooper in the posh English accent that the years in Australia had not diminished.

"Got a letter for you – though why your mail still finds its way to our address, I'll never know!"

Meg dipped into her bag and took out the envelope. She had brought it with her almost as if she expected to see Jimmy that evening. She handed it over, triumphantly.

"There," she said, "I've got it with me! It's from England."

James took the letter from her outstretched hand and

saw the names of Parker, Jones and Winstanley. He recognised them straight away. Even though he had last seen those three names when he was in England, they still struck a chord of hatred in his heart.

"Thanks," he murmured, "I'll read it later." And he stuffed the letter into his trouser pocket.

"Hope it's not bad news!" Meg smiled sympathetically.

"They're always bad news," he commented ruefully.

The evening broke up soon after, with them all promising to meet again soon. James said his goodbyes and slipped away to his house. He was thankful that no one in England had his present address – indeed, he only wished that Henry and Meg had moved at least once since their marriage and then perhaps he would be totally untraceable to any English person.

He got himself a beer and examined the printed address of the solicitors on the front.

"Parker, Jones and Winstanley," he said to himself. "Well, well – when was the first time I saw your name? Back in '48 when I was five. Young, innocent and five! But not so young that I couldn't read the letter sent to my mother, eh. Not so young that the words you wrote were above me."

At five, James had been an avid reader. He was similar in looks to his elder brother Charles but at five he was far sweeter than Charles had ever been. At five, he was far cleverer than Charles had been – he was also better looking and better tempered. However, in spite of all that, he was not the apple of his father's eye like Charles was. Perhaps it was because he was not the first born but just the second. Perhaps it was because his mother adored him.

It had been a normal day until the letter had arrived

by the second post. Father had gone to work; Charles was in his final year at Eton and Mother was reading the newspaper. It was December 17th 1948, a day he remembered quite clearly because it was the day after his birthday.

"I was five and one day," recalled James.

Mother had picked up the letter up from the salver that the butler brought in. She used the letter opener that came with the salver and carefully opened the envelope. She then replaced the letter opener and dismissed the butler. She removed the contents of the envelope and perused them carefully. All the while, James had remained seated, reading a book.

The next thing he knew, his mother had collapsed and the letter had floated down to the carpet next to her.

Whilst attending to his mother's vapours, he could not help but read the letter. Ever since that day, the name of Parker, Jones and Winstanley spelt trouble. The letters that came from them that day onwards further increased the doom that James had felt when he read the first letter. The doom did not go until he had reached the freedom of Perth thirteen years later.

* * *

It had become an almost daily ritual for Fiona to relinquish her world of leisure for a couple of hours, in order to explore the world of financial gain. She enjoyed this new found power, particularly the status that she thought she had obtained within the household.

"I'm afraid that you'll just have to catch the bus!" was a frequent refrain when the teenagers requested transport during the long summer holidays. "Unless you can delay things for an hour or two. You see, I have a little business to deal with." To begin with her offspring were astounded; they just could not believe that their mother had anything other than their immediate needs to attend to. Then their astonishment turned into frustration as they were forced to beg lifts from friends' mothers and even, horror of horrors, to actually catch a bus. Finally, as their mother let slip the amount of money she was really managing to coin in with her mere couple of hours a day, they started to admire her.

They knew nothing, of course, of the legacy. Children can be a little greedy and selfish and the prospect of Blayborough House coming into the family might have resulted in a severe upset in the delicate balance that operated in the Pearson-Cooper household; they might have been tempted to indulge in a little feverish money making activity themselves in order to increase the pot of cash and win the house. This, Charles had admitted to Fiona, could result in an over zealous claim to the house – a sort of "if it hadn't been for us…" form of demand. Fiona immediately recognised the attitude her husband described, reflecting that perhaps their children had inherited a double dose of it from their parents!

So the morning after the visit to the ever-so-helpful Mr. Bates, saw Fiona once again locked in the study, busily at work, as she liked to refer to it.

She was interrupted by the telephone ringing. On answering it she was pleased, though a little bit puzzled, to find that she was talking to their bank manager.

"Fiona, Peter Dawes here, Midland Bank," he announced.

"Oh, good morning, Peter, what can I do for you?"

"Well, to tell you the truth, Fiona, I'm – or should I say we, the bank, indeed it is we in the situation we are talking about…" and he paused, for he was just a little bit in awe of the aristocratic Fiona and her magnificent English accent.

"Peter, do get to the point!" admonished Fiona.

"It is the account that you and your husband set up some months back – I believe you opened it with a £100,000 cheque?" It was a rhetorical question that requested only a helpful "Yes, go on" from Fiona.

"Well, the overdraft that we agreed with your husband…"

"What overdraft?" queried Fiona.

"The overdraft of £25,000," answered Peter, unaware that on the other end of the line, a great deal of consternation was occurring.

"And?" prompted Fiona again.

"We have received a cheque this morning which extends it beyond that limit. If you want to negotiate any further extension, we shall have to ask for additional security."

"Additional? Additional to what? Please remind me, I can't recall what the original security was." Fiona was becoming ever so slightly tense. She twirled the telephone cord around her finger.

"Just hold on a minute and I'll take a look." The phone went quiet for a moment and then there was a rustle of papers. "A cottage on the Blayborough Estate… Tangle Trees Cottage, they call it. Anyway, seeing as you are both such good customers, I'll let this cheque go through but you must arrange some further security. Goodbye." And without waiting for Fiona's response, he put the telephone down.

Amelia had got to grips with the Wilkinson Engineering Works. She had stemmed the flow of clients that were departing and had managed to reverse the fortunes of the factory. However, the reversal was not sufficient enough to provide a permanent future. It was only a temporary measure that merely put off the eventual day of closure. What was needed, she knew, were fresh ideas, new thoughts and enterprises. Now were the days of the Thatcher Enterprise Culture, apparently sweeping through Britain; unfortunately, it had largely swept on past the Wilkinson Engineering Works.

She often turned to John Spencer, of Spencer and Spencer, solicitors to the Wilkinson family and firm, for advice. Not that he could get the factory going again, whirring and humming like the second coming; she leaned on him for more thoughtful consideration, not for energetic revamping ideas. It was largely in his capacity as an advisor that Amelia consulted John Spencer. After all, it was John who had made sure that she had the majority shareholding in the engineering works. A particular piece of advice had been given during the summer of 1986 and Amelia could recall the conversation almost word for word.

"I don't like to be sexist about all this but an engineering works needs a man," suggested John Spencer to his client, Amelia.

"There is Ralph…"

"A man, Amelia, a man – it needs a man!" John Spencer smiled indulgently and then he added, "And how often is Ralph at the works?"

"He comes in every day!" Amelia said stoutly.

"To work? Does he actually come to work?"

"Well…" replied Amelia.

"Precisely!" stated John, as if the whole thing was a fait accompli. "Just what I meant!"

"But I can't sack him," said Amelia. "Can I?"

"There is no need to sack him… just supplant him!"

The idea of supplanting and planting another in his place began to grow on Amelia as she thought about it on and off. John Spencer was rather pleased with how he had handled this situation so far. The consultations he had readily given had become numerous in the past few months as he tried to persuade her the wisdom of, as he thought of it to himself, giving Ralph the boot. He had spent quite a bit of time reminding her of the employee shareholder scheme. This had not proved an attraction to the present set of employees. This was due, John Spencer judged, to the fact that the present employees were somewhat reluctant to take up shares in an ailing company, even at the cheap price that they were being offered at. The shareholding democracy, so prized by Mrs Thatcher, did not attract the rank and file of the Wilkinson Engineering Works. They knew that buying shares, however cheap, in a company that was heading for the rocks was not a sensible way of spending money. So far, only twelve percent of the shares had been taken up, the rest lay in trust waiting for eager employees to snap them up in a fit of foolhardiness.

Naturally enough, John Spencer had advised his client of the marvellous package that could be given to the lucky candidate who secured the position of manger of the works. The salary could be reduced and the shares given as an incentive for the newly appointed manager to work harder and thus share in the profits.

"With thirty-seven percent of the shares, he would want the company to succeed and if you own fifty-one percent and the remaining twelve percent his split between four others, you would still retain overall control," he advised.

Amelia, quite naturally, was delighted with the idea and promptly reduced the amount of salary on offer by £3,500. In late September, she placed an advertisement in the *Yorkshire Post*, sat back and waited for the replies.

Revenge was sweet and revenge on Ralph was even sweeter because it was all quite time consuming and so there could be a rather hefty bill for all those delicious moments! John Spencer wanted his own back on losing out by not marrying Amelia and thus not marrying into money. Though there was obviously less money now, the issue still rankled with both father and son. Remove Ralph, revenge complete. And now I can be the one to instigate the removal of Ralph, thought John Spencer to himself with a smile.

* * *

After the telephone call from the bank manager, Fiona did not feel like working any longer that day. She wondered just what had been going on with the money in the account that was supposed to be financing the acquisition of Blayborough House. She had long since suspected that Charles had another woman but doubted that even he could shower her with quite so much money. Not only was there the original amount missing and spent but so was the profit acquired so diligently by herself from the sales of the plots. Now, it even turned out that an extra £25,000 had disappeared too. Charles had some explaining to do.

She locked the study door behind her and decided that a game of tennis would take her mind off her problems until Charles deigned to return home. She played no mean game but today was distracted by other thoughts and so her partner won easily.

Setting off for home before 3.30 meant that a short detour would take her to the Midland Bank branch where their account was. She could collect copies of statements, just in case Charles had conveniently forgotten where he had put them.

The statements showed just what she had feared. Money had disappeared from the account on a regular basis. The only money that had entered the account had been put there herself. She swept up the drive in her car, relieved to find Charles' car parked in the driveway already. Slamming the door behind her, she stormed into the house, shouting for Charles as she went.

"Hello, darling – had a good day?" he asked.

"No," was her reply and she thrust the statements from the bank in his face.

He smiled, which annoyed her even more.

"An explanation, I want an explanation," she demanded, putting her face just two inches from his.

He grinned even more.

"What about some cottage that you don't even own – Tangle Trees or whatever? I mean, it's a cottage on the estate that we have yet to win!"

Still he offered no reply; and this time he laughed.

"There is nothing to laugh about!"

"Oh, yes there is," he replied, "you think I've spent the lot and more besides, don't you? You think that I've squandered it all on some woman I've got tucked away somewhere?"

"Well, those thoughts had crossed my mind."

"But you're wrong – on both accounts. I've invested it all on the stock market. In fact, I've just been doing a few sums and I see that our original £100,000 is now more than doubled and those dribs and drabs that you have been adding – well, I just put them to work. It was meant to be a surprise for you. When this stock account period ends, a cheque will be coming to clear the overdraft. Tangle Trees will no longer be in jeopardy."

"How did you…?"

"Get a loan, do you mean, on the basis of something I've yet to possess? Ask John Bates – you just would not believe how devoted he is to us. Rather like a dog or fag at Eton – I had one who would do anything for me, I think he had a sort of crush on me, well I am rather handsome. Anyway, whatever, Bates is just like that. We are in his debt but the silly fool doesn't realise it at all – just sees himself as doing his job, like he said to us yesterday."

* * *

The next day, Charles went off shooting somewhere in the Vale of York, as he put it. "Can't give you a contact number, you know these events – all men together out in the wilds." Unfortunately for him, as Fiona noticed when she went past the gun cupboard and checked its contents, he had forgotten his guns and left the labrador behind…

Fiona had an appointment with Mr. Page that day anyway, so what Charles was getting up to did not bother her too much. She had taken to visiting Mr. Page on a weekly basis. It was at his request and she agreed readily. She readily agreed to anything he said or wanted to do. Sometimes she had to dip into other bank accounts to pay the fees he demanded.

* * *

James had just enough time to leave a message on Henry's answering machine to say that he was leaving for England, before making a dash for the airport. The Quantas flight to London took eighteen hours from Perth. This gave him ample opportunity to consider the contents of the letter.

The gist of the peculiar legacy was conveyed and the letter ended in a request that he should make an appointment with Mr. Paul Winstanley if he wished to take up the challenge. If he had no desire to do that, then the writer of the letter requested that he should inform the solicitors so that arrangements could be made.

During the long flight, James' eyes kept straying to the names of the solicitors on top of the letter. The style of letter heading had altered, as anyone would expect considering the length of time that had elapsed. The names were just the same, except that the names of the partners no longer contained a Parker or a Jones and the Winstanley was not the original Winstanley that used to inscribe the letters to his mother and who had signed that first letter, and the only letter he had managed to read, with a flourish.

That first letter – how those words seared him! It had been written so simply, it was almost as if they had wanted a child of five to understand.

"Would you like another drink, sir?" the stewardess asked.

"Just a beer will do," he replied as he went back to his thoughts. Then the letters that followed – always letters, never face to face contact; quite a lot of them came, at least every other day until after a month they stopped. As one letter came, so a reply had to be formulated. There was no one to guide his mother, no help was given. It was a relief when the letters stopped and mother started to smile again. Then he remembered the packing, the tea chests, the trunks from the attic.

"Here you are, sir," smiled the stewardess, "and if you want anything at all, just let me know!" He assured her that he would.

The interruptions by the stewardess had given the man sitting next to James the ideal opportunity to break into James' reverie and start a conversation.

"So you're going back to the mother country?"

As the plane was flying to England, where else would he be travelling, James wondered but chose not to reply facetiously to the question which he presumed was a rhetorical one in any case.

"Family or business?" continued the fellow traveller.

"Family or business, what?"

"Are you returning to visit relations," answered the man a little impatiently, "or is it business?"

"Business, and family, I suppose. A bit of both."

"Oh, I get it," replied the man with a knowing wink, "the firm is coughing up the bill and you're getting in the chance to look up some relatives while you're there!"

"No."

"No, what?" this conversation was getting a little bit difficult for the man sitting next to James. Heaven knows, the man thought to himself, I was only using the line about England, business and relatives as an opening gambit! You'd think he'd jump at the chance to chat during a long flight!

"No, I'm not going to look up relatives," answered James.

"So, it is purely business!"

"Unfinished business," replied James.

"Unfinished business?" queried the man.

"Yes," James said, "unfinished business with relatives."

The fellow traveller decided to look out of the window, peruse a book and watch the movie, all in that order, for the rest of the journey. Polite conversation could sometimes be very heavy going.

* * *

Ralph could not believe his luck with the horse. He mostly won and did sometimes wonder if he might end up getting banned from the booking shop! Going to work, casting a bored eye on the proceedings at the Wilkinson Engineering Company and then spending the rest of the day studying the form filled the time up very nicely for Ralph.

He had decided that the chairman of the board should run the show, considering she had wittered about the downward turn of the business. Ever since then, he had had amazing luck with the gee-gees and put it down to a lack of distraction – a slow dying company can be very distracting and can take up an awful lot of one's energies until one felt one was dying with it.

Amelia, he judged, found the need to apply artificial

respiration to the Wilkinson Engineering Works. Giving the kiss of life to a nearly dead company was something that you only contemplated when you owned fifty-one percent of it. It was rather like a life insurance policy that one might take out on one's partner – except that in this case, the money was only secure if the partner lived!

Betting was just about the most exhilarating thing he had ever found. His heart would race and gallop with the horse he backed; his mouth would go dry with fear until the horse, jockey and his money were safely past the winning post. Then he would collect his winnings and lock them away in the building society until the next time. On occasions, he contemplated going on to the nearby casino when the betting shop closed but he was no fool. He was winning with the gee-gees, so why lose on the turn of a dice?

At the end of the period, when the books were open for inspection by Parker, Jones and Winstanley to see who had created enough profit to win Blayborough, he doubted if he would even come near enough to grab a wing. What he hoped was that he would make enough money over and above the £100,000 he would have to return to the winner to provide for him in the future, when Amelia discovered that the company, and her fifty-one percent along with it, had really died.

Pat O'Reilly, or rather Councillor O'Reilly as was his correct title, became the social angle of the betting shop. His strident socialism was no barrier to their friendship. Ralph was too lazy to be a Thatcherite – being enterprising was an exhausting process – and so they could often find the occasional common ground, which eased their arguments whenever their conversation strayed into politics.

Pat's socialism was of the militant form. He had so far escaped the notice of the national Labour Party but he doubted whether his luck would last too long. Meanwhile, he was steadfastly undergoing a public conversion to mainline socialism, so that when the plug was pulled on him, he could re-emerge in a different form. Of course, he would keep his militant connections, for when the party ousted That Woman, they would need all the ideals they could muster. He knew that he could pull it all off, for he had the luck of the Irish!

Pat, though, was not as lucky with the horses as he was convincing the Labour Party that he was undergoing a transformation. He was even less lucky with the roulette wheel. For a socialist, he was a practised decadent but unfortunately his socialism had not allowed him to amass money through capitalist means. He had no successful business to finance him during his gambling; he had no rich daddy who had left him a legacy. This was why he was a socialist – he wished to have other people's money for his own use, for when he had gambled away the little he had. Unfortunately for him, his party had not managed to achieve power for a while and so he had not been able to grab and squeeze the pips of the rich, so to speak, and catch and use their juice for his own.

Yet, in spite of their different philosophies, Ralph liked Pat. He enjoyed his chatter, he loved his banter and cheerful optimism when things went wrong. The two of them developed a very close friendship, so it was no surprise to Ralph that when Pat was in trouble, it was to him that he turned to.

"What's up, mate," inquired Ralph on seeing his friend so glum.

"Things are a bit rough at the moment," answered Pat.

"Have you tried prayer?" laughed Ralph. They often joked together about the tips that Pat got from the horse's mouth – "God himself told me, during Mass last night!" he would declare, as he placed £100 on another loser.

"I'm past prayer."

"Then you must be ready for confession, if you're beyond prayer!"

Pat did not laugh. His face was showing more wrinkles than normal; his eyes had lost their Irish sparkle. Ralph knew that something serious was up.

"The bank has pulled the rug from under me, they are wanting to repossess the house."

Ralph glanced up at Pat in astonishment. "Repossess? You own a house?"

"Of course I do – we've got to live somewhere!"

"But I thought you lived on a council estate?" queried Ralph.

"I do, I do, but I bought the house a couple of years back when they were offering those big discounts."

"You bought your council house? I thought that you lot were supposed to be against that sort of thing?"

"Look, I haven't got time to discuss party politics with you," Pat said by way of an answer, "I need a loan quickly or else I'll be made bankrupt."

"But if you're made bankrupt, you can't be councillor."

"I know," agreed Pat, "and so I'll lose my only means of support. It'll be a disaster for the lot of us!"

"What does your wife say about all this?"

"How can I burden a woman with five kids and

another on the way with troubles of this sort. Isn't it enough what she has to put up with already without my problems as well. And before you ask, my parents live in a back to back terrace and haven't two pennies to rub together. You're my only hope. You've got to help me. Please, in the name of the Holy Mother of God, help me!" His eyes were pleading and Ralph could not turn away.

"How will you pay me back?" At that Pat's eyes lit up. He had the answer he needed, the money he wanted, and life would go on.

"Look, it's like this – you have money but no information; I have no money but, as a councillor, I have information… So I will pay you back in kind… You will see your money double, treble, quadruple I promise you…"

Pat, Ralph thought, could be the best thing he had ever backed!

* * *

Roland Peterson, broker's representative to the Westbury Group and other large concerns, adjusted his black bow tie. His wife was resplendent, as usual, in a shimmering dress that said designer at a hundred paces. His dinner jacket was hand stitched all down the lapels in a minute black embroidery-like pattern. The same design was copied on the shirt, but this time, the stitches were in white. He had to admire himself in the mirror just once more; it was an amazingly beautiful sight that greeted him.

His second wife, Amanda, had been a model for three years before becoming his mistress. Then Amanda was promoted to wife when wife number one was thrown out (Roland had discovered number one and best friend cavorting together under the bed clothes). As wife number two, Amanda was lusty, cunning, greedy and deliciously attractive – all qualities that Roland admired. Wife number one, meanwhile, had gone off to live in sin with a Scottish laird having abandoned Roland's best friend in a fit of pique at being caught out in such an uncompromising situation.

Luckily for Roland, the first wife had no need of any settlement, which was perhaps just as well for Amanda had the spending powers of many wives put together. Roland, though, was a generous provider. His wealth knew no limits. Their lifestyle was ostentatious. They had so much money that they really did drip it.

"Do you like Charles Pearson-Cooper?" asked Amanda, while rubbing her hands down the line of her dress. She never wore panties with this figure-hugging outfit, a fact which some men guessed.

"He is the director of about six PLCs, reputed to be worth a lot of money – Blayborough House is his, so they say."

"So why do we go to dinner at that neo-Georgian pile of modern rubbish he is living in at the moment?" Amanda pouted at herself in the mirror.

"Search me – perhaps he's having repairs done. I don't know. Maybe there is a hitch with the will – look what it was like when my father died. Who would believe that anyone would have such problems getting money out of the Cayman Islands?"

"I would, darling, I would," simpered Amanda. "After all, I'm half Caribbean myself!"

"Do you think I'd forgotten about that," he said, and

he grabbed hold of her backside, squeezing it hard. "That half is your erotic half!"

After that brief interlude, the two of them set off for the Pearson-Cooper household for a small dinner party that Fiona had been instructed by Charles to arrange.

* * *

John Bates did not have a wife, or a live in girlfriend. He indulged occasionally but had never had the time to find the right woman. Office girls were too plain, for the most part; women solicitors – too bossy. He was not interested in a chain of little Bateses to follow in his footsteps so he never felt the need to acquire a wife with a view to fatherhood. Women were, he considered, pathetic and inclined to cry at the least little thing or else become avaricious... The type of woman he really fancied was the one who could best be described of as like a bowl of plump strawberries, with lashings of cream...

So he only had himself to please, apart, that is, from his clients. Pleasing his clients was his main occupation in life. As the only lawyer who dealt with company law in the practice, he was very keen to extend his range of clients. After all, the more clients he brought in, the more his chances were increased in the partnership stakes. The names of Parker, Jones and Winstanley were bywords in the area. They were the most expensive and the most successful solicitors in the conurbations that littered West Yorkshire. To be a partner in that firm was a passport to riches for ever more! John Bates had set himself the task of achieving that. He knew that Paul Winstanley did not like him, in fact it could be said that

Paul Winstanley hated his guts. Mr. Winstanley, of course, did not hate the fat fees that John Bates brought in. Mr. Winstanley drove a Rolls Royce largely on the back of those fat fees.

The partnership was nearly in the offing. There were just a few more deals to clinch, just a few more national companies to bring under the wing of this provincial firm of solicitors.

It was with this in mind that John Bates set off for the dinner party at the Pearson-Cooper household.

* * *

Meanwhile, another dinner party guest was getting ready. Glenda was putting the finishing touches to her face. She had been given £400 to buy herself a suitable dress and by suitable, the donor of the money had meant that, the dress had to adequately cover her ample proportions. She had chosen a vivid shade of electric blue, a colour that seemed to give even more emphasis than anyone would have thought possible, to her shape.

She was, she knew, voluptuous. So voluptuous that people had been known to gasp on seeing her for the first time; her figure, her mannerisms, her pure sexual dynamism. She was all woman, from the tip of her head to her painted toe nails.

Glenda had no need to pout in the mirror for approval, her lips we so full and round that they permanently pouted but not petulantly, never petulantly. She liked what she saw looking back at her in the bedroom. Every wall in the bedroom had a mirror on it – but the best mirror of all was on the ceiling.

She locked the front door of her cottage and scrambled into her 2CV, which her large frame managed to fill with only a small amount of room to spare. In her mind's eye, Glenda saw herself as a buxom wench or a mother earth figure, which is why she had a cottage and a French peasant car – she even voted Liberal because she was a very liberal woman...

Glenda chuckled to herself as she set off. How naughty of Charles to invite her to a dinner party at his house! She wondered if his wife would guess just who she exactly was.

* * *

Charles adjusted his jacket, it was just a little tight and he resolved to diet just as soon as this night was over. He admired his own reflection in his dressing table mirror. He was still handsome, he thought, nicely tanned and with quite a lot of hair for a man of his age. On closer examination, he could see that his jowls were rather slack, and his eyes, once very piercing, were now encased in puffy skin which was none too flattering. Yet if he pulled in his stomach muscles and tightened his brow, he appeared, to himself at least, as formidable as he did thirty years ago. Age was a peculiar thing – it crept up on one, made its implant and then moved on ahead, waiting in the mirror until noticed. Charles moved on to the landing mirror where the smoked glass complimented his reflection wonderfully.

He further congratulated himself on inviting the luscious Glenda to this little bash. He did consider, when contemplating asking her, whether it was wise to bring her into the lion's den. Supposing Fiona guessed

– what would she say if she knew just who Glenda was? Would she laugh? Or sneer? She definitely would not cry, for Charles judged that Glenda was performing a duty that Fiona did not enjoy; her presence could be an interesting aspect to the evening.

As to the other guests, Charles thought about them one by one. Roland was a creepy corrupt creature; Amanda, reputed to be his wife, was a dusky lusty type; John Bates – "Can I really trust that man?" thought Charles out loud.

"What was that, darling?" asked Fiona.

"Just thinking about our Mr. Bates – do you think we can trust him?"

"But he has been so helpful!" replied Fiona, which was about the extent of her thoughts on him.

"Precisely – why has he been so helpful?"

"He's probably after a back-hander," suggested Fiona. "After all, he knows all about our money, so I expect he'll be wanting a cut!"

Charles merely grumbled in reply.

"By the way, who is this Glenda?" inquired Fiona sweetly.

"She's Bates' cut!" replied Charles, feeling that perhaps the sacrifice of the gorgeous Glenda to the Bates Altar was worth it… what luck that he had found out while they were both at Eton that Bates had a penchant for a couple of ample bosoms!

* * *

Fiona smiled to herself when she heard Charles' remark. So he was getting rid of his bit of stuff, handing her on to someone else, she thought while applying her lipstick.

No doubt he had tired of her, as he had of others before her. She was glad that he could find someone to amuse himself with, someone would share his tastes.

"After all," she commented to herself, "I have my Mr. Page, so I mustn't deny him his extra comforts."

There were times when she did wonder if they would ever find enjoyment in each other again. The nearest that they had got to it was this little escapade, this competition for Blayborough House. This had brought them together in the search for the many ways of making money. It was a shared delight in greed and a need that they both recognised in each other for the lifestyle and home to match their dreams. Except that in her case, the dream was an attempt to replace reality with what she had had in the past – before death duties had forced her family to donate their all to the nation.

Her marriage to Charles Pearson-Cooper had been something of a charade from the moment that she had found Charles eyeing the waitress on their honeymoon. He had not taken it any further, that was true, but she quickly realised that his tastes lay not in the realms of the English rose. His sexual capacity was fulfilled in the arms of the nearest barmaid. This is why she knew that Glenda would be a bit on the common side – she might have virtues and features that could be additional attractions but basically she would be more like the English earth than an English rose like herself grows out from and blossoms. In other words, she would be as common as muck.

* * *

Fiona had installed Mrs Armitage in the kitchen to clean

and had brought in a firm of outside caterers. She had been told by Charles that his dinner party could seal Blayborough House for them, but on no account was she to mention the weird will in front of Roland, Amanda or even Glenda for that matter. Blayborough House, in the eyes of the two main dinner party guests, was already theirs and was undergoing some internal refurbishments prior to them moving in.

Fiona checked the table in the dining room. A flower arrangement adorned the centre and the very best china and silverware graced the linen tablecloth. No one could fail to be impressed by the sheer splendour of it all.

The doorbell went and she dispatched the waitress (she was attired in black and white and came with the caterers as a package) to open it. John Bates was standing there in his dinner jacket and with his briefcase bulging as instructed by Charles.

Fiona welcomed him in with a peck on the cheek. The two of them then fell into pleasantries about life in general and Leeds in particular until Charles sauntered in.

"Do you have it?" he asked anxiously.

"Of course," John Bates replied.

Fiona smiled, for she was in on the secret.

The doorbell rang again and the waitress opened it to an immaculate pair. Roland was beyond handsome – he was almost beautiful. Amanda was slinky, erotic and, past beautiful, was now handsome. The Caribbean half of her spoke volumes to the welcoming Fiona.

"My dear," smiled Fiona, "you look quite something!" Fiona was English, aristocratic and dignified and so felt that she did not need to enlarge on what that 'quite something' was…

As the five of them indulged in little aperitifs, the doorbell went again.

"This will be Glenda," Charles whispered to Roland. "A friend!" he added before Glenda entered the room.

Roland and Amanda both smiled as the ample woman tripped in. John Bates drew a breath in amazement – what a woman!

Fiona mumbled to her husband out of the corner of her mouth, "She's a bit of a floozy, dear!"

* * *

The Quantas plane docked in England during the evening and James alighted. While waiting to go through immigration and customs, James thought of the names of his two brothers – Ralph and Charles. All three were contestants in this most amazing will. He wondered how the other two were doing – how much had they amassed? He had decided his tactics on the plane.

First things first, though, he must visit his mother's grave. Then he would deal with Ralph Pearson-Cooper.

* * *

The six of them sat down at the dinner table and awaited the first course, which was tomato, carrot and orange soup served with wholemeal rolls and finesse by the catering team. Glenda tucked in with gusto and John Bates could not help but notice that as she ate, her bosoms moved up and down. It was quite fascinating and was the only reason he did not contribute much to the conversation that was going on around him.

Roland was informing the others about how he made his first million in under two years. It had obviously been surprisingly easy.

"But what type of help did you have initially?" inquired Charles, thinking that perhaps he had been left a fortune or had stepped into his father's business.

"Help? I had no help."

"But you must have had some help – no one can make money that quickly!" Fiona added.

"Of course you can – if you haven't, you just haven't been trying!"

Fiona was tempted to reply to that, but politeness forbade her for the moment to put the man in his place and so she merely smiled.

Amanda tore off a little section of bread and chewed at it erotically. Her lips were full and dark, and their movements made watching her eat a voyeur's experience. Fiona cut her roll daintily and carefully coated it in butter.

The fish course arrived and was, in turn, devoured. The conversation turned to each other's origins. Fiona always enjoyed this subject. The reason being partly because she could boast dramatically, cause unseen amounts of envy and then castigate her husband for not returning her to the station she was born into. The trips to India, knowing various cousins of the Queen, half, step and otherwise (although as the Queen had many cousins and other assorted relations, that was not too difficult to achieve), and having led a charmed childhood, left most listeners dripping with unconcealed jealousy. Unfortunately for Fiona, these particular listeners were not too impressed. Amanda and Roland both felt that they had surpassed and outpaced anything that Fiona had experienced in the past. Glenda considered that it explained everything about Charles – his constant need for her for one thing. John Bates tried to look interested – Fiona did not really count for anything in the game of chance that he was playing, it was her husband who held the key; it was Charles who would give the key to him, John Bates, which would unlock the golden door to the Bates fortune! Charles did not even try to look interested – he had heard it all before and patiently waited for her to come to the bit at the end.

"I do hope my little tales of the past are not making you too jealous!" she said when she had completed the finale – the bit about when she encountered the Queen at Royal Ascot ("I was so touched, she remembered my name from two years previously!").

Roland was not jealous, merely amused. He did not try to hide the fact that her found her pathetic. When she had finished her little diatribe, he asked if she thought that such a life had been of any help to her.

"How do you mean, help to me?" replied Fiona, somewhat frostily.

"How do you equate your background with your position today?" continued Roland. Sensing the beginnings of a few choice words, even Glenda called a halt to her chewing of the rolls to listen.

"My position?"

"Yes, your position," Roland did not care that he was treading on dangerous ground. He was used to upsetting people – that was how he had got where he was today. He also recognised that Fiona was used to upsetting people, so the two of them were meat and spice to each other's sandwich. "Do you think that your initial little childhood sortie into the faded ranks of the aristocracy prepared you for your life now?"

"Absolutely!" answered Fiona. "For thanks to my excellent breeding, I can sniff an East End barrow boy at a hundred paces!" Her nose twitched and she whispered in tones loud enough for her guest opposite her to hear, "Goodness, yes!"

"I'm not ashamed of my background."

"Of course not, nor am I," smiled Fiona.

"And I'm proud that I'm a self-made man!"

"Indeed, I'm sure your are – in fact, I can see 'Established 1980s' printed all over you!"

Roland smiled and then laughed – he had met his match, or at least he was not prepared to take the matter any further considering that he was a guest in the redoubtable woman's house.

"Alright, I am an East Ender but I saw my dad was taken care of – I created a little fortune for him and he lived like a lord in his last years! Can you say the same about your dad – did you make enough money for him to live like a lord again?"

Charles thought that he had better try to defuse the situation. He needed Roland's goodwill, and so he did not want his wife upsetting the man. Charles could never understand why Fiona insisted on goading people – she was such a snob, that he knew, but did she have to be rude as well? What is more, she knew well enough why Roland had been invited so why provoke him? Yet, as Charles pondered about his wife, he knew that Roland was not really upset, more amused.

"Is your mother still alive?" asked Charles and the other non-combating dinner party guests heaved a sigh of relief.

"No," answered Roland, "my mum died twenty years ago and after that, I set up a fund for my dad just as soon as I had made some money. I invested it in the Cayman Islands – that's where I met Amanda!"

Amanda smiled succulently and seductively. The male dinner party guests were all impressed with the apparent twin advantages of the Cayman Islands.

The rest of the meal proceeded amicably enough and at ten o'clock, when the meal had ended, Fiona let the other two women in to the study for coffee. The three men stayed behind to discuss business.

However, first of all, Charles felt the need to apologise for his wife. There was too much riding on all this for Roland to be peeved over anything that Fiona had said.

"Excuse Fiona, Roland," began Charles, "but she has this thing about her youth – getting a bit bitter, I think."

"No need to apologise – all forgotten! Let's get down to business, shall we?" Roland smiled at Charles, as he was expected to do. Actually, all Fiona had said had been water off a duck's back to him. He did not care what she thought of him, whether she liked him or not. He never allowed personal feelings to come in the way of business and he saw this relationship as strictly business. He also knew that Fiona and Charles were just the types who would realise disaster was coming when it was too late and thus could be relied upon to be the ones who would be left behind to carry the can.

Roland put a reassuring hand into his jacket pocket. He could already see the extra passports – the ones that he would need when the going got tough, and the tough got going!

* * *

James checked into the hotel next to the airport. The flight had been exhausting and arriving in England in Autumn was miserable. If he had not had a good reason to leave his mother country in the first place, the weather would have given him enough impetus.

The hotel receptionist was friendly and welcoming. The last time he had stayed in a hotel in England was the night before he had left for Australia. He remembered how bored all the staff had been – they had showed no interest in his needs, barely looking up when he had asked for a single room. It was only when they noticed how young he seemed that they awakened to the possibility that he might not have enough money to pay. He had had enough, of course, for that was the least that his father could do. His hotel bill, his airfare and accommodation in Perth with a couple who used to work for his father – all those things had been arranged and paid for.

James lay on the bed in the modern Posthouse and reflected that at the age of eighteen and two weeks after his mother's death, he had been dispatched to Perth.

* * *

The three women eyed each other without mercy. They sat in three separate seats and crossed and uncrossed their legs in mused silence. Fiona was trying desperately to think of some conversation point that would draw them together but her mind was a complete blank. What topic could there be that could begin an hours bewitching chatter between three totally different women?

"So, you are from the Cayman Islands?" began Fiona to the exotic Amanda. It was a rhetorical question which Fiona hoped would produce a long reply, extolling the virtues of the tropics, the beaches, the natives, the best places to stay and so on.

"That area," replied Amanda.

"We went to Bermuda for a holiday a few years back. We had a super time! Have you been to Bermuda?" she asked Amanda.

"No, but I went to Jamaica for a month last year."

"I've never been to Jamaica," replied Fiona, "only Bermuda."

"I haven't been to either," put in Glenda.

"So, which exotic island have you been to then?" inquired Fiona politely. She had a feeling that this conversation was not going to run for long – they did not seem to even have a tropical island in common.

"I went to Jersey a few years back," offered Glenda, as an additional talking point.

"Jersey? I've never been to Jersey," began Fiona with the faint feeling that she had been down this conversation road before.

"We have bank accounts in Jersey," Amanda mentioned.

"So you have been to Jersey then?" Glenda asked Amanda.

"No, we just have a couple of bank accounts there."

"I expect you'll be going on holiday there soon, then, if your bank is there. I mean to say, if you went to Jersey, it would be quite handy to have a bit of local cash to call on," Glenda remarked.

"Oh, they are not that sort of bank accounts," replied Amanda with a sultry smile.

"Oh," said Fiona and Glenda together.

The three of them shuffled in their seats for a few moments, as a way of distraction. Fiona then had a bright idea. "Fancy watching a video?" The other two nodded in agreement. Fiona put the only pre-recorded video that she and Charles possessed into the machine and the three of them all settled down to view *The Sound of Music.*

* * *

"Right then, now that the women are out of the room, let's talk business," Roland suggested.

The other two men nodded and Charles passed the port to John. With their glasses recharged, the three of them leant forward in their chairs. This was the whole point of the evening, the reason for the three of them coming together.

"As you know, I'm the broker for the Westbury Group of companies. I have been assigned the task – if you remember, Charles, – of looking out for other suitable companies with a view to takeovers." Here Roland paused for a moment; he took a quick sip of port and then continued, "The Westbury Group is asset rich now that they have sold some of their properties to a subsidiary company. They have money in the bank ready to invest in shares of other companies."

Charles smiled. His idea that he had put forward to Angus in the spring had been acted on. This was the first that he had heard of its fruition, after it had been grudgingly accepted by the chairman, Angus McNeil. His position as a director in the company was generously financed and did not require his attendance at many board meetings. There had been no mention of any possible takeovers in the offing when he had visited the company during the summer, so he was glad that he had revived the old friendship between himself and Roland Peterson.

"I've drawn up a list of possible companies for Angus to consider," he said as he handed the list to the other two sitting around the table.

Charles scanned the names – he recognised a couple of them but the rest were mostly small firms.

"The top two are a couple of sleeping beauties," stated Roland. "They are really the best takeover bets – very attractive and no one has spotted their potential yet!"

John Bates passed the list back to Roland, who replaced it in his pocket.

"Now I have put my cards on the table and shown you something," stated Roland, "what have you two got to offer? Charles?"

Charles smiled back and reached into the breast pocket of his dinner jacket. He had his own list.

"These are companies I am a director of," he said as he passed the piece of paper to Roland. John Bates pretended to look at it but it was not really necessary for he knew off by heart Charles' financial and other positions.

"Now you, John, what can you offer us?" asked Roland.

"I specialise in company law – at Parker, Jones and Winstanley, I find out about any moves that a firm has to make before anyone else does. I handle their legal work. I am privy to the thoughts of the chairmen and directors of a number of companies with headquarters in the West Yorkshire area. When they want advice about property purchases, or sales, impending legal issues that might affect their share price, possible takeovers of other companies by themselves or potential takeovers of themselves, when they want advice, they come to me. I offer them confidential help to assist them in their ventures. I hear about everything, when it is just a gleam in a chairman's eye; all confidential, of course!"

"Confidential help that will assist us too!" Charles laughed out loud. The other two men joined in with his laughter, partly as a result of the drink that they had been consuming, but mostly due to the thought of the potential profits that they could make.

"You see," began Roland, "this is where others make the mistake – when they use information gathered for their own advantage – they buy a few too many shares from too few brokers during too few days…"

"Phew!" cried out Charles – the drink was adding to his bewilderment (a case of a few too many!) – then he had the idea of drinking a final drink to the venture: "Gentlemen, let's have a toast!" and the three of them recharged their glasses. "I give you the toast to insider dealers, long may we all flourish!"

"To insider dealers!" the other two said and the three of them clinked glasses together to confirm their friendship based on mutual cooperation.

* * *

Glenda shed a few tears when *The Sound of Music* was on. She had seen the film twice before and had never failed to be moved by it. She adored a good love story.

She did sometimes wonder if such delights would befall her. Whether she too would fall in love with some rich and handsome man and become the mistress of some large house, instead of being a mistress full stop. She did not, however, fancy becoming a nun in order to achieve this. Nuns tended to fall for priests, and that path looked a little bit stony and narrow for her to climb. *Climb every mountain… till you find your dream* – Glenda considered that she was still climbing what was turning out to be a whole mountain range!

Amanda had never seen the film before. She had heard about it and on the basis of what she had heard, she knew it was one to miss. How could anyone be so foolish to fall in love with a man who had a whole tribe of children? she wondered to herself. It was incomprehensible and ridiculous and very long. Fiona congratulated herself on having chosen such a suitable film for the three of them to watch. It was innocent and pure and best of all it was long, so now there was no need for any of them to try and think of conversation for the rest of the evening.

Fiona let the film drift over her head. She smiled to herself and contented herself with pure thoughts of money – lots and lots of money!

* * *

After midnight, the dinner party broke up. The men had sorted out their bits and pieces of business and the women had watched enough of the film to keep them amused while they were waiting.

"Shame we missed that bit near the end, when they are singing on the stage," said Glenda wistfully.

"Singing on the stage?" inquired Amanda.

"You know, as the Von Trapp Family singers or whatever they called themselves. "

"Such a shame!" agreed Amanda sarcastically. The sarcasm was lost on Glenda and she merely began to wax lyrical about the youngest member of the Von Trapp family. Fiona gently guided her to the door with a suggestion. "Why don't you have the video – to keep?"

With extreme gratitude, Glenda accepted and went cheerfully on her way. John Bates guided her to her car and slipped his telephone number into her pocket. This pleased her more than the video did.

Roland and Amanda were the next to go and they sped away after pecking Fiona on the cheek.

John Bates remained, as requested by Charles. The three of them retreated to the study where they looked at the information that John had brought with him. They thought that they knew exactly what was in the briefcase and were looking forward to viewing the various bits and pieces; their thoughts, unfortunately for them, were not quite accurate…

He took out of his briefcase various envelopes and documents. He knew that he had the two of them in the palm of his hand. He could just squeeze and they would squeal but, as they would now find out, they could not get out and instead would have to put up with what he planned. He started to begin his squeeze now.

"What we are going to have to do is a spot of rationalisation," began John. Fiona, in spite of having watched the video, was still slightly pickled and could not work out what exactly rationalisation was but it sounded interesting!

Charles knew it to be the shorthand for streamlining, getting rid of and simplifying things. It was a policy of rationalisation that had caused the redundancies of 350 men at the firm he was a director of, so he was quite familiar with it.

"What do you propose to do?" he asked.

"At the moment, you have many different building plots and half finished houses waiting for buyers to complete before you have to complete with the builders and so on and so forth!"

"Yes, we know, go on," urged Fiona.

"The other day I suggested that we should obtain loans on the strength of these assets," continued Bates. "Well, I've talked to a number of banks and that is no problem – we could have over a million pounds to invest!"

"A million? A million!" exclaimed Fiona. "So Charles and I are millionaires!"

"No, you are not!" replied John firmly. "You are borrowing a million. With that money, you must turn it very quickly into real money – that is, money that you actually own and belongs to us."

Charles' ears pricked up when he heard that little word: 'us'. His heart began to pace somewhat as he realised that they were coming to the nitty-gritty of it all – the pay off, the cut, the fee that John Bates would require. He would bide his time, he decided, before challenging John on this. First of all, he thought, he must get one fact clear.

"Why should we borrow from the banks? I know you mentioned it the other day but you did not say what the purpose was. Why can't we continue to do as we have been doing? It seems like a good way of earning a bit to me!"

"The building companies are starting to sniff a rat. The firm is getting telephone calls from them and the letters from their solicitors are becoming more searching. You've done this little scam for six months now and I think you should call a halt to it. You should get out of the housing market – or perhaps I should say the un-built housing market – and use the money gained, and the loans that can be obtained, to invest in shares; shares such as the type that the three of us discussed tonight!" He smiled at Charles, who took the hint and did not mention anything further about the little plan hatched over the port. The fewer people who knew about it, the better! Fiona, in any case, as Charles knew, possessed a lower level of sophistication (based nearer to honesty than Charles' ever was) that could not appreciate the gains to be made from inside knowledge.

"So, to recap: we move out of the plots and into shares using other people's money – the banks' money. We make large profits from shares, repay the loans and hey presto, we are rolling in money," said Charles.

"Precisely," agreed John.

"Sounds good to me!" echoed Fiona. Anything that involved large increases in money sounded good to Fiona.

"Just one thing, John," began Charles.

John stiffened slightly. He notices the edge in Charles' voice. He spotted the firmness of the lips and the steel blue gleam in his eyes.

"Yes?" he prompted.

"You mentioned a few moments ago 'the money that you actually have' and 'belongs to us.'" Charles smiled encouragingly, "who is this 'us'?"

"We three!" answered Bates promptly.

"Yes, but, how can money that belongs to us two," he pointed to himself and his wife, "suddenly belong to us three?"

"Because I have arranged for an account to be started in each of the four High Street Banks in our names. No one will be able to withdraw money from that account without the other two signing and agreeing to it. It is protection against one of us running off with the money."

Fiona was sobering up pretty fast here. "If Charles or I ran off with the money, okay, it's our money to run off with; but I don't understand where you come into this – why do we have to protect ourselves from you running off with the money – it's not your money?"

John Bates smirked at her and narrowed his eyes. "But it is just as much my money as yours! You see, you seem to forget that I know about everything. I am the only one who knows how you made your money and how you will make even more; Tangle Trees – that cottage on the Blayborough estate, you remember – false documents, false valuations, different names – you agreed and signed the lot of them…"

"But you produced them, you did it. You are just as much to blame as we are!" interjected Charles.

"Oh, no – that is not the case! You seem to have forgotten – when you used different names, you wrote and spoke to different conveyancing clerks, not me. To Jane, you were Mrs Cooper, to Mrs Earnshaw, you were Mr. and Mrs Pearson-Cooper and so on. Parker, Jones and Winstanley are a very big firm. No one ever needed to see you about the houses, you were just names. The clerks did not know that they were dealing with fraudulent names! I am the only person who can connect the names with you two. However, the actual transactions were nothing to do with me for I deal with company law, not houses!"

"But we came to see you – we had appointments!" protested Charles.

"About the will, you had appointments about the will." John Bates produced a piece of typewritten paper from his briefcase and showed it to Charles and Fiona. It was an alleged account of the meeting that they had had a few days ago. It spoke of questions that Fiona had asked about the will, points that she was unclear about.

"But we did not come to discuss that – we did not visit you to talk about the will!"

"That is what it says here!" John put the paper back into his briefcase.

"And the letter you sent to us asking to see us – that is proof that you were involved."

"Proof of what?"

"Proof that we are your clients!" stated Charles.

"Yes, it is proof that you are my clients," agreed John, "clients with regard to the Pearson-Cooper will."

"And Tangle Trees," Charles shouted out, "what about Tangle Trees?"

"Have you a letter about Tangle Trees from me? I don't think so. I was on holiday, I believe, when you signed the documents concerning Tangle Trees. I know nothing about it. I did not deal with you and Tangle Trees!"

"It was your idea!"

"Prove it."

"You suggested it on the telephone…" Charles said lamely.

"What telephone call was that? I don't remember any telephone call. How could I possibly agree to letting you use Tangle Trees as security when you did not even own it?"

Charles and Fiona realised that he had covered himself enough for them to be exposed to what was covert blackmail. How naïve they had been to think that someone would do it all for small potatoes. What was narking Charles even more was the fact that he had sacrificed the gorgeous but gaudy Glenda to the toad Bates. His original estimation that Bates was slimy was correct. Charles acknowledged that he and Fiona had made a serious error of judgement. They had let their love of money cloud their thinking and allowed someone to take advantage of them. What they could do about it, he did not know. All that he knew was that there was probably no option but to carry on. Once Bates shared an account with them, he would be implicated just as much as they were! They would then sink or swim together!

Fiona and Charles sat down. By sitting themselves down, they demonstrated that John Bates had won. It was a climb-down. John allowed one corner of his mouth to move slightly in a smug grin before he also sat down opposite them.

"It's not too bad," he began, "after all, it is only money and if you pull this off, you will get Blayborough House!"

It was the only comforting thought that Charles and Fiona could think of to cheer themselves up.

"Think of money as a commodity – tins of baked beans or whatever. The trick is not to think of money as the means of purchasing something but just as, well, numbers on a balance sheet. Never actually visualise pound notes. That's my advice, for what it is worth!" stated John. Charles and Fiona just nodded. He then continued, showing them bits of paper form Barclays and so on. "These are the accounts I am in the process of setting up. If you would like to sign here and here, next to my signature, then I will take them back tomorrow."

The couple duly signed the forms for the four bank accounts that were to be created in their three names.

"I have arranged for all the securities to be spread out between the four accounts, so if you could sign these forms here…"

"What are these?" questioned Fiona.

"Please read them and you will see that they are just charges on property and land; just normal forms to back the loans."

Charles made a point of glancing through each one. It was a gesture of defiance but only a gesture. What could he do? If they refused to sign then Bates would withdraw his support and who knows what charges of fraud they would be up against. The Inland Revenue and the police would be round in double quick time; and before the authorities would have a chance to work out everything backwards and eventually trace the lot to Bates, the blackguard would have slipped the country.

It ran through Charles' mind that perhaps he and Fiona could slip the country but he dismissed the thought. They were too near to gaining everything to throw it all away now. Bates was right; without his help, they would be nowhere near to making a mint and grabbing the goods. Charles signed everything he was asked, including the form that closed their present account and transferred all the money that they had both carefully accumulated since spring into the new accounts. Fiona copied Charles. Protest, she knew, would be useless.

"Lovely!" exclaimed Bates once everything was duly signed and completed. "Now, whenever we need to invest or withdraw any money, we can only do it with the agreement of each other!"

He got up to go and then paused by the door. "Oh, just one more thing," he began.

"What?"

"All share dealings will go through Harrison and Harpers – same basis as the bank accounts. Total agreement!" He produced a typewritten letter with spaces for signatures ready for the three of them to fill in. "After all, where money is concerned, you can't trust anyone!"

* * *

Amelia dressed herself suitably for the important day ahead. She always tried to look smart, now that she was an active player in the company. Today, however, was especially important. It was the day of the big interview.

She had interviewed personnel before – workers for the factory floor, a cleaner for the morning shift and so on. Those had been easy occasions, a more of a general getting-to-know-you type of thing. This time it would be different.

She had sifted through the assortment of application forms that had arrived in response to her advertisement in the *Yorkshire Post*. Nine people had replied. At first, she had been most gratified at the numbers interested in the position. However, on further examination, she discovered that seven of the applicants were absolutely unsuitable.

It was not that she was looking for a paragon of expertise or for somebody with a string of qualifications. What she wanted was some indefinable quality, which would show itself in success in a previous post. The winning candidate had to be someone who had previously retrieved an ailing firm from the ashes and brought it back to life. She was looking for an ability to rejuvenate, a believer in reincarnation and a person to whom achievements mean more than remuneration.

When she had whittled the respondents down to two, she had examined their CVs with the utmost care. The other seven were sent polite notices of thank you but no thank you. Percy Albert Jenkinson was fifty-seven years of age and had previously owned a similar company in the Midlands, until he had sold out to a large multi-national firm. His firm had undoubtedly been a success but, as he said in his CV, retirement was now beginning to bore him and he longed for a challenge. Amelia was immediately attracted to that statement, for she had a challenge she longed to give someone.

Tony Driver was forty-three and was a manager for a large company in the south. He wanted more responsibility, more opportunity to make decisions. His expertise were rounded and wide but more in the luxuriant fields that a major firm could offer. Amelia wondered if he would miss his expense account lunches, his dealings with large concerns in the UK and Europe. She considered that perhaps Wilkinson Engineering Works would be small potatoes to him.

Today was to be the day when she would find out. She was attired for the event. Ralph had been and gone at the office. She had assigned him his usual tasks of picking the children up from school, as well as vacuuming and generally cleaning up. Their cleaner had been sacked as part of an economy drive. Ralph was shaping up nicely in that field. What he did the rest of the day, she had no idea. He kept out of mischief, that she knew, and a regular check around his clothes for perfume and any other evidence of a sexual liaison showed that he was not indulging in women in his spare time. It made no difference to their income who turned up at the works. It made more sense that someone who was actually committed to the firm should roll up and take charge. She had grown quite used to being the man about the house. Ralph made a good wife.

Percy Jenkinson put on his three piece suit. It was of excellent quality. His house was as expansive as it was expensive. His Jaguar, which he could afford to renew every three years from his investments, was the sleekest around. He drove from Staveley, near Knaresborough, to the appointed place for his interview – it had not been many years ago that the boot had been on the other foot and he had been the one to do the interviewing! That experience had given him all the wrinkles he needed to get the position – if he wanted it. He was not sure whether he did indeed want it.

As he drove along the lane towards the A6055 that would take him to Harrogate and then onto Leeds, he congratulated himself on coming to North Yorkshire to retire. It was a beautiful county, quite understated and so quite unknown to many. This merely increased its beauty in his eyes for it meant that many areas were relatively untouched by tourists.

He had checked out the route the night before. The firm was in Armley, Leeds. Apparently, it was quite near to the prison… this thought had not inspired him one little bit. His Jag wormed its way around the ring road that would take him to Armley. The weather was brilliant when he had left home – bright sunlight had caused the leaves to literally drip in golden rays. But storm clouds gathered as he approached Leeds. It was raining in Armley.

It did not take Percy long to find the works. They were not as near to the prison as he had first feared but they looked prison-like. He parked his car in the staff car park and then entered the works. It was a grim building, made worse by the now torrential downpour.

The receptionist was not waiting in the hall, as she should have been. There was only a slight hum of activity coming from the works – a fact that his experienced ear picked up straight away. The place was run-down, down at heel and he now was feeling distinctly down in the mouth. Did he really want to take on this at his age? he asked himself. No he did not!

"Tell Mrs Pearson-Cooper that I have changed my mind and do not want to be considered for the position," he told the receptionist when she finally deemed to turn up.

Percy sped off home as fast as he could. When he parked his car outside his small mansion in Staveley, he could not help but notice that not a drop of rain had fallen in this neck of the woods…

Tony had driven up from his house in Colchester the night before. He had stayed the night with some old mates of his from university days – the same friends who had sent him a copy of the jobs section of the *Yorkshire Post* a few weeks back. He was glad to get out of the house. It was quiet and strange now that his wife had left him for another man. Thank God for the other man, he often said, for taking her away! The quietness without her haranguing him every night was weird though; and it was strange to go to bed alone of an evening – for though she had been an unwilling bed partner, she had at least been there.

He was not at all familiar with Leeds, in spite of going to university – or rather college of advanced technology, as it was then known – in Bradford. Leeds, he knew from what he had read in that morning's edition of the *Yorkshire Post*, was the financial centre of Yorkshire, it was revived and up and coming. Well, that suited Tony down to the ground for he was up and coming – up and coming from Colchester! What luck that this Mrs Pearson-Cooper had not checked his references out. The fact that he had been sacked for misappropriation of funds would not be uncovered and he could slip into a new position, suitably chastened and reformed!

Amelia greeted the news that there would be one candidate less to interview with dismay. She needed to fill the vacancy as soon as possible and could not afford a delay while she re-advertised. It would have to be this Tony Driver, there was no one else to choose from.

"Where are his references? I've been going through the file and I can't find them," she asked her secretary.

"References?" the secretary replied to her boss.

"Yes, I asked you to get them last week!"

The secretary shook her head, nothing rattled and went back to her typing.

"Well, I'll just have to appoint without them," murmured Amelia gloomily. "References very rarely tell you much, unless it is something dreadful, such as he's been caught with his fingers in the till."

Tony Driver, being the only candidate, was offered the job. He accepted and surprised Amelia by saying that he could start the following Monday.

* * *

Ralph was handling the vacuum with the utmost care. He had found that if he swung it around too much, the bits were not picked up and he had to do it all over again. After the vacuuming, he was planning to clean the windows. The window cleaner had been sacked at the same time as the cleaner. Being at home gave him the chance to reflect that things were just a little unfair. For example, when Amelia was the housewife, he had provided her with a cleaner and a window cleaner; now that the roles were reversed, she had sacked them both.

Furthermore, when she was at home, he did not once imagine that she would be doing anything other than keep house and socialise; now that he was at home, he had on two occasions caught her sniffing his clothes – for perfume, he presumed. Had he ever in the past questioned her faithfulness even once? No he had not. He even wondered, in his darker moments, whether the sacking of the cleaner and the window cleaner were more to do with her wanting to make sure that he kept busy than with the desire to economise!

Ralph picked up the ringing phone. "Hi, it's Pat here," came the unmistakable Irish voice at the other end.

"Hello, how are things?" was Ralph's reply. It was a rhetorical question which required a positive answer, not the truth.

"Fine, and you?"

"Oh, not too bad."

Pleasantries over, Pat then launched into what he had really rung about.

"Want to see you, Ralph, as soon as you are free."

"Lunchtime – I'm free lunchtime. What if we meet at that new wine bar that's opened up off Park Street?"

Pat quickly agreed and then hung up – he had an important Labour Party committee meeting to attend before he disappeared off for his lunch date.

At half past twelve, Ralph was to be found sipping wine at the aptly named Park Wine Bar. He had gone into Leeds on the bus, which was a novelty for him. Parking in Leeds was a nightmare that he did not wish to indulge in. The metro bus was cheap and quite regular, so he had plonked himself next to an elderly man who was off to the shops for the day.

Pat arrived in a hurry. He only had time for a lasagne and a pint of lager before he had to be back for a full council meeting.

"Did you manage to stave off the bailiffs?" asked Ralph in a whisper.

"That's what I wanted to see you about," replied Pat.

Ralph moved back in his seat slightly – he was hoping that Pat was not going to touch him for another few grand. He needed that money to make more.

Pat noticed the look of apprehension on his friend's face and grinned at him.

"Don't you worry there," he said comfortingly, "I have no need for any more!"

Ralph smiled back in relief. "So what do you want?" he inquired.

"To return the favour – if you remember, I said that I would give you information in return for the money," he was whispering so that no one could hear. "You know that I'm on the Highways Committee, well the Labour group have decided which route to go for, you must have heard about it, they've been thinking about it for years!" Pat dropped his voice even lower, so that Ralph had to bend forward to hear the next few words. "It's going through Castle Street. Now, it is the same Castle Street that has a block of offices on it, all unoccupied and dilapidated and right in the way of the new road. Buy the block and put in plans to do it up. Get a valuation on the basis of those plans by the end of next week."

"When is the announcement due?" whispered Ralph, sotto voce.

"Government approval is expected in two months' time – enough time to give your scheme credibility. Make sure the papers know about it and the local residents' groups, so it looks genuine – but don't make out that there will be lots of jobs in it. Then when the announcement is made, sit back and await compensation!"

Ralph took another slurp of his wine and sat back in his chair. Betting took many forms and this bet, backed with inside knowledge, looked a winner!

* * *

James had been in the old country for three days before he made the journey north to pay his respects. It had taken a bit of getting used to, this new England. It was vibrant and active and people seemed to be enjoying their smell of success. James planned to visit Bradford first, to lay some flowers on his mother's grave. Then he had an appointment with Mr. Paul Winstanley at Parker, Jones and Winstanley in Leeds.

In his hire car he set off for the council crematorium. Nab Wood Cemetery was in a valley. It had often occurred to James, during the fortnight before his banishment to Australia when he visited it every day, that this could be likened to the Valley of Death, except no one charged down here on horseback; they came in large cars and in wooden boxes.

The crematorium was smoking today and wreathes, honouring the dead person who lay a-smouldering in his coffin, were laid out on the grass outside the small chapel. As James went past, the chapel started to empty and people came out, some clutching their hankies, others chatting away.

They all inspected the wreaths, just to make sure that the flower shop had sent theirs and it looked worth the fortune it had cost. Then as James walked on to the rows of graves, he imagined that now, floral tributes viewed, they would be setting off to the funeral tea. There would be roast ham sandwiches and trifle to finish off with. They would all be telling stories about how marvellous the dear deceased was, before falling into great discussion as to which piece of furniture they would most like to appropriate.

His mother had not had a funeral tea to view from up above. His mother had been buried without much ceremony. There had been few at the graveside to witness things.

James found the headstone that marked her spot quite quickly. Her body had filled the final space in the grave and she was put to rest with her parents, who had died before her. It came as no surprise to him that the grave had been left untended. He knew that Charles and Ralph lived nearby – and his father when he was alive – but they had obviously not been near for a long time, if at all.

"Our time for revenge has come," he mumbled as he lay the flowers on the mound. "But I shall bide my time until I can be sure of good results – I'll make them regret what they did to us!"

PART THREE
Spring 1987

Fiona tingled with excitement as she stepped into her car for the journey to Bradford. For some reason, the mere setting off from a beautiful home and very splendid surroundings (albeit not quite as splendid as Blayborough), to arrive at a run-down and dingy building just off Lumb Lane was enough to make her feel stimulated. It was the contrast – the sumptuousness compared with starkness; the soft as opposed to the hard; the layers of pastel finery against the bareness of black flesh.

Mr. Page had of late been more demanding. Fiona knew that she had become more compliant. As his demands increased, so her subservience grew.

Before arriving there, she called in at the bank to withdraw the rest of the month's housekeeping. She made mental plans about how she was going to replenish the funds. Perhaps she could borrow the mortgage money?

* * *

Charles was on the way to yet another board meeting. It always amazed him that the more directorships one held, the more meetings one is asked to hold. It must be that – he had deduced in the past – companies thought that experience went hand in hand with quantity. For some it might, for Charles it did not. Fees and perks went hand in hand with quantity as far as Charles was concerned.

"Actually," he thought out loud to himself, "experience did give one marvellous advantage – it taught one how to negotiate the best deals for oneself!" In this respect, he had John Bates to thank, for he had given him a few wrinkles that would protect him whatever the fortunes of the company.

The relationship with Bates had settled down after the first initial shock last autumn. They had managed to pull it off and now the large profit was sitting in the one bank account. Splitting the money three ways, and protecting your back from the daggers held by others, through mutual agreement, did have its advantages. Bates had been right, as far as money is concerned, you cannot trust anyone; even one's wife, pondered Charles. He had left Fiona looking flushed and nervous that morning; he had found her in that state quite regularly these past few months.

The car phone went as he wondered about what his wife was up to. He picked it up and continued to steer the car with his right hand.

"Charles?" said the voice. "It's Roland!"

Now it was Charles' turn to feel flushed. Whenever Roland rang, it was always to tell him about some deal or other; and it was always a rushed job. The three of them – John, Charles and Roland – spoke in code, just in case someone was listening in. This especially applied to car phones, which are notorious for sharing lines with all and sundry. Charles personally thought that the code was so obvious that if someone was really listening in to their conversations, they would be able to crack it. However, he was bound to agree with the other two, who insisted that a code would protect them from the casual listener but no code could protect them from the professional, for the professional was armed with personal information relating to the three of them.

So, they each had a list of companies, firms that they had connections with. The list was numbered. The days of the week were also numbered. It was thus quite simple to make the whole conversation out to be a tip for the horses!

"Got a tip for you," began Roland.

"Great!"

"Number seven at eight to four at 3.30," continued Roland.

"Thanks – I'll put one on!" And that was that.

Charles replaced the telephone and put two hands back on the steering wheel. He had need to rest his hands, for he found that they were shaking slightly. He decided to pull in at Hartshead Moor for a coffee and a sit down.

Once off the M62 and parked, Charles fumbled in his pocket for the list of companies. He needed to see the list in order to find out which company number seven was. In his breast pocket, he found only a couple of tranquillisers – tablets he was now taking every day – and a pound coin. The rest of his jacket pockets were empty, so were his inside pockets.

"My wallet – it must be in my wallet," he muttered out loud. He retrieved his wallet from his briefcase and opened it up. There were notes in one compartment and pieces of paper with important messages in the other. His credit cards were all present. There was no list of numbered companies. In vain, Charles searched his briefcase. Company information, documents awaiting his perusal (they had been awaiting that for many months – their next step was destined to be the wastepaper bin,) and his extra supply of tablets. He took one of these to steady his nerves and immediately felt just a little bit easier, even though he was aware that the effect could never be instantaneous.

The contents of his case were now scattered all over the floor of his Jag. The petrol receipts thrown on top of the pile did not hold a list in between them. Charles started his frantic search all over again. His pockets, his wallet and a further scramble amongst the papers from his case revealed nothing. It was now nearly 2.45 – he had three quarters of an hour to find the name of the company before the deadline of 3.30 on the 8th of the fourth month. Perhaps Fiona had emptied the pockets of his suit and ditched that important slip of paper in the bin. He remembered then that he had put on a different suit that morning – the list was, no doubt, in his other jacket.

"Fiona, I'll ring Fiona, and then she can find the list and tell me which company is number seven."

However, the telephone at their home rang and rang – no one was about to answer it.

"Where does she get to? When I want her, she's never there," he shouted into the receiver, before banging the mouth piece into his fist in exasperation. "Where the hell are you, woman?" he cried. Fiona was not in hell though, for at that precise moment she was in heaven, a dark and erotic heaven...

Charles decided that all this was too important to miss by going to a board meeting. He had to get that information, so he turned back onto the motorway and headed for home, after having first given his apologies for non-attendance. He put his automatic Jag into drive and swung into the fast lane. He tore past lorries that were lumbering towards the coast or the industrial centres of Yorkshire. He sped past the Mercs and the BMWs. He raced faster than the steady pace of the police patrol car.

As he touched 110mph, he saw a blue flashing light

in his mirror; he heard the noise as he gradually reduced his speed to a more respectable 70mph. When he changed to the middle lane – in the fond hope that perhaps the police were chasing some villain and wanted him to move out of the way – he saw the wagging finger of the policeman.

"Do you realise what speed you were doing?" inquired the policeman when Charles eventually stopped on the hard shoulder. Charles wondered whether he was being invited to answer that question. If he said that he knew what the speed was, wouldn't that mean he did not care a fig about the speed limit? If he said that he did not realise what his speed was, wouldn't that imply that he was a careless driver?

He was on the horns of a dilemma, so Charles made up his mind to give a smile, rather than reply.

"I don't see anything to smile about," replied the policeman. Charles stopped smiling.

"I've got to get home, officer," began Charles as a way of an apology.

"Why, have you got your own funeral to attend?" answered the police officer.

"No," replied Charles somewhat lamely. Policemen can be a trial at times, he thought to himself.

The whole procedure with the police did not take too long and Charles was allowed to drive away once all his particulars had been taken down. Just as soon as he was out of their sight, he stepped on the accelerator and revved up, switched lanes and hurried home.

It was 3.25 when he entered through the front door. He barely noticed Fiona propped against the fridge door, sipping wine. He went straight to their bedroom where, in his other suit, just as he expected, was the all important list. He glanced down it until he found number seven. Then, pressing the buttons on his bedside phone, he got through to their stockbroker and placed the share purchase request, after having checked that Bates had also rung.

That evening, at five o'clock, he noticed on teletext that their newly acquired shares had leapt up thirty-eight pence each. The papers the next day noted that Northern Manufacturing was the subject of a takeover bid and that there had been a late surge in their share price once the news had been announced during the late afternoon. Charles breathed a sigh of relief. The shares had been bought in time – twenty-five minutes before the bandwagon had been started!

* * *

Tony Driver was proving to be an excellent manager in the six months that he had been appointed. On that very first autumn morning in 1986, he had walked in and taken one look around the shop floor and announced to Amelia that the workforce needed pruning.

"Dreadfully overstaffed!" was how he had phrased it. Amelia was impressed that someone could come to a conclusion so quickly and, what's more, be quite prepared to do the dirty job of sacking! She had, herself, been aware that they might just be a bit overmanned but could not pluck up the courage to get rid of anybody. She was hoping that natural wastage would do the job but it is very indiscriminate in its application. Often the best person left and had to be quickly replaced; or perhaps the only man capable of a certain process decided to take early retirement – then he had to be persuaded to carry on and teach an apprentice his skills, thereby creating an extra job. The areas where there were two men to do one person's work, those were the sections where Amelia hoped that there would be a mass exodus, but no such luck! Re-training one person to do a different job involved time and expense. So, Amelia was heartily glad when Tony quickly recognised the problem and set about solving it. The redundancies that ensued were a little bit expensive though. Then Tony went to visit every client, both old and established and potential new ones. These visitations began at the customer's work place and extended over lunch. Lunch, quite naturally, took place away from the customer's base and though they were not at the largest restaurant in town, they were at the most intimate one. Intimate restaurants tend to come a bit dearer than the less cosy types. However, a lot of clients were comforted by the delightful meal and thus a stampede to various competitors was halted, to a certain degree anyway.

Finally, Tony reorganised the office and brought it up to date. Unfortunately, the two typists employed there left as the company was in the middle of its reorganisation but, as Tony remarked, it was perhaps just as well because now they could employ office staff competent in word processors and computers. This did have an effect of putting up the wage bill but the cost of buying the new equipment was mitigated by leasing it all. This allowed the firm to buy the most up to date machines, capable of handling accounts at the touch of a button. It impressed Amelia tremendously and she found herself quite wooed by the attractions of lease-hire.

"It is the most tax efficient way," Tony Driver advised

her and it certainly seemed to be.

Once the six months qualifying period was up, Tony was given the option of buying company shares for a nominal amount. Amelia was delighted when he took up his option. She was especially pleased when he informed her that, due to the fact that the other employees were not interested in buying into the company, he was going to snap up the remaining shares.

"This firm is going places!" he announced. Amelia was exceptionally gleeful at this thought and decided that as it was now spring 1987, she would rejoin her tennis club and take a back seat with regards to the firm.

She felt she was putting her engineering works in safe hands.

* * *

Meanwhile, spring was having an effect on the generous Glenda. She was a great lover of spring. She physically enjoyed the rejuvenation that took place when the new shoots pushed their way into the world. Spring, in her cottage, nearly ten miles from the beauty and medieval splendour of York, was overwhelming. The flowers enticed birds and insects into her garden. The colours and scents to be found scattered in heady clumps here and there caused the eyes to be dazzled by the sheer variety. The wildlife pond, woken from its slumbers of winter, came to life when frogs and newts could be spotted in their pre-metamorphic forms.

Glenda spent many wondrous hours between bird and bee. With her coat wrapped around her generous bosom, protecting herself against the sneaking winds, she took her fill of nature and the natural world. She picked blossoms and posies and carried them resplendent into her rooms where they graced every nook and cranny. She delighted in the sticky buds opening and observed their progress on the kitchen windowsill.

In the bedroom, she had two vases – one was full of narcissi and the other of forget-me-not. The narcissi reminded her of Charles because he was inclined to be somewhat narcissistic. This arrangement she placed by the mirror, where he always went to just before they made love, to admire his physique. The forget-me-nots she placed on the bedside table. These flowers were gathered and put in a prominent place so that John Bates would be reminded not to forget her. Not that there appeared to be any chance of him doing that. He was totally besotted with her; he enjoyed every ample inch; he savoured all the moments they spent together. Once in her company, he was like man reborn.

Unfortunately for poor Glenda, it was not possible for John to pay her too many visits. He was under intense pressure at work, by all accounts, and needed every spare weekday minute to promote himself within the Parker, Jones and Winstanley hierarchy. However, at the weekend, he more than made up for his lack of attention to Glenda during the week. At the weekend, he spent all day Saturday and most of Sunday worshipping at her altar. So during the week, Charles came to see Glenda, to worship at his own altar. Charles was quite convinced that Glenda had rejected the overtures that John had made at his dinner bash in the autumn, and John was absolutely sure that Glenda had finished and disposed of Charles. Glenda, generous to a fault, considered that she had ample enough love to spread between the two of them.

* * *

So the Wilkinson Engineering Works was, by the springtime, newly adorned. The offices had been refitted with the latest equipment on lease-hire and Tony Driver was now turning his attention to the shop floor.

He made out that he knew what was needed there and spent many hours making frequent enquiries as to the exact cost of new machinery. Amelia trusted him completely, she was confident that he would make the right decision. A number of Midland companies were invited to the factory to quote for the machines. Tony Driver, after showing the second company around, was warming to it all.

The third and final company were coming to begin the hard sell. After all, they depended on refits to keep them in business, so they needed to make sure that they sold the best, the most and the dearest. They arrived on Tuesday morning, ready to court the man and woman in charge. They had done their homework. They were obviously not going to make the mistake that the first company had done, by presuming that the woman before them was really the secretary when in actual fact she was the owner. Asking her to 'make some coffee, love, before the boss arrives – we're gagging!' did not endear them to Amelia. She had replied quite haughtily that she was the boss. After that, it was a waste of time for them. This third firm had made enquiries. They had found out that the owner was a woman, her husband rarely put in an appearance at the works these days, and the power behind the throne was the newly appointed manager – a Mr. Tony Driver.

Amelia had intended to be there, to make sure that fair play took place and to see that she was given the respect due to her. That morning she woke up feeling ghastly, her legs ached and her head throbbed. She got Ralph to ring in and give her apologies.

Tony tried to hide the glee when he answered the telephone and heard that Amelia would not be in that morning. He felt a sudden surge of power enter his body. After replacing the telephone on the hook, he examined his face in the mirror. It was so handsome that even he could not fail to be attracted to his reflection.

The receptionist, sitting behind a magnificent new desk within the now immaculate foyer, welcomed the visitors. She urged them to sit down and they did so, placing themselves in the comfy grey leather seats. The carpet was in pink and grey, with the new logo woven into it. The desk, behind which the receptionist sat looking busy, was in toning shades – once again the logo featured, this time painted on the front.

The men from the Midlands glanced around and loved what they saw. The managing director leant forward and whispered to his deputy, "I think we've found our crock of gold!"

Five minutes later, Tony's secretary ushered them into her boss' room. She introduced them to Tony and they all shook hands. In those intervening seconds, the three visitors – the managing director, Mr. Wilmott, his deputy, Mr. Greenwood, and their technical representative Mr. Mansfield, – took in the surroundings.

They noticed that the colour scheme in the offices was in shades of green, complimented by plants that would not have been out of place in Kew Gardens. They spotted the brand new office equipment which had sprouted in every available office space. In the midst of all this splendour was the man himself. Tony Driver was wearing a sharp suit. He sported a natty beard. He was slim and eager looking – a veritable panther on the prowl.

Such men always impressed the worldly wise managing director of Midland Machines and Co. Ltd. They were the new breed of men. They were eager and thrusting, dynamic and, above all, spendthrifty. It was something about their appearance that gave them away. At face value, they seemed to be wealthy. Underneath, they wore the shabby underwear of the newly rich, not literally, of course – for the underwear of the nouveau riche was the best silk boxer shorts – but metaphorically. They had no substance behind their facade. There was never any actual money. It was credit, credit, credit all the way.

It was not a case of Mr. Wilmot not admiring the newly rich, he did. He loved them all, for they had brought prosperity to his company. However, at sixty-two he was old enough to have experienced enough booms and busts in the British economy to realise that the nouveau riche had better move from borrowed to real money before the next downward gyration of the British Big Dipper Economy took place. It was always a race against time in post war Britain; rationing, booming, consolidating, near bankruptcy, mismanagement, union rule, European salvation, inflation, unemployment and now low interest rates fuelling a credit inspired boom.

He had seen it all. He had sheltered from all the storms and enjoyed all the periods of heady sunshine. He knew the signs. He knew that Tony Driver was ready to buy, or rather borrow in some form or other. Another storm weathered and then he, Mike Wilmot, managing director, was going to get his managers to buy him out. One final big sale and retirement beckoned. Today would be the beginning of the end of work for Mike Wilmot.

"Where is Mrs Pearson-Cooper?" he enquired.

Tony smiled and gave her apologies to the men. He assured them that he had total power to make decisions, that finalising things did not depend on the Chairman's say-so.

"I enjoy her total confidence," he stated, which indeed he did. Much relieved, Mr. Wilmot gratefully accepted coffee, which was served in the very best Wedgwood china.

"Before we all go in, I would like you to tell me just what you are hoping to achieve with this overhaul?" asked Mr. Wilmot of his client.

"I want our factory to be equipped with the very best, so that we can move forward into the nineties, ready to take on Europe and the world. We need the most accurate and up to date machines manned by computers, so that the workforce can be cut down and efficiency increased. I want the old Wilkinson Engineering Works to be completely modernised. At the moment, the ghost of Ezra Wilkinson hovers around the factory. I removed him from the offices, now I want to exorcise him off the shop floor."

The three men replaced their coffee cups and laid them to rest on the marble coffee table. "Mr. Driver, we will be able to make your shop floor be completely unrecognisable to Ezra. We will transform your factory and open up its gates to profits and markets unheard of before. If you award us the contract, you will be able to play the Japanese at their own game."

Mr. Wilmot then gestured with his hands towards his technical representative before continuing, "Mr. Mansfield, here, has visited the top Japanese companies. He is the most experienced man in his field outside of the Pacific Basin. And not only do I say that but those are also the words of one of the executives of Toyota."

Tony Driver was impressed and he did not think to press this Japanese connection too far, which was perhaps as well for once pressed, total evaporation of all evidence would result. Mr. Wilmot was a poker player who loved to hold all the cards and more.

Tony led them to the shop floor where there was the usual vague lack of activity. Tony's answer to any problem was to refit. He never really knew how to tackle the difficulty in any other way. A refit represented a fresh start and did have the effect of covering up any small problems, such as a complete lack of orders. When he had been working for his previous company, refits had been the order of the day. There was so much money sloshing around that anything other than a complete and fresh start was out of the question. The underlying difficulties were not ones he cared to explore. He did not know how to begin to unravel the real reasons behind the lack of orders. He always thought that he had missed his vocation when he had not applied for the job of principle buyer at Harrods. He would have loved that. As it was, he had to make do with buying such things as computers, coffee machines for the workers, cars for the senior staff (himself, his boss and his boss' husband) and various pieces of office equipment. Shop floor machines did not really interest him but he was prepared to go ahead and order them on the basis of the bigger, the more modern and the more expensive, the better.

Mr. Wilmot and his two minions tut-tutted when they saw the out of date machines. They drew in their breath quite noisily when Mr. Wilmot had the temerity to touch the largest and oldest and find his forefinger covered in black grease. They quoted government legislation that Tony had never heard of. They murmured about fire regulations and "How ever did you manage to get away with that when the inspectors called?" They shook their heads in amazement when they actually saw the best of the old machines in operation. "Can you really find someone to buy something of this quality?" was the question which greeted the arrival of the finished product at the end of the production line. Finally, at the end of their guided tour, Mr. Wilmot whispered to Mr. Driver, while pointing in the direction of the resting workers, the fait accompli "And most of that lot, you'll be glad to hear, will be thrown out on the scrapheap with the old machines!" Just the words that Tony wanted to hear! He was a great believer in the concept that when you brought in the new, you swept out the old.

Over lunch, which was served in a private suite at the nearest Trusthouse Forte hotel, Mr. Wilmot's deputy outlined some brief plans.

"Streamlining the works and bringing it up to date – I believe that that is what you have in mind?" Tony nodded. "We will endeavour to produce the most cost effective method of doing it. It is no good having a newly equipped factory if you have to sell off the family silver to pay for it." Tony nodded again.

"The answer lies in lease-hire. That way, you need not touch your assets, you can pay for the equipment as it is earning money for you and you can offset all the payments against tax. It's making your money work for you. The interest rates will be fixed, of course, so you can take advantage of them while they are low! The initial down payment can be decided on to suit the firm. What is more, we can arrange for you to have a payment holiday, so that the machines can be earning their keep before you are keeping them! At the end of the day, there is a residual amount which will be more than offset by the second-hand value of the machines. You will be able to re-equip with new technology at the beginning of the twenty first century without any major reinvestment at all!"

Tony gently wiped his mouth with his serviette. He needed no persuading to lease-hire. After all, hadn't he already restocked the whole office area on that basis? Even the plants. Not forgetting the cars, of course!

"I'll look forward to receiving the details, gentlemen," murmured Tony, "and now I must leave you."

Mike Wilmot did not smile gleefully until Tony had left the room and was heard squeaking his way down the steps. He then grinned from ear to ear. With the profit from this little deal, he knew that the figures for the year end would look tremendous. The managers and their venture capitalist backers would be eager to grab the company off him. He would feign unwillingness to sell for enough days to appear genuine and then would, with reluctance, sign away the firm he had so studiously built up.

"Bless you, bless you," he whispered under his breath, "a hundred times, bless you Tony Driver!"

* * *

James Pearson-Cooper had watched the comings and goings at the Wilkinson Engineering Works all day long. He noticed the arrival of three men in a chauffeur driven Bentley and their departure two hours later. They had been closely followed by a chap who strutted like a peacock, or so James thought. This man had got into his own Daimler and followed the Bentley down the road towards the centre of Leeds.

Two and a half hours later, the same Daimler had returned and parked in the car spot marked manager. The man with the beard then leapt up the steps two at a time and went in through the front entrance. Meanwhile, in the intervening period there had been a few comings and goings – girls off for their lunch, men in grubby overalls in pursuit of sandwiches and postmen delivering packages.

At three o'clock, a woman of about forty was seen leaving the building. She was clutching a cloth bag. "That's my girl!" James was heard to whisper. He got out of his car and made his way down the street on foot. The woman was quite a bit in front but the road was quiet and he knew that he would not lose her.

At the corner of the road, she turned left and then went straight on towards the row of modern shops that are to be found in the main street in Armley. She then entered the bank. James doubled back to his car and set off for the cottage he was renting near Harrogate.

He had all the information he needed at present

about the firm connected by marriage to his brother Ralph. He would visit his brother's bank the next day.

* * *

Ralph had spent the day as he always did these days – in a state of glorious contemplation. His life had slowly altered these past months – in actual fact, since he had obtained his £100,000. Somehow, the money – fraught though it was with complications – had freed him. He now no longer felt any necessity whatsoever to show even the slightest bit of interest in the wretched engineering works. He had broken away from the chains which had imprisoned him for all those years.

Breaking away had not been an overnight achievement. It had taken a while not to feel responsible for the few ups and the many downs that occurred. To begin with, he had put in a daily appearance – on the way to the betting shop, while he was waiting for it to open. Then, forever prompted by Amelia insisting and reminding him that she was the owner, he volunteered to take over her duties in the morning if she wanted to totally assume his mantle at the works. Then, along came Tony Driver – the saviour of them all, the man who could alone mastermind the revival of all their fortunes. Now, even Amelia no longer felt the need to be present all and every day. After all, as she pointed out, you don't keep a dog and bark yourself!

Thus, contemplation was now the order of the day. He was still a dab hand at the gee-gees and had temporarily indulged in the dogs but soon stopped that. He was not a doggy man. His greatest achievement to date though, was the little arrangement that he had with his friend on the council. To that end, he had increased his original amount left to him by quite a large degree. Not that Pat had showered him with ways of benefiting from the council, he hadn't, but the one he had initially given him had proved to be quite lucrative.

In preparation for more little gems, Ralph had set up a company, a holding company, to look after any tasty investment tips that Pat might throw his way. After his successful deal with the projected office building, Ralph had then advanced into land speculation, green belt acreage. He was not contemplating being a farmer. Not for him the mud and muck. In any case, the land in question never struck him as particularly good for farming. Ralph's vision of good farming land coincided with Constable's depiction of the English countryside. This land that he had bought was just about good enough for a few mangy sheep.

Sheep, though, were not going to be farmed here, not on this land. There was something so special about this land that even the farmer who originally owned it did not know. It did not have minerals hidden under the stumps of grass. There was no coal seam that could be mined. The farmer was highly delighted to get shot of it and pronounced it as excellent for keeping horses on (which was what Ralph had said that he wanted the land for). The documents that went through listed the owner as Wilkinson Engineering but that was a name of convenience. Wilkinson Engineering – the company so beloved of his wife and her new protégé, Tony Driver – was kept totally in the dark about its new acquisition. (Ralph had contemplated using his own name but decided that suspicions may be aroused if his name appeared once more as the owner of something that would benefit from a council decision and he could not bring himself to use a fictitious name, as he was basically an honest sort of person.)

The value of the land that the firm had unknowingly bought lay in its change of use from farm land to industrial land. The council wanted to create more jobs; it needed flat land – near to motorways and main centres of population – for factories and warehouses to be built on. Pat O'Reilly, who was in the thick of Labour Party politics and decision making, was privy to the master plan.

"And that is the last one, the last tip – when you sell this little bit of land, I'll have more than repaid my debt to you," he had stated when passing on the information to Ralph.

* * *

The cashier was wearing the bank's uniform. It fitted her badly as she neither had the figure nor the looks to suit it. James noticed with interest that she was bursting out of her blouse.

"How can I help you?" she inquired while toying with her pen.

"I want to open a bank account, in the first instance, but really, as I have a substantial amount to invest, I would like to see the bank manager."

James had withdrawn his legacy from the building society where he had lodged it on being given the money by the solicitors. He gently passed the cheque to the cashier, who visibly blinked on seeing the figures; the rows of noughts that graced the piece of paper impressed her. She smiled at the man, who was tanned and athletic looking, and he smiled back.

"I'll go and see if he is free," she said for a cheque for that amount and made out to an individual was not something that you saw every day in Armley. It definitely warranted the bank manager putting away his spam sandwiches and administering the free coffee that was reserved for important clients.

"Tim," she called as she spotted the errant man disappearing down the corridor. Calling the bank manager by his first name was something that was positively encouraged. It was supposed to foster good customer and staff relationships. Customers, though, more often than not felt bewildered when invited to call the bank manger by his Christian name, especially when 'Tim' wrote them nasty letters about their overdraft. Staff enjoyed calling their boss Tim, it made him seem less aloof, more like them, on their level – a factor which influenced their attitude to work, which became slack and laissez-faire. After all, could someone you were expected to treat as an equal one minute, really tell you what to do the next?

Tim hastened along the corridor, trying to ignore the frequent calling of his name. He knew that he only had two more yards to go before the men's toilets and then there would be peace for quarter of an hour. The cashier lengthened her stride and just managed to halt her boss before he entered the safe refuge of the bogs.

"Tim – there is a chap downstairs who wants to see you."

"Tell him I'm busy – get him to make an appointment," was the reply and then he added, as a precaution, "unless he is massively overdrawn, in which case I'd better see him now!"

"He's got a cheque for over £100,000. He wants some advice on investments."

Tim's eye sparkled. Investments meant commissions. Commissions for the bank meant brownie points for the bank manager. Brownie points meant promotion. And promotion meant, to Tim, moving away form this God forsaken branch and getting into something bigger and remoter where he could just sit in his office and tell his minions to dish out the dirt. Joy, joy!

"Send him up!" was the reply.

James was sent up and soon found himself sitting comfortably in the manager's office, sipping coffee and being advised to "call me Tim – everyone else does!"

James wafted the cheque in front of Tim's face, so that the manger could smell the money. It smelt good.

"You are interested in investments, you said to one of my cashiers?"

"Well, this little legacy I received is rather a large amount to leave in a building society – thought perhaps of unit trust?" James left the cheque on the desk and gave the manager the benefit of his honest face.

Pound signs raced around Tim's brain as he clocked the amount written on the cheque – commissions, commissions he murmured to himself. Tim spotted the appearance of honesty that faced him and tried to check his enthusiasm.

"First things first, you must open up an account!" And then the manager asked the person opposite him his name.

"James Pearson-Cooper."

"Pearson-Cooper? That's strange!" announced Tim, with his pen poised mid-air.

"Why?"

"Well, no, you can't be," stuttered Tim, "no, I mean,

you're obviously from Australia!" Tim was an avid fan of Neighbours and could recognise an Aussie accent at a hundred paces.

"Yes, I'm from Australia, but what is the problem?" replied James innocently.

"Well, nothing really – it's just your name. Pearson-Cooper. I mean Armley is not the sort of place where you get two Pearson-Coopers, and there is a customer with that name at this bank already!"

"Not called Ralph is he?"

"Well, yes, I must admit he is. Though I shouldn't be telling you really, it is supposed to be confidential, the names of customers and all that. Why, do you know him?"

"He will be my brother," and then James adopted a crest-fallen look, "but please, please do not tell him I'm back in England. There was a bit of a fall out years ago and we don't speak."

"Oh, shame about that," Tim said and then added, "but have no fear, I won't breathe a word – my lips are sealed!"

"Thanks," replied James and he looked suitably relieved.

"What brings you to England then?" inquired Tim, trying to change the subject.

"To collect my legacy."

"Legacy? This is your legacy?" Tim cast an eye on the cheque to make sure that his vision was not deceiving him. In his part of the banking world, most individuals inherited only debts and the right to a council flat.

"Yes, but then you must know about it, if Ralph banks here…"

"Know about it? How do you mean?"

"Well, Ralph will have inherited £100,000 too."

Tim straightened his back and stared at the man sitting opposite him.

"Ralph has inherited money, has he?"

"Yes, from his father, like I have. A straight £100,000 – he must have told you!"

"Probably, it will have slipped my mind."

The two of them then went on to complete the formalities, with James placing the coveted money into a high interest investment account while he examined the various unit-linked proposals.

After James had departed, Tim got out the Wilkinson Engineering files and glanced through it. He then called for a statement of the account that was held there. He checked through the security that was backing the borrowings; a house worth at the last valuation £32,000. He made a mental note to tell the Pearson-Coopers' to get the house re-valued, and the factory buildings, loans, overdraft… then he added a pencil note to the list. £100,000 he wrote, underling it heavily and adding a question mark at the end of the row of noughts.

* * *

John Bates unlocked his filing cabinet and took out the file about Charles. The list of directorships was the most interesting item in the file and John cast his eyes covetously over the names. He needed to be in those companies. He needed to have them. He wondered if he could do a deal with Charles. Quid pro quo. Charles liked quids.

* * *

John Spencer rarely thought of his wife. It wasn't that his wife had never loved him. She had, with all her heart, many years ago. It was that he had never loved her. He had only ever loved one woman in his whole life and she was married to a certain Ralph Pearson-Cooper.

Amelia was the woman and he kept the flame of love burning for her in his heart. She did not realise this, of course, and thought that his constant desire to see her was due to his concern about the company she was now chairman of. He was concerned, naturally, and this excuse served him well. It also meant that when he was giving the amorous Amelia (as he remembered her) the benefit of his advice, he could charge for the pleasure of seeing her. This was a double advantage.

He often wondered what made her marry Ralph. The fact that she was pregnant by him had probably been part of the reason, he did admit. What made her submit to the man in the first place? Why had she given her all to him – before he, John Churchill Spencer, had a chance to dip into the well? His father had been none too pleased when he found out, by virtue of a wedding invitation landing on their doormat, that John had missed the boat and lost Amelia to another suitor. His father had wanted to see the two families hitched together in permanent wealthy wedlock.

When it became apparent that the Wilkinson Engineering Works was not as wealthy as the Spencers' had first supposed, Spencer Senior was a little relieved. It removed the initial annoyance. It did not alter the fact that in his eyes, and in his son's eyes, Ralph Pearson-Cooper was an upstart who wanted squashing. It had taken many years to arrange it but now, John Spencer noted, his old flame's husband was frozen out of the firm: marginalised, as they refer to it nowadays.

John Spencer considered that now was the time for his wife and himself to call it a day. Then he would be free to court Amelia and win her away from Ralph.

* * *

Charles pleaded guilty to speeding and accepted the fine as a sign that it was the end of the matter. The fine was small and posed no problem to him. He wrote out the cheque there and then and left the courthouse to grab a bite to eat before hastening to yet another board meeting.

For some reason or other, very little had been happening in the vicinity of late. Wayne, the cub reporter, who had joined the local paper only a month previously, was feeling just a shade bit disappointed. He had hoped that there might have been some news, a mass murder with bodies scattered to the four winds of the city, or perhaps the mayor could be caught kerb crawling in the mayoral limousine. He knew, though, that his editor would not allow him loose on these juicy items, even if they were happening, which they were not. The cub reporter was given the number one boring job. He had to be at the magistrate's court, making a note of the names of those who had not paid their television licences, so that the paper might shame them that evening and parade them before their readers.

He had been joined by a journalist whose job it was to take pity on the youth assigned to serve out their apprenticeships on the local newspaper. The two of them sat next to each other and shared a bag of sweets. The experienced journalist took one look at the information that the youngster had scribbled down and declared it to be mind bogglingly uninteresting.

"I know, but what can I do?"

"Just sit here and hope we get a flasher and then we can interview the victims."

The thought of that did little to raise the youth's spirits. He knew the rules, never photograph a flasher, it gives them prominence. The two of them then fell into chatter about the apparent irregularities of the legal world.

"What really gripes me is the system of fines," began Ed as they sat waiting for the next case to begin.

"They do seem a bit unfair at times."

"Unfair? Unfair! That's not the word I'd use. Disgusting is more like it. Last month, I was up before them on a speeding charge and got stung well and truly. The chap after me got let off, said he was late for an interview or something. He was doing exactly the same speed as I was – albeit on a different stretch of road – but I got done and he didn't. Now, I ask you, is that fair?"

Wayne agreed that it was not.

"What's next?" asked Ed, his anger subsiding now that he felt he had made his point well and truly known.

"Someone caught speeding," announced Wayne with a sidelong look at his neighbour.

"Right, let's see what happens to him!"

The two of them sat there and watched as the case unfolded in all its petty ways. It was over quickly and justice was done. The accused had pleaded guilty and had even made motions to pay the fine there and then, to the judge himself!

"Pearson-Cooper?" began Ed. "I've heard of that name. He's got a few directorships. I'll run it through the computer and see what comes up."

Then he touched his nose in a knowing fashion. "There's a story in this somewhere, Wayne me lad, a big one!"

* * *

Charles returned from his board meeting feeling well satisfied with the day's events. He had managed, in between appearing in court and greasing up to the chairman of the board, to overhear a conversation between two people. Those two had discussed the possibility that there might be a hostile takeover bid in the offing. The chairman gave no hint to his fellow board members but instead of lingering to chat to everyone, had hastened away in the company of the two conspirators.

Roland and John Bates welcomed the news with open arms, and by dint of suggestion, agreed to invest in both firms. It might be a long shot but they all agreed it was worth a gamble on both the horses in the race.

On the way home, Charles picked up a copy of the local evening paper and scanned every page. There was not one mention of him. "Thank God!" he whispered under his breath.

* * *

The editor received the finished copy of the article and beamed. It would fill tomorrow's editorial page nicely – as long as the Queen Mum didn't go and peg it or something – and he immediately set to work on his column, which would compliment the prose next to it. First of all though, he thanked Ed and Wayne. "Nice work – a good bit of digging there. Like the way you managed to list his earnings in one column and his fine next to it; sort of profit and loss account! And where did you find that poor soul on £106 a week with a fine greater than Peason-Do-Dah, whatever his name is, eh – masterstroke!" The editor picked up his pen and the two reporters turned away to go toward the door.

"I've been thinking," continued the editor. He put the pen down and the two men stopped in their tracks. "Why don't you two work together a bit more? You make a good team. See what you can dig up at the council – always good for a story there!"

* * *

James was quite enjoying his sojourn in the mother country. He had rehearsed the tactics that he had thought out on the plane for winning this amazing competition. His first move, in all its subtlety, had been successful. He was surprised at how easy it had been to drop the information into the bank manager's lap. He would leave the little gem there to ferment awhile. Then he would give the mixture a little stir.

In the meantime, he decided that he would take a part time job, just to amuse himself. He had no actual intention of physically increasing his legacy himself. He intended to win by reducing the other two's legacies; by far the easier method. He was never the business man. In Australia, he felt no need to make his fortune. He had never married and had no children – that he knew of anyway. Making money never appealed to him – a sort of reaction that he put down to the way his father had made money hand over fist. In any case, when the sun was shining and there was enough money for a beer and a good meal, why should you need to go on making more money? If you had enough money for a few pleasures, then why kill yourself for extra bits and pieces that you would not normally need or ever use?

The cottage that he was renting was well-equipped for four people, with three big bedrooms. He could spread himself out and feel at home – well, nearly feel at home, for the grey skies were somewhat depressing when he was used to shades of blue. The trees, in verdant splendour, did compensate for the clouds and the garden was a gem. There were a few items of what was referred to on the inventory as patio furniture, with an umbrella to protect the folks sitting on the plastic seats against the sun. James was waiting for this sun to come out in sufficient ferocity to justify the umbrella!

What a contrast, he thought, to that factory of Ralph's in Armley. It was all grey there. Soon, it would be under a heavy black cloud of financial problems, James thought. All he had to do was to stir things up a little. Then he would be killing two birds with one stone. The first little bird was the one that fluttered on the wing of hope; the desire to win Blayborough House – that bird would soon have its wings clipped. Just a screw or two to turn, then it would tweet no longer and collapse in a lump of feathers in Queer Street.

The second little bird that was due to meet its maker was Ralph, the prime cause of his mother's death. James could remember clearly and distinctly the letters that kept arriving while his mother was pregnant with Ralph. The letters were from Parker, Jones and Winstanley and were written by them on behalf of Sir John Augustus Pearson-Cooper, James' father. They accused his mother of having an affair. Again and again they arrived, preparing the grounds for divorce and causing such distress that his mother went into early labour. It was a long and difficult labour, made worse by the fact that she had no support from anyone. The baby, Ralph, was healthy and strong, but his mother was weakened by the trauma.

The two birds that were to be killed with the one stone were in fact one and the same bird. Ralph was the healthy baby. His father had caused the distress which eventually resulted in his mother's death. If he upset Ralph's financial applecart, not only would it increase his chances of gaining the Blayborough Estate but he would ruin Ralph. Thus he would have revenge over his father and his brother and thus put things right concerning his mother.

* * *

Fiona was sitting in the drawing room of her home and was doing her nails. She cared for each and every one of them and nurtured them to grow long and strong. Using only the best nail polish remover, she gently wiped the old colour off in preparation for the next stage of the process.

Mrs Armitage was in the next room, having a break. She was supping a cup of weak tea and glancing through the local evening paper. Normally, she came to clean in the morning but due to what she had described on the telephone that morning as unforeseen family circumstances, namely her husband falling down the steps and busting his ankle, as she told her employer later, she had been unable to turn up in the morning. So her breaktime was spent inspecting the hatches, matches and dispatches of the evening paper, instead of the comic cuts in the morning paper. There were no names that she recognised, so she did not dwell on the lists for too long. Then she turned over the pages to reach the entertainment section.

Something on the editorial page caught her eye. She gave the photograph a closer look. It looks like… yes, it is! she thought. Yes, it was indeed a very unflattering photograph of Mr. Charles Pearson-Cooper. Right next to a box that listed his earnings. "Good God!" she proclaimed – this time out loud. "He earns a fortune!"

Fiona was busy with the nail file, gently filing the sculptured points, when Mrs Armitage rushed in and stuffed the newspaper in front of her employer's face.

"Take a look at this!" she demanded. Fiona took a quick look.

"Good God!" she exclaimed.

"Just what I said!" agreed Mrs Armitage.

"Oh, no!" she cried, for in her astonishment at seeing her husband emblazoned across the local rag, the file had slipped and her prize nail had splintered.

* * *

Charles had already admired himself in the mirror and he had liked what he saw. Glenda was still in the bathroom pondering about which perfume to use. She was taking stock of herself at the same time, deciding that she wasn't too bad looking for her age. Moments after, the two of them lay in bed, supping a glass of last year's elderflower wine, as a warm up to the events to come.

Charles had a number of set routines, which he alternated on the occasions that they met together to enjoy their voluptuous but illicit relationship. Glenda believed in letting the spirit take her. It was method versus madness and it worked quite well for them both.

Afterwards, Glenda popped into the bathroom to run them both a bath. Pouring Radox in – to relieve any tensions that the love session might have missed – she swished the water around to increase the bubbles. Then, testing the water with her toes, she lowered herself in, submerging herself up to her breasts with a mixture of bubbles and water.

"Charlie!" she called. The bed heaved as Charles swung his legs out. This time, as he passed the mirror, he did not glance at his image. The flaccid state held no appeal.

"Be an angel and find the soap, Charlie darling!"

Charles rummaged around the bath, eventually locating the missing bar in a place where Glenda had strategically hidden it. They played this game every time – it never failed to amuse! Then in he stepped, taking his usual position by the taps.

Just as they had got themselves thoroughly wet, Glenda thought she heard a noise downstairs.

"Did you hear that?" she enquired.

Charles, who by now was covered in bubbles, had not heard a thing.

"I'm sure I heard something," she continued.

"Well, I didn't," replied Charles while loading the water pistol.

"Do you think I'd better investigate?

"No!" And Charles took aim.

The pistol squirted water all over her hair and she squealed, flicking water over her partner in reply. The ensuing fun stopped her from thinking about the noise anymore. Half an hour later, when the bath water was well and truly cold, Glenda stepped out and wrapped her body in a flamboyant scarlet robe. She wandered downstairs, where she saw the evening paper lying on the doormat. Picking it up, she sauntered back up to the bathroom, where Charles was already getting dressed.

She skipped through the paper as he fastened his buttons and adjusted his tie.

"It must have been the paper coming through the letterbox that I heard – it's earlier than usual!"

As she turned over the pages, something caught her eye… the photograph, though a poor likeness, was definitely… yes, must be – "Charlie? What have you been doing? You naughty boy!" She grinned at Charles.

Charles stopped mid-button and paled slightly.

"What do you mean?" he asked naturally.

"There's an article in here about you. Hey, you're pretty wealthy!"

Charles grabbed the paper off her and quickly read the words printed there. He soon grasped the gist of it all. He was glad that they had obviously missed a few thousands off his quite substantial salary. He was exceptionally thankful that they knew nothing of his even more substantial investments, and he was extremely grateful that they had not uncovered his expenses and his share option schemes – thank goodness they had not found out about those! However, what was listed was bad enough – he suddenly felt dreadfully naked and exposed. His mind achieved instant sobriety before anxiety took hold.

He reached for his tranquillisers, which he kept in his jacket pocket, and swallowed two. After all, he thought, who knows what reporters might dig up next?

* * *

That afternoon, Mr. Page was calculating just how much money he really had. He congratulated himself on two accounts: firstly, he had kept his drug taking under control. He never allowed it to affect his performance, nor did it interfere with his lifestyle. Drugs were the cherries on the cake to him. Sometimes though, he liked a lot of cherries. Secondly, he had managed to extract a tremendous amount of money from a number of old bints, particularly one of them. He could never work out the psychology behind it all but for some reason, white women liked it from black men – that was his experience anyway. Often, it was vice versa too; often but not always. Where he worked, the white women who arrived in search of paid fun were old and unattractive. In their prime, they might have created a stir but past their prime they were like mutton in a field of lambs. Money helped though. When a woman pays well, anything is possible. The trick is to make her pay – pay for the pleasure and the pain. Yes, Fiona had improved his finances wonderfully. He knew that there would come a point when she would turn around and say no more but until then he would continue his demands. There was a limited amount of time in this game before they grew tired of each other. She was twice his age. Her thighs had stretch marks and her breasts sagged. Her face was still attractive though, but now only with the twinkle of lost youth instead of the full bloom of womanhood. When he was with her, he shut his eyes and thought of the money. The money inspired him – that and the humiliation that he could inflict.

He poured himself a double rum and filled the glass up with coke. Tonight he would forget all about old women. Tonight he would hit the town. He had bought a copy of the evening paper to see what was happening in Leeds. He fancied a night out in Leeds, perhaps kip down at a friend's house in Chapletown afterwards.

"Entertainments," he murmured to himself, looking for the page in the paper, "where the hell are entertainments?"

He stopped going through the paper as the name Pearson-Cooper caught his eye. There was an article with an accompanying photograph of Mr. Charles Pearson-Cooper. There was also a list of his income.

"Bloody old bint's more rolling in it than I thought!"

Then he knew just what he would do. Screw her one last time – and screw her for every penny her husband had.

* * *

The usual morning task bored the manager at the bank in Armley. It was tedious in the extreme to have to go through all the accounts that were 'being brought to his attention'. The action livened up when, on examining the account in question, he could write a mildly cross letter. Better still were the ones that invited the customer to make an appointment at their earliest convenience to discuss the situation. There was something rather enjoyable about dictating such a letter – was it the thought that the recipient would start to sweat and shake on reading it? Or was it the thought of the extra fee that the writing of the letter produced? Tim was not sure but which ever it was, writing letters was certainly more than marginally better than examining the accounts.

Wilkinson Engineering's account received such undivided attention the moment a cheque that they had issued bounced. It was not normal bank procedure to scrutinise an account on a daily basis after just one cheque had been 'returned to the drawer'. If the account holder had paid some money into the bank which rectified the situation then everything would carry on as normal. However, Tim was paying particular attention to the customer after the James' visit a month ago. The bounced cheque merely caused his weekly overview of the Wilkinson account to become a daily scrutiny.

One month after requesting it, he had received the new valuation of the house that Amelia and Ralph owned. The bank had a charge against the property to cover the loans that they had made to Wilkinson Engineering but theirs was not the only charge against the house. There were also other interested parties forming a queue behind the bank. Tim was aware that a number of new direct debits had been started very recently. These monthly amounts went to finance companies, who were even less friendly than banks when the chips are down.

Salaries had gone up too – in particular Tim spotted the standing order that sent money into a certain Tony Driver's bank account.

"He's getting a huge whack!" Tim commented to his subordinate. "A nice little earner!"

The subordinate, who was learning the ropes with ferocity, suggested a letter to the owner of the firm.

"A strongly worded one!" he advised with all the sagacity of a twenty-one year old straight from college.

"No, let's get a copy of the provisional accounts instead," Tim said. He did not want this new boy to steal a march on him. He had his position to think of, after all, if he fell in with every idea that the wretched new comer thought of, he would lose face very quickly.

So it was decided to request a copy of the provisional accounts, as a shot over the bows.

* * *

John Bates totted up his share of the proceedings so far. He had become a very wealthy man. The idea of the three of them – Roland, Charles and himself – pooling information about companies with a view to making a killing on the stock exchange was brilliant, even marvellous. Especially so because he, a company solicitor to quite a number of small but thrusting Northern firms, had not compromised his position at all. He had not actually given any information that was in any way truly confidential.

He had offered tit-bits. He had dropped tasty morsels. Little gems which could never, ever be traced back to him. Now was the time to call it a day and do a deal with Charles.

John had thought about this for quite a few weeks and given tremendous consideration to how best to use the leverage he had over Charles to his own advantage.

In the end, he came to the same conclusion he had reached in the first place: he had to appeal to Charles' and Fiona's greed.

That morning, he rang them up at their home and made an appointment to see them both the following week. So during the second week of May, he would see them and put his idea to the couple. They would agree and stage two of his master plan would begin!

* * *

"Who was on the telephone, darling?" inquired Fiona.

"Just that Bates fellow," answered Charles as he came back into the kitchen, where his wife was loading the dishwasher. Mrs Armitage was away for the week, so Fiona found herself having to do all the chores. However, as Fiona was fond of remarking to herself, it was now Friday and the Armitage horse would be returning to her yoke on Monday morning.

"What did he want?"

"To see us, can't see why," replied Charles. "Anyway, I've told him to come here on Thursday afternoon at two."

"You could have checked with me first!" protested Fiona. "I might have been busy!"

"Well, you're not, I checked your diary, you left it by the telephone," Charles said in reply. "By the way, who's the Mr. P that you have an appointment with on Monday?"

"He does my hair," she said quickly and then made a bee-line into the hall, where she picked up the diary and put it in a safe place, away from prying eyes.

Charles wandered off into the garden to pull a few weeds that the gardener had inadvertently left behind. Fiona disappeared upstairs and rang the 'clinic' to confirm her Monday appointment. She always did this, in case her session had been cancelled. Once it had, and her disappointment had been acute, so ever since then she had rung to confirm the booking a couple of days before.

"Oh, yes, I have a message for you," the receptionist began once Fiona had introduced herself.

"A message?"

"Yes, Mr. Page cannot make it on Monday at the clinic and would like you to go to his other surgery instead." The receptionist was obviously adapting the words that were written on a piece of paper.

"Surgery?" questioned Fiona.

"Well, that's what it says here. Anyway, I'll give you the address. It is for the same time, just a different place, for some reason."

Fiona took down the address in Chapletown, Leeds. Her mouth was dry and her hands were trembling. It was the thought, the thought of him…

* * *

Tony Driver spent Friday morning taking stock of the situation. A month ago, he had managed to get Amelia to award him a larger salary, with a performance related bonus. The bonus was related to turnover; up the turnover and the bonus ups dramatically. Profit did not need to enter into it. Turnover was king!

"There is nothing like a bonus to get a person out there, grabbing the customers in!" stated Tony to the acquiescent Amelia. She was a ready listener to all his plans. The concept of a bonus related salary was dripped into the frequent conversation that they enjoyed together over a good meal with the best wines. Tony called them power lunches.

Amelia could see the reasoning behind the bonus. She wanted to reward him properly for all the work he was putting into the factory; the reorganisation, the ideas, the pure sparkle. She adored the sheer power that emanated from her manager. She would come into the works to chat to him, to see how everything was progressing. It was always progressing well. Tony was a dynamo. She could see that. He had transformed the place into a modern, up-to-date, state-of-the-art factory. The new machines were now in situ and three workers had been given their cards, so they were saving money already!

She appreciated the effort that Tony was putting into his job. The way he liked to avoid worrying her about the day to day problems. It left her more time to enjoy herself. After all, why shouldn't she have a bit of fun – her husband was! What a contrast Tony's attitude to the business was to Ralph's. It was amazing to talk to him. He made the factory seem alive and buzzing.

Tony, for his part, rather liked Amelia. She had a certain appeal for his ego, which grew the more she fawned over him. To begin with, the attraction was based on Amelia's position – she was the boss and from her money, decisions and power descended. Tony had soon altered the iniquitous situation so that the tables were turned, for he preferred being the one who wielded the power, without actually having it. He appeared to all and sundry to be the man in charge but, in reality, appearance was a facade. He made many decisions, but largely spending ones. He made authoritative gestures but largely empty ones, such as making out that he had got rid of some of the workers ("without giving them a penny in redundancy pay," as he had remarked at the time to Amelia. "You've just got to have the knack.") when in actual fact they had left of their own accord. True, he owned shares in the company, but shares had been dirt cheap to buy! In fact, he could not believe the price when they were offered to him. It was the very best way to dispose of the money that he had 'acquired' during his last job…

"Yes," he said to his image in the mirror, "things are looking up!" The awarding of the contract to refit the works had been decided a few weeks back and the winning firm had soon got cracking. The task of choosing who should get the job to refit had been quite easy. The third company was by far and away the best. Their managing director, Mike Wilmot, had been overjoyed to have his quotation accepted without question.

Naturally enough, he also readily agreed to slip a backhander to the man who smoothed the way for them.

* * *

Ralph had spent Friday morning studying the form. Then he thought he might take a wander around the neighbourhood. The format of his days suited his lazy nature. Few demands were made on his time – or on his body! At the works or in bed, at home or on the social circuit – his wife, beloved as she had been, followed her own sweet pattern and left Ralph to follow his. It suited them both.

She still knew nothing about his legacy or the profit (quickly becoming quite vast by Ralph's standards) he was making out of it. She was totally unaware of Pat O'Reilly, though she did ask Ralph on a couple of occasions how he knew so much about town hall politics. He said that he read the newspapers and kept up to date.

Pat O'Reilly was gambling again, he just could not keep away. Lately, though, he had been having more luck and so Ralph did not need to feed him with fivers, or tenners and more! The land purchase that Pat had suggested was going through very quickly. A personal local authority search sped the whole proceedings up and Ralph expected the whole conveyance to be completed by Monday of the following week. Then he, or rather Wilkinson Engineering, would be the proud owner of the acreage of low grade agricultural land. It was a good job that he could still sign documents on behalf of the works. He did not like telling lies and could never have made himself sign documents on behalf of something or someone that was absolutely unconnected with him.

The announcement about the change of land use, to be coupled with a few other important measures that would promote and bring jobs to the area, was due to be proclaimed on Thursday of the following week. It was vital, therefore, that completion was finished on Monday, before the farmer got wind of it and held out for thousands more.

There was one thing, however, that he did not like about Pat O'Reilly these days – the way he always seemed to stink of drink; Irish whiskey, apparently, was his tipple – he was patriotic to a fault. He was still good company though, and that counted for a lot.

* * *

John Churchill Spencer, to give him his full title, partner in Spencer and Spencer, solicitors to the Wilkinson Engineering Works, decided to divorce his wife. Get rid of his wife and make way for the love of his life, his first love, the one and only Amelia Wilkinson. It was rather unfortunate that the said Amelia was already married to Ralph Pearson-Cooper but, reasoned John, she would divorce Ralph just as soon as she realised how hopeless he was!

However, first things first; John obtained a quickie divorce from his wife of many years.

* * *

The Monday morning post arrived early at the Pearson-Cooper household, well before Mrs. Armitage arrived. Thus Fiona and Charles missed the bringing in of the mail session, a feature of their morning which they enjoyed. For a moment every morning, Fiona imagined that she was back in the mansion she used to live in as a child. There the butler would carry the letters in on a silver tray and her father would open them with a silver letter opener. Mrs Armitage, transporting the mail in by hand, although a poor substitute, was better than stooping down oneself for the scattered missives on the hall floor.

This Monday there was the usual splattering of bills and a letter postmarked Cambridge. It was from their daughter and she wrote of days boating on the Cam, drinking at parties and generally having fun. The only mention of work – which, after all, was the whole point of her being there – was a passing reference to her tutor right at the end of the letter: *By the way, I'm off to France for a month just as soon as term ends. Peter (he's my tutor – remember meeting him?) knows of a super little resort in Brittany where we can stay. It'll do my French no end of good! Love and kisses, Emma.*

"Do her French no end of good? I thought she was supposed to be studying German?" demanded Charles after Fiona had read out the letter to him.

"Well, perhaps she's got to brush up on her French as well. How should I know? It will be something to do with the Common Market!" suggested Fiona.

"Common Market? Common Market!" spluttered Charles. "How the hell can her going off to France with a man twice her age be to do with the Common Market?"

"You know what I mean! Improving her languages and all that! Anyway, I haven't time to chatter to you, I've got an appointment at the beauty salon this morning!"

With that, Fiona sped off upstairs to shower. She liked to start off fresh when she paid Mr. Page a visit. She used no perfume on these occasions. The shampoo was a natural type without any additives. She always wanted to go to Mr. Page as pure as possible.

* * *

The post at the other Pearson-Cooper household always arrived after nine. This was very convenient for Ralph, who had arranged for the mail concerning his land purchase to be sent to his home address. Thus, when an envelope came marked to Mr. R. Pearson-Cooper, Wilkinson Engineering, c/o 26 Laburnum Close, only Ralph would be there to pick it up.

This Monday morning, the mail that pushed through the letterbox and was picked up by Ralph on his return from the school run included a letter from his solicitor. His solicitor for this purpose practised in Scarborough – well out of the reach of Leeds. It informed him that the land was now the property of Wilkinson Engineering – in other words, his. Ralph smiled the contented grin of the Cheshire cat who was viewing bowls of cream. With the change of use announcement due to be made on Thursday, he could confidently predict that his little purchase would make him a tidy sum! At the end of the allotted time, he may not make as much money as his other brothers, but he would have enough over and above the £100,000 and interest to buy his independence.

* * *

Fiona dressed simply for her trip to the dark wonders of Chapeltown. She studied her A-Z in order to acquaint herself with the maze of streets and picked out the one she had been told to visit. She was unfamiliar with this part of Leeds, as one would expect of a person in her position.

As she entered the area, she slowed down to a crawl and read the street signs. A quick consultation of her map book showed her that she had two more roads to pass before the one she wanted. Two minutes later, found her parked outside number 4. She locked the car and knocked on the front door and then walked in, just as she had been instructed.

She entered the first room on the left. The curtains were drawn. The lights were on. On one side of the room, there was a dividing door which was partly open. She noticed the two West Indians. One of them was Mr. Page and she nodded to him by way of greeting. The other was a friend of his. The friend shut the door behind her.

Fiona did not see the camcorder that began filming two minutes after she entered the room. Nor did she hear the shuffling that was going on behind the dividing doors.

* * *

The letter from the bank requesting the provisional accounts arrived on Tony's desk by second post. Amelia – his co-boss, as he called her – had already been and gone. She had signed a couple of cheques which Tony had presented to her.

"Just sign here, Amelia," he had said and she signed. He wrote in the amounts when she had left for the tennis club. It was a good arrangement, which worked well.

Tony read the bank's letter with a little alarm. Until he thought about it all again and comforted himself with the fact that provisional accounts were what you wanted them to be. They were creative accounting by the person running the firm; this is not to be confused with creative accounting by the professionals. Their form of make-believe has to have some semblance of truth. Tony knew that provisional accounts were what you wanted them to be; for the bank manager – especially if one was in hock to him – they were demonstrative of high turnovers and big profits; for the tax man, they showed big expenses and losses occurred in varying operations in different spheres; for the potential buyer, they spoke of increasing business and healthy trends. It could be very hard work producing provisional accounts, keeping track of what one told the bank, which was a very different story from the tale told to the Inland Revenue and so on.

Tony put the letter in his briefcase. He would attend to that in the privacy of his own home and concoct the answer that he knew the bank would like to hear.

* * *

On Wednesday, Mrs Armitage picked up the post as usual. She glanced through the mail and made her own judgements about whom each one had come from. There were two letters which she knew from her vast experience were electricity and telephone final demands. She could see the red writing through the window in the envelopes. There was a letter for Mr. Pearson-Cooper marked private and confidential and bearing an Amsterdam postmark. That would be a timeshare circular. She had had one herself the day before and had made her appointment that very morning. They had promised her that she would definitely win a video recorder and, as her old one was on the blink, she was quite looking forward to carrying home her loot from the session arranged. The fourth letter was for Mrs Pearson-Cooper and was postmarked Leeds. Her scrutiny completed, she took them all into her employers, who were still breakfasting.

Fiona carefully slit open the envelope that was addressed to her. She read the contents slowly at first and then again and again. As she poured over the typewritten letter and the other contacts in the envelope, her face paled.

At the other end of the table, Charles examined his mail. The timeshare went straight into the bin. He then opened the red demand letters.

"Haven't you paid these bills, Fiona?" he asked just as soon as he had scanned their amounts.

"No, I never got round to it," she said as she read her letter once more.

"But you've still got the money for them?" her husband asked.

"I think I spent it," she replied apologetically, barely glancing up at him.

"But you have some money in the household account, haven't you? I mean, I give you £2,000 a month so it can't have all gone. Then there is the mortgage money, on top of the £2,000, that I hand over. As well as all the extra bits and pieces you seem to be requesting these days. It was £250 the other day for a new dress – did you get the dress? You didn't show me. Then, last week, you said that you desperately needed £400 for something or other, so I gave you £400. And now you tell me that you've spent the money that was supposed to be for these bills! It really is too bad, Fiona. You seem to be spending as if there is no tomorrow, and then, the other month…"

"Shut up, shut up!" cried his wife. "Just shut up!"

"No, I won't! I won't shut up! It seems to me that just as fast as I make money, you go and spend it."

Fiona rose up from her seat and stared Charles straight in the eye.

"Why don't you go and piss off," she suggested before disappearing out of the room, holding her letter and leaving her husband dumbfounded in the kitchen.

* * *

Pat O'Reilly had a gigantic hangover on Thursday morning. He had been on a huge binge the night before, when his cumulative bet he had placed in the afternoon had failed. His head throbbed from one side to the other. It ached beyond pain and any sudden movement sent a hundred thuds through his cerebral hemisphere. It was just as if someone was using his head as a football.

Feeling like that, he could not face the important committee meeting which had been arranged for that morning. In any case, he felt that his attendance was not too vital. The whole thing was just a formality and was bound to go through on the nod. He would slink back to bed until the afternoon. A further telephone call would confirm the situation and then a little walk to the bookies. There he would meet up with Ralph and celebrate his good fortune. Unfortunately, further headaches prevented him from informing the whip's office that he would be unable to attend. Had he rung, he would have been told to turn up as someone had come up with a site that could also benefit from investment by the council and that, as they could not back two sites at the same time, a choice had to be made between the two of them. He would have been told that his presence was requested, for his own sake. Without him there, the vote was in danger of being split equally between the two proposals. Both ideas would create much needed jobs but if Pat O'Reilly wanted to keep faith with his voters, he should be in attendance, making his mark and supporting the proposal which would provide jobs in his constituency.

Pat went back to sleep and slept the sleep of the wicked; peaceful and contented. On waking, he felt much better and immediately looked at his watch.

"Hell, I never rang in this morning. Never mind, I'll just get a weather check to see how things have gone."

The house was empty and so there was no one around to hear him talk to himself. He picked up the phone and dialled City Hall. He got straight through to the Labour leader of the council.

"You should have been there!" rebuked the leader.

"Ill – you know how it is."

"But we needed you!" continued Frank.

"Why? It was quite straightforward, wasn't it?"

"No. At the last minute, another site was suggested, in a Labour marginal seat as well and equally as good as the site in your seat!"

"What happened?" inquired Pat, feeling cold all of a sudden. Ralph's face was appearing in ghost-like form in front of him, ready to haunt.

"Well, we managed to delay the decision for a few months. Someone put forward an amendment suggesting that the officers should examine both sites in question and report back and so most of the councillors voted for it. Anyway, you'll be able to hear all about it on the television – there was a team from Calendar there!"

Pat put down the phone and felt miserable. What on earth would Ralph say?

* * *

Dead on the dot of two o'clock, John Bates rolled up at Charles and Fiona's house. He stepped out of his car, inwardly grinning. He knew that the two of them would never be able to resist what he had to offer. The deal would be safely delivered and he would be acknowledged by all and sundry as the company law specialist in the north of England!

Mrs Armitage – who had been persuaded to stay behind for an extra two hours in order to carry out the role of 'butler' – opened the front door. She announced his arrival to her employers, who had seen him drive up anyway. They pretended otherwise, but nothing fooled Mrs Armitage. She knew that they were putting on an act; but then, as she often remarked to her hubby, they were a permanent double act, those two!

"John, didn't hear you arrive," commented Charles.

"It's my new Jaguar, it purrs!"

"Oh, yes, perhaps; but then, when you have had a whole collection of cats – new of course – for years, you'll notice that they all make slightly different noises. I just can't recall off hand how many we've had! Have you got leather seats in yours?"

"No, cloth," replied John.

"Get leather next time, worth the extra," advised Charles and then he added, "if you can afford it, of course!"

Pleasantries over, the three of them settled down to discuss business. Fiona kept a back seat while this discussion took place. Her mind was on the letter she had received that morning and its contents. She had been desperately thinking of a way out of the mess but nothing was springing to mind. She had thought of going to the police but knew that such a course of action would automatically involve Charles. She could not keep it quiet; she needed some support from someone. How could she have been so foolish? she wondered. How could she have done all that? The still photographs that were enclosed were graphic enough so she could only imagine what the video would be like. Would they really keep up their threat of making copies and hiring it out? If she gave in, where was she going to get all that money from that they were asking for?

All these thoughts were raging around her head. She could not contribute to the conversation. All she could think about was the shame. Here she was, at fifty, the subject of a porno video. She suddenly felt old. An old, foolish woman who had allowed herself to be used by four different men, one after another, again and again.

"Fiona, come on. What do you think of his idea?" Charles tried to jerk his wife back to reality. "What's up?" he asked when he noticed she was trembling.

"Oh, I just feel a bit sick,"she answered and rose from the chair and left the room. As he opened the door, she turned to Charles and said, "I'll agree to anything you think is right."

"Oh, okay," replied Charles and then when the door shut behind his wife, he turned to John and commented, "Unlike her to be so amenable!"

So, a bargain was struck which suited them all down to the ground. It suited Charles and presumably Fiona too, because it gave them eighty percent of the proceeds, shares, profits or whatever; it suited John because Charles promised to push the various companies he was working for into either using a new firm of lawyers or else appointing a new director – an expert in company law. The two of them shook hands on it and set a date by which they would cut the ties which held the three of them together. It was a gentleman's agreement which they both trusted each other to honour, as Old Etonians!

The date agreed on was November 1st 1987.

* * *

Ralph spent lunchtime fiddling with his pocket calculator trying to work out exactly how much profit he was due to make from his little deal. It all depended on how much per acre he could now ask. It was great fun, working out just how much extra you would make if you could sell the land for just that little bit more.

After lunch, he thought that he would wander down to the shops before placing a little something on his favourite jockey. It was about three o'clock before he set off and the evening newspapers were just hitting the stands. Naturally enough there was no mention of job opportunities that were to be created in the newly designated industrial site! That decision, Ralph knew from what Pat had told him the other week, was due to be made that afternoon. The evening papers were printed too early to carry it.

Funnily enough, Pat was not at the bookies in the afternoon. He must have got held up at the council, Ralph thought to himself. The jockey failed to win but that did not deter Ralph's excellent spirits.

He wandered home in time for the children to arrive; he was glad that someone else was transporting them this week. The school run was tedious. The children rolled up in a Range Rover and flopped down on the comfy sofas in the lounge to watch television. Ralph had planned fish and chips for tea, so he had no cooking tasks to do. He joined them as they sprawled in front of the set.

He was in the toilet when the local events that the Calendar team had covered that day were advertised in preparation for the programme after the national news.

He was supping a cup of tea as the local newscaster started outlining what had been happening in the region that day.

"First of all, we'll go to Leeds, where local councillors have been arguing among themselves over which site should be earmarked for industrial development. Both sites have good motorway access and are level. Both sites are in areas where jobs are needed. So council officers are to examine them and report back to the council in the autumn. Sue Timpson is at one of the proposed sites now…"

Autumn? Autumn! I can't wait that long, thought Ralph. "I thought it was cut and dried! I'll wring his neck, the git!

* * *

Friday's edition of the local paper carried a full report of the controversy. Apparently, both sites had their virtues. Opinion was equally divided between the two. The newspaper carried an excellent article, written by one of their main reporters, Ed Fitzpatrick, with extra material provided by Wayne Brownlaw.

The editor was pleased that he had assigned the two to dig around at City Hall. Not that the article was a result of the digging – it was just straight forward reporting. The editor advised the two to look a little deeper into these new and proposed areas. After all, as he said to them both, there may be some reason which makes one site better than the other.

"Have a look at who's aligning behind which and why. There's quite a pretty bob to be made from the outcome of this little number! And you know what I always say – where there's muck, there's brass…"

"And where there's brass, there's corruption!" finished off Ed.

* * *

Tony Driver had spent the month of July cooking; it was very important for the firm that employed him and for himself that he got the recipe right. To correctly cook the books you need invoices and receipts to back up whatever claims you make in the second set of accounts. Such activity is a long drawn out process that is better started right at the beginning of a firm's existence, not when it had been going for many a year. To produce two sets of books after a number of decades of trading involves knitting the second set to the previous, and correct, year's accounts. A difficult job and one best left to those who show a natural adeptness at such tasks. However, the creation of a set of provisional accounts is a far simpler action. It takes time, that is true, to make sure that the figures add up and balance. Then you have to set it all out – a projection of the trading figures, ahead of the certified accounts. What sets the seal on it all is a real live accountant scrawling his signature at the bottom – with that, you can face the world, wave your piece of paper and announce "Profit in our time!" or something like that.

July had seen such an action take place and, luckily for Tony, a friend of his was able to add the necessary gloss by rubber-stamping the profit and loss accounts projected for the next year. There are some accountants who are well known by the Inland Revenue for their tendency towards the artistic; thankfully for Tony, the accountant friend of his, though well known to the Inland Revenue Service, was not known to the bank manager at the Armley Branch where Wilkinson Engineering Ltd. banked.

They were suitably pleased to see such provisional accounts and took the company off the scrutiny list; for a while anyway.

* * *

There had also been a flurry of financial activity at the home of Charles and Fiona. There were two levels of financial action here. The first was the level well known to both members of the household, involving the ordinary domestic matters and the wheeling and dealing that was taking place; the second was only known to Fiona.

Ever since she had received the stills, she had been at desperation point. Finding some way to halt the blackmail was uppermost in her mind. She had burnt the photographs, watching the edges bend and smoulder as the evidence went up in smoke. It was more of a gesture, and an empty one at that. The negatives were in their hands and any attempt by her to burn the prints and thus remove the incident from her mind was a waste of time, that she knew. They held the negatives and, what was worse, they had a video master copy.

She had tried not to recall what would be shown on the film. Was it as explicit as she feared it must be? Blotting the event from her mind was proving impossible. Each humiliation, every action was imprinted on her brain just as it was videoed on a cassette. She did not need to see the video; she played it every evening in torment, in fear. When she went to sleep, it haunted her. When she awoke, she felt their laughter, their sniggers and their hatred.

Above all, she knew that she was alone in her torment. She realised that, like all blackmail victims, her actions were the reason behind the blackmail. If she had not been so foolish, then the extortion would not be occurring. How could she go to the police when the first thing that they would want to know was the reason behind the blackmail? She would have to face their looks, their sniggers, their "You did what? And you did not realise that you would be set up?" questions; further humiliation to add to the present plight. Then there would be Charles, who would divorce her, no doubt finding some crafty way to leave her penniless. All because…

"What a fool I've been!" she moaned into her hands, running her fingers through her hair. She automatically felt the strands, noticed their dryness and glanced in the mirror. A fifty year old woman peered back at her, with puffy eyes and sorrow lines etched deeply; a woman at the onset of menopause. The shoulders were rounded. There was no lustre in the eyes or expression in the lips. The skin sagged a little around the neck. There were grey hairs clearly visible in the new growth that showed in the parting, the golden streaks hanging limply in reminder of hair care past. The image that showed itself in the looking glass was of an old bag; a hag.

Fiona knew that she had no option but to pay up. The amount that they asked for was large. It was especially a problem after the quantities that she had previously been doling out to him. It had been hard enough to cover up those tracks and she had to dip into other accounts to make up the difference. Dress money, that Charles had given her on asking, went straight over to Page; every last penny. So at the beginning of June, when they had an important function to attend, Fiona had to hire a dress.

"So that's where my £600 went that I forked out in April!" exclaimed Charles.

"Do you like it?"

"Fantastic!" was his reply. It really was an amazing outfit and she returned it to the hire shop the next day. The £600 had already been handed over to Page back in April, just as soon as Charles had paid it into her dress account. The cost of the hire was met by not renewing the television licence. It was a case of robbing Peter to pay Paul. It was a balancing act that she had done for many months for services rendered, until, that is, the blackmail demand came.

She had never seen Page again after that. She had not wanted to. She could not face him. However, it had not stopped him writing to her. More photographs arrived when she missed the first deadline. She wrote back and pleaded for more time. She knew how to plead. When Page answered her – there was no name on the paper, but she presumed it must be him – he enclosed further prints with the caption *This is how you begged. Remember? One week.*

Fiona had a week to sort the money out. The first week in July, when the nation was watching Wimbledon, Fiona was scanning the newspapers for adverts.

Put all your debts in one basket.

No questions asked!

Fast loans!

It was lucky for Fiona that Charles' signature was so easy to copy, for all these loan companies wanted was a charge on the house.

PART FOUR

Autumn 1987

"Where's the boss?" Tony called out down the office towards where Amelia was standing chatting.

Amelia turned and smiled. "Here," she called back in a girlish fashion.

Tony grinned back at her, whilst thinking that she was an inane fool. He knew that she loved being referred to as the boss. It was a courtesy title only, though. She was no more the boss at the moment than he was. The Wilkinson Engineering Works existed in a power vacuum. Decisions were taken, that is true, about buying or concerning colour schemes, or whether the company cars should be upgraded or not (they were, of course). Concepts were floated and ideals listed. Aims were produced after expensive lunches. Office staff were given five star treatment at a nightclub, in case the changes that had taken place over the past number of months had disrupted their working lifestyles. The changes, of course, had not disrupted anything except their expectations. These had risen, for when money is being spent as if there is no tomorrow, then all and sundry jump on the bandwagon and demand a share of the action. Decisions, real hard decisions, had not even been considered. They had been glossed over, papered over and filed under T for Tomorrow. Amelia had handed over all her responsibilities to Tony. Tony considered himself responsible to no one but himself, and in that regard he was highly responsible and saw it as his duty to look after number one. There was no number two, or three or four.

When he called out for the boss, he was merely being

polite. She was not the boss, for she did not have a clue what was going on. He was not the boss either, for he, as he pointed out frequently whenever the going was getting sticky, was just the manager. Therefore, hard choices were never made. The underlying problems were not tackled. The firm just bobbed along on a sea of glitz, troubled waters being skilfully avoided by Tony, until he could abandon ship safely.

Troubled waters were increasing. The firm was getting deeper and deeper into debt. Not obviously so, for the debts had been artfully disguised even though they had multiplied at a fast rate. The company owed money here and there; it had commitments to various interested parties and had undertaken these largely at the same time. Therefore the extent of the problem was disguised because money had been applied for over a few months and from a number of places, with each financial institution blissfully unaware of the others! It was quite complicated and taxed Tony tremendously. However, if things got a little too confused, he solved the problem by filing it under something such as M for Muddle, Mess or Mistake or F for Finance, Foe or…

"I've arranged for you to meet some important potential clients, Amelia," Tony told her.

"Super. Where?"

"I've found a rather nice little restaurant, a bit pricey but worth it. Very nouveau! You'll love it!"

Amelia simply adored nouveau cuisine. It always arrived looking like a picture and made one feel somewhat frightened to eat it, in case one destroyed perfection.

"Have you got last month's trading figures?" Amelia inquired in a fit of inquisitiveness.

"They are being prepared, remind me tomorrow and I'll get you a copy!" replied Tony, knowing full well that she would forget by tomorrow. He had seen the trading figures and they did not look so brilliant. In fact, they were grim. It did not help when one order, which constituted over half of the production, was returned. Apparently there were mistakes and not for the first time either. The finished goods had not matched the criteria requested. Tony had disassociated himself from all this. Such tasks were the responsibility of the works manager. Unfortunately, there was no officially appointed works manager and Tony instead had delegated duties to someone on the shop floor. He, lacking any experience whatsoever, saw no reason to question the criteria given, despite it seeming a little odd. The goods were produced, the buyer rejected them and went elsewhere, Tony blamed the 'works manager' and he, in turn, did not give a damn.

The potential clients that Tony and Amelia were due to meet over lunch later that week were really rather small fry compared to the major customer just lost.

* * *

James had spent the summer as a part-time barman at the local in the village where he was staying. The villagers took to their new barman immediately. They flocked in on those English summer days, when one feels that the sun ought to be shining but it is not, to hear tales of the great Outback. James fed them stories of derring-do, telling them in lurid detail about how he encountered this creature and that insect whilst out on walkabout.

"But how did you sleep at night?" one customer asked.

"With my arms around my sheila, how else!" he replied, and they laughed as he knew they would. He exaggerated his Aussie lifestyle and accent when he was behind the bar. It amused him to see them listening to his every word and in turn he made them smile and think of other lands away from the pushy materialistic England.

His still tanned complexion and ready smile, his patter and banter with the folks who propped up the bar, made him an asset. He held the drinkers in a state of rapture and they bought more crisps and beers as he related further adventures. Crocodile Dundee had nothing on James! The landlord wanted to take him on in a permanent capacity but James refused, he had a job to do outside the King's Head.

He had to remove the two Pearson-Coopers from the running. They did not deserve Blayborough House; he did not need it but he was going to make sure that his two brothers did not acquire it. He was out to smash their chances. In the spring, he had laid his little trap for the youngest brother, Ralph. He had fixed the bait and now it was time to spring the trap and catch the animal.

To this end, he needed to leave the genteel village during the daytime and head for the city of Leeds. He arranged with the landlord that for the next week he would do evening duties instead. This suited the landlord, for he had grown to trust the friendly Australian/Englishman and relied on him. He knew that he could leave the bar safely in his hands and spend the evening watching the television for a change.

James therefore planned to take his hire car to the

metropolis of Leeds, carefully avoiding the centre he intended to hang around Armley. Not that Armley was a place that one really enjoyed hanging around, but for his purpose it suited well.

The comings and goings of the Wilkinson Engineering Works was under his observation. He knew from past experience that at about noon, someone would leave the building and head for the bank. That someone, as noted in the spring, was female and quite young. He hoped that she was not engaged or married, or else it would make his plans that much harder to put into practise.

The sun was shining that September morning and James hung around waiting. The strong light made a slight bit of difference to the rather grim surroundings but in reality it really failed to obscure the air of industrial depression that hangs around such places. At five past twelve, a woman wearing a green skirt and matching blouse come out of the door. She was carrying a cloth bag and James kept a watch on her movements as she headed down the road.

He followed at a discreet distance, only hurrying as she got near to the bank. As she strode up the steps and opened the door, he was just one yard behind her. In the queue, he was right behind.

At the counter, the cashiers seemed to have their work cut out, counting loads of cash and making it tally with what was written on the bank slips. This gave James the opportunity he wanted.

"Long queue!" he said and smiled at the young lady in front of him.

"It always is," she replied and then told him how long she had to wait the day before.

"Need some more staff on, I'd say," James commented.

The young lady in question gave James a close look and then asked him the obvious question.

"You from Australia then?"

"Well, I'm from England originally but I've been out in Oz for years and years."

"So you're over here visiting relations, are you?" she asked, presuming that no one would come all this way for any other reason.

"Sort of," he replied.

Still the queue had not moved. There were girls in summer dresses, as the day was warm for autumn, lining up, waiting to bank the week's monies; a couple of men in smart suits stood posing with mobile phones in their top pockets. The queue was increasing and had barely moved an inch. People were shuffling around from foot to foot, flagging in the warm air. It was suiting James' plan ideally.

"I've got an uncle over in Adelaide," continued the woman. James knew from vast experience that every single British person had some relative somewhere in Australia.

"He's called Jim, Jim… can't remember his full name. Anyway, he's been in Adelaide for ten years or more. Are you from Adelaide?"

James shook his head.

"Pity," she replied, "because if you were, you might have met him. That'd be funny! Anyway, he came from Leeds originally and went out on the assisted passage for £10. That's all it cost him, £10! All the way to Australia for £10!"

"It was a real bargain – for both sides," commented James.

"Oh, yes, I know – I mean England got rid of some real dross with that assisted passage lark!" James smiled at her remark – what else could he do?

"This is really bad, this queue," she said and then turned slightly away.

James noticed that and immediately made attempts to rectify the situation. He did not want to lose her. "By the way, I'm James. Thought I'd better introduce myself, after all we might be here for the duration!"

"Jenny – pleased to meet you!" They smiled at each other, the introduction temporarily halting the flow of conversation.

"So where do you work then, Jenny?" inquired James in an innocent fashion.

"Oh, down at Wilkinson's. Hate it there, really. I mean it's better than it was. It's all been done up for one thing but it's dead boring there. All potted plants and first names! Does that make sense to you?"

"Yes, it does – I know just the type of place you mean. All facade, all front!"

"Yeah, that's right – nothing behind it all!"

At that moment, the bank decided to alleviate the queue by requisitioning one of the many back room boys and sending him into the front line. Suddenly, the queue started to move and they all edged forward a bit.

A little while later, James and Jenny were dealt with simultaneously by two cashiers and they both left the bank at the same time.

"Going off for my lunch now," stated Jenny while lingering on the steps. "Expect I'll see you again in here, waiting!"

"Probably, mind you, a bloke could die waiting in there!" And then he added, as if by afterthought, "Listen,

I'm going for my lunch now – why don't I take you out and buy you a bite to eat?"

"Oh, no, I couldn't let you do that – I mean, I don't know you or anything," she replied.

"Don't worry, I'm not going to kidnap you and drag you off to Australia or something!"

"Pity!"

James laughed and then continued, "There's a place across the road that does snacks, we'll go there."

Jenny looked mightily relieved when he suggested something close by. She did not want to get into his car but she did rather fancy him.

James took her arm and guided her across the busy road. She was to be his spy in the Wilkinson company, his mole who would burrow away for him, getting information that would ruin his brother Ralph.

Slowly, slowly, catchy monkey!

* * *

It was called a repayment holiday. There would be no money to pay back until the beginning of September. However, as with all things relating to finance, it was no holiday, no picnic. Fiona had arranged, in July, a loan secured on the house that she and Charles inhabited. She had easily copied Charles' signature. The money from that loan went straight to the agreed building society account. Two days later, in the same month of July, she awaited the master video copy.

Fiona would not have recognised a master video copy if it had stared her in the face. She presumed that it was a video that would be perhaps especially strong and robust, maybe in a different colour. Anyway, it would definitely, she decided, be easily identifiable.

Fiona waited and waited. As each day passed, she raced to the front door just as soon as she spotted the postman wandering up the avenue. She was in so much of a hurry that Charles commented on it and wondered why she did not let Mrs Armitage transport the mail from the hall to the breakfast table. Fiona mumbled something about Mrs Armitage's bad back. Charles went back to his *Daily Telegraph* and chewed his toast.

July passed by and August did too. No communication came and slowly Fiona calmed down and told herself that it was all over. All that remained was for her to pay back the money that she had borrowed on the house. The video probably did not even exist... there was no such thing... she could relax...

In the second week in September, the postman rang the front door bell. He could not get the parcel through the letterbox. He held in his hands a jiffy bag addressed to Fiona. She took it from him and shut the door without saying a word.

She carefully opened it in the privacy of the cloakroom. There was a video tape inside and a letter. It was a letter of thanks, a thank you for the £90,000 that she had deposited. She leant against the wall and sweat poured from her. Relief was great. She was free. He had sent her the evidence and now all she had to do was destroy it.

She removed the tape from its cover and prepared to pull out the film, to unwind it and mutilate it. It was then that she noticed the sticker on the cassette: Postman Pat.

"No, no, no," she stammered, "oh, please no!"

She took the video into the drawing room and

inserted it into the recorder. She did not want to see herself, she was trembling but she prayed that the film would be the one she had paid so dearly for.

It wasn't.

* * *

The provisional accounts, endorsed by the new firm of accountants that Tony had persuaded Amelia to employ, impressed all who looked at them. There were times when Tony even believed the figures himself. He, by September, had got to the point of conviction – he was convinced that the firm was prospering, as his concocted accounts showed. This state of belief had been reached through having to go discuss the figures with various groups. The bank had temporarily abated their interest in the company – the projected profit and loss accounts having persuaded them to turn their attentions to other businesses; Amelia was terribly impressed – she readily agreed to yet another rise and bonus for Tony! the merchant bank, who Tony was approaching with a view to changing to, showed signs that they would welcome the company – it was their sort of firm, thrusting, daring, a devil take the hind-most type of works.

John Spencer, as the solicitor to Wilkinson's, was not swept up in this euphoria; not that he was a figures-man, he was not. It was just that he was automatically suspicious whenever people changed accountants and banks and produced glowing projections at the same time. He was also just a teeny bit jealous too.

"Mrs Pearson-Cooper is here, Mr. Spencer," announced a voice over the intercom.

"Send her in, will you please."

The door opened and Amelia walked in. She looked stunning and John's heart gave a little flutter.

"Hello, John, you keeping alright?" she asked.

"Not so bad."

"Sorry to hear about your marriage," said Amelia.

"Just one of those things – I'm not upset or anything!"

John offered his client a seat on his sofa. He moved away from his desk and plonked himself next to her. There were a few beads of sweat on his forehead. He was nervous and she could detect it.

"You wanted to see me?" she began, wondering why he was sitting right next to her.

"Oh, yes, yes I do," he stumbled a bit on his words and a few more drops of sweat appeared on his brow.

"Nothing the matter with the company, is there?"

"No, no," he answered and then added, "I mean yes, yes there is!" He was trying to collect his thoughts. All his old feelings were coming back to him; his passion for this woman. Flames were emerging from the embers of yesteryear. He was blushing embarrassingly. Worst of all, he felt his stutter beginning to affect his vocal patterns.

He knew that he would have to revert to matters in hand. If he began by discussing the firm, then he would overcome all his personal problems and be able to pursue his quest for Amelia's heart free of difficulty. Yes, that was it – he would begin by discussing the engineering works and then tell Amelia that he still loved her after all these years, and luckily he was just recently divorced!

He rose from the sofa and sat on a hard chair opposite her.

"How do you feel about Wilkinson's?" It was an

open-ended sort of question that put the ball in her court.

Now it was her turn to stumble. "Well, you know – I mean, it looks good," she stuttered but she recovered her composure when she added, "Tony is a marvel!"

Straight away, John Spencer spotted the gleam in her eyes. He wondered if she was already having an affair with the man. Perhaps they were engaging in some sort of sordid romance behind the filing cabinet. Maybe he was touching her up as he sauntered through the office. Or indeed, was she already planning to ditch her husband in favour of Driver? These thoughts ran through John's head at lightning speed. The hated conclusion – that he had missed the love-boat again – emerged.

"You're not? You and Tony? You and Tony aren't? Are you?" he inquired.

Amelia was startled. She had not been expecting this line of questioning. "What do you mean?" she asked, feeling affronted.

"You're not…"

Amelia rose from the sofa majestically. "How dare you! How dare you ask such things! No we are not!" she turned to go and John was horrified. It had all gone so wrong. He grabbed hold of her elbow but she pulled away.

"Please, don't go!" he pleaded.

"I'm not staying here to be insulted by you – who do you think I am?"

"I'm sorry, I'm truly sorry – I didn't mean it, please believe me!"

Amelia glanced crossly in his direction before once more heading towards the door.

"I wanted to speak to you about the firm – I'm worried about it, I'm worried you might be going under."

By now, Amelia had reached the door and had her hand on the handle. She turned to him and gave him a withering look. "You aren't worried about anything of the sort. All you wanted to know was whether Tony and I were having an affair. And why? Because you were planning to have one with me. Well, I'm not going to be your bit on the side, your replacement wife now she has gone and done a bunk. You and I won't be flitting between the sheets because I am not interested in you one little bit. So you can stop your pretend concern in the day to day events at Wilkinson's."

With that, she opened the door and marched out. John slumped in the chair and tried to work out just what had gone wrong. Where had he messed it all up? Yes he did fancy her and not just a bit but as much he had in the past – it wasn't just that though, he was also concerned about the business and still wanted to advise her. He saw problems ahead and felt that he could assist as the trusted tried and tested family firm of solicitors. Just as he was coming to the conclusion that all was lost, the door to his office opened again. His heart rose when he saw who it was but sunk again as Amelia spoke.

"In fact, I think I'll swap solicitors. Tony knows an excellent one who charges half your fees."

* * *

The letter that arrived by the second post was quite clear. It demanded another instalment of the same amount as the first. Fiona was beyond panic; she was in despair. She put her head in her hands and tried to blot it all out.

To make matters worse, the repayment holiday on the loan was nearly over. In order to pay the first instalment, she knew that she would have to acquire the money from somewhere. All ideas about where had disappeared when the letter came outlining the second demand. She was given a week to find it. If she did not, then the film would be sent out. This time where it was going to be delivered was made quite clear. The chairman of the local Conservative party, her neighbours, friends of hers that she had inadvertently mentioned on those sessions of wild abandon she had indulged so foolishly in. Also, she was warned, it would go out on general distribution. She tried to comfort herself with the thought that all this activity would make his capture all the easier but she knew that unless she went to the police and made a complaint, the receivers of such lurid films would only know who the named star was and not who the men were.

A week is not a long time. All that she could think of doing was borrowing the money. It had been so easy last time and, after all, the house was worth well over £500,000. As she reached for the morning paper, where those tempting adverts always were, she noticed her nails. They were torn and colourless, scraggy ends to wrinkled hands.

* * *

Charles amused himself with the *Financial Times*. Armed with a pocket calculator, he regularly assessed his worth.

"I think I'll soon have to invest in a machine with a capacity for larger figures!" he commented to himself. True, he had to divide everything by three but that division was only until November and then eighy percent would be his and Fiona's.

The tips were coming in fast and furiously. It was money for old rope and stocks and shares were zooming up like there was no tomorrow. There was one thing which niggled him and that was missing out on a particularly good gem from Roland. He had been enjoying the delights of Glenda when Roland had tried to get in touch. Fiona had been out and John Bates was away in Scotland for a few days. Circumstances had contrived against them and quite a large sum of money had been lost or rather missed.

As the broker to the Westbury Group, Roland was privy to all sorts of information that he was not supposed to use to his own advantage. However, as with all other information that the three of them had pooled together, this Chinese Walls scenario held no fear. Roland had found out that Angus McNeil – the chairman of the Westbury Group – was looking to sell his stake and get out. The chairman had spotted this opportunity, as every day he saw his shares rising and rising and thus judged now was the time. What he needed to do was find a buyer for the company that would delight all the shareholders. He had instructed his brokers to search around for a suitable company. It was to be a hush-hush operation until all the negotiations were nearly complete.

Angus McNeil, as chairman of the Westbury Group, used to think that he would carry on forever. He could hardly imagine not turning up to work. It was only a year and a half ago that he thought a takeover was out of the question! Put out to grass, was how he saw it. Now, the situation had changed. He had been sufficiently narked with running a company with what he saw as a committee of people, instead of by himself. Owning thirty-five percent of a firm is not quite the same as owning one hundred percent. He was open to offers now. "Take the money and run!" was what his wife had said. He fancied running to Florida.

However, he was still the man at the helm and an honest man. That is why when, shortly after receiving what was supposed to be confidential information about a firm that was interested in buying him out, the shares of Westbury rose on a rumour, Angus smelt a rat. Someone was trading on insider information.

He asked the registrars to send him details of names and nominee names. He circled a few for further investigation. He hated insider dealing and was determined to bring whoever it was to justice. And then, who knows who else may be caught in the net?

* * *

James had soon gained the confidence of Jenny. She loved being taken out for lunch by him, that was apparent. She enjoyed chatting about this and that. In reality, she had very little conversation. She talked endlessly about the same things – her mum, her dad and her brothers and the firm she worked for.

Being moved from the position of confidential secretary to being in charge of the accounts had miffed her.

"I really liked Mr. Pearson-Cooper. He was so easy

to get on with! And I was quite good at my job so I don't know why I was moved!"

"Perhaps they thought you'd be good at accounts also," suggested James, while toying with the salt-cellar.

"Hardly, I mean, maths was never my strong subject at school."

"So, how do you manage?"

Jenny pulled a face and admitted the truth. "I don't! Tony Driver, the wonder boy, does all the accounting. I just sort out the invoices and the sales ledgers!"

"So, why do you think you got the job then?" asked James.

"Oh, I just think it was a case of moving people around in the same way he moves the pot plants around. I think that he shifts someone just as soon as they know too much about the job they're doing!"

James jerked himself awake. "Why?"

"Well, the firm's going bust. That's my opinion, for what it's worth. Going under, yes, that's it!"

"Going down? Are you sure?" James was suddenly all ears. This was too good to be true.

"Has to be!" she confirmed in a whisper. "Even I, with my limited knowledge of accounts, can see that we are spending more than we are selling."

"Yes, but surely he doesn't let you see the bank accounts, so how do you know?"

"I found a whole load of them when I was searching through the files! And now guess what is happening?" she asked James.

"What?"

"We are changing banks and solicitors. And guess what else?"

"I don't know."

"It was only a short while ago that we changed our accountants." Jenny then glanced at her watch and let out a squeal. "Christ, I'm late!" With that, she dashed off.

James realised that he only had a short time left to deal his master stroke against his brother and his wife. He had to pull the plug before they were re-financed by another bank.

* * *

"I want to see you!" demanded Ralph that Tuesday. The voice at the other end faltered but the Irish accent was unmistakable.

"Sure, sure," agreed Pat.

"Well, then – when?"

"Next week, I'll see you next week!"

Ralph shouted down the telephone, "No, not next week – today!"

"Well, okay then, today."

"Today at two o'clock in Bradford."

"Why Bradford?" asked Pat. He never usually went there, preferring Leeds, where he was well known.

"Because no one knows you in Bradford and there will be no one watching us."

Pat mumbled yes to that and inquired where.

"Outside Cartwright Hall, in Lister Park. There are some seats and lots of flower beds. I'll wait there for you at two o'clock."

"Shall I wear a carnation in my button hole and carry a copy of *The Times*?" asked Pat, trying to lighten the conversation.

"Not necessary – I'll spot you because you'll be the

one looking worried." With that, he put down the telephone and got himself ready for the car journey to Bradford.

Ralph had demanded a meeting with the reluctant Pat for two reasons. Firstly, he wanted to make sure that the decision on the land would go his way and secondly, he wanted to pile the pressure on this Irish leprechaun. In the intervening period after the debacle with the land, he had lent Pat some more money in order to settle further gambling debts. Now, he wanted to make sure that he was definitely getting a return on his investment. After all, if the land deal failed then he had no come back. One could hardly take a person to court for failure to ensure a crooked deal went through!

* * *

As Ralph got into his new car, with its brand spanking new registration plate, for his two o'clock appointment, his brother James was waiting outside the bank manager's office for his appointment.

"James, do come in!" welcomed the manager. Such friendliness! Such comradeship! Such falseness.

"Well, I thought I'd come and have a little chat about various investment ideas; thought perhaps the bank might have a few schemes that might be of interest to me."

What a delicious worm James had dropped! Tim grabbed it in mid-air and chewed the bait. "We have some excellent investments – you can't go wrong with them!"

"Really?"

"Yes, really. I mean, if you compare our unit trust

with the profit that can be made on houses, you would be better living in a tent and putting all your equity with us!" Tim produced a series of graphs which were sufficiently vague as to prove anything and everything.

"That's amazing!" agreed James, as he thought he should.

"Yes, but let me show you something which is even more amazing." And Tim produced his piece de resistance, which was a comparison of unit trust performances showing his bank's trusts to be the top performers. According to the graph, anyway!

"I'm glad I came to see you!"

"Oh, you will be even more than glad – you can't go wrong with stocks and shares! Providing, that is, you take good advice and place your money with this bank!" Tim delved into his drawer and found a form and pen. With this poised, he prepared to take details which would lock away his client's money for ages. That is, all except for a large slice – this would be commission.

James leant back in his chair and pretended to weigh the prospects up.

"Funny thing, isn't it?" he began.

"Funny thing? What is a funny thing?" Tim asked. He did not like his clients pausing before signing up, it was ominous. He did hope that James would not start asking awkward questions as he had no answers for them. It had taken him long enough to master the basics – which included how much money the bank would earn in commissions – without someone pondering on advance points.

"Money, money is a funny thing."

Tim did not think money was amusing at all. It was

deadly serious to him but he thought he had better humour the client.

"Why is money a funny thing?"

"Well, here I am, thinking how I am going to invest £100,000 after safely placing it on deposit. Here I am, wondering about money in my old age, preparing and being careful…"

"Yes and what is funny about that?" interrupted Tim. "Sounds most sensible to me."

"Well, it does sound sensible and it is, but well, you know Ralph…" and he paused for the words to lingering the air.

"Ralph, your brother?"

"Yes, Ralph, my brother. I mean, he is the opposite of me."

"The opposite?" echoed Tim. "Why is that?"

"Well, I like to prepare and put money by and he… no, I shouldn't tell you this!"

Tim's appetite was well and truly whetted.

"If you know something that could affect the bank, then you must tell me!" asserted Tim, who by now was sitting bolt upright in his chair.

"But surely it would be a breach of confidentiality?" queried James, watching the man opposite him carefully.

"Oh, no it wouldn't be," the bank manger reassured his client. "It would only be that if I told you something about Ralph Pearson-Cooper. If you tell me, then you can't be breaking any rules because you're not bound by any."

James was inwardly jubilant. Tim had really eaten the tempting worm. He pulled on the line and landed the fish.

"If you are sure then?"

"Absolutely!" reassured Tim – by now twitching for the knowledge.

"Well, it's not about Ralph personally..." James began.

"No, it's about the Wilkinson plant, isn't it?" prompted Tim.

"Yes, that's right – how did you guess?"

"Just call it bank manager's intuition. Go on."

"Well..."

"Yes?" urged Tim.

"They might be going bust!" announced James.

"How do you mean, might be going bust?" Tim pronounced each word very slowly, to emphasise them as he awaited further elucidation.

James did rather think that this bank manager had a frightening lack of financial know-how but ignored the fatuous aspect of the comment.

"Trade is difficult!" stated James. "You know how things are with these engineering works."

"But I have a set of provisional accounts..."

"Endorsed by a new firm of accountants?" asked James and Tim nodded in reply. "And, what is more," continued James, "I am given to understand that they are asking another bank – a more dubious bank than your good selves – to lend them money!"

"But they can't do that! We're their bank!"

"I'm just passing this information on to you – for what it is worth. Sometimes, if someone in a position like yourself could talk to Ralph and his wife, persuade them to take stock and think about things. Perhaps put a halt to some new investment or see if they can make savings somewhere. If I were you..." And here he paused.

Tim jumped in with the answer, "Yes, I bet if you were me, you certainly wouldn't grab some extra security, tighten the screws or anything like that; but there's a time for hand-holding and a time for letting go!"

James smiled back at the man, who was by now looking rather worried. It suited James to let the bank manager think that he was just saying all this for Ralph's own good. Businesses going under were bad for the bank's own business. What they really liked were businesses that were successful but risky – that way they could up the interest rate charge for any loans offered.

"I think I've said too much – I just thought that perhaps you'd be able to help him, give him a lifeline or something!"

With that, James rose to go, his investment requirements put to one side by the ever eager bank manager.

"Don't worry, you did the right thing. I'll offer him a lifeline," assured Tim.

James appeared to look relieved. As he left the manager's office, he thought to himself, a lifeline long enough to hang himself with!

* * *

The flowers outside Cartwright Hall looked particularly resplendent. The Parks Department in Bradford did an excellent job and it would have been quite enjoyable just sitting there, if one had nothing better to do. But Ralph did have something better to do. He had the Irish question to sort out – his own personal Irish problem.

Pat was as slippery as an eel. Though to begin with their relationship had been one of friendship, lately the two of them were not on the best of terms. Pat had turned even more to drink and was gambling heavily again. The differences in their backgrounds were beginning to show up more and more. It was not just that one was Irish and the other English – heavens knows, the two nationalities had not been the best of bed fellows for the past hundred years. It was all to do with class. Ralph was of a different class. His education was not an Etonian one, unlike his brothers. His mother could not afford that, even if she did want him to board, and his father was unwilling to fork out too much money in the circumstances. However, a private day school in England is far removed from the rough and tumble of an Irish city school.

The differences of class and indeed culture played their part in separating the two of them. Ralph was no longer feeling lonely and a loser, as he had done when they first met. He had developed into a winner in his own way. Pat always felt a loser. Ralph had time to contemplate their differences as he waited. He was not even sure if Pat would turn up. Would he have turned up, if the boot was on the other foot? he wondered. Time ticked by and watching the bees venturing in and out of the flowers held only a limited appeal, as did viewing the countless parents wandering off in search of the children's playground and the old men with empty days spending an hour or two on the park bench. It was now half past two and he still had not arrived. Ralph rose to go, now determined to sort him out – just as soon as he could catch him, that is.

As he left the area of formal flower beds, Ralph

spotted a figure running in his direction. It was Pat.

"You're late," he admonished as soon as he reached him.

"And what else do you expect me to be when you arrange to meet here? Did you really think I'd be on time? Holy Mother of God, I'd never even heard of the place, let alone visited it!"

"I presumed…" began Ralph, the wind taken out of his sails.

"Yes, you presumed! You presume too much." Pat took a look around. "What is this place anyway, some sort of stately home?"

"It's an art gallery."

"It's one hell of an art gallery then!"

With that, the two of them settled down. The ice had now been broken and Ralph's anger had subsided. Perhaps this little episode was going to be easily solved.

"So," started Pat, "what do you want that requires me to leave Leeds and sit amongst the flowers outside this, this – are you sure it doesn't belong to some English lord?"

"Quite sure," answered Ralph. "I brought you here because I want to know what is happening to my little investment."

"You mean you brought me all this way to find out that? Couldn't you have asked me over the telephone, like a normal human being?"

"No, I couldn't. Supposing the telephone was tapped?"

Pat pondered on that point and dismissed it as stuff of spy thrillers. "So why here then?" he asked.

"Take a look! Everyone is either old, deaf or can't understand English. It's the perfect place!"

"Okay, you win."

"Now then – what about my land investment? After all, if they don't choose my land, I'll want my money back!" Ralph turned his steely gaze onto the man sitting next to him. Pat turned away, unwilling to look him in the eye.

"With interest!" Ralph added.

"Yes, alright, I get the message!" said Pat. "But it's not easy, though, not easy at all. Sure it may seem easy to you, sitting there waiting, but I've got to be careful. I've got my reputation to think about."

" Reputation? What reputation have you got?"

"I'm a highly respected councillor."

"You're nothing of the sort!" retorted Ralph.

"I might be next in line for Lord Mayor!"

"Next in line for Lord Mayor? What's happened then – they've run out of normal blokes, onto the scrapings, are they?"

"You can mock but let me tell you, I've put a lot of work into being a councillor. It is my only occupation…"

"Only because you can't get another!" replied Ralph.

"No, it is not, it is because I want to put my constituents first and devote all my attention to them!"

"Bullshit. Deliver me the goods, you drink-sodden corrupt thing." Ralph started to wander off, turning as he did to add a last retort, with the additional accompaniment of a wagging finger, "Or else I'll have your balls boiled for breakfast!"

* * *

Tony had a feeling. It was strange sometimes how these feelings appeared in his mind but when they did appear, he recognised them straight away. It was probably experience that caused him to notice the tick-tock of worry that would begin inside his head, the gnawing feeling that something, somewhere was starting to happen – wrongly.

Experience was something that he had a lot of. His life had been quite charmed, by anybody's standards. It was not that he had been a great success, that was true. Nor had he been born with a silver spoon in his mouth; but it was a charmed life, or so he thought. After all, hadn't he lost his pest of a wife to another man – a very rich man who just wanted a fuss free divorce for his new partner and therefore was willing to forgo any rights to a settlement? That was lucky. As was the previous company not taking him to court for nicking their money. (He did think at one time that they might hunt him out when they found out just how much he had taken, which was a hell of a lot more than they first thought.) Then there was the question of the insurance company he had worked for prior to his little sojourn with the firm in Colchester. Lucky for him they were so negligent in finding out just where some of the funds had disappeared to!

Yes, indeed, life had served him well. However, now he knew that there came a time in everyone's sessions of scams that they realise that they must put a stop to it all. Just one last go, one last big one, and then peaceful retirement!

The little pangs of worry were presenting themselves and Tony knew he must make his plans quickly. He had quite a good shareholding in the firm. His standing with the largely inept Amelia was high and her husband took very little notice of him. Tony was rather glad about that. He had plans which did not involve Ralph Pearson-Cooper.

* * *

John Bates rolled over on the king size bed and embraced Glenda. "What an amazing idea it was of mine to come here and surprise you!"

Glenda, totally bare and amply laden with flesh, agreed whole-heartedly. It had amazed her and totally surprised her. Tuesday was her day for household chores, but to Glenda they were not chores. The collecting of fruits and flowers, the bottling and jamming, the arranging and placing were all delights to Glenda. Mother Earth rewarded her, year after year, as she in turn thanked her and paid homage to the bounty given so freely.

There she had been, busy picking and plucking, when she heard a car purr up the drive. She recognised the engine noise and, as it was a week day, presumed it to be Charles. Imagine her surprise when she encountered John, breaking with tradition and visiting her mid-week!

She quickly abandoned her gathering of garden produce and led him inside. A thought did cross her mind, concerning the awkwardness of the situation should Charles also turn up, but she dismissed it as too dreadful to even consider.

However, she was greatly relieved to hear that he only had half an hour to spare. They swept upstairs, leaving the apples and pears on the kitchen table. Once in the bedroom, they enjoyed a different type of fruit.

Glenda had more than a soft spot for John. To her, he

was like a fox cub with a broken leg, or an owl lonely in the woods; to her, he was a vulnerable man in need of love and attention. She never spotted his reptilian nature.

John, in turn, adored his mistress of the plains. To him, she was a vision of beauty, a mist-shrouded Venus, a Diana who had hunted him and ensnared him with her ardent love. To John, Glenda was his reason for living, his reason for grabbing as much as possible and his reason for being a slimy toad. Soon, he knew, he would shed his outer skin, his snake-like appearance and be just the person she knew him as. Soon, when he had everything he planned for he would give himself over to her totally. Until that day, he knew he must continue to plot and deceive and always try to make his fortune.

When the half hour was up, they rose and got dressed again. Glenda returned to her gardening and John to his soliciting. As his Jag disappeared down the drive, Glenda picked up her basket and managed to fill it full of fruit before she heard another car come up her driveway. The car door shut quietly and the occupant could be heard treading on the small stones as he made his way to the back of the house.

"Glenda," he called out.

"Charlie, this is a surprise!" she replied.

It was a good job for the two men in her life that she was a warm hearted woman.

* * *

By the end of that week, Tim, the bank manager, had decided on a course of action. He would write to Amelia and Ralph Pearson-Cooper and demand that they come and see him as soon as possible. The letter was dictated on Thursday and arrived, as luck would have it, on Friday morning. Tony Driver opened it because Amelia and Ralph, to whom it was addressed, were not in just then. Letters from the bank were considered his domain, by virtue of the fact that they might pull the plug on the company and thus also on him. Once he had read the letter, he replaced it in its envelope, re-sealed it and hid it.

Just as he had done that, Amelia walked in through the door.

"You look great," Tony commented.

"Thanks!" she replied, glowing with the compliment.

"Let me take you out for lunch today, on me."

"Fantastic, where shall we go?"

Tony pretended to glance at his diary and then stated that he had nothing on all day and, as she had a blank day too, why not go to the seaside?

"I've not been to the seaside for years!" Amelia admitted.

"Right then, I suggest St. Anne's!"

The two of them set off straight away to St. Anne's, pausing only for Amelia to phone her husband and tell him that she would be out all day at a meeting.

The journey was not too arduous and the sun shone all the way. When they arrived and parked the car near the pier, Tony insisted on buying a bucket and spade.

"No seaside trip is complete without a dig on the sands!" he announced.

Indeed that is true and the two of them wandered onto the beach in search of suitable castle-building sand. They were like two young children, they both had their shoes off and he had rolled up his trouser legs. They set to work with bucket and spade, digging and laughing as they were building, topping with shells a turret moulded out of wet sand.

"Now then, you go and fill the bucket with sea water while I get the crowning glory," said Tony.

Amelia viewed the walk out to where the sea was with a certain amount of trepidation, as it was a long way out, but she gamely set off in the general direction. Tony wandered off towards the pier.

When he returned, he found that Amelia had not reached the sea and had instead decided that the castle should have a dry moat. They both agreed that that was the best plan and then Tony produced his piece de resistance.

"Flags! No castle is complete without them!"

Amelia gave a squeak of delight as the Royal Standard and Union Jack were put in their places and fluttered in the breeze.

"Super!" she said and she turned to Tony, eyes shining. "Thank you for suggesting this trip. I haven't had so much fun in years."

Her eyes fastened their gaze onto his. She opened her mouth slightly and, as he cupped her chin with his hand, they kissed.

"Stay the night with me," he murmured.

"What will I say to Ralph?"

"Tell him you are going onto another meeting…" he suggested, while gently running his fingers through her hair.

"On a Saturday… he wouldn't believe me!" she protested but his kisses stifled her protests and she felt as a young lover does on her first date.

"Stay the night with me," he pleaded with her.

"Yes, oh, yes!" she agreed and they rolled on the sand, squashing the flags and oblivious to the old man and his dog walking nearby.

* * *

That Saturday morning produced the usual crop of post for Charles and Fiona. Contract notes from brokers dominated the mail. Sometimes Charles would wonder just how he was going to sort it all out and work out the capital gains tax involved. There was a lot of it, that was for sure; but then, if you intend to make a fortune, it is only right that you should be prepared to pay your whack to society.

"What's in that envelope, Fiona?"

Fiona, looking as unkempt as she usually did these days, mumbled her reply. "Just an advert, it'll just be an advert!"

Charles stared at her. She seemed old these days. He compared her with Glenda, who was only a few years younger. Glenda held the secret of eternal youth, compared to his wife. If it was not for Blayborough House, he did sometimes wonder about trading her in.

"What an apt expression," he thought to himself, "trading her in!" Out loud, he did ponder one thing, "You don't seem to yourself these days, old thing!"

"Old thing? I'm not an old thing!"

"I know you're not – it's just a saying."

Fiona looked frantic and protested that it isn't just a saying.

"I didn't mean it," protested Charles, trying to wriggle out of the situation.

"Yes, you did. You looked at me and called me old thing!"

"Well… well, you haven't been yourself lately, have you?" admitted Charles.

"So I was right! You did mean it; I am an old thing to you!"

"No, no you're not! It's just that, well…" And then he rather unfortunately added, "Perhaps you need to visit that beauty salon you used to go to. You haven't been there for ages."

Fiona burst into floods of tears and left the room, clutching the letter that she described as an advert.

Charles returned to his toast and newspaper, making a mental note not to mention age or beauty salons or whatever again. He put it all down to the time of life. The change or whatever they called it. "Never realised that it would be so dramatic. Always thought it was a gradual thing," he muttered to himself and as he turned the pages over to the Peterborough column, he comforted himself with the fact that he always had Glenda!

* * *

Fiona wrapped her dressing gown around her even more tightly. She had stopped weeping now. She slit open the letter and surveyed its contents. Another loan had been arranged; another load of money waiting.

This would be the last, she decided. Not a penny more would he get.

The house that Charles and Fiona had been so proud to call 'nearly their own' now had extra mortgages. What worried Fiona was how was she going to pay all the money back.

* * *

Pat had gathered up his courage and made arrangements to see his leader. The Labour leader commanded a great power over fellow councillors as did the Tory leader over Conservative councillors. Unity was the watchword. United we stand!

The question of the two opposing but equally attractive sites was posing a problem for the leadership. They favoured the site that was not in Councillor O'Reilly's constituency because it suited their plans to see Pat O'Reilly embarrassed and scorned by local party activists.

What they had in mind was the removal of O'Reilly from the council; a sort of gentle elbowing out. Pat O'Reilly was well known for his drinking and gambling; he was equally as well known for his militant stand. The more he drank, the more militant he became.

So when the Labour leadership heard that Councillor O'Reilly wanted to have a chat, they prepared to tell him the unfortunate news.

"Pat, how are you this Saturday morning?" he was asked just as soon as he walked in.

"About the same as I am every other morning – hung over!" he replied.

The threesome sitting in the room laughed – at him. Pat presumed that they were laughing with him and joined in the merriment.

"You wanted to see us?" they prompted.

"Curious to know if you have heard about the new industrial site. Is it in my area?"

"Wish it could be! Wish we could do that for you!"

Pat froze with fear. "What do you mean?" he asked.

"We wanted it where you represent, believe me!" began one.

"But the officers…" continued another.

"Came down in favour of the second site," continued the third.

"Why?"

"You know council officers! Got weird reasons of their own," explained the first man.

"But we'll do what we can, believe us."

"I'd be grateful. If I don't get this, I'll…" trembled Pat.

"I know – they'll de-select you. That's our fear. We don't want to lose you, you're a good man!"

Pat looked up and thanked his comrade. "If you could do your best…" he murmured.

"We will!" the three of them stated in unison.

Pat rose and left the room, feeling near to tears. He knew that Ralph would want the money back and he did not have it – thousands were involved, literally thousands. He knew that his local party would throw him out in favour of someone else. There would be a power struggle between left and hard left. He held the mantle for the hard left, or so he used to think, but just lately he had noticed that someone else had become the standard bearer. Did drink remove reality? Did drink obliterate the truth of the situations? It seemed to. The trouble was, as anyone could have told him, that just as soon as you lose control through drink and create a mess, you need more alcohol to blot the trouble from your mind. It was a vicious circle and Pat was going round and round that circle. The noose was getting tighter and tighter round his neck.

As soon as the door had shut behind Pat, the three

men smiled at each other.

"That's dealt with him nicely!" said one.

The other made for the internal phone and dialled a number.

"Let the press release go out first thing on Monday," he announced, "you know the one I mean – the report that you have done on those two sites!" He put the receiver down and turned to the other two men. "I can just see the newspaper headlines now: 'Late contender Wins Council Approval' or something like that anyway!"

* * *

The couple in the king size bed sipped champagne. They had no night-clothes, so when room service had arrived with the bottle, they told them to leave it outside. Breakfast similarly had been left on the landing. Amelia felt years younger. She had forgotten about the children, the business and her husband. She was in a state of delirious excitement that Saturday morning. Tony joined her in those moments of ecstasy. He was a bit of a preener and poser himself, so pretending enjoyment did not come too hard for a man of his acting abilities. He had given her his best shot. She had taken it with rapturous enjoyment. Now he knew he had her, body and soul.

"It's funny you and I being here!" she had said as soon as they had woken.

"Natural, I'd call it!" he had replied and she agreed with him, just as he wanted her too.

Later on, they made love again. It was rare for Amelia to indulge so often. She and Ralph were not ones to frequent that activity. Tony was attentive in his lovemaking. He fondled and caressed her, stroked and touched her in such a way that she just wanted him all the more.

By half past eleven, the strings of home were pulling at Amelia. She started to feel the twinges of guilt that accompany such illicit affairs.

"We'd better think about going home," she suggested tentatively.

"Home, where is home?" he replied.

"Home is where your heart is," she quoted.

"My heart is with you."

"If only…" she began.

"If only what?" he prompted.

"I was just thinking out loud."

"Tell me," he suggested.

"If only home was with you and not Ralph!" She stopped and turned over to look at him. "There, I've said it!"

"Then we must see what we can do about it!" he replied. How easy it all was. How easy to make someone your own. Could he do the next stage, though? That would be the test! He knew that he had little time to achieve it because the bank was starting to breathe down the firm's neck and all his little indiscretions would come to light. He had laid some of the groundwork but he had to build fairly quickly.

He faced her and stroked her hair. "You could make your home with me."

Amelia smiled and asked, "How? What could we live on?"

"You tell me – you're the boss!"

"The boss! I'm not the boss. I haven't a clue about the wretched firm. You have though. Just look at the accounts you showed me."

Tony thought rapidly about those accounts and was pleased to notice that she had already forgotten that they were merely provisional ones. Soon the real ones had to be produced but they could be manipulated to look good. "Yes, I am really the boss, aren't I?" he stated.

"I know you are – you make all the decisions. You find the clients. You are Wilkinson Engineering Works! Without a doubt – you are the boss."

Inwardly, Tony's heart missed a beat. It was all too easy, too easy for words.

"You know my shares…" he began but she interrupted him in full flow with praise for him.

"That's another thing – you have a stake in the firm! My father was right, when someone has an interest in the firm, they work harder. Just look at Ralph."

He did not particularly want to look at Ralph but he forced himself. "What about him?"

"He has no shares and he just could not give a damn about it. It really grieves me, it really does. I mean, he is related by marriage to my father and worked for him – to what end? Eh? To nothing! He has washed his hands of the business. But you! You are different."

"Maybe it is because I love the boss!" Words were cheap to Tony.

"No, I love the boss, you just love your servant…" and she turned towards him and gave herself to him once more.

It was obviously going to be tiring business for Tony, trying to get his own way with Amelia.

After the third performance, Tony tried once more to return to the subject matter in hand.

"I was thinking about my shares…" he began.

"Yes?"

"Well, I want to buy a house and I could borrow against the shares, I'm sure I could."

"A house? A house!" And she gave a little shiver of delight. "If you had a house, we could make love all the time!"

"I know, that's what I've been thinking!" Then he turned to her with a worried frown on his handsome face. "But I need the shares valued!"

"Get them valued. First thing Monday morning, fix it up!"

Having successfully dealt with that, now he could make love with a clear mind. She had her attractive points, he decided; on balance, she was not too bad!

* * *

There were moments when Fiona came to her senses and almost called the police. She even got to the point at one stage of dialling the number. But as someone answered on the other end, she put the telephone down and sank back into despair.

She knew that she needed help and needed it fast. The amount that was now owed could never be paid back and who was to say that more would not be demanded? Who was to say that a further letter would not arrive, with more instructions?

Blackmail never stopped unless the perpetrators were brought to book. They could only be brought to book if the one who was being blackmailed grassed on them. The first step, she knew, was to realise that she was totally out of her depth. It was then that despair always set in.

"Depth? I was out of depth when I first started! I lost my dignity on day one – the day I paid him to have sex with me." When she reached that point in her self analysis, she invariably broke down in tears and her harsh discussion with herself got no further.

Another loan, another sum of money obtained through deception. Who could help her now? The police? Would they help? Could they find all that money from their hardship fund? They might be able to bring the wretch to justice but would that get her the money back? Would that pay for the two mortgages she had fraudulently obtained?

Yet she knew that she could not let the matter go on. She would be found out anyway, just as soon as the demands for money kept coming in. These loan companies – they were as bad as any blackmailer. She had to tell the police and she had to raise some real money and raise it fast.

But in what order should she do the two tasks? If she told the police first, then Charles would have to know about it all – then there would be one hell of a row; if she sorted the money out first, by some miracle means she had yet to work out, then that would defuse the situation somewhat. She was never quite sure whether Charles would be more cross about what she had done or about the money.

The money, she guessed, so that is why she decided to seek help to alter the precarious position that she was in.

* * *

Angus McNeil needed to speak to someone in confidence about the problem in his company. It was one of those delicate situations that made one go down and down a list of people, crossing off those you could not trust. The person who he should talk to about it was the last person he could trust. But then, if I can't trust him, just who can I trust? he wondered. He would be glad when the Westbury Group was taken over but he did not want anyone profiting out of it – certainly not prior to himself.

There was only one person left on the list. Angus was a straight and honest man. He never cheated anyone. He paid his taxes – even when there was a Labour government in and he could have moved his money elsewhere. He could hold his hand on his heart and say that he never lied, never diddled someone out of something.

He dialled the number that got him through to the police department that handled such cases.

* * *

Ralph tried to ward off the feeling that ticked over and around in his mind. He would resist all temptation and not ring up Pat to see what was happening. That Monday morning, he had examined his building society passbook and noted with a certain amount of alarm that the original £100,000 had shrunk. If the state of affairs continued then he would have to dip into his own personal savings to repay the ultimate winner.

"I'll just wait and bide my time," he said to himself over coffee.

Of late, he and Amelia had been receiving the local evening paper. It was not exactly the highlight of the day for Ralph but occasionally there were articles of interest. It generally arrived in the afternoon at about four o'clock. Usually, it remained on the mat until one of the children picked it up when they returned from school. Today, however, when it plopped through the letterbox, it fell onto the floor in such a way as to reveal its leading article.

Ralph, who happened to be going through the hall on the way to the garden, spotted the black and heavily typed words. The truth shouted out to him. He had backed a loser.

"Where's that man?" he shouted out loud. Luckily, there was no one in the house; the children had been taken by a friend's mum to another home for tea.

"I'll have him!" he said through clenched teeth as he dialled Pat at his home number.

"Hello," Pat mumbled, sounding half asleep when he eventually answered the telephone.

"What the hell happened?" cried Ralph, not bothering with introductions.

"The officials preferred the other site," was the reply, for Pat knew exactly what Ralph was talking about. "Look, don't get mad with me, I did my best!"

"No, you didn't. You didn't do your best at all. You never turned up for that important meeting."

"I'm sorry but I wasn't feeling too good, in fact, I don't feel all that well now."

Ralph just shouted down the phone in reply, he was not going to waste any sympathy on what he viewed as a scoundrel, "Ill? You weren't ill and you're not ill now! You're just an alcoholic in a permanent stupor!"

Pat protested that he was not an alcoholic, "I can stop drinking any time I want."

"That's what they all say," Ralph answered, "let's face it – you're a drunk!"

"I'm not and I'll prove it. I'll stop tomorrow – you just see if I don't!"

"Tomorrow never comes, fool!" stated Ralph.

There was a pause in the conversation as the two of them regained their strength.

"I want my money back – all of it, every single last penny!"

"I haven't got that sort of money."

"Well then," began Ralph, "you'll just have to find it. Maybe there will be some other mug who will lend you it. Perhaps you can find someone else to con some money out of."

"You took a gamble," said Pat, beginning to fight back. "You thought that you'd profit out of some information, make more money than you'd lent me. It was your greed that let you down."

"I want that money back!" stated Ralph.

"What money?"

"Don't play funny with me! The money I lent in return for those tips."

"Let me draw a parallel," began Pat. "Last week, I had a tip from a crooked trainer as to who'd win a race. I backed it…"

"With my money no doubt!" interrupted Ralph.

"Probably, but the fact is, I followed a tip and backed it. The horse lost. Did I go back to the trainer and say to him 'that was a dud tip you gave me, I want you to give me the money back I spent backing the tip'. No, I did not!"

"Not the same," said Ralph, fearing that he was losing the moral high ground.

"But it is similar!"

"Listen, O'Reilly – I want my money back by this time next week. Understand?"

Pat did not reply. He put the telephone down and mopped the sweat off his brow. The pressure was getting to him. No sooner had he replaced the receiver than the phone rang again.

"Jack here, Pat," spoke the chairperson of the local Labour Party.

"Hi, Jack," replied Pat, feeling relieved that it was not Ralph again.

"There's an extraordinary committee meeting tonight. Be there!" Jack's voice was serious, his tone brooked no refusal.

"Sure I will," agreed Pat. "What's it about?"

"They're gunning for you, Pat."

"And why might this be?" Pat asked innocently.

"It's this new industrial site. They are using it as an excuse to get rid of you."

"Get rid of me?" Pat was worried. "But they can't do that!"

"Yes they can!" replied Jack.

"And will they succeed? Tell me, will they win?"

"Would they have called the meeting if they hadn't thought that they'd have a good chance of winning?"

"But why tonight? Why so soon?"

Jack just gave a false laugh in reply.

"No, tell me – why now? Why not wait until the proper time?"

"If they hold the meeting tonight at short notice, they can be sure of passing a vote of no confidence in you. Once that is established, getting the members to support someone else is easy. Once you've told people that, in other words, your local elected representative is inept, as can be seen from the fact that a vote of no confidence has been passed, they soon desert you. It gives them time to badger folks to switch allegiance from you to another candidate."

"But why tonight?"

"Normally you could muster just over half of the committee in your favour…"

"Half? Only half? But I thought I was popular!" protested Pat.

"You were, you were, but when was the last time you attended a local party meeting? When was the last time you showed your face around here?"

"Well, I don't know."

"Precisely!" stated Jack. "And that's what I mean. It's all changed now, down here. A lot of the old men have bowed out. It's all university types and such like!"

"But I can muster half, though, you say?"

"Usually, yes, but not tonight. That's why the meeting has been called for tonight."

"So where are my supporters going tonight? Having a quiet drink while I am roasted alive, I bet."

"Two of them are on holiday, they come back tomorrow, and the third is on night shift this week. If their side all turn up, which they will, then they will have the majority."

"So what does that mean?" inquired Pat, fearing the worst.

"It means that it is the first step toward you not getting selected to fight next May. It's the beginning of the process to push you out!"

"Where does that leave me then?" Pat was feeling low and in need of a large glass of hard stuff, neat and golden.

"Out on your ear!" Jack said, not showing the greatest amount of sympathy. He did not feel the need to get too het up about his one-time friend Pat O'Reilly. There were plenty more fish in the sea and as far as Jack was concerned, the main thing was to save his own skin. He enjoyed being in the thick of local Labour Party politics. He loved the cut and thrust, the intrigue and the plotting – there was no way that he was going to go down with the sinking Pat O'Reilly ship! Like the best rats, he was jumping over board!

"Got to go!" said Jack. "You can rely on me to do my best for you. Remember, we're old mates, old comrades you and I. I'll try to get them to see your side. I'll ring around the rest of the committee and see what I can do!"

"Will you?" said Pat hopefully. "I'd be ever so grateful if you would do that. If you could do your best, perhaps…"

"No promises, mind!"

"No, of course, but if you could just give it a try. I need the money. I have to be a councillor – I haven't got any other job."

"Trust me!" assured Jack.

And, foolishly, Pat did.

* * *

Tony was doing just as he had been instructed to do on Monday. He was going to get his shares valued. What joy such a procedure was going to be for the likes of Tony! He had a compliant friend, a professional person who was willing to look leniently at such requests. He requested an immediate appointment and considered himself lucky to have his request granted.

Monday afternoon saw Tony motoring over to

Manchester with his portfolio in his briefcase, along with a selection of important papers concerning the Wilkinson Engineering Works. On arriving there, he went straight to see his old friend and colleague.

"Hello, Harry. How's tricks?" Tony said as an opener.

"Marvellous! In fact, I'll go further than that and say bloody marvellous!" replied Harry Carpenter. "Sit down, Tony, and tell me all abut it!"

Tony sat down on a leather seat and got out the information he had brought with him.

"There isn't much to tell, really," he began.

"No? I gathered from your telephone call that it was urgent. I put off two appointments to fit you in. One of them was a particularly important and rich client," grumbled Harry. The blood vessel in his neck was throbbing with the beginnings of anger. It did not take much to upset him these days.

"Well, when I say not much to tell, I don't really mean that!"

"Good, I'm glad to hear it. I thought that perhaps we were sitting here discussing some wild goose chase." Harry was starting to calm down; his ruddy face was looking less vibrant and his corpulent body was heaving only with the normal breathing processes which are so obviously displayed in portly people.

"I am the manager of an engineering works," began Tony.

"An engineering works? Not the best type of firm to be in! Has it been restructured?" inquired Harry.

"Well, I've been doing that myself…"

Tony was interrupted by Harry's laughter, a real belly laugh.

"It's not funny!" protested Tony.

"Yes it is! You, of all people! You haven't a clue. Who the hell is employing you? Must be a total cretin to even give you a second glance!" asked Harry, still barely managing to keep his mirth under control.

"The boss is a woman, actually," offered Tony by way of an explanation.

"A woman? A female boss of an engineering works! There! Told you. It just had to be someone odd to employ you!" Harry was an avowed chauvinist and very proud of it too.

"Very funny. Anyway, this woman – Amelia Pearson-Cooper – her dad started the firm," explained Tony. "And what is more, I've got shares in the company, lots of them! What I want you to do is value the shares for me. Produce some sort of document which will purport to put a price on the holding."

Harry leant back in his chair and surveyed the man sitting opposite him.

"Okay, but it'll cost you," he announced.

"I'm prepared to pay," Tony said and then he got out files with various bits and pieces of information on. "These are the projected figures…"

"Pretty good recipe, I presume you cooked them up?"

"Well, I had a hand in it but the accountants will be able to back most of them." Tony mentioned the name of the new firm of accountants.

"Oh, they'll back and support anything you tell them to. I suppose it was your idea to use them?"

Tony nodded and Harry grinned.

"Like I said, I'll do it for you but it will cost you. I will have to employ valuers to place some sort of value on the assets. The site might be worth a bit, if it is in the right place and so on. I'll produce something good for you."

"How long will it take?"

"First or second week in October should see it done."

With that reassurance, Tony left Harry Carpenter with photocopies of all the relevant documents and drove back to Leeds.

* * *

Ralph was feeling very morose by the time Amelia ventured home. She had spent the day chatting with friends, confiding in them and informing them about her exploits over the weekend. She had been just bubbling over with the joy of it all. Her friends shared in her enthusiasm, pressing her for more details. The whole day was better entertainment for one and all than an X-rated movie.

Ralph had given lots of thought in between the hours of four and six; and the result of those two hours of contemplation? The conclusion reached was quite simply that he did not have a leg to stand on as far as Pat was concerned. He had no proof of lending him the money. If he took Pat to court, would he not have to mention the purchase of a piece of land using insider information with a view to gain? They both could end up in the soup then!

Pressure was the only way – he would have to exert pressure on him. Therefore, just as Amelia came in through the front door, Ralph disappeared upstairs to use the telephone. Once again, in no uncertain terms, he demanded his money back. Or else!

* * *

Tim from the bank had spent a fruitless Monday trying to get hold of someone at Wilkinson's. He knew that the letter had only just gone out and it was highly improbable that a reply would be sent back straight away. He was, however, more than slightly concerned about the Wilkinson account and did feel that the whole process could be sped up if he could contact them personally. That had proved impossible. He therefore dug out their home telephone number and rang them that Monday evening. Ralph was busy gardening when the telephone went. He was venting his frustrations out on the soil. Amelia was daydreaming in the kitchen and so she answered the phone.

After introductions and apologies for disturbing them at home, Tim got straight to the point.

"It's about my letter I sent to you the other day," he began.

Amelia had to admit that she had no knowledge whatsoever of any letter, but then, as she explained to him, she had not been in the office today at all.

"Just a bit concerned and wanted to have a chat with the two of you."

"With Tony and myself?" replied Amelia.

"Tony? I thought your husband's name was Ralph!"

"What do you want to see him for?" Amelia could not understand why anybody should want to talk to such a deadbeat.

"It's a question of security," explained Tim.

Amelia could not understand at all what security and Ralph had in common. To Amelia, security was burglar alarms and such like. Perhaps Ralph had arranged to have a new alarm fitted? Or, more likely, perhaps Ralph was a security risk!

"Security? What do you mean?"

"The security that you guaranteed to the bank in order to back up your business borrowings."

"It's not our business, it is my business! Ralph has nothing to do with it. He doesn't even work there anymore, you know! He has opted out of it," protested Amelia.

"That may be so, but the fact is, the two of you gave personal guarantees of security when you took out loans for the company."

"So you want to see us then?"

"Just for a chat. Will tomorrow do?"

Amelia agreed on behalf of Ralph and herself.

"Just a formality," was Tim's parting remark.

* * *

The meeting was held in a smoke-filled room over the bar at the local Labour club. Pat O'Reilly got there five minutes early but he was the last one to arrive, the others were already sitting in their places discussing events.

"Am I the last?" he asked, by way of an apology.

"Don't worry," soothed Jack, "you're not too late!"

"But I thought that the meeting was due to start at half past?"

A man unknown to Pat looked up and remarked, "It was felt that as we were all here, we might as well begin."

Pat did not bother to add that they were not all there because he had not arrived and it was not even time to start the meeting.

Pat was handed an agenda. After apologies, the second item was minutes of the last meeting and the third item was any other business. Pat suddenly felt glad. His heart missed a beat and relief flooded all around his body. There was no motion concerning him. He felt sure that something of such importance would not be placed under the heading 'any other business'. It would be given its own separate section, black bordered probably! Jack had done the trick. He had got them to think again; thank God the chairperson was on his side.

The meeting went smoothly on and Pat even managed to contribute a bit to it here and there. It was largely about things that he did not care a great deal about. He was a member of what they referred to as the hard left but drink and gambling had taken their toll. He could no longer speak their language. It was newspeak and the left-wing language he was familiar with had its roots in the terraces of Ireland.

At the end of the meeting, when it broke up and the various components which made up the committee there, split up into factions, Pat thanked Jack for his trouble.

"Don't thank me. I'm just sorry that I couldn't do more!"

"But you did everything. You were marvellous. They didn't even mention me!" exclaimed Pat.

"What do you mean?"

"The motion of no confidence – it wasn't mentioned!"

"Oh, but it was," stated Jack.

"No, it wasn't," answered Pat. "I was there. It wasn't even on the agenda!"

"Yes it was," began Jack.

"Where?" asked Pat, picking up a copy of the agenda that someone had left behind. "Show me!"

"The typist made an error when she was typing it

out. We had a vote at the beginning of the meeting and it was agreed that the agenda should be amended. It was thought – the committee agreed one hundred per cent – that as it was so important, and the reason for the meeting in the first place, that it should go straight after the apologies for absence."

"So I missed it…" remarked Pat mournfully.

"Sorry, but I did my best!" And Jack walked off, leaving Pat trying to pick up the pieces of his life.

* * *

The police were glad that some of the spade work had already been done by Angus McNeil. The unit specialised in crimes of this nature. The sudden rush of financial activity that had happened during the past number of years had greatly increased the temptations that some brokers and dealers worked under.

They decided to mount a watch on a number of names on the list. Some would prove to be false leads; some would prove to be big fish.

* * *

No amount of beauty work can prevent nature taking over when you are asleep. Two o'clock Tuesday morning, saw Roland and his wife snoring away. Not a pretty sight! But when you're the brokers representative to Westbury's and other big conglomerates, you have to drop your front at least on some occasions; you can't pose for the full twenty-four hours in a day.

The telephone ringing broke Roland's slumber and he turned over in bed to answer it.

"Roland, it's me, Fiona,"

"Fiona?" questioned Roland, unable to work out just who Fiona was. Amanda had not woken, so he had to speak in whispers in order not to disturb her.

"Fiona Pearson-Cooper," announced the caller.

"Fiona, just what are you doing ringing me at this hour of the day!" Roland had just been able to figure out the time on the bedside clock.

"I need your help, desperately!"

"Tomorrow, I'll help you tomorrow!" he assured her.

"Now, I need it now."

"I can't help you now – it is the middle of the night!" And then he added, just in case it was some deal that she had uncovered (though he doubted it), "What's it about anyway?"

"I need to make some money quick; I thought that you'd know how!"

"Oh, is that all? I'll see you tomorrow at your house. Nine o'clock." With that agreed, Roland put the receiver down. Before he went back to sleep, he thought he might just take a peep through the window to see what the weather was like. It had been raining heavily and he wondered if it had stopped yet. From their bedroom window, one could just make out the avenue at the bottom of the drive.

It was still raining and there was a car parked near to the entrance of his house. A man was sitting in the car and was just lighting up a cigarette.

* * *

The next morning, Roland discreetly did another check. This time, a van from the gas board was positioned in the road. There was a workman with a gas board uniform on busily inspecting the pavement.

Very strange, thought Roland, for a road that has yet to have gas installed, and as we are the only people who live up here, they are unlikely to be installing gas without telling us first, if only to get us to pay for it!

He remembered the telephone call from the night before and his promise to go and visit Fiona. He was a little bit worried about the situation. He felt that he might be being watched for some reason or other. If he went to the Pearson-Cooper house, he might be implicating them, he might be followed there. But he could not just leave the matter as it was and not speak to her – she sounded so desperate.

If he telephoned her from home, the phone might be tapped. If he rang her from a box, her phone might be tapped. He deduced that there was only one thing for it for he had to get a message to her somehow.

He would send her some flowers! He would not order them by credit card just in case the police were keeping tabs on that. It was lucky that he had an account with the local florist and thus a bouquet could be arranged quite easily. He would ring from a public telephone box and the message would be quite simple – to ring from a call box to a call box at noon. Box to box!

* * *

Charles was planning himself a delightful Tuesday. First of all, he would examine the pages of the *Financial Times* for details of how all of their investments were doing. Then he would telephone John Bates and inform him of the good news: he was to be granted some various corporate positions. Then, after all that hard graft, he would wallow in Glenda.

Bliss!

* * *

John Bates also took the *Financial Times*. He also scanned the pages listing the stocks and shares, the news snippets about various companies and the articles. He, like everybody else, daily notched up the gains and smiled bigger smiles as the share prices rose as the weeks went by.

However, John Bates also lived by the maxim 'what goes up must come down'. No rise goes on forever for no apparent reason. Optimism is a reason, for a while; expectations are good enough reasons in themselves, as long as they are met at some future date; and indeed, rising for the sake of rising because that is what the rest of the sector is doing is a good enough reason until the rising stops and the questioning begins.

John had read – no doubt like many other people – the article by Kevin Goldstein-Jackson in the *Financial Times* on August 1st but unlike other people, he took the message on board. It talked of the fear of a crash. What goes up must come down – nothing rises forever, pondered John on that Tuesday morning in September.

The telephone rang just as he was thinking that thought.

"Mr. Pearson-Cooper for you, Mr. Bates," said his secretary.

"Put him through."

"John!" cried the excited voice at the other end.

"Charles," replied John, less enthusiastically, "what can I do for you?"

"Nothing, more a case of what I've done for you!"

John's ears perked up at this. Was music about to be played? Were dreams about to become true?

"Yes?" John replied.

"Just fixed up a few things for you – remember?"

John did indeed remember and suggested that Charles should pop into the office, perhaps this morning if he could.

After they had said their goodbyes, John did think that perhaps now would be a good time to sever the partnership that existed between himself, Charles and Fiona. He never really approved of a ménage a trois!

* * *

Fiona waited and waited. She had dressed early, which was unlike her these days, and had not breakfasted. Instead, she sat in the drawing room and scanned the drive for the arrival of Roland. He had promised he would turn up at nine o'clock and it was now half past.

By ten o'clock, Fiona was just giving up hope and started to move out of the room. Just as she reached the door, a van came into the driveway and parked right outside her front door. It was a florist's van and the man driving it opened the doors and brought out a magnificent floral bouquet.

For a moment, Fiona forgot all her troubles and rushed to the door. Someone did care about her – the flowers must be for her, there was no one else they could be for.

She met the delivery man on the doorstep. "Mrs Pearson-Cooper?" he asked.

"Yes?" she replied.

"Been asked to deliver these for you," he said, and with that, he handed over the spray and went back to his van.

Fiona felt momentarily young again. She carried them inside and placed them on the kitchen table. She searched for the message to show just who the flowers were from. Instead of some note of love, or promise of affection, she just found a card, decorated with painted pictures of roses. There she read a message asking her to go to a public phone box and ring the given number at twelve noon.

Fiona went white with fear.

"No, no, not him! Not him again," she cried out loud.

She shoved the flowers into the bin, breaking all the stems in anger before tears eventually took over.

* * *

Ralph and Amelia set off to the bank together. They talked very little in the car; each was wrapped up in their own thoughts. Amelia was still in dream-land with Tony; Ralph was trying to overcome the urge to go out and strangle Pat with his own bare hands.

They were ushered into the manager's office quite quickly. This rapidity was a trifle worrying; shouldn't appointments be made a few days in advance, shouldn't there at least be a decent interval between arriving at the bank and being taken into the inner sanctum? These thoughts were starting to race through Ralph's head.

They were both surprised to see not one but two men present. There was Tim, who they were quite familiar with, and his new assistant, a pushy Bernard

Walker. Tim was often given assistants to help him; each one was invariably keener than the last.

"Please sit down," invited Tim, after introducing them to his new protégé. Bernard, apparently, would be looking after their account while Tim was transferred to a more central office. Bernard was, or so they were told, a very experienced bank official in the field of small businesses. Bernard also had very sharp eyes, like a weasel, and lacked even a morsel of humour.

"You wanted to see us?" asked Ralph, hoping to speed things up a bit.

"Your account," began Tim, "is not very healthy…"

He stared at them with accusing eyes, waiting for some sort of explanation to emerge.

All Amelia could say was, "Isn't it?"

That was probably not the right answer to give. It caused Bernard to roll his eyes towards the ceiling and Tim to rest his chin on his clenched hands – the pose of someone who wants to help but must be stern!

"But surely you know it isn't?" inquired Tim in a pseudo-kind voice. How he loved these little games!

There was a pause as the two in the first stages of being grilled alive tried to think of an answer. Bernard interrupted their frantic thoughts with a suggestion.

"Recall Mr. Micawber!" he urged.

"Oh, don't tell me he works here as well!" Ralph laughed. A grave mistake. No one else laughed. Not even a titter. Tim produced statements to prove the situation was more than a little dodgy.

"Even you two can see that there is more money going out than there is coming in."

Ralph and Amelia nodded their heads.

"You are spending more than you are earning."

They nodded again. Suitably chastised, they avoided looking either Tim or Bernard in the eye.

"However…" began Tim. There was a glimmer of hope rising from that word, however. It was the way it was said. Tim had pronounced it slowly and his voice had gone up slightly on the final syllable. Ralph and Amelia felt the faint flutter of hope.

Bernard now sat down. He had been standing the rest of the time but now decided that the moment had come to draw up a seat and wade in. Tim and Bernard had got the two naughty children cowed and now he, as an expert in small businesses, would offer them a life-line. He was so glad that he had been dispatched to this office. What opportunities there were here to demonstrate his effective handling of accounts! Soon, in a matter of days, he would be in sole charge and could pull the strings, manipulate the customers and practice an active, hands-on style of bank management. Not for him the laid back, take it easy type of control exercised by Tim. He, Bernard, was going to be in the forefront, the ghostly vision of the commercials, breathing down the necks of the customers!

Bernard adopted his earnest expression as he leant forward in his chair. Tim moved out of the way, glad to be stepping out of the limelight. All he wanted to do was to extract commissions and charges and other bits and pieces that took his fancy from the customers. He detested the hands-on approach that was finding favour with head office. It sounded too arduous. It also had its own attached problems. Tim had deduced these pretty quickly when he read the directives that had filtered down from above. The problems lay not in the customer. The poor customer still had to carry his own can. The problems lay in wait for the bank manager. If one was expected to adopt a very interested role in the affairs of one's clients, it also followed that, should the client enter difficulties that caused the bank problems, then you should have spotted them. Thus the proverbial can, which previously the customer carried to the bankruptcy courts, could now be shared with the friendly, I-am-here-to-help bank manager. Not that he personally would be held responsible for any shortcomings that the bank had to make good when a customer went bust; no, he would not lose money, only precious Brownie points. Tim felt that he had sweated enough, and collected enough points, under the old system without losing everything under the new. Bernard the Beast of the Bank, as his less than devoted colleagues were calling him, could handle all that.

"Bernard has been giving your problems some thought," Tim said, and with that, he practically bowed out.

"What you need is an extended overdraft, in order to manage your day to day problems."

Amelia smiled; this was all beginning to sound promising to her. She was starting to like Bernard.

"A loan to cover all your payments, so that in future, we will pay your lease hire charges etc. etc." Bernard paused, all the better to judge the effect that his words were having on the couple. "All you do is pay the loan off. Exact amounts and the term, we can discuss later, but you need the bank behind you. Backing you. Supporting you."

Ralph did reflect that perhaps the bank was becoming totally all embracing but decided not to say so, just in case he ruined the flow that Bernard was now in. Never ruin the flow of money, when it is coming your way, that is!

"But we can't do all this for you on our own." Bernard's voice had lowered slightly. A bad sign. "We can't take all the risks. We can't shoulder total responsibility."

Those three statements were just the overture to the second act. Softened up by the hope and joyful picture presented initially, Ralph and Amelia were not ready for the roll of drums that was to come.

"You must be our partner in this financial package," stated Bernard.

"Partner?" questioned Ralph. "What do you mean?"

"I mean this: if we are to help you, provide you with the cash that will get you through this little crisis and towards those big orders your manager has described," and with that, he wafted a letter with Tony's signature on, "then we must have your backing!"

Both Ralph and Amelia were now just a little bit confused. They had been under the impression that it was supposed to be the bank that was doing the backing, not they themselves backing the bank. It was just a little twist that Bernard had made, a twist that switched the responsibility from bank to customer.

"Well, yes," assured Ralph and Amelia murmured her assent too.

"Good!" And with that, Bernard leant back in his chair. "Then we are all agreed, we will lend you sufficient funds in the form of an overdraft and a loan to sort you out!"

"Great!" was the reply from the two customers.

A moment of silence ensued until Bernard dipped into the file and produced the current valuation of Ralph and Amelia's home.

"We will need to take a charge on your home for an unspecified amount, to be fixed or otherwise at a later date," Bernard announced.

"But you already have a charge on our home," protested Amelia.

"But only for a fixed and rather inadequate amount!" replied Bernard. "If you want us to help your business prepare for the nineties then you must put your money where your mouth is. We are quite prepared to put our shareholders' money at risk on your account, so you also must take a certain amount of the risk too."

Amelia had a sudden guilty vision of shareholders up and down the country preparing to lose everything on her behalf. She could do nothing else but agree to a revised charge.

"But," began Bernard, "if a businessman personally injects some of his own money, he has a stake in his company, and this inspires him all the more. After all, limited liability is all well and good but you can't beat a bit of personal liability!"

"You mean you want some money as well?" asked Ralph. Such a missionary zeal as displayed by this Bernard in the field of entrepreneurship was a bit awe inspiring.

"Yes!" replied Bernard quite emphatically.

"How much?" asked Amelia.

"We will get down to the fine details at a later stage but I'd say we are talking in terms of tens of thousands."

"Tens of thousands? You are joking!" stated Amelia. She was genuinely astounded. "But why so much?" she asked.

"We would like you to try to match us pound for pound; for every pound we put in, you must provide the same in terms of security or cash."

"But we don't have that type of money!" protested Amelia. "We have a couple of hundred put away in the Bradford and Bingley and perhaps a thousand in the Skipton but that's it!"

"But surely not!" Bernard stated firmly.

"Surely so!" replied Amanda.

"But you appear to have forgotten your legacy," and with that the intrepid Bernard grinned, "the £100,000 that your father-in-law left you!"

* * *

It was quarter to twelve when Fiona came to a conclusion. She would put up with it no more. She would go to the police and face all the consequences. This time, she had a deadline set, a telephone number to respond to. The police would be able to step in. They would arrest him and deal with him.

She told her story to the officers and was surprised at how sympathetic they were. They frequently told her, in the short space of time she had allowed them, that she had done the right thing. They assured her that she would remain anonymous. All that she had to do, they told her, was to make that telephone call. It had taken them only minutes to find out where the call would be going to and they had dispatched a local squad ready to pounce on whoever answered the telephone.

"Just keep him talking," they advised her as they quickly equipped her with microphones.

"Can't I ring from here?" Fiona had asked but she was told that someone who was used to public phones would soon realise that she was ringing from a private line – it was those initial funny tones, apparently.

Reluctantly, Fiona entered the booth outside the police station and dialled the given number.

* * *

Just before twelve, Roland parked his car in the car park behind the library in Baildon. He walked down the hill, noticing as he went that the same car that had been following him from Leeds had just pulled in and parked.

A coincidence? No way, he thought.

He knew the telephone box well for a number of years back, when he had been having financial difficulties, he had used that same booth for his business calls. The number was somewhat familiar to him. He spotted the police car parked in the pub car park straight away thought it a little strange.

Surely the police would be a little more sensitive to the publican's feelings than to park there at the time of his busy lunch trade? He dismissed the thought as he strode to the red box just as the phone was ringing. He rushed to answer it, knowing it was for him.

"Fiona," he shouted down the phone, "you want to know about money!" Just then, the phone started to crackle and Roland could not hear Fiona's reply.

"Can't catch what you are saying – is it money you want?" shouted Roland.

At the other end, the policemen listening in could make out very little due to interference. The words 'Fiona,' and 'Money' were quite clear but nothing beyond that. Fearing they were going to lose him, they sent word out to their colleagues waiting in Baildon to arrest the man immediately.

Roland slammed the phone down in disgust,

mumbling complaints about British Telecom, and left the box only to be faced by two policemen, intent on arresting him.

* * *

While his wife was attempting to bring her blackmailer to book, Charles was treading gaily towards the office of John Bates. He was feeling remarkably pleased with himself. He had set out and achieved what were great accomplishments in the field of providing the reptilian Bates with enough goodies to remove him from the incestuous relationship that the three of them had.

Charles felt a bit like Little Red Riding Hood, off to see her grandma, except in this case, the grandma and the wolf were one and the same! He entered the room and greeted John like an old friend – which he hoped he soon would be!

"I think you'll like this!" began Charles and he showed John all the strings he had pulled on his behalf. The gems collected sparkled before the pleased Bates. He showed himself only too willing to sign the forms which released his hold on the account and the shares. Arrangements were made for the broker to sell an appropriate amount that would satisfy the agreement reached.

"To be done at the close of trading," suggested Charles, "so that you can't accuse me of selling you short by making the broker trade before the next rise. I just can't believe the share prices. It is just amazing. I mean, when will it stop?" Charles was not asking a question, so John felt no need to give an answer; instead, he let Charles gush on.

"And house prices! When you think how much you paid for your house and how much it is worth now. And what will it be worth next month? Yes, next *month!* Where we are, people are having the valuers in so many times, they are becoming part of the fixtures. We had our house valued a year ago and I tell you that price is just ancient history now. Bricks and mortar, could be gold, for the value of them!"

With that flow, Charles bade John goodbye and assured him that he would be the first to get an invite to Blayborough House.

"That place is in the bag!" stated Charles. "And what is that worth, I ask you? Eh? How much has that gone up since we started this little caper? Eh, how much? Well, I'll tell you – a fortune, that's how much!"

And with that rather imprecise value impressed on both their minds, Charles left for a pub lunch at a nice little watering hole in the country, after which – Glenda! He never asked about how his other two brothers were getting on. He knew that Bates, horror that he was, would never break his promise not to tell; and in any case, neither of them could possibly be doing as well as he was.

* * *

The police kept Fiona tucked away as they brought Roland into the station. She was left to enjoy a cup of tea as they interviewed the alleged blackmailer. Her quiet was brought to an abrupt end when a police woman asked her a question.

"You told us that his name was Page, didn't you?"

"Yes, that's right," replied Fiona.

"And that he was West Indian?"

"Yes, he is black," agreed Fiona.

"Well, the chap they they've brought back from Baildon is English and goes by the name of Roland Peterson. He tells us that he knows you as a friend. Now is there any way that you could have been mistaken? I mean, even in a poor light this fellow does not look at all dark!"

"Roland? You've arrested Roland?"

"Yes, and he does admit to sending you some flowers!"

Suddenly the truth dawned on her. The flowers had come from Roland and not Page. She had made a fool out of herself. What was she to do? Apologise? Say that is was all an error? Or tell the police all the truth, the bits that she had not had time to describe before the noon deadline arrived.

She decided on the latter course, explaining it all. She also informed the police woman about Roland's innocent role in it all, so that at least he could be set free. The police once again assured her that they would do their very best and she left the station feeling better then she had done for ages. Roland too was relieved to leave the police station. The man following him had disappeared when he had been arrested.

I wonder just when he will reappear? thought Roland as he strode down the steps in search of a taxi back to his car in Baildon. The police had given Roland his taxi fare and he was just about to enter a vacant cab when Fiona called him.

"Go away," he called out, half in jest and half truthfully.

"I'm so sorry!" she said just as soon as she reached him.

"Not half as sorry as I am!" he replied.

"I'm still in trouble," she looked worried and Roland reluctantly agreed to help her. He dismissed the taxi and went to sit on a bench so they could talk things over.

"I need to raise some money easily; I thought you might know of some method."

Roland thought for a moment and then, noticing the same car that had followed him earlier in the morning park further down the road from where they were sitting, answered hastily.

"Try this," he produced a card with a London number on it.

"What is it?"

"Basically, it is betting on the F.T. and so on – you can make a fortune doing it. I made £20,000 in a day once!"

That said, he grabbed a vacant taxi and went back to his abandoned car.

* * *

It was a very frosty lunch that Ralph and Amelia shared. Neither of them spoke to the other. Amelia was poker-faced. Ralph was silent. He wondered to himself just how that bank had got to know about the money. He suspected the building society but then thought, no, they would not tell other institutions willy-nilly about depositor's accounts. In his mind, he questioned the confidentiality of the solicitors – could the information have come from there? A secretary who talked too much? Perhaps Bates or Winstanley? Whoever it was, that was of minor importance compared to the result of the bank knowing. Now he suddenly found that his little fortune could become committed to a lost cause.

What did occur to him was the fact that the bank had not mentioned the little matter of the competition. If they knew about that, it would have been in their interest not to take the legacy as security but instead to take a gamble on him winning Blayborough House.

Amelia still did not know about the Blayborough Estate. Ralph judged that if he told her now, so long after the will had been read, she would presume it was his intention to ditch her and keep the estate. If he kept her in the dark still, there was a faint, and very faint at that, glimmer of hope that he might be able to retrieve something out of all the mess. Either way, he was going to have to kiss the money goodbye for a while. This brought his mind back to Pat O'Reilly. It was not as if Ralph still had the money sitting in an account somewhere, totally intact. The money was greatly reduced. The winnings that had been accumulated on the horses and the exploit with that office block had increased the amount – that was on the profit side; on the loss side, Ralph had deducted the cost of buying the land and the money he had loaned to Pat.

Just how was he going to explain all that away?

* * *

Amelia cut through the cucumber slices that she had arranged on her plate and grimaced. Trust Ralph to deceive me! she thought as she stabbed an egg. Why did I ever marry him? was the next question she put to herself. She knew the answer; because I was pregnant, that's why!

Chewing on a spring onion, she stared at his head,

bent over the plate. He's got no business sense, no energy, nothing! she muttered to herself.

Ralph, who was slowly shovelling food into his mouth, glanced up and tried to avoid her eyes.

Useless lump! Amelia thought. But with £100,000 tucked away that he did not want me to know about. Me, slaving away night and day at the factory and him, sitting at home doing nothing but counting his fortune! Been silent about it ever since we left the bank and no word of an explanation! He doesn't even apologise. Probably got some bit of stuff he was planning to run away with. No doubt someone with a blonde rinse and big boobs, stupid man like him will go for middle-aged bimbos. Well, I'll teach him a lesson or two! I'll show him that he can't mess me around and get away with it.

Out loud she told him to produce the money or else.

"Because without that money, the bank won't lend us a penny and then we'll go down and you'll lose it anyway."

Ralph knew that he was going to lose it either way, so perhaps on balance it was better earlier than later.

* * *

There was a certain little watering hole that Charles always frequented when the sun was high, the birds were singing and everything in the Pearson-Cooper garden was wonderful. At the pub, the theme of which was a carefully chosen rustic style, Charles unwound with a glass of cider. He rejected the inaccurately termed beer garden, which was really a number of patio tables with jaunty umbrellas in a section of the car park, for the lounge bar. He conversed with the landlord about the price of farmland, the value of sheep and other assorted country topics. Here, Charles frantically practised for the day he would become the master of Blayborough Estate.

"Not long now!" he was heard to mutter out loud. "Soon be mine!"

That afternoon, at the close of business, the ties that bound Bates to the Pearson-Coopers would be cut. Charles intended to head straight for Leeds later that afternoon to hand the letter over to the broker himself. Then, thought Charles to himself, I will never need to see him again, except for the day I have to collect the keys!

* * *

"I am going out!" announced Amelia. "And I shall not be back until late! And it is your turn to pick up the children!"

With that, she stormed out of the house. Ralph was glad to see the back of her. It had been a bad old day for him. Things had not gone at all well. To put it mildly, he was in a bit of a mess.

When a person is in a mess, the first thing that they should do is find someone else to share the blame. A mess shared is a mess halved. Ralph therefore got straight on the phone to his old mate Pat.

There were no introductions to break the ice. Just as soon as Pat picked up the phone, Ralph said, "Well, then?" in a tone that brooked no refusal or apology for inaction.

Pat decided that attack was the best form of defence and launched straight away into a blistered bombardment of all and everyone.

"I can't help you because I've been set up!" was his first statement.

"What do you mean, you can't help me because you've been set up? What's all that about?"

"I've been set up, ambushed. I tell you, they've only gone and passed a vote of no confidence in me. Me, a sitting councillor who has served them loyally. Aren't I left-wing enough for them? Don't I buy their magazine and dip into my pocket on a Monday morning, regular as clockwork, to pay some money over to the cause? Will they find someone else as generous with their time and money as me? Well, will they?"

Ralph was a bit flabbergasted by this outburst. So amazed was he, he did not reply to Pat but as it was a rhetorical question, Pat ignored the lack of an answer and carried on unchecked.

"Of course, I know what it is. I know what they are up to. It isn't fashionable to have an Irish person representing the poor and oppressed anymore. An Irishman is white, we're practically English, we can't possibly feel what it is like to be the underdog! As if we haven't known anything else! I'm telling you, I've been the underdog for so long, I'm beginning to sniff lamp posts!"

There was another two second pause.

"Then there is the question of what I'm going to do when I'm no longer councillor. Do they care? Are they interested? No, they're not! You think you've got problems, just you work out the worries I must have, being passed over by a black man, just because I am European. It was a sad day for Irishmen when we joined the European Community, a very sad day. We gave away our second-class citizen status for a bag of money, now, whenever people think of us, which isn't very often, they think we are the same as the other Northern Europeans. It is a question of geography. We're badly placed, stuck out in the sea but near to the devil incarnate, Britain, and other God forsaken Protestant states. Anyway, enough of my troubles, I've got to go!"

"You can cut the crap, O'Reilly, you don't fool me one minute. I didn't ring you for a lecture on nationhood. Find that money! I'll be round at your place tomorrow!"

"And where will I be able to find a sum like that?"

"Your problem!" Ralph slammed the telephone down and sat down in the lounge to think things out.

Pat turned to another drink. The first drink of the day always revived him. He had had the first drink when he had awoken from his sleep at midday. The second drink made him feel talkative and merry. He had had that shortly before Ralph rang. The effect was always short lived and he drank thereafter in order to re-acquire the effects achieved with drink number two.

He spotted the note pinned to the door. Why he had not seen it before, he did not know. It was written by his wife. She wrote that she and the children were going to stay at her mother's for a while.

A while? What does that mean? wondered Pat as he reached for a glass. He looked at the nearly empty bottle of Irish whiskey and the new one he intended to break into today. He poured himself another drink and then he thought of how his wife was coping with everything. The lack of money for her household expenditure, which was caused by him not being in full time employment and drinking the attendance allowances he got from the council. The neglect, which was due to him turning to drink and the horses in an attempt to shut out the problems. And in the past, when the good times were rolling and he was cock of the midden, did he share them with his wife? No, he spent his time and money chasing some lunatic left-wing cause, which involved all talk and cigarettes in the pubs but no action afterwards. The revolution was postponed for another year! Then Pat thought of the children; was the eldest seven or eight now? How well was he doing at school? And Lizzy, did she still suck her thumb at night? "What happened? What have I missed?" he asked himself.

The tears started to flow as he realised that his wife, whom he had neglected and ignored, had obviously left him. No wife or children, soon no status and never a job for an Irishman with a liking for the drink; and a friend, yes, a so-called friend demanding money off him.

Pat sank into his daily depression. Today, however, it was deeper than ever before.

* * *

Bates was delighted with the way Charles had ferreted away and produced all those rabbits. He was especially pleased when the second post brought a letter from a large local concern inviting him to visit them informally with a view to further contacts – they were venturing into the big time and had been told that he would be able to advise them. Then, the telephone call that sealed it all. The words "Charles Pearson-Cooper told me all about you. You're just the type of fellow we've been looking for!"

John Bates was mightily pleased with everything. With all these advantages, he would soon be able to present himself to the partners at the firm and say:

"Turn me down for a senior partnership this time and I'll set up on my own and take all these clients and contacts with me!"

He needed to share his good fortune with someone. He needed some warm person who would rejoice with him. Glenda!

* * *

Tony was busy working when Amelia arrived. When he saw her through the glass partition, he blew her a kiss and she managed to smile back at him. She longed to tell him of her problems but thought better of it. Why spoil a good relationship? Why burden him with the difficulties she was going through at home? Wasn't he her release from all that?

"Tony, great to see you."

"I can't stop thinking about you," said Tony, and he smiled his most charming smile. "Instead of working, I find myself day dreaming about Friday and Saturday!"

"If only everyday could be like that!" exclaimed Amelia. She really meant it.

"I wish it was," agreed Tony. He did not really mean it. Well, he did sort of. He found her quite enjoyable between the sheets. Her company was engaging, for the most part. The truth was, he had found that in all the relationships he had experienced, his own company was the best, but did appreciate that someone else, such as a wife or mistress, filled those little gaps that his own company missed quite nicely.

"I've had a bloody awful morning!" Amelia stated.

"Tell me all about it," invited Tony, patting his knee and inviting her to sit down on it.

"No, I wouldn't want to burden you!"

"Not Ralph playing the heavy husband, was it?" Tony asked.

"Ralph never plays the husband, heavy or otherwise!" she replied.

"Well, then," comforted Tony, "forget about it all! Come out to dinner with me and we'll make love, before and after!"

Amelia quite readily agreed.

* * *

Glenda was quite busy that Tuesday afternoon. She had decided to embark on a mammoth and much delayed spring clean. She had removed all the many ornaments that hung around the house, taken the curtains down and hung the loose mats on the line for a severe beating.

For the occasion, she wore her hair up in two large clips and put on her old cheese cloth blouse with a pair of jeans. The blouse, though it covered her generous backside, showed large glimpses of cleavage. The jeans were a tight fit. It was a magnificent sight that welcomed John when he knocked on her back door.

"What a surprise!" she remarked as she ushered him in.

"You're wonderful!" He could hardly keep his eyes off her.

"You've caught me at it!" she said and then, by way of an explanation added, "A late spring clean."

John grabbed her. "Leave the cleaning for another day," he pleaded, "come to bed! I've got such wonderful news to tell you."

Glenda peeled off her jeans in the kitchen and threw

her blouse on top of them. Now, as she wore nothing underneath her clothes, she was totally nude.

Rapture!

* * *

Charles left the pub and went slowly towards his destination. His favourite pub followed by his favourite woman. That was his idea of a good, relaxing day. It was not a long drive from the one place to the other and Charles soon found himself parking his car at the front of the house and making his way around the back.

It was there that he noticed a fellow Jaguar, shiny and bright. He peeped through the kitchen window and saw abandoned cleaning. The back door had been left ajar and there was a blouse and a pair of jeans lying discarded on the kitchen floor. Next to those items of clothing, a pair of black shoes and a tie lay and in the hallway, Charles could just make out trousers, pants and a shirt. There were sounds of laughter and gaiety coming from the upstairs window.

Charles could hear his woman, his mistress, the one person he trusted above all others, squealing with delight. He could hear that man, that hated man, bouncing around on top of her.

"I shan't stop until you say you'll marry me!"

"No, no!" laughed Glenda.

"Say yes you'll marry me!" demanded Bates. "And then I'll stop!"

"But if I say yes, you'll get off me and I don't want you to. I want you to make love to me forever!"

"Alright, then how about this – if you say you aren't going to marry me, I'll stop making love to you and abandon you – I'll leave you feeling all frustrated! All nude and alone on the bed!" Further grunts and groans could be heard and then Bates' voice again said, "Right, now will you marry me, or do I leave you to your fate? Say yes, or else!"

"Yes! Yes!" Glenda screamed. "Oh, yes, please, please…"

Charles stormed off in a fury. He would ruin their plans. There would be a different type of squealing soon! He touched his inside pocket where the letter that John Bates had signed was waiting to be posted. If I post it, he will come into money and everything will be all jolly for the two of them. Off they'll go, having fun, getting married! What the hell do they want to get married for? he thought.

Charles jumped into his car and drove off. If I don't post it, there will be no ready cash. No wads of money for exotic honeymoons. That will cramp his style a bit! and he chuckled to himself at the thought.

He took to the open road with a roar. Then, I'll let him sweat a bit. Gradually blacken his name so that all those tasty golden morsels turn to dust! I'll make sure that no one will want him ever again. He'll be short of money and then let's see how long he'll last with that whore! Life out in her cottage won't seem so much fun in the middle of winter when there is no cash to pay the coal man. There will be no running around starkers then! It'll be all goose pimples and woollen sweaters! Let's see how long they last then. Especially as I won't be dropping the occasional large doses of funds into her bank account! I wonder how he imagines she manages to keep living there, without working and with no means of support.

With that thought of pulling the plug on Glenda and John, Charles now felt much more cheerful. There was just one final notion which kept a smile firmly fixed on his face. In fact, this thought made the sun shine again; it made the world seem a much rosier place than it was a mere ten minutes previously.

"Then, when they've struggled a bit through winter, I'll demand my cottage back!" He announced out loud.

* * *

Roland found an empty telephone booth and arranged the sale of all his shares, every last one of them. He then managed to contact his wife in London at the agency she used and told her to do likewise. At the end of the accounting period, the money would be credited to their bank account, which was decidedly offshore.

One final telephone call to a friend in Paris and everything was sorted out.

* * *

Pat reached once more for the bottle. There were only a few drops left. "What good is it to me?" he stuttered through a blur of drink. "Drops! Where's the new bottle?"

Searching for more whiskey, which he found behind some baked beans, he discovered a container full of medicine hidden away in a kitchen cupboard. They were for his wife and he recognised them straight away as being her prescription for sleeping tablets, which she had been on for many years; a whole bottle of them, untouched and waiting for those in need of eternal sleep to dip into.

"I'm depressed. God, I'm depressed," Pat muttered to himself. He opened the bottle, unscrewing the child-proof cap. He tipped the contents out onto the table. They scattered and rolled slightly.

"I've nothing, not a penny, not a wife, no children – all gone... how could anyone be as stupid as me? What did I do wrong? When did you leave me, God? I can't help myself. Look at me, Blessed Mary. Why didn't you help me? I know I didn't go to church often but why did you desert me too? I'm at the bottom now, so where are your guardian angels? I thought that they were supposed to be there all the time, waiting and watching. But they aren't, are they? Just a story to keep us on the straight and narrow. Then when we stray, when we wander from the path and ask for help, you don't come. You aren't there, Holy Mother of God, where are you? I need you now. Where are you? You should be at my side. They said that you'd help me – that's what the priests said to us, 'when you're down, Mary will be there, never fear, she will always help you.' But I am afraid; I need your help now, Mary, Holy Mother of God. You're not here. You've left me too."

Pat put the first capsule in this mouth and washed it down with some drink. "When you can't sleep because you're sick with worry, what do they give you – medicine; no help, just medicine."

The second capsule quickly followed the first and Pat started to blub, "If you really existed, Mary, you would be here and you would help me, if you were real. If... you are not, it's all a story, it isn't true. There is no such thing as heaven, is there? Just hell. Hell on earth."

Slowly, Pat took the capsules one by one.

* * *

Amanda Petersen arrived home late that evening. Her day had been hectic, going from one assignment to the other and then catching the train home. She adored modelling and took up every opportunity to do it as she knew her days were numbered.

Roland was already home when she entered the house.

"Darling," she murmured, placing a kiss on his cheek, "home already?"

"It's been a bit of an odd day!" began Roland.

"Lucky old you – mine has been exhausting! I'm absolutely whacked! By the way, I did as you said and sold the lot."

"Good. Did you notice anybody outside?" asked Roland.

"Where? Outside the house?"

"No, on the avenue. Hanging around or someone in a car."

"I passed a van, but couldn't see inside," she replied while lighting a cigarette for herself. "But talking about that, I'm sure I've been followed today. I had this weird feeling a few times that there was someone a few paces behind me."

"Following you?" inquired Roland.

"Yeah, it was sort of creepy, like something out of a spy movie. Anyway, I took no notice of it until on the train I spotted this chap and I'll swear blind that he was the same man who got on the train this morning when I left for London."

"Could be a coincidence, but I doubt it," suggested Roland.

"That's what I thought, a coincidence, until I saw him watching me when I left the station."

"Did he come after you?"

"No, that's it. He just watched me take a taxi."

Roland invited his wife to sit down and he told her that he had something serious to talk to her about.

"You see, I think that you have been followed. I also think that there is someone watching our house and I reckon I've been followed too."

"Who? Who is it?" she asked, concern etching her forehead.

"The police probably," he replied and he outlined the reason why he thought they might be interested in him. She knew that he had amassed a fortune and some of it had been gathered illegally. What she did not know and what he told her now was how he had been speeding up the process up recently. During the last year, he had become bolder.

"I thought if I could just do a few last scams then I'd stop. We'd get a little place somewhere abroad and retire."

"But I don't want to retire just yet, I'm sure I've got a few more years left at the top."

"Oh, come on, Amanda, apart from today, which was an exception, haven't your bookings dropped recently? How many sessions did you have last month? You weren't exactly run off your feet with work, were you?"

"No, but I put that to living up here. The work isn't up here, maybe that's why – if I went back to live in London, I bet the phone wouldn't stop ringing!"

"Rubbish! You're past you're prime, over the hill."

"No, I'm not!" she protested. "I've got at least another year left!"

"Anyway, it's all beside the point. The fact is, the police are hanging around outside and I think we've got only hours before they come hammering on that door!"

"What do you mean?"

"I mean this: my bet is that they'll pounce tonight, or rather, early tomorrow morning, and arrest us both!"

"Both of us!" exclaimed Amanda. "Now come on! I've done nothing wrong, they can't arrest me! That's not right, it isn't fair! I haven't committed any crime!"

Roland smiled weakly at his wife, whose beautiful face was contorted with the beginnings of anger. "Oh, but I'm afraid that you have. You see, a lot of investments were in your name. Documents that you signed and shares that you owned… investments that you made…"

"But it isn't a crime to own shares!"

"But it is if you bought them on the basis of insider information!" explained Roland.

"But I didn't! I bought them when you told me to!"

"Precisely!"

The truth was slowly dawning on Amanda. She was up to her eyes in the mess, along with her husband. They could stay, she reasoned quickly, and fight it all out in court; but would the courts believe their innocence? She doubted it! Or they could flee the country…

"I think it is about time I retired…" began Amanda.

"To warmer climes?" suggested Roland. "What luck, I arranged with a friend in Paris today to book us some air tickets. I must have been reading your mind!"

They spent the rest of the evening thinking things out. With their personal shareholdings now sold and the money heading towards those financial havens on the open seas at the end of the accounting period, all they had to do was decide quickly how they were going to get to Charles de Gaulle Airport in Paris. Once they were out of the country, they had funds aplenty.

At half past ten, they turned off the lights downstairs and put the bedroom light on as usual. Then they turned off the bedroom light.

Quietly, they slipped out of the back door. They tip-toed down the garden path and clambered over the fence into the field behind the house. After that, it was a short walk to a busy pub where taxis waited ready to ply their trade.

By Wednesday, they would be sunning it up on the beach somewhere decidedly foreign and untouchable!

* * *

"A bit of dirty work for you here, young Wayne – delicate stuff this, do you think you can handle it?" Wayne's mentor had just come off the telephone to City Hall and was looking worried. "No, on second thoughts, I'd better take care of this one!" Ed Fitzpatrick added.

"How can I ever learn to be a top newspaper hack if you take all the goodies away from me?" protested Wayne.

"This one requires tact, Wayne, and careful handling. I mean, one wrong sentence and it could all explode in your face and therefore mine too!"

"What's it all about then, this mysterious matter?"

"Suicide, my dear Wayne – a councillor's just topped himself!" Wayne pulled a face and then said that he thought, in the circumstances, it was best left to the senior reporter.

"Thought you'd think that. I'll just let the editor know about it, then he can leave a tasteful column free for the details to be described."

"Details? What details? You mean how he did it?"

"How he did it? Good God, no. You never describe how to do it or else you have all and sundry copying. Then for the next month, all you are doing is attending coroner's courts as the world and his wife decide to end it all. No, not that type of detail. Tasteful details, such as how much he'll be missed and what a good chap he was – that sort of detail!"

"And will he be missed?" asked Wayne innocently.

"By the bookies and the beer off shops but that's about it."

"But why do you think he did it?"

"That," replied Ed, "is for us to find out. Tactfully, of course!"

* * *

SHOCK DEATH OF COUNCILLOR

Pat O'Reilly was found dead at his house this morning by his wife as she returned home to collect some things. Councillor O'Reilly (46) had been a Leeds councillor for the past fifteen years and was a popular member. The chairman of his local Labour Party said that he was a much respected member and would be a great loss to Leeds.

A man of strident left-wing views, Pat had spent his childhood in Dublin. When Pat was seventeen, his family left Ireland in search of work. It was when they all settled in Leeds that Pat became involved in Labour

Party politics, championing various causes, in particular the plight of the miners and the NHS. Police today say that there are no suspicious circumstances surrounding the death of Councillor Pat O'Reilly and stated that they are not looking for anyone in connection with his death. He leaves a widow and two young children.

* * *

Ralph had to read it through three times before it sunk in. Only a short column really, suicide not even mentioned; but Ralph knew.

Ralph felt cold and hot at the same time. He had driven a man to kill himself, all over some money. He had pushed him into it. He had pulled the trigger, turned on the gas and selected the knife for Pat to choose the method to end it all.

"And it was all because I wanted my money back."

* * *

Just as her husband was blaming himself for Pat's suicide, Amelia was enjoying a late afternoon session with her manager. They had not got much time, so it was a question of a quick grope behind the filing cabinets. This took Amelia back in time to when she first entered the world of office work.

"There was a rather attractive man who used to fancy me like mad!" she said as she rearranged her dress.

"Oh yes?" replied Tony.

"And every time I went past him, he used to beckon me into the filing room – it was a big room with no windows and you could lock the door from the inside. I really used to enjoy filing in those days!"

"Tell me more!" urged Tony, pretending to play the injured husband.

"There's nothing more to say, except I called a halt to his little game when I found out that I wasn't the only one he used to entice in there."

"You mean he kept a harem of filing clerks?"

"Something like that!"

Amelia went back to her desk just as the telephone was ringing.

"Mrs Pearson-Cooper?" inquired the receptionist who had taken the call.

"Yes, speaking," replied Amelia.

"I've got a Bernard on the phone for you."

"Put him through," said Amelia. She did not want to speak to him at all. She really just wanted to return to the delightful and engaging little jaunt she had just been on, but duty called and she knew that she had to put away such childish things, for the moment anyway!

"Amelia, how are things?" asked Bernard. This was bank shorthand for 'have you sorted out the security yet?'

"Well, there's a little hitch, I'm afraid."

"I think you must get something sorted as a matter of priority, you know," warned Bernard. He deliberately slowed down the pace of his voice as he spoke those words in order that the full implications should sink in. It did.

"I'm trying."

"We can't really hold the situation as it is for much longer.." continued Bernard, once again in measured tones.

"Ralph has the money; it is just a question of extracting it!"

"If you could ring me by Friday and let me know the situation. It is very important that we put your account with us on proper footing, you know."

Amelia was starting to feel just a little bit annoyed by his tone. She thought that she would hit back – perhaps then he would not be so smug! "Well, I'm sure that if you won't play ball then some other bank will!"

"If you can find a bank ready to take on your account, feel free," he replied frostily. "But they may look somewhat askance at the overdraft and borrowings that you have already, and the leasing arrangements… you would not be in a very strong position, not at all; but if you want, we will be more than willing to release your account, more than willing!"

Amelia did think that perhaps he was being a bit too eager to get rid of them. This caused a certain amount of worry to emerge in her mind, so she assured Bernard that she would do her best and get back in touch with him on Friday.

"Damn that husband of mine!" she exclaimed as she put the receiver down, "Damn, damn, damn him. I'll have to sort him out, and that means tonight. Oh darling, no love session for us tonight… instead, you'll think of me, won't you, while I berate that husband of mine and get that money off him? Fancy him not telling me that he had all that money tucked away. Do you know what I reckon – I think he planned to leave me and go off with someone else. Well, she's quite welcome to him – she can have him, whoever she is. With pleasure!"

Tony smiled; he loved to hear Ralph being castigated. After all, if Amelia was busy blaming Ralph, it meant that she was seeing him in a good light. It was a new version of make hay while the sun shines – in other words, if you want to make quick but shady cash, do it while people think you are beyond reproach!

"After all, darling – I've got you now!" continued Amelia.

Tony still managed to smile but it was a little weak.

* * *

That evening, Amelia arrived home to find a more than usual dejected Ralph. He was sitting on the sofa feeling very miserable. To him, Pat's suicide was entirely due to the pressure he had applied. Ralph felt guilty.

He also worried that now he would have to explain all to Amelia. This was not a prospect that he was looking forward to at all. He and Amelia had become very detached of late and he did not expect to find much sympathy from her about his plight. On the contrary, he expected fury.

She began on a less than promising tone. "The money?"

"Oh, yes. The money," replied Ralph.

"Where is the money?" she continued as she took off her coat.

"Well, the money isn't, it isn't…"

"Isn't what?" A harsh note was creeping into her voice.

Ralph glanced up and then down at his feet again.

"Isn't what?" demanded Amelia.

"Isn't all there!" muttered Ralph.

"How do you mean, isn't all there?" Amelia was still standing. She now took two paces forward, ready to confront her husband.

"Some of it's gone…"

"Gone where?"

"I've lent it," answered Ralph.

"Well, unlend it then, get it back! We need it for the firm!"

Ralph decided to tackle this head on. He stood up and faced her. "*We* need it? For the firm? As you have been so fond of reminding me, Amelia, it is *your* firm! You find the money!"

Amelia let a little smirk run across her face. "You seem to forget a little point. The fact that I own a substantial shareholding does not alter the original agreements signed. We have to provide personal guarantees – and by we, I mean you and I. Don't you remember a few years back when we both had to sign the agreements?"

"When I signed that, I didn't think…"

"That you would inherit £100,000?" suggested Amelia. "No, I bet you didn't. And why didn't you tell me about it? What were you planning to do with it?"

Ralph refused to answer that and instead inquired as to just what would happen if he did not stump up the money.

"I don't know, but things could get very tricky and we could lose our house. It is just a question of backing the money that they are going to lend us with a little bit of our own. It shows our commitment. Where is the money, anyway?"

"I've lent quite a bit of it to a man…"

"Get it back then!" demanded Amelia. "Tell him you need it now!"

"It's not quite so easy…"

"Of course, it never is easy with you. Nothing is ever easy with you, is it? Why isn't it easy?"

"He's gone and killed himself!" stated Ralph.

"Oh, bloody typical," shouted Amelia, "just like you that is, to go and lend some money to a chap with suicidal tendencies!"

"I didn't know he would go and top himself, did I?"

"And I suppose you didn't get a receipt for this fortune, did you?"

Ralph chose not to answer the question, so Amelia took the lack of reply to be an answer in itself.

"No, you didn't. Great! Now we can't even squeeze some money out of the widow!"

* * *

Bernard had little to do that Friday morning. He was thoroughly enjoying himself, being a small business advisor at the bank. He had always wanted to have a little bit of a business himself but thought that the risks were too great. He was a great considerer of risks. He always weighed up the risks very carefully before coming to any conclusion about anything. Risks about this and that were entered into imaginary columns in his mind and balanced. He always weighted the balance first, of course, in favour of the bank. Then he added the known risks, those that the small businessman described. After that, he added the unknown risks, those that the small businessman chose not to describe. Then, he upped the interest charges accordingly until it all balanced in his mind.

On that Friday morning, Bernard was awaiting a telephone call from someone at Wilkinson Engineering. Preferably someone with authority and the cash to back the loan that he might, only might, give out.

The internal telephone rang and the voice of a

receptionist in the banking foyer down below asked him if he had a moment to see a Mr. Tony Driver from Wilkinson Engineering.

He had a moment, so he agreed and a few minutes later, Tony wandered into the office.

Bernard was immediately impressed with Tony's appearance and air of authority. He contrasted that with the air that Ralph Pearson-Cooper had exuded.

"Bernard!" began Tony. "We haven't met before, but I'm Tony Driver. I run Wilkinson Engineering!"

They shook hands and Bernard offered him a seat and coffee.

"How do you mean, you run it?" inquired Bernard, for he was really still finding his feet in his capacity as small business advisor.

"I took over the management last autumn. I thank God I did, for the sake of the company! I overhauled it! Straight away, I noticed what it needed and I tell you, it needed radical action fast!"

"Well, I can see that just by looking at the statements – there are plenty of commitments that you have entered into. Plenty of risks," commented Bernard, as he got the weighing scales out in his mind and loaded them up.

Tony lent forward and then stated, using his hands to emphasise various points, "I took the firm by the scruff of its neck and shook it! New machinery, redundancies, new organisation – that company is ready for the nineties, ready for Europe and beyond. What is more, I turned that order book round and filled it!"

Bernard smiled happily. He liked what he heard; those buzz words – Europe, nineties, redundancies – were music to his ears.

"In a year's time, I anticipate we will be ready to

apply for a stock exchange listing. Back us, Bernard! Be there!" Tony sat back now, satisfied that he had appealed in the right manner to this so-called advisor.

"But what about the money, the security?" asked Bernard, not too easily put off his chosen track but impressed all the same by the spiel that he had heard.

"Give us a couple of months, Bernard," pleaded Tony. "That money is tied up but it will be here, in the bank, in a couple of months' time. I can promise you that you will be backing a winner." Then Tony dealt his ace, "After all, we are the only British company that Ford are even considering for their new small parts production pieces!"

"Ford Motor Company?"

"Yes, but if we don't get your backing, they'll go abroad for the parts!"

Bernard was impressed. He drove a Ford himself, he always drove Fords. If the Ford Motor Company considered Wilkinson Engineering to be suitable then shouldn't he consider them too?

"A couple of months then," agreed Bernard. "You can have the loan but I want the backing by the end of November, and I want proof that Ford are buying from you."

Tony leant forward and shook hands, "that's all I need, a couple of months!"

It is always very easy to pull the wool over the eyes of an essentially simple but very puffed up small business advisor. All that you had to do was to lie and look convincing. Never look like a failure, or else they will treat you like one. Success breeds success, which in turn spawns loans, money and backing.

Amelia knew a man when she saw one and she certainly saw one in between the sheets at Tony's flat that Friday evening.

"You told him that!" she exclaimed.

"Yes, I said Ford is considering us."

"But they're not!" she squealed with delight at his cheek.

"I know that, you know that, but he won't ring up the chairman of Ford UK to check it out, will he?" stated Tony as he gradually worked his hands down her body.

"But supposing he wants to see a letter from them or something? I mean, he did say that he wanted proof!" wondered Amelia, still trying to concentrate on the issue in hand.

"Well, then he will have his letter, won't he?"

"How?" she removed his hand from her leg in order that she could fully attend to the matter.

"Don't you worry your pretty little head about that," replied Tony. "I've got a letter in the office from them!"

"From Ford? You mean they really do want to buy from us?"

"No, of course not!" said Tony. "I have a letter from them about a query I had concerning a car I bought a few years back. I kept the letter for some reason or other and now, with the careful use of the photocopier and some suitable typing, we can concoct a letter which purports to be from them!"

This time Amelia did not stop Tony getting his own way with her. What a man! He had saved her company single-handedly. Ralph was just not in his league!

* * *

Ed and Wayne went with notebooks in hand to the briefing that the local Labour councillors held on Wednesday the 14th October. They spent a lot of their time at City Hall nowadays, following this lead and that. They had almost completed their investigations into the two competing sites when the untimely death of Pat O'Reilly halted things for a while. However, as luck would have it, the two issues appeared to be connected.

"Unfortunately," Ed mumbled to Wayne just before the briefing began, "we cannot make much out of it."

"Why ever not?" wondered Wayne. Being much younger, he was not as susceptible to delicate situations as his older friend was.

"Suicide, you know…"

"But they delivered an open verdict," Wayne protested, as if that was the answer to it all.

"Open verdict! Everyone knows that an open verdict is just another term for suicide but unproved!"

"Can't we even hint at possible dirty deeds?"

Ed shook his head and said that is was impossible in the circumstances . "It would be a bit like grave digging, you know, getting a story printed knowing full well that the accused can't answer back. The editor would not agree to it at all!"

"But supposing O'Reilly was just one of many?"

"Oh, that would be different! Then we would go for the jugular! But he isn't – there is no evidence to suppose that this is no more than just an isolated incident, someone selling information to pay for his drink and the gee-gees!"

"Pity he had to go and kill himself," suggested Wayne just as the briefing began.

"Yes, well, there it is – poor chap had problems, wife just left him, only returning the next day to fetch the rest of her stuff, a vote of no confidence passed against him, money problems; sounds just the stuff to make anyone reach for the pills and booze!"

"Ladies and gentlemen," began the speaker, "if I could just have your attention for a moment, please!"

Ed and Wayne listened to the details with great interest. It was a surprising briefing and was certainly a turn up for the books.

"If only Pat O'Reilly had waited a while before finishing himself," commented Ed when the briefing was over. "He wouldn't have needed to end it after all!"

* * *

Fiona rang up for the spread on the index. She knew that it was going up and she wanted to buy at £500 a point. She was flushed and excited. The voice on the other end of the telephone confirmed her feeling that the market was moving yet again. The spread that he offered was much higher than the actual position of the Footsie. She bought at the highest figure given in the spread, confirming her account number on the recorded telephone call. She prepared to watch the screen and wait for the market to move up. Time went by and the Footsie moved up. Her heart gave a jump as she knew that the trend was upward. When it reached a certain level, she would ring up again and ask for the spread. The lower price given would be her selling price. As long as the selling price was at a higher level than her buying price, she was quids in. £500 a point to be precise. For every point that the spread moved above her buying point, she was due to get £500; two points above and she would get £1,000; ten points above, £5,000 and so on. No tax to pay – just lovely, lovely money. She was getting a dab hand at this. She had found her medium at last, her means of getting the cash back that she had handed over to that Page man.

The police had been as discreet as they promised and she had been delighted that up until now, she had been able to keep the whole messy business out of Charles' way. The court case had not come up yet, so she had that to face, but the police had managed to get what had turned out to be the one and only video copy. They had not managed to get their hands on any of the money she had paid over to him though, that had all been spent. Betting on the index was Fiona's excellent way of replacing that money.

Of course, should the market not move the way you thought it would, should the market move against you and their spread become unfavourable to you, then you had to pay the spread index betting firm £500 a point.

* * *

Charles had spent the previous number of weeks mooning around. He had felt the loss of his love Glenda to the foul Bates very badly. It had taken Bates a few weeks to realise that his portion of the shareholding had not been sold. Foolishly, he had not checked up on whether Charles had delivered the letter. He had presumed that he had and had therefore waited for the cheque to arrive at the end of the accounting period. When it did not come, he rang their stockbroker to see what had happened. They denied all knowledge of any letter. This had led Bates to wonder just what was going on. Furthermore, some of the contacts that Charles had arranged for him had disappeared into thin air. In fact, the whole situation was looking decidedly grim and was not something that he could present to his superiors as a reason for offering him a partnership.

At the beginning of October, he had tried to ring Charles but was unable to get hold of him. Twice more he tried but with no luck. Then, via Fiona, who was back to her normal self now, he arranged a meeting with Charles for Friday 16th October.

Charles was not at all pleased when, on Wednesday morning, Fiona told him about the meeting.

"I shan't be there!" he stated quite emphatically.

"Why ever not?"

"Because he is just a toad!"

Fiona shrugged her shoulders and thought of the hundreds of pounds she was steadily accumulating.

"By the way," asked Fiona, "I haven't heard of much activity on the share front just recently."

"No, we're just letting them grow!" replied Charles, in an attempt to cover things up. He did not want his wife to know the real reason why he and Bates had fallen out.

"Anyway," he continued, "thought it better if we laid low for a while, until that Roland Petersen thing has blown over."

"Do you think that the police might have others that they are interested in?" inquired Fiona worriedly.

"Could have, I've no idea, so that's another reason –

apart from the fact that Bates is an annoying toad whom I want to avoid at all costs – the police might have some tenuous links between Petersen and us. You never know, so it's better to be safe than sorry!"

"You want to leave the shares alone in any case, they have just been soaring! It's unbelievable!"

* * *

The evening paper covered the briefing in two ways: the first reported the news item itself; the second was an article about Pat O'Reilly. Ralph, still feeling miserable about being given the cold shoulder by his wife for his failure to produce the money and also about the Pat's suicide, read both the articles with great interest.

Pat O'Reilly, the paragraph said, had personally backed the proposal to have the industrial site in his constituency. He had taken it very badly when the council officials had supported the other site. Then he had become distressed when a vote of no confidence had been passed against him – due, in part, to what was seen as his failure to secure the site for his constituency. He had been fond of drink and gambling and there were a number of court orders outstanding at the time of his death and it was thought that he owed various people money. Added to his misery was the fact that his wife had left him, taking his children with her.

Suddenly, Ralph felt one hell of a lot better. It was like a load had been lifted from his mind. So it had not been just his pressure that had caused the death of Pat – there had been other things as well!

The main article was directly related to the subsidiary

column inches. It was about the new industrial site and how the original decision taken just a short while ago was to be reversed, in favour of the site in Pat O'Reilly's constituency. The council had neglected to check a few rather important points which affected the viability of the original site – for example, the site was criss-crossed with footpaths; it was also in an old mining area, with all the attendant difficulties that such things create, like disused shafts and subsidence. Therefore, the industrial site was to be placed in Pat O'Reilly's old constituency; council approval was to be given the next day.

Ralph had nearly finished the article when a smile and then a grin gradually appeared. At last he was going to make a fortune! Golden eggs were hatching into golden chickens! Bless you, Pat, he thought, whereever you are!

The words at the end of the paragraph caused a jolt in Ralph's jubilations. He was stunned and then horrified as the full implication of the disclosure hit him. There it was, in black print on white paper:

'The proposed industrial site is owned by Wilkinson Engineering Ltd., a local firm in Armley.'
Gone was any attempt to keep things secret!

* * *

On Thursday morning, Fiona rang up and checked the spread. It was up – she was in the money but only just. Therefore, she decided that it was prudent to leave her bet in a little bit longer, to reap even greater amounts.

* * *

Bernard had his own little pip-squeak to assist him and prod him. Just as Tim had had a succession of assistants, so Bernard was going to have some. They were there to keep the advisor, or whatever his current title was, on his toes. They were there on occasions to report back to the powers above when groups of them were called together for training sessions. A skilled person did not take long to work out how and why a budding manager got his ideas. Enough hints were dropped that sealed the fate – up or down – of many a manager. This particular pain in the backside sent to assist Bernard was called Piers. The name did cause Bernard a little bit of worry for it implied a privileged background. Indeed, Piers did come from the upper echelons of society ; in fact, he had had so many silver spoons put in his mouth at birth that he must have choked on them and spewed out the few brain cells that he had. Piers was somewhat thick – he spoke beautifully but lacked intelligence. Bernard gave him the job every morning of searching through the previous evening's papers. This saved Bernard the hassle of finding out which of his customers had done anything special, naughty or nice; such information was then added to the files. It also kept Piers occupied for an hour.

Piers emerged from behind the paper to inquire of his superior whether Wilkinson Engineering banked with them or not.

"Yes. Why?"

"Oh, nothing really – it's just that it says here that they own the proposed industrial site," said Piers.

"Industrial site?"

"Yes, apparently the council are going to approve change of use today. It was a few fields belonging to a farmer but with it being so near the motorway and all that, the council have decided to turn it over to industry. Do you think it will be worth a lot more now they are going to put industrial units on it?"

Piers did not get an answer. Bernard had already picked up the telephone and was dialling away.

* * *

James was getting a bit desperate. He wanted to see how his plug-pulling was coming along but the only contact that he had inside the firm was dear Jenny. He rang her up at work, giving only his Christian name, and spoke to her.

"How about I take you out for lunch?"

"Great!" she replied. "Where have you been recently, anyway? I keep looking out for you in the queue."

"Tell you all about it when we meet!" he promised and they made arrangements to have lunch at one that day, Thursday 15th October.

* * *

Charles had no business meetings that morning, which was very unfortunate for it meant that he spent his time thinking about Glenda in bed with Bates. It still troubled him because he had a little dream about ditching Fiona, if they did not manage to get Blayborough, and going to live with Glenda in the cottage that he owned. If Fiona and Charles did not get Blayborough, Charles had planned to still maintain Glenda as his mistress, but he would then be able to visit her more often.

Thus, on Thursday, he had time to dwell on the

implications of Bates and Glenda, Bates and the shares, his cottage and Bates lying with his mistress in the bed that he, Charles, bought and so on.

"I can't stand that man!" he said thinking for a while after.

"Well, I know that you haven't been exactly very keen on him in the past but I didn't know you detested him!"

"I won't see him tomorrow – I don't know what you were thinking of when you made arrangements for me to see him. Don't you know I've been trying to avoid him for the past few weeks?"

"I hadn't realised," admitted Fiona. The truth was, she had not noticed, she was too busy wrapped up in her own plans.

"I'll ring him up and tell him not to turn up. I'll tell him that because of this Petersen thing, we'd better keep a low profile share-wise and not buy or sell anything. That's what I'll do. It'll be a good excuse not to see him."

"You can't keep putting him off forever!"

"No, but in the spring we will be selling everything anyway and then we need not see him again!"

John Bates did protest about it. He stated that he wanted his money and that Charles had no right not to deliver that letter. "And," continued John to Charles on the telephone that morning, "you've broken your promise. What's happened? One minute, there were chairmen ringing and writing to me, wanting me to come along and advise them or whatever, next minute, nothing! It all dissolves into thin air!"

"Not my fault, Bates, not my fault. I set it up for you – hardly my fault if they get into contact with you and then change their minds! They mustn't have liked what they saw!"

"Anyway, whatever, I'm not happy and just as soon as this Petersen thing has died a death, I want out! Just supposing the market drops, it might, there have been articles!"

"Doom watchers! Take no notice!" advised Charles.

"Well, I think they might have a point. If it wasn't for this Petersen business, I think we should have sold."

"I'll talk to you in November," promised Charles, trying to make his voice sound convincing. He had no intention of speaking to him in November at all.

* * *

Bernard of bank fame was not able to get through to either Ralph or Amelia, so he spoke to Tony instead.

"Tony!" began Bernard enthusiastically. "What news!"

On the other end of the telephone, Tony's face had a blank look on it but his tone managed to convey total knowledge of the news in his reply: "Great! Yes!" and while he spoke those few words, he was racking his brains, trying to think what this news could be. At the time of the phone call, he had been drinking coffee and reading the newspaper. He had cleared up the morning's mail and poked his head around the factory door. The workers were busy producing an order. They did not know, of course, that there were no more orders in the pipe-line. Everything appeared around the factory to be full of life with brimming order books. The workers breathed in this air of expectant good fortune and thought it was real – instead of a puffed up image.

"How did you do it?" asked Bernard. "I mean, I knew when I read it that it just had to be you who had obtained it!"

"Well… you know…" replied Tony whilst thinking, What is this man talking about?

"I know, you can't reveal your sources!"

"Yes, that's right!" Tony agreed.

Bernard went on talking, oblivious to the fact that the man at the other end had no clue as to what he was going on about.

"When I read about it in the paper this morning, I said to myself, I must ring Amelia Pearson-Cooper up straight away!" Bernard announced. "I must put her out of her misery!"

"You read it in the paper?" Tony queried.

"I always scan the previous evening's papers – I personally take an interest in our clients' little, or in your case big, triumphs!" Piers was busy picking a juicy spot, out of earshot of the conversation, so he did not hear how his own clever sighting was being high-jacked by his superior.

"Tell Amelia," continued Bernard, "that she can have her loan, we'll take a charge on the land's deeds!"

"The land's deeds…" echoed Tony.

"That's right, if she could make arrangements with solicitors etc. etc."

"Yes, I'll tell her," assured Tony. They bade each other goodbye and Tony replaced the receiver.

"Land? What land?" he asked himself. "And where is last night's newspaper?"

Tony dashed out of the office and flew down to the newsagent hoping to find a copy that had not been sold. He was out of luck. He did consider knocking on someone's door and asking them if they had a copy that they did not want any longer but thought better of it. He returned to the office and grabbed his car keys. There was only one way to get a copy and that was to go straight to the source of the newspaper – the press. In his eagerness to get out, he bumped into Jenny, who was leaving for her lunch date.

* * *

"Hi James," she called. "Take a look at that!"

James examined her right arm; it was red and there was a slight cut.

"What happened?" inquired James solicitously.

"Tony Driver crashed into me and caught his car keys on my arm. Not a word of apology or anything. That man is all top show, you know, a sham."

James got the drinks in and guided Jenny to a seat in the corner.

"So, what's new then? Apart from the arm!" asked James.

"Tony is really getting above himself. He thinks himself it – especially now he's having an affair with Mrs Pearson-Cooper, the chairman of the company, herself!"

James' ears pricked up at this; it was music to him, sweet music! "What makes you think that then?"

"Saw them at it – behind the filing cabinet the other day – and, what's more, I heard them discussing what a great time they had had in St. Anne's. Poor Ralph, he doesn't deserve it."

James had no sympathy for poor Ralph. In his eyes, Ralph deserved everything he had coming to him. Revenge was slow, but it was all the sweeter for it.

Ralph had been the cause of his mother's upset. Ralph had been the cause of his mother being thrown out and her subsequent ill health. Now Ralph was being similarly treated.

"There are two sides to every coin," cautioned James.

"Not in this case there isn't," Jenny loyally stated. "And another thing, I reckon that Tony is on the fiddle. Things just don't add up and I'm not an expert book-keeper but even I can see when someone is trying to hide things."

"Time will tell," replied James prophetically. He had suddenly acquired a great liking for this Tony fellow – he realised that he would be an extra instrument in the downfall of Ralph. Delicious double revenge – personal and monetary!

"He's up to something," continued Jenny, "and it certainly isn't getting more orders in. There are no more orders in the offing, not one single screw or bolt or anything! Mrs Pearson-Cooper doesn't know, she's so besotted with the man that she believes all the hype he is putting out. You know what I think I'll do?" Jenny began thoughtfully.

"What?"

"I think that I'll go and see Ralph at home and tell him my suspicions!" she stated. "Yes, I will!"

James was worried. He did not want this slow plan of his going astray because of some overzealous little bookkeeper with a crush on her previous boss. He decided to squash the idea immediately, using the affair as an excuse. "Oh, I wouldn't do that. I mean, no husband wants to hear that his wife is having an affair!"

"Oh, I wasn't going to mention that! I was just going to tell him about the firm – how I think that it's going bust. I mean, he has a right to know – after all, he still has personal guarantees, signed along with his wife of course. You know, like you do when you marry."

"Personal guarantees, has he?"

"Oh, yes. I know it's a limited company but Amelia and Ralph had to back the firm with money and their house and so on." Jenny smiled and then admitted to James that she had found it all out a few weeks ago when she was searching for a file on Tony's desk. "He'd got all their details, every single one of them, on his desk. I smelt a rat right away!" Jenny said. "Something fishy here, I said to myself. Heavens, is that the time?" She had glanced at her watch and found that she had overstepped her lunch hour.

James watched her dash off and then, feeling smug, ordered himself another drink. The next part of the plan would involve his elder brother; he had the plot nicely worked out in his mind.

Time to show an interest in the life of Charles Pearson-Cooper, James thought to himself. Time to put spokes in his wheel!

* * *

Tony managed to get himself a copy of Wednesday evening's paper and quickly scanned the articles. It did not take him long to find the relevant section and he whipped through the information until he spotted, there as an after thought, the name of the owner of this potential lucrative site.

Armed with the paper, he dashed back to the office and rang up his pal in Manchester.

"How's it going?" he asked. "Is the valuation complete?"

"Just putting the finishing touches to it," answered Harry Carpenter. "It's looking quite good. Not brilliant, but quite good. Your main asset is the actual land that the factory is on. That is worth a bit in itself because it could make an excellent site for a supermarket, you know, one of those great big drive-in types. I've got a friend of a friend whose job it is to search for suitable sites. He is just gasping for it!"

"Marvellous!" agreed Tony.

"More than that – a bloody gold mine that site is. The beauty is that the council could be so easily persuaded to let this supermarket company build there, if they are offered the carrot of light industry attached, especially as it seems you're going bust."

"Going bust?" queried Tony.

"You did realise that, didn't you?" answered Harry and Tony could hear him puffing on a cigar. "I mean those figures don't fool me one minute!"

"Yes, well never mind about that," replied Tony dismissively. "What about this then. Just you listen to this bit of news. It only turns out that Wilkinson's own a lucrative proposed new industrial site!"

"When did you find out about that then?"

"This morning, when the bank manager rang and said that of course the loan would be alright, just have to arrange for a charge on the industrial site! You could have knocked me down with feather – I knew nothing of it at all!"

"Get the details in the post right away!" advised Harry, "I'll wait until they arrive and then arrange a valuation based on that. Then, do you know what you should do?"

"No, go on," urged Tony.

"Bail out! Get the hell out of it! Grab your money and run for all you are worth, which, with one definite industrial site and one potential, will be quite a large amount!"

* * *

Amelia came into the factory in the afternoon. She had been shopping for some particularly attractive underwear to entice Tony with.

Tony greeted her with a little kiss. "Good news!" he said.

"You're free tonight?" Which was Amelia's idea of good news.

"Yes I am but even better news than that," replied Tony. "The bank will lend us the money!"

"Without the £100,000 being lodged there?"

"Yes," answered Tony, "all they want is a charge on that industrial site you own."

"What industrial site?"

"The new one, the proposed one – you must know! After all, you are supposed to own it!"

"I own it?"

"Well, not you exactly," said Tony, "Wilkinson's, really I suppose own it – you know what I mean."

"You mean this site, this land here, the land we are standing on now?"

"No, I don't mean that." Tony was beginning to get worried. He could see his fortune diminishing before his very eyes. He produced the paper and flicked through it until he found the paragraph that backed his statement.

"Look. Here,"he said and he pointed to the words.

"Ralph! It must be his doing!" And with that, Amelia dashed off home to confront her husband with the article.

* * *

Fiona congratulated herself on her good luck. It was holding out well and she was overjoyed at having bought in when the spread was so much in her favour. Once more, the spread was in her favour, this time for selling her position. She counted up the points – each point did not mean prizes but pounds, lovely, lovely pounds, in groups of 500!

Should she sell, when all was going so well, and take the profit? Or should she wait for even greater profits to come?

* * *

Ralph had the whole morning to decide his tactics. The best thing to do, he concluded while watching the children's education programmes on the television, was to pretend that it all was meant to be a surprise for her.

The door opened and Amelia strode in. She held the paper in her outstretched hands. "Do you know anything about this?" she demanded.

"Yes, of course!"

"Well, what do you have to say about it? Why didn't you tell me?"

Ralph just shrugged his shoulders and replied, "It was meant to be a surprise. I thought that with that, we could offer the bank security and the firm would be saved!"

"But why didn't you tell me about it before?" she demanded, not wholly satisfied with his answer.

"The decision went against us to begin with, that's why! I mean, you were hardly in a mood to appreciate that I had speculated with that legacy and lost! Your tirade against me would have been greater!"

Amelia quietened down and even began to look at Ralph in a new light. Perhaps he was not such a bad husband after all, perhaps he had his moments! Maybe she was hasty to be disloyal to him... maybe she should think again...

Ralph plonked himself back down on the seat and continued to watch the screen, not taking the programme in at all. He had lost most of his money. Now he had lost the site as well. Ralph concluded that he was now worse off than he was when he had received the money, for now he had just a few months to find the £100,000, plus interest, that the winner would want.

* * *

The winds were starting to get up and the weather was turning nasty. People had it in their minds that perhaps the end of the world was nigh, that maybe they were paying the penalty of the years of good living that they had enjoyed in the eighties. The weather forecaster assured the listeners that there were no hurricanes on the way, but the winds increased, taking no notice of the expert's advice that they were not supposed to come!

The telephone went and Charles rushed to answer it.

"Daddy?" went the voice at the other end.

"Is that you, Emma?" asked Charles. He was right to

wonder for it did not sound a bit like his daughter at all. Her voice was faltering and seemed shaky.

"Oh, Daddy!" she said again and this time Charles could hear the unmistakable sound of sobbing.

"What is it? What's the matter?"

"Please, Daddy, come and get me, please," went the voice, usually so confident but now so nervous.

"Of course I will – I mean we both will, Mummy and I," assured Charles. "I could come over at the weekend, how about that?"

"No! No!" she replied almost vehemently. "Come now!"

"But I can't come now! It's the middle of the night – well, it must be ten o'clock, at least!"

"Please Daddy…" she pleaded.

"What's up, sweetheart?" he asked.

"I had an abortion, Daddy, and I can't stop crying."

"We're setting off now," Charles assured her, "wait in your room for us. Don't worry, we're on our way."

* * *

Havoc had been wreacked by the hurricanes that were not supposed to be coming. It was a dreadful scene that people up and down the land woke up to on Friday morning. Glenda had half her roof off and had terrible problems trying to get someone in to fix a tarpaulin on. Still the winds blew. She was glad that she was getting married the next day and would be off on her honeymoon.

She tried to contact the agents who usually arranged repairs on behalf of Charles but they were not very helpful at all. They told her to ring up the owner herself as they were no longer paid to act as go-betweens on this particular property. No one had told her that the situation had altered. This did worry her a little, especially as she had not heard from Charles at all just recently. It did make her wonder about her position as a tenant. Then she realised that she was not really a tenant at all, for she had no agreement and paid no rent. The agreement was between the cottage letting business that Charles ran and Charles himself. It was all rather incestuous and Glenda, who was not a legal expert, did tend to think that her rights to the cottage were somewhat shaky. She paid no rent; she had no lease; the person who had the lease really owned the cottage, albeit in a nominee name of a business. Glenda decided to dismiss these worries from her mind. She was going to get married tomorrow and would be Mrs Glenda Bates. Then perhaps John would buy a house for them both to live in.

So she thought that she would have just one more try to contact Charles at his home address and then, to hell with it, she would leave the roof as it was, with the tarpaulin covering the hole! When she was back from the honeymoon, well, John would dip into his pocket and then, bingo, they too would be members of the home-owning democracy!

It wasn't a good thing, she concluded, to keep ties with Charles after she was married to John. He could have his cottage back then, leaky roof and all!

* * *

Charles and Fiona held their daughter's hand that Friday morning and comforted her through her misery.

"I thought it would be so simple," she said through her tears.

"Nothing is ever simple!" murmured Fiona.

During the previous academic year, Emma had enjoyed a deep relationship with her tutor. He was separated from his wife and much older than her. Emma adored him; she regarded him as the source of wisdom, the font of knowledge and the giver of sexual pleasures. She worshipped him so much that when he suggested that they should go to France together for a holiday, she readily agreed. They had been to bed before, but in France there was the opportunity to abandon their all, to eat the fruits of their forbidden love. The ties that bound her to him were tightened during their sojourn in France. On their return, she had found herself pregnant and gladly told him the good news. Now he had a reason to get divorced. Now they had a reason to get married. However, when she related the information, he had been horrified and had not shared her delight. Slowly, he distanced himself from her, rejecting her advances and not returning her calls. When she eventually told him that she thought that an abortion was the best alternative, he offered her money – blood money. With no one to support her during the termination, she felt deserted and at prey to her thoughts. Loneliness bred fears and worries. The word murderer crept into her mind on those dark days and nights that followed the termination of her baby. Perhaps, she would think when she was at her lowest, if she could kill her own child, she could kill herself. Her mind fought against the idea but it popped up again and again, until she was no longer strong enough to resist it. Then, summoning one final bit of determination, she rang home for help.

The tears flowed and flowed throughout that Friday

morning. When they would come no longer, Charles suggested that the three of them should go away for a few days, somewhere quiet and where the world could not touch them.

At lunchtime, with the winds still sweeping the countryside, they drove off to a thatched cottage in Norfolk which Charles had managed to rent that very morning from an agency. It had no television, no newspaper delivery and was isolated from civilisation.

The wind, the world and life passed them by until the middle of the following week.

* * *

All the way to the church, John Bates worried. He had hardly been able to eat his breakfast. He had been alright when he had woken up that Saturday morning. The thought of tying the knot with Glenda was enough to make him jump out of bed with delight. He had gone out of his bedroom and wandered to the postbox to pick up the morning's papers. Clutching the *Daily Telegraph* and the *Financial Times*, he had sauntered into the kitchen of his flat to prepare a small repast.

With the F.T propped up, he dug into his cornflakes and thought once more about how lucky he was to be marrying Glenda that very morning. Unfortunately, his eyes caught sight of another article warning of a probable fall in the stock market. This brought out John's hidden fear of losing all his money. He was not a particularly rich man. His assets lay in two areas: firstly, they were tied up in the account he shared with Charles and Fiona, which he had wanted to dissolve and take the profits from; secondly, they lay in his career, which he had hoped would take off when he presented the senior partners in the firm with his achievements. Both those assets were not looking so good at the moment. So it was with a heavy heart and troubled mind that John got ready for the Big Day. He tried to contact Charles a number of times but with no success. He had to make sure that his shares had been sold. He had to secure his money. He had dialled so often that he was running late and the friend of his, who was acting as best man, warned him that it was the bride's prerogative to be late, not the groom's!

The bride wore white. It was a great surprise to all the villagers that she chose such a virginal colour and the gathered throng did admit to themselves that the pureness of the colour was tainted by the deepness of the cleavage. Glenda sported a dashingly cut bodice, which showed her attributes to great advantage. Naturally, being eager as she always was, she was on time for the ceremony. John was late, but he did have the decency to leave the *Financial Times* in the car, for a later, more detailed, inspection. He had tried again to get hold of Charles before he had set off but had received no reply. As he approached the village, he stopped at a phone kiosk and rang once again but still no answer.

The wind, still strong, left the couple flushed and tangled as they struggled against it. John insisted on using the phone before they entered the village hall for the reception. When he came out of the box, he still looked as worried as he was when he went in. Glenda took no notice and led him by the hand to introduce him to all her friends. There was nothing more that John could do about his fears, so he just decided to hell with it and enjoyed the feasting and the one week honeymoon on a remote Greek isle to follow.

* * *

James considered his position carefully. He had only a few months left to execute the final part of his plan. He was quite satisfied that the first part was well on its way towards success. The second part would be slightly easier, in that he could control it absolutely from the onset. The trouble with trying to ruin Ralph was that it involved dropping large hints to other people and awaiting the results. It was a slow business. It would be far quicker dealing with the ruining of Charles.

Once again, James was forced to consider the events of the past. He had been over the same ground many times when he was younger. Now the opportunity to cleanse his mother's torment was presented by dealing with Charles for good. Just as Ralph had been instrumental in his mother's expulsion from the family home, so Charles had also played a part.

There were two things that had tormented James during his years in Australia. He had dealt with one. He had yet to deal with the other. His mind went back to those years at Eton. All had been well and things had settled down to some sort of normality after his parent's divorce had finally come through; he had followed in his elder brother's footsteps and, though he was not as forceful a personality as Charles had been, he made his mark because he was more intelligent than Charles. He had enjoyed the stability of the place which gave him roots. The way that father followed son, brother followed brother, gave the school a strong sense of tradition and loyalty, which family ties only served to increase.

He had stopped worrying about who had informed on his mother and accused her wrongly of an affair. He had long since presumed that it must have been a jealous streak of his father's that had developed into a moment of madness, leading him to accuse her of adultery. The fact that his father had admitted that he was wrong confirmed that presumption in James' eyes. His mother's failing health was more of a concern to him. He tried to do his best and gain reports and marks that would make his mother proud of him. He saw his father on occasions but never managed to become close to him.

Then, when he was eighteen and a short while before he was due to take his exams, he was taken to one side and told of his mother's death. He felt broken and openly wept. That night, he returned to his books but did not study – they remained opened at the same page while James tried to come to terms with the loss of a parent, the one relative who really loved him. It was during that evening that a fellow pupil came to chat to him to try and cheer him up. James told him about how his mother had never recovered from the divorce and had been ill on and off since the birth of Ralph.

"Messy things, divorces," consoled the boy, whose name was Peter.

"You're telling me!" agreed James.

"Did you know that my brother and your brother shared a room together here?" said Peter, trying to lighten the conversation.

"Did they?" answered James. "What, they shared a room when the divorce proceedings started?"

"Yes," said Peter and then he asked, "So, how do you think Charles will take it?"

"I don't know. He wasn't close to mother," replied James.

"Well, I know he can't have been in the past, but I thought perhaps, you know, maybe they got on better now!"

"How do you mean?" asked James, growing alert to what Peter was saying.

"I mean that he was obviously not close to his mother or else he would not have done that!" Peter was oblivious to the fact that the two of them were talking at cross purposes.

James, in spite of being upset, realised that he was on the verge of a great discovery. He knew that if he questioned his friend too aggressively then he might never know the answer to the question that had been dogging him for years. Was it just a jealous streak that had caused his father to accuse his mother, or had someone (as James had first suspected) pointed the finger at his mother? "Oh, that, yes! I mean he can't have been close to her – I mean he just wouldn't have done it would he, if he was," he said by way of encouragement. James paused, knowing that Peter would carry on and spill the beans.

"I mean, fancy shopping your own mother!" Peter had said.

"Yes, I know." James was now starting to shake with rage, inwardly, and all the hatred that had been bubbling up over the years began to ferment. Hatred towards a person who had dealt the blow to his mother; hatred towards the one who had accused his mother of a crime she was innocent of.

"I couldn't believe it when Freddie told me what Charles had said. I don't know why he did it, perhaps it was because he loved his father?" And then Peter looked up and saw James' face. He knew straight away that all he had just said was totally new to his friend.

"You… you did know about that?" he asked.

There had been no answer.

"Oh, my God. I'm so sorry, James; so sorry."

Still no reply.

When Charles had arrived the next day to take James home and prepare for the funeral, James went berserk. He tore pictures off walls, smashed windows and piled all the bedclothes from one dormitory and started to set fire to them.

"I'm sorry," his father was told, "but in the circumstances, we don't feel that your son should return to Eton."

James had refused to stay with either of his brothers or his father as the family prepared for the funeral. It was a quiet ceremony and quickly dealt with, the immediate relations going their separate ways after the burial was over. Only James knew just what his mother had gone through. She had been betrayed, wrongly and unjustly, by her own son.

His father had declared that the best thing for James would be a fresh start. James had said most emphatically that he did not wish to live in England anymore. He could not trust himself as far as Charles was concerned. He felt like slitting his brother's throat and came to the conclusion that he should leave the country.

"I want to live in Australia," he had announced on arriving at his father's mansion that evening after they had buried his mother.

His father, glad to be rid of the problem, supplied the money and the contacts for James to start again.

Now, back in England and older and wiser, James knew that slitting his brother's throat would not have been the answer. Revenge should only destroy his brothers, not bring trouble and heap destruction onto him as well. Subtlety was the key word. It was such subtlety that was bringing the end near for Ralph. Now James would ruin Charles' life in exactly the same way that Charles had ruined his mother's life.

* * *

"Feeling better now?" Charles asked his daughter.

"Much, thanks,"she said. She was starting to smile again now.

"I'll tell you what, let's go out for a meal! We've been cooped up in here for days and a meal out will do us all the power of good."

Fiona and Emma readily agreed and the three of them got ready. They decided to head for Norwich that Tuesday evening, where they could saunter around before picking a restaurant which took their fancy for dinner. They parked the car and walked in the direction of the market square. On the way there, they passed a newsagent's where the newspapers still screamed the facts that had hit the headlines throughout the world, flashing across television screens the day before. Black Monday they were calling it. The stock market was in free fall, they said. Shares were plummeting all over the world. Would capitalism ever recover? the papers asked.

Fiona stopped in her tracks and the colour drained from her face. She had forgotten all about her position she had opened and watched so hopefully a few days ago. The stock market was in free fall, and with it, at £500 a point, was her bet.

Charles froze in horror. To think that only the previous week he had been happily counting his money, his gains and glowing with the thought of all that wealth. How were his shares doing? What had happened in those few days? Why had he been so greedy?

* * *

PART FIVE

Epilogue

It had been, for Charles and Fiona Pearson-Cooper's household, a winter beyond discontent – it had been a winter of disaster. The evening that they had found out that an earthquake had hit the world's capitalist markets had not been an easy one. For the sake of Emma, they each put on a brave face and tried to keep the conversation light, though neither of them had any appetite left after having digested the news. Luckily, Emma never spotted the doom ridden fears lurking below the façade. Fully recovered, as much as one can be after such an event, they took her back to Cambridge the next day and left her in the company of friends.

However, before they set off for Cambridge, Fiona and Charles both went in search of a telephone box. Charles just wanted to satisfy a nagging annoyance – had the foul Bates married Glenda? A phone call to Bates' employers confirmed his fears – Glenda Riddings was now Glenda Bates and was probably baring all on their honeymoon. Fiona, who had to go further to search for an empty phone box, was armed with a fistful of coins. She rang up the Index and asked for their spread. She found out that they had closed her position for her. An ominous sign that she had gone way over her agreed credit limit by at least three times.

"Didn't you receive our letter?" she was asked.

Meanwhile, Charles reflected on his position: it was only a short while ago that he had a fortune tied up in the stock market and he was all cock-a-hoop about it; just a matter of weeks ago he had had that and a luscious mistress to boot. Now he didn't have either.

They had both withered away on the vine. Maybe it was true, the moral of the story about the monkey and the nuts – maybe if he had not tried to have everything, he would not have lost the lot.

He fumbled around in his pockets, trying to find his car keys. He was going to meet up with Fiona and then head north to their home. He felt through his trouser pockets and his jacket pockets. Just as he was going through his inside pocket and pulling out the contents, he spotted the keys on the floor by the edge of the kerb and picked them up. He was stuffing the bits and pieces back into his inside pocket when he stopped, grinned and laughed uproariously.

"I may have lost lots of money but so have you, Bates!" In his hand, he held a letter. "This will take the shine off your marriage, Bates," Charles was heard to mutter, much to the amazement of passers-by. "Now to well and truly cook your goose for good!"

* * *

James wondered what Fiona would be like. He hoped that she would at least be attractive, for that would make his little plan so much more pleasant. He also hoped that she would be sexually compliant or else he would have to woo her, and that would be tiresome.

James was starting to find England a bit boring. He was longing to get back to Australia, where his heart truly lay. During those grey Autumn days, he saw the surf, the blue skies and the bobbing yachts dancing around in his mind, teasing him. It constantly annoyed him to realise that when the days were short, dark and damp in England, they were long, warm and dry in Australia.

Plan number two had to be accomplished mighty quickly, he considered, for Australia was beckoning.

* * *

Harry Carpenter, the valuer appointed by Tony Driver to give a glossy assessment of Wilkinson's worth, went through the figures once again. He checked them over with his calculator and then reached for the phone.

"Tony, get off your butt and get over to Manchester right away!" he had said as soon as he had got through to him.

"You've finished then?" asked Tony. "You can put a value on my holding?"

"Just get over here!" advised Harry.

* * *

Charles took a detour on the way home and stopped at their broker's office. There he left Fiona in the car and bounded up the stairs to the palatial suite to deliver the letter in person. The situation that greeted Charles could best be described as chaos. It seemed that no one had predicted what had happened, though, naturally enough, after the event, all were muttering words to the effect that the markets cannot go on the up forever, and there was bound to be a correction sometime etc. Charles was the only person to be happy about it all. His broker just could not understand why, for the value of the shareholdings they held had dropped like a stone.

"Thank God you're in!" exclaimed Charles, a little breathless from his exertions.

"What can I say?" began the broker. He had said

these words so many times during the hours that had followed Black Monday that he was word perfect. "If I had known, if anybody had known, we would have told you, advised you. It was a complete surprise. It was the Americans, they had fixed their computers to buy at certain levels and then sell at certain levels; when the market started to slip, the machines when into auto-drive. It was sell, sell, sell… but don't worry, please don't worry…"

"Oh, I'm not worried!" announced Charles, just wondering when he was going to get a word in edgeways.

"Good lad," replied the broker, oblivious to the fact that Charles was older than he was and so could hardly be called a lad. "Take heart! The companies are still the same ones. Their value is just the same! It is only their shares which have dropped! Now, the shares will seem cheap and everyone will be out buying again! Just you watch!"

"Perhaps you're right but that is not why I've come to see you," said Charles.

"No? Oh!"

"No, I've come to see you to deliver a letter from John Bates. He wants out!"

The broker read the letter and remarked on the date.

"Well, his intentions are quite clear but he did write this a few weeks ago. How can I be sure that he hasn't changed his mind?"

"You have my personal assurance," said Charles, sitting ramrod straight in the chair and fixing the broker with his very best 'trust me' look.

"I have no option but to do as the letter suggests," the broker said, and he removed another letter from his file and compared the writing and signature. They matched and, satisfied, he began the process that would see Bates' share of the holding sold at the low, low prices the market makers were offering.

Charles bounded down the steps and ran to the car. Jubilation!

* * *

Tony arrived in Manchester and went straight to see Harry Carpenter to hear the news.

"You're a rich man, Tony!" announced Harry. "How did you do it?"

"You know, I'm not quite sure but it seems that everything I touched since moving to Leeds has turned to gold!"

Harry grinned at his friend and then offered him this advice, "Gold made in these circumstances has a habit of changing back into base metals. Witness the fortunes lost in the City these last few days!"

Tony nodded his head and assured Harry that he had no share holdings to worry about.

"Except the one in Wilkinson's!" cautioned Harry. "You need to worry about that. You are sitting on a gold mine, my dear Tony, which is about to close down!"

"You really reckon?"

"I truly do! It is time to cash in your chips, before, as they say, you have your fish and chips!" Harry laughed like a drain at his witty comment. Tony did not join in; he was considering the best way to approach this delicate situation. There was the added complication of Amelia. To effect a payout, she would have to be

319

informed and that could make life difficult. She might drag her heels; she might think that he wanted the money in order to disappear, leaving her behind.

"There is one point," began Tony after Harry's laughter had subsided.

"Oh, yes, and what is that?"

"Amelia Pearson-Cooper!"

"The owner? So?" asked Harry while leaning forward to find out more.

"We have a bit of a thing going… you know…"

"Well, you dirty old devil!" exclaimed Harry, starting to laugh once more. "Not only are you nicking money from the firm, and you are running it so disgustingly that bankruptcy is on the horizon, and you want to be bought out but you are also knocking off the boss as well! I can't believe it! You know what you are, don't you?"

"No," replied Tony, somewhat lamely.

"You're a swine, that's what you are!" And Harry spluttered and roared so much with laughter that he nearly burst a button off his shirt.

"It isn't that funny," said Tony.

Harry still chuckled.

"If you could stop it," Tony continued crossly, "your hilarity is costing me a fortune."

Harry's amusement started to subside and he managed to speak. "String her along," he advised when he had finally recovered.

"What do you mean?"

"Tell her that you are building a little nest for her; tell her that you are planning a future for the both of you. Whatever she wants to hear, tell her! Then she will gladly pay up and buy you out!"

"And then?"

"As they say in the best American movies, go West, young man – or South or East, in fact, anywhere as quickly as you can before she realises that the end is nigh!"

* * *

After being out all morning, Fiona returned in her car and entered the house, picking up the mail that Mrs Armitage had left on the hall table. Then, with the day's post in hand and a pad of writing paper, so that she could pen a letter to Emma, she went into the drawing room. Opening the mail was not a task that delighted her at all. Some people grumble about junk mail but she wished that was all she got – stuff that could be binned.

She sat at the writing desk and took stock of the situation that Wednesday afternoon. To say that she was in a mess would be an understatement. There was no way that she could raise the sort of money that she had lost by betting on the Index by the deadline that was set. She cast a glance over one of the envelopes that had arrived by that morning's post. She knew what it would be about. They would want money up front, a bit of cash on the nail to show, on her part, willing.

Fiona started to feel the fear and nerves that she had experienced only a short while ago, when she was being blackmailed. Once more, she wondered if she had not been just a bit stupid, getting involved with betting on the Financial Index. If she did not manage to raise the money by the settlement date, they would charge interest on it and she would owe even more.

There was another letter, this time addressed to both

herself and her husband. Fiona unwittingly opened it and saw that the payments on the mortgages she had taken out were just about to begin.

The good times were over.

* * *

Charles whistled most of the afternoon. Joy was in his heart and he felt decidedly light-headed with all the achievements of the day. What did it matter that he had lost a lot of money? The shares would bounce up in time and in any case, he doubted if his brothers were anywhere near to him in acquiring the fortune. What mattered most of all was the pounding of Bates and the total undermining of the marriage that he and Glenda had foolishly entered into. There was nothing like a financial crisis to push even the most lovey-dovey marriage to the brink of disaster.

Charles gave a thought about the scene when dear Mr. and Mrs. Bates returned from their honeymoon. There they would be with stars in their eyes and confetti barely out of their hair, entering their little abode. Perhaps he would be carrying her over the cottage threshold? Charles dismissed the thought as physically impossible considering the size of Glenda in proportion to the size of John. Then, Charles imagined, John would return to his flat to collect some stuff. There on the doorstep would be a letter informing him of the value that had been obtained by the sale of the shares.

The beginnings of penury!

* * *

Tony arrived back at the factory to find Amelia waiting for him. She was frowning slightly and appeared a little worried.

"Oh, thank goodness you're back," she said as soon as she spotted him coming up the stairs.

"What's up?" he asked, feeling the twinges of alarm in his body. Was it already too late?

"I've been waiting here for you to come," she began.

"Oh, darling, is that it? You've been worried about me!" interrupted Tony with relief.

"No, I mean yes. I've been worried about you but…"

"But what? I'm here now, so let's go. Let's get away from here!"

"No, listen. We must talk," she said, pushing his arms away. "While I've been sitting here, I've been looking through the order books."

"Yes?"

"And that's it! There are no orders, the book is empty!"

"Oh, no – it's not empty. You seem to be forgetting something here, Amelia," Tony replied sternly. He wanted to nip this dangerous situation in the bud straight away. "You charged me with modernising the place, didn't you?"

"Yes, but we still need orders, there are wages to pay, bills to settle!"

"Yes? So?"

"Well, I can't see how we can do either if there are no orders coming in!" said Amelia. By now she was looking very much the boss; she was coming on strong and feeling cross.

"Don't you trust me?"

"Yes, of course I do but," began Amelia.

"You don't trust me, do you?" continued Tony, his face was etched with pretend harshness, his body stiff with contrived annoyance.

"Of course I do but where are the orders – that's what I want to know!"

"And what is this?" Tony tapped the computer.

"It's a computer, I know that!" retorted Amelia.

"Well then, there is no point of having all this high tech equipment if you don't make use of it!"

"You mean the order details are in there?" asked Amelia.

Tony just smiled. He did not say yes and he did not say no, so nobody could ever accuse him of lying.

"That's amazing," said Amelia. To her, computer illiterate as she was, such things were amazing. "How do we get the information out then?"

"You don't want to sit here watching me press buttons, when we could be back at my place… enjoying ourselves…" suggested Tony.

Easily side-tracked from the issue, Amelia linked arms with her manager and sauntered off to their respective cars. Tony breathed a sigh of relief. Saved again!

* * *

James had a good vantage point, sitting in his car and spying on the comings and goings from his elder brother's household. He deduced that the woman with the faded looks must be Fiona. He watched her leave her car and enter the house. Ten minutes later, she emerged with a letter in her hand. This was the opportunity that James had been waiting for. He needed the element of surprise, to find her on her own.

He saw her step off towards the postbox and waited until she was out of sight before alighting from his car. Then, when he judged that she would be coming back, he walked into her.

"Hello?" he said questioningly.

"Hello," she replied, barely looking in his direction.

"Excuse me, but don't I know you?"

Fiona stared at him. "Maybe," she answered, unsure as to whether she recognised the man or not. There was something familiar about him.

James smiled and he was gratified that she smiled back at him.

"We do know each other, don't we?" he said. The truth of the matter was that they did not really know each other at all. James had deduced that the woman must be his sister-in-law by virtue of the fact that she was of the right age and living at the correct address. This knowledge gave him the advantage over Fiona; it meant that he could pretend to know her, to have met her before. Fiona merely saw her husband echoed in the look of James, the face and the build were familiar enough to her for her to think she had met him before.

"I'm James Pearson-Cooper," he announced to the startled Fiona.

"And I am Fiona Pearson-Cooper," she replied and then added, "I can't believe it! I thought you were in Australia. Did we meet, I can't remember but your face is so familiar – you have a look of Charles."

"Let me buy you a drink," James added warmly, "and then I can answer all your questions!"

Everything was going smoothly to plan, to James' plan that is!

* * *

Fiona had felt down and low as she wandered towards the postbox. She had written to Emma, telling her that everything would be alright and so on. In the letter were little bits of social chit-chat concerning the local conservatives, what funny thing Mrs Armitage had said that morning and other bits such as 'do you remember when…?'; it was the type of letter that Fiona knew would cheer her daughter up.

If only someone would cheer me up, Fiona thought as she plodded off to post the missive.

On the way back home, she spotted a rather attractive man who was slightly bronzed and bore an uncanny resemblance to Charles. She noticed him staring at her and tried to avoid catching his eye in case he thought her forward. However, after he had said hello, she took the opportunity to give him what her mother would have called 'the glad eye'.

She was pleased to accept his offer of a drink. She really needed someone to take her mind off life at present. Money owed to various institutions was growing at an alarming rate and she did not have a clue as to what she was going to do about it. A drink with her newly found brother-in-law was a form of escape for an hour or so.

Then maybe, she reckoned, she could pump him for information that would be of help to Charles.

* * *

There was a pot of tea waiting for Amelia just as soon as

she had got dressed and re-applied her make-up. Tony had laid out the cups and saucers on the table and arranged the tea tray next to them. Then he awaited her arrival in the lounge of his flat.

Patting the seat next to him, he urged her to sit down.

"It's wonderful having you here," he simpered just as soon as she had seated herself.

"I love being with you," was her reply. She did love being with him, she adored him in bed, she admired his work at the factory, she looked up to him as a manly example of all that a husband should be. It was true that Ralph had managed to secure a valuable site for Wilkinson's but, she considered after the initial euphoria had worn off and she began to view Ralph with the same faded look as before, just what wonders would Tony have achieved if he had been lucky enough to have been willed £100,000? Ralph was a soon forgotten being when she was with Tony; Ralph's years of steadfastness, his years of being a loyal husband faded into insignificance when compared with Tony.

"I don't think I ought to tell you this," began Tony.

"What? Tell me what?" Amelia loved to be teased and she saw this as the beginnings of a tease which might – she hoped – result in a little session right there on the lounge floor… she was game for anything!

"No, no!" Tony said, laughing at the same time.

"Yes, yes!" was the reply.

"No, because if I tell you, that would be it! You would want to do the same and then what?"

"How do you mean?" asked Amelia, her voice becoming slightly more serious.

"Well, if you knew, you'd be doing the same and

then off we two would go to – where? The West Indies, or perhaps France or maybe a villa in Spain!"

"What is all this about? You've got to tell me – a villa in Spain! Yes please!" she announced.

"See? That's what I mean – if I tell you then you'd be packing your bags and we'd be spending the next number of decades drinking wine and making love, as well as spending money, that is!"

Amelia's eyes had lit up. She loved to hear him include her in his plans. At times like this, all thoughts of her husband and children were firmly shut from her mind as she selfishly considered number one.

"Sounds great! Now tell me how?"

"Well," began Tony as he launched into his final play for a large slice of money – her money, "do you remember that I told you I was going to have my shareholding valued? You remember – I told you I wanted to buy a house for us to share our love in."

Did she remember? She most certainly did – she had thought of nothing else during those sterile days and nights she had been forced to spend with Ralph.

"Yes, so you've bought a chateau?" she asked in a teasing fashion.

"No, I haven't bought anything yet! It is what I could buy, that is what is interesting!"

"I don't understand, explain yourself," she demanded.

"You and I are sitting on a gold mine! I've had my shares valued. If my shareholding is worth a fortune, yours must be worth a fortune plus more!"

Amelia was amazed. She could hardly work out the sudden change in events. It was only a short while ago that the bank was breathing down their necks and behaving in a threatening manner, then with Tony talking to the bank manager and now… a fortune! A fortune plus more!

"So, I mean, what? What happens now? How do we get hold of the money? And where shall we live?" asked Amelia. She always believed totally in everything that Tony said. If he said that they were worth a fortune then they were. If he said they would live together in France then they would! To hell with Ralph – he could keep the house, the miserable house in Leeds, and the children if they wanted to stay with him (they were happy in their schools and Ralph was a good 'mother' to them, she concluded).

"Steady on, steady on," cautioned Tony and he held up his hands to halt her flow of enthusiasm. "One thing at a time!"

"First of all, you must buy me out. Look, I'll show you!" He produced the figures to back his claims.

"You must get the company valued too, so you have an independent valuation for comparison – but I assure you that this is what it is worth! Aren't you staggered?"

Amelia was indeed staggered. She could see that the wealth of the company lay in two areas: firstly, in the new industrial site and secondly, in its own site, the actual land that the factory was built on.

"The easiest thing to do would be to sell the industrial site first and pay me off. That would give me the money to purchase a property for us both abroad. I thought perhaps a chateau in France with cottages, gîtes I think they are called, for holiday lets. We could run the business from our mansion and spend our time having fun!"

Amelia was tickled with the plan, she just adored the

word 'our', but saw one immediate problem. "The bank loan is secured by that site – they would want their money back."

"No problem! Just tell them that you are ceasing trading and selling the factory site to Asda or Morrisons or whatever. In the interim, while you are waiting for the planning permission to be passed and for the supermarket company to buy, you can get a bridging loan from another bank, not a high street type; they will soon lend you the money to tide you over. No problem! Just as soon as they see Asda sniffing around your site, they'll want to help you out, I know these bank people. They're far more pliable than the high street chaps. They'll charge but it will be worth it. Just look again at this letter here and see what that valuer says someone like Asda will pay for your site! Can you believe it? Now, work out what your shares will be worth if you cease trading, settle your loans and sell up. You will be a very rich woman and then you can come and join me! I'll be keeping the bed warm and the wine cool!"

It was an invitation that Amelia could not refuse!

* * *

The pubs were not open yet, so James and Fiona went into the Northgate Tea Rooms for a pot of tea and a cake each. It was all very civilised and seemed just right to Fiona. In her mind, she saw the sordid episodes of the past number of months, the blackmailing and the debts, and she compared it with the dainty cakes and the Laura Ashley decorations. James was like a breath of fresh air.

"Funny, isn't it?" he began just as soon as the waitress

had deposited the teapot and other bits and pieces. "How this will business has brought us all together…"

"Well, not really all together," corrected Fiona.

James glanced at her and caught a slight glimmer of sadness flitting across her face. "You're right," he agreed, "but you know what I mean – before, we never made contact, now we are forced to compete. You know what?"

"What?"

"I've been in England for quite a while and I've not seen Blayborough House. I think I'm scared to have a look, in case I love it. I have vague memories of it, but that's all."

"Well, I'll tell you, it is marvellous! It is beautifully proportioned with the most magnificent parkland around it. Then there are the farms and the cottages – all set in acres and acres of gently rolling countryside. It's no wonder we are all fighting over it!" Fiona looked at him and smiled. He smiled back; his eyes were warm and loving.

James stared at the woman sitting opposite him and gave her one of his best looks. He considered that perhaps there was more to this sister-in-law of his than met the eye. He reckoned that she was about five years older than he was but sometimes, when he caught her unawares, she appeared ten years older or more, and then on other occasions, she seemed ten years younger. He had half a mind to ask her outright just how Charles was getting on but decided against it because he thought he might frighten her off. He did contrast her with Jenny, which had been the only other female contact he had had since coming to England (he had become quite celibate, a state which was a trifle frustrating to a red-

blooded Aussie like he considered himself now to be).
Jenny was a mere child. Fiona was a woman, with depth
and experience; she was also a lady and an aura of
refinement surrounded her.

"And how is Charles?" James asked, hoping she
might drop some information that would help him,
information as to how she saw Charles. People became
quite unguarded if you offered them friendship when
they needed it badly.

"Charles is full of himself, as usual," she replied. Her
face told him a fuller story...

James continued to stare at her and she melted, right
there in front of his eyes.

"And how is Fiona?" he enquired gently.

Fiona's tears trickled down her cheeks. James paid
the bill and led her away.

* * *

"Sometimes just talking to a complete stranger
helps," suggested James, "and the best thing about me
is that not only am I a complete stranger, but I am also
your brother-in-law!" He laughed a little, hoping that
the remark would lighten the situation. It did and Fiona
opened up slightly.

"I don't think I know where to begin!" she said as
they walked around the park together.

"At the beginning," said James, holding her arm in
his and guiding her towards a vacant bench.

Fiona wanted to talk to him. She found him friendly
and warm. Yet she knew that it was unfair to burden
him with her troubles and also to tell him before she
informed Charles. It was Charles, after all, who would

have to sort it all out, not his brother James. In the back of her mind was the niggling worry that to confide in James would be a betrayal of confidence. She decided to resist him and not open up.

"I feel better now," she lied, "I think it would be better if I went home."

"And I can see you again?" he asked.

"In a fortnight," she suggested. "Here, at this time in two weeks."

James nodded his head in agreement and watched as Fiona walked away. He looked forward to her return, to prising her away from her husband and doing to his brother a similar deed that Charles did to their mother.

* * *

Fiona knew that she must tell Charles everything within two weeks. It was not just that she had promised to meet James in two weeks' time, it was also for other good reasons too. For example, the court case was due to be heard and she wanted to witness Page being sent down on all accounts; also, she had been given two weeks' grace to find the money she owed various people.

If it had just been the question of the blackmailing then she could have perhaps got away with not saying a word. Unfortunately, there was the money and that would take a lot of explaining!

Between now and two weeks' time, she had to tell Charles everything!

* * *

Fiona left it until the very last day. She could not carry the burden any longer. She needed the sting of being told off. The police had been very understanding. The attempt to recover the money through various means might have helped to reduce the feeling of hopelessness. However, no one had actually told her off, she had never really felt the expunging of her guilt through someone punishing her. She felt as though she could not continue her life until a person had said to her, "You've been bad. You must suffer." She had suffered, through guilt, and she had suffered with the worry about the money, but they were self-induced sufferings. What she needed was someone to sit in judgement on her and find her guilty; to serve a sentence and put it all behind her. She had to tell Charles everything. He would find her guilty. He would pass sentence.

Fiona invited Charles into the drawing room and then closed the door behind him. She told him to sit down as there was something she wanted to tell him.

She told him about Page and the blackmailing. His reaction was as predictable as she hoped it would be.

"What the hell were you doing with him?" There was nothing short of contempt written all over his face.

Fiona could not reply – how could a wife tell her husband what explicit things she did with other men, things that she would have never done with him in a million years?

"Well then? Come on now," he began, his mouth sneering at her. "I've a right to know! Did they…" and he started to list acts that were both repugnant when crudely described and true when matched against the events that Fiona recalled.

There was no answer.

Charles taunted her again, "Is it true what they say about black men? I mean, you should know, you must be an expert!"

Fiona sat in her seat with her head bowed in shame.

"Do say, Fiona dear, is it good with more than one?" Lines of hatred showed themselves and his eyes pierced with disgust.

"Lost your tongue, or have you had it wrapped round a penis so much…"

Fiona couldn't take anymore; she rose swiftly from her chair and struck Charles across the face. He grabbed her hands and putting his face within an inch of hers, shouted, "So that's what you like now, is it? Scum…" And he started to walk out of the door.

She called out after his retreating figure, "You've got to help me, I owe a lot of money, I had to pay him, I had to buy him off!"

"Your problem!" Charles answered.

* * *

"Have you got in contact with the landlord yet?" John asked of his wife.

"He won't fix the roof, I've told you time and time again," protested Glenda. It was raining again and she had had to rearrange the buckets to catch the ever increasing drops.

"Well, perhaps he will listen to me!" suggested John threateningly. "Of course, if you would tell me just who owns the property then perhaps I would be able to get something sorted out!"

"I can't see why finding out who owns the house will help you. I've told you that he refuses to have the roof mended, can't you just leave it at that?"

"No, I can't. Your legal position is quite clear..."

"Legal position? Legal position!" Glenda puffed out her cheeks and expelled the collected air, as if to demonstrate just what she thought of the legal position.

"There is no point in pooh-poohing what I say. If it is anything about the law, I should be handling it," and then he added as an afterthought, "he might listen to a man!"

"I very much doubt it!" replied Glenda, knowing Charles very well. Charles only listened to Charles.

"Look, Glenda, it is now the beginning of November and this roof has been leaking since the day we got married. That tarpaulin had been on for over a fortnight! You are the tenant, he is the landlord; he should fix the roof for us!"

"Can't you get the roof fixed?" asked Glenda, trying hard to find a solution to this tricky situation.

"Why should I? In any case, you know I haven't any money!"

Glenda reflected on that fact. How could she tell him that the cottage was owned by Charles? The very same person who had delivered a letter to the stockbroker that her John had signed previously when the times were good; a letter that had resulted in a very low sum of money finding its way into the bank account. The very person John had thought was responsible for spreading the dirt around about him.

The amount of money was not dismal but it certainly was not enough to help them through the present circumstances. When they returned from their honeymoon, John had come home and told her that his dreams of being made a senior partner, of having a massive salary, injected with directors' fees and so on, had all come to nothing. He would remain as an important, but not particularly well paid, company law specialist. He had decided not to approach the other partners, as he had planned to do all those months ago, because he did not have those ingredients. He could not offer them tasty morsels which he thought he had managed to capture a few weeks previously, for there had been a slur campaign against him and though he could not point his finger exactly at Charles, that is where he thought the blame lay. The slur campaign had resulted in important clients defecting to other practices. He felt that he was lucky, in the circumstances, to keep his job. He did ponder, in the days that followed the realisation that his future was sealed in its present state, that perhaps he could return the 'favour' and throw the muck around about Charles, but he decided against it. He might pull himself into the mire with that man and make his life worse than it already was.

"Look," began Glenda, "I'll give it one last try and then you can have a go!"

John, satisfied, went off to work and left Glenda to tackle the landlord. Married life, they both reflected to themselves, was not a bed of roses!

* * *

The telephone rang and Charles picked it up. He recognised Glenda's voice straight away and knew just what she was ringing about: the blasted roof!

"Oh, Charles, thank goodness you're in!" she began.

"Enjoying married life, are we?" asked Charles. There was a bite in his voice, which Glenda detected right away. This was the first time that she had talked to him for quite a while. He had disappeared mysteriously from her life. She did not even have the chance to explain to him the reason she had accepted the marriage proposal that John had made. She had not had the opportunity to tell him that she was not getting any younger and that she could not keep going in the same fashion for ever. She needed constant companionship and love and friendship that would endure through her middle age and until her death.

"I'm sorry. It must have been a shock to you," she murmured.

"No shock! You women are all the same!" he replied with vehemence in his voice.

Glenda did not know what to say. She knew nothing of the shock that Charles had just received at the hands of his wife. She thought that she better begin with the task she had set out for herself, the job of trying to get Charles to do something about the roof of his cottage.

"Fix the roof? No way!" was his reply.

"But you have to!" she exclaimed, "I live in the house; it's your duty as the owner. You are legally bound..."

"Legally bound?" he retorted. "Good God, you're even beginning to sound like him! Let's get the facts straight: Cottage Holidays Ltd owns the house and I rent the cottage from them. I am the tenant!"

"Oh, so what does that mean?" asked Glenda.

"It means that I have every right to come and live in that cottage with you two."

"But you can't..." replied Glenda, feeling dreadfully worried.

"But I can!" was the answer she feared.

* * *

Amelia was delighted to accept Tony's advice concerning who to appoint as a valuer. She was not surprised at all that the man knew Tony, after all, Tony, as she had discovered, was a very popular businessman, with friends in many professions. The valuer did not take long to prepare his report.

"Mrs Pearson-Cooper," he began, "I am loathe to admit it but really the best thing for you to do is to shut up shop! You could always start again in one of those enterprise zones, if you have a mind to, but please, while the going is good, go out for the top value you can get for this site!"

"How do you mean, while the going is good?" questioned Amelia. She had invited the man into her office to give her a preview of the situation, prior to him having the report typed out.

"While the supermarkets are on the up and up; they are desperate for new sites and are very keen to increase their share of the market. At the moment, the supermarket giants are pegging out the country, marking out their patches. Get in there now! Look, Mrs Pearson-Cooper, I have prepared you a map."

He produced a map of that part of Leeds, demonstrating the catchment areas that the groups were looking at. In varying colours representing the different companies, he had drawn in the sites that were already occupied and the populations they called on.

"Yes, I can see," agreed Amelia. It was all so wonderfully clear; there on the map was her factory and there was a gap in the grand and expanding scheme; the ever increasing supermarket tentacle had not quite covered the factory's area. It was almost as if they were just waiting for her to release the land!

"I cannot say for definite, I do not know what they already have boiling away in the pot," said the valuer, disclaiming himself from a situation that he might not realise was happening. For all he knew, protracted discussions could already be taking place in the area, and so he did not want Mrs Pearson-Cooper coming back to him at a later date, threatening all hell and fury.

"Indeed, indeed," agreed Amelia.

"But my advice to you would be go for it!"

Amelia, tired of playing at factory owner and longing for the good life, decided to take his advice.

"Could you open up negotiations with Asda, Sainsbury's or whatever and see what the state of play is?" suggested Amelia.

"Of course," he agreed, "I'll prepare the groundwork for you!"

* * *

That afternoon in November saw Fiona waiting on the park bench for James to arrive. Having told Charles, she felt a lot better. Charles had not spoken to her since but that she could bear, for his conversation was not the most uplifting at the best of times. They had long ceased to enjoy intimate chats about this and that, private jokes and innermost fears. Of late, they had engaged in a certain amount of frankness about their daughter Emma and her sufferings, as well as how to rectify the tremendous reductions that their share dealings had suffered. However, as Charles had pointed out, they had increased their net worth in spite of the crash. That remark was before she informed him of the losses that she herself had incurred. Though he remarked that it was her problem, it was, of course, a joint problem. The mortgages were in both their names and disentangling himself from the situation that his wife had put him in might be so awkward and costly as well as fruitless, that is was not worth his bother. Charles had not inquired as to the exact amount of debt that Fiona had incurred; no doubt he would decide that he had better take an interest when the threatening letters multiplied.

"Fiona, glad to see you!" said James.

"James," she replied by way of saying hello.

"Let's walk down here," he suggested and together they wandered around the park. James wanted to coax her into telling him everything. He needed to know just what her position was with her husband. Had they quarrelled? Was he having an affair? Had he already made a fortune and secured Blayborough House? Once he had the information, he would know just how to act.

"Feeling better now?" he asked.

"Much," Fiona replied.

"You know, everybody makes mistakes in life. There can't be a person in the whole country who doesn't feel shame at something or other. Guilt haunts many a man and woman – if it didn't then that person must have no conscience! Sometimes I look back and shudder at the things I have done!"

Fiona smiled and admitted that she shuddered more often than she cared to admit!

"There you are! You suffer from a guilty conscience and that is a good thing! It means that you'll never do that thing again!"

This was the first time that Fiona had seen it that

way. She had never realised that the feeling of absolute abhorrence at what she had done was in fact good in itself – it was her mind's method of making sure that she never went that way again!

"You could be right!" she admitted.

"Of course I'm right!" he said, and then he added, "Look, first of all you have to tell yourself that everybody makes a mess, everybody has their own private hell; then, you have to see that the sufferings that you are going through are all part of your mind telling you not to go down that path again!"

Fiona was perking up at all this. At last it was being explained to her and she could start to put it all behind her.

"So what did you do that was so terrible? Did you murder someone?"

"No, of course not!" she protested.

"Well, that's a relief, because if you had said yes then I might not have wanted to continue to walk down this lonely path. I mean, you can see how weak I am and how easily you could overpower me!"

Fiona laughed at this and felt even better.

"Have you pinched something or battered an old lady on the head?"

"No, but I have signed a document pretending to be Charles and acquired rather a lot of money because of that…" admitted Fiona. James' ears perked up at this; at last he was getting to the nub.

"Well, Charles is your husband so that isn't really pinching in my book – what's his is yours and all that."

"I don't think Charles sees it that way!" said Fiona, mindful of the attitude that Charles had displayed when she had told him about owing some money.

"So what did you need the money for?" asked James, wanting to get to the nub of the problem.

"I was being blackmailed," she answered. Oh, how easy it was to talk to this man, she thought to herself. How she could tell him everything and get it off her chest! It was true that by telling Charles, she had felt the pain of being punished, but now she needed to be fully expunged of her guilt. James squeezed her arm as he led her around past the now empty flower beds.

"Blackmail is a horrible thing," he told her, "you are caught between the guilt of what you have done, the horror of having to admit it to the authorities in order to put a halt to the blackmailer and the constant hope that if you pay him off, he will go quietly away!"

"I paid him off but he just wanted more!"

"Of course, you see, a blackmailer knows that the fear of the sin that you feel you have committed is what makes you pay up. He does not see what you have done as particularly bad, he does not see it in the same light as you do. He knows, however, that you see it as something dreadful and thus begins his extraction of money!"

"You can say that again!" Once more Fiona smiled. Here was a man who understood what she had gone through!

"So what terrible thing did you do then?" asked James. It was not that he wanted to have a hold over Fiona; it was just that he needed to know so that he could judge just what the position was between Fiona and Charles. Once he had that type of information, he would know exactly what to do.

There was a pause and it was apparent that Fiona did not want to answer his question.

"Okay, let's play twenty questions!" he suggested. "Were you being blackmailed by a man?"

Fiona nodded her head.

"Question number two," asked James, "had you been to bed with him?"

"Sort of."

"Interesting!" laughed James, relishing his little inquisition.

"What type of man was he?" asked James. He was trying a different tact now.

"He was a charmer, I suppose," admitted Fiona, for indeed he had been a bit of a charmer in the beginning.

"Was he a rich man?"

"Heavens, no! I mean, I think all his money went on drugs! Or rather, I should say, I think all my money went on drugs!" she admitted somewhat ruefully.

James had sufficiently softened Fiona up for her to tell him all about it, for once he had started questioning her, she began to feel the need to give him all the details. She spared him nothing. Every little gory detail she told him about.

"Well, that's nothing much to get ashamed over," said James quite truthfully. "Let me tell you just what I got up to last year. Now that will really make your hair curl!"

James told her all about his trip into the heart of Australia that he had undertaken with a group of men and women.

"Now, that certainly would have given someone something to blackmail me over!" Fiona laughed and he joined in and held her even tighter.

* * *

During January 1988, negotiations were nearing completion and the sale of the industrial site was about to go through. Amelia had entered into preliminary talks with another banking organisation about transferring the loan and overdraft as a temporary measure. They, naturally enough, wanted the marital home as security and the original lenders agreed to release it once their loans were repaid.

By spring, she hoped to have the factory shut and the site sold to become a supermarket. The bank was quite happy to be shot of Wilkinson's, Bernard having decided privately that the whole thing might just as easily go down the shoot as not.

Ralph was less than happy. He had just over £20,000 in the building society and had very little chance to make up the difference by April. He hardly saw anything of Amelia; she seemed to spend all her time elsewhere. The children were left constantly in his care and were not easy to look after at the best of times. At the worst of times, when his mind was distracted with the worries about money, Amelia and so on, they were a real handful.

One Monday morning in the middle of January, he had taken them to school, along with a couple of their friends. When he returned to the empty house, he made himself a coffee as a prelude to his usual tasks of bed making, washing up and so on. His wife, who had disappeared very early in the morning, had given no indication as to when she intended to return that day.

"She never even tells me how things are going at the factory – and it is my money which is bankrolling it all! Without that site, she would never have got that loan! What is going on there, that's what I'd like to know?" Ralph mumbled to himself.

Ralph did not have a clue how trade was. Amelia had become very evasive when he asked. He did not know, for example, that she intended to buy Tony out. Naturally, he was also unaware that she was entering into negotiations that would result in the closing of the factory altogether and the sale of the site that the factory was built on. The idea of a chateau in France was one thing that was kept very private between Tony and Amelia. It was the little flame which kept Amelia going.

Just as he was starting to drink his coffee, the telephone rang.

"Mr. Pearson-Cooper?" began a female voice. "It is the Headmistress of your daughter's school here."

"Yes?" answered Ralph, already alert to a possible problem.

"I am sorry to have to tell you but your daughter has had a slight accident during a PE lesson. It is nothing to worry about but we think she may have broken a bone in her leg. Now, we have called an ambulance but we would be grateful if you could make your way over to Leeds General and perhaps take over from the games mistress. Naturally, we are very concerned about the accident but I must assure you that we feel the school was in no way to blame."

"I'm not interested in who is to blame! I just want to comfort her and be with her!" exclaimed Ralph.

"Of course, of course, but I was just making the point because there will be questions asked – by yourself perhaps..."

"Goodbye!" Ralph put the phone down on the woman before she could extricate herself any further from blame.

He quickly phoned the factory to get in touch with

his wife but was told she was not there, so he left it at that and went straight to the casualty department of Leeds General.

* * *

Charles had been in a furious state for a number of weeks. His anger was becoming so commonplace that Fiona had begun to forget just what his normal mood was. He did have a right to be angry, that she had to admit, for the full extent of the financial misfortune to hit the household was coming out. He had managed to secure stay of executions on a number of the debts that she incurred on their behalf but he was none too pleased at having to waste his time sorting out the mess.

"You do realise that I'm having to use the money that has been amassed to win Blayborough? I mean, this little bit of action with half the male Jamaican population is costing me a fortune. If I lose this house or indeed Blayborough …" and with that threat hanging in the air, he stormed off.

There was only one thing that had cheered him up and that was the little escapade he had indulged in on Christmas day. The memory of this incident kept his spirits up throughout the dark winter days of January. While all the family were tucking into their turkey – Emma included, now fully back to her normal self – he had set off on a mission. He was smiling, for once, and Fiona was delighted to see it.

He drove his car to visit Glenda. All the way there, he was barely able to drive at the thought of what was to come. He slowly pulled up and parked in front of the cottage, and, noticing the tarpaulin still there, he got out of his car. He then opened up the boot and dragged out a large suitcase.

As he went around the back of the house, he heard strains of the Queen's speech. Glancing in, he noticed Glenda and John, sitting down on the sofa wearing paper hats, thick woollies and other assorted warm clothing. Charles knocked on the door.

John Bates answered it and was surprised to see who was standing on the doorstep, complete with suitcase.

"John, nice to see you!" said Charles, grinning falsely.

"Charles is here…" shouted John, wondering just what on earth Charles was doing standing on the doorstep with a case in his hands.

Glenda froze. It was the very thing she feared. She started to rise from her chair to try and defuse the situation before Charles could get into the cottage, but it was too late.

"Glenda!" said Charles. "I'm here!"

"Here?" questioned John. "What do you mean, here?"

"Can we talk privately?" asked Glenda, trying to push Charles and his large case out of the living room.

"There is nothing to talk about!" Charles said, determined not to budge one inch.

"Can someone please tell me just what is going on?" asked John, highly mystified as to what Charles was doing there on Christmas afternoon and looking as though he was intending to stay a while.

"Simple, old chap," began Charles as Glenda sank back into her seat, feeling her age. "This is my cottage, I pay the rent, my company owns it, and I am coming here to live!"

"Glenda? Do something, Glenda?" John begged as Charles stood there, master of all he could see.

"Glenda? Is it true? Is he the landlord? I mean, does he own it? And is he the tenant as well?" John asked and then, realising the full implication of it all, said "Glenda, you and him? You weren't, were you?"

"We were, weren't we, Glenda? I believe I had the lion's share, being the weekday boyfriend; you were Saturdays only, I understand. Glenda, Sundays – who came on Sunday? Not the vicar, Glenda, surely not the vicar!"

Charles stayed long enough to see John pack his bags and leave for his own flat, muttering about needing time to think it all over. The flat he was returning to was empty as if it was just waiting for its master to come home.

In the weeks that followed, John and Glenda patched things up on one condition: Glenda had to find another house for the two of them to live in. She could only get one in Ripon, which was disappointing for her.

"Ripon is not a place," she concluded in the weeks after the incident with Charles, when the sting of it all had died down, "that one runs around in the garden starkers in! I'm going to miss my little bit of private paradise!"

* * *

Ralph actually managed to arrive at the hospital before his daughter did. He waited there for the ambulance to bring her in and was overjoyed to see her still chirpy.

"Where's Mum?" was her first question. Ralph promised to try and get hold of her again and went off in search of a telephone. When he found one, he spoke to the receptionist at Wilkinson's. She was quite new and she had never heard Ralph's voice before.

"Is Mrs. Pearson-Cooper in?" Ralph asked.

"I'm sorry but she is out with her manager," replied the receptionist.

"Is there any way I could get hold of her?" continued Ralph. "Do you have a number I could ring?"

"You could try Mr. Driver's number, I did hear that they were going to his house," she told him, so innocently.

She gave him the number and Ralph felt himself going cold as he murmured his thanks. He then reached into his pocket and got out some more change. Dialling the number, he wondered just what would happen when someone answered the telephone.

"Tony Driver here," the voice went.

"Is my wife there?" Ralph asked in a small voice. There was a pause and then Amelia came to the phone.

"Ralph! I just called in here to collect some documents, Tony's car had broken down and he needed someone to run him over to his flat. You just caught me – dashing in and dashing out!"

"I'm not interested," said Ralph. "Kirsty is in hospital…"

"Hospital!" interrupted Amelia. "Why? What's happened?"

"She's broken her leg. She is in Leeds General and she is asking for her mother – though I am surprised she can remember what her mother looks like!"

Ralph replaced the telephone and went back to where they were treating his daughter. He felt strange; both sad and dejected but free and unencumbered at the same time. It was a weird feeling.

"Daddy, was she cross with you for disturbing her?" was the first thing Kirsty asked.

"No, of course not darling," was his reply. "Whatever makes you say that?"

"Because she doesn't seem to love us anymore, does she, Daddy?"

Ralph squeezed her hand and, smiling through his tears, said, "True but I love you and I always will."

* * *

Charles had sorted most of the financial mess out by the end of January. He still barely talked to Fiona. Life in the household was conducted by a series of nods and grunts. He had decided to leave one large gambling debt for her to settle, as a sort of penance for the suffering that she had caused him. The sale of his two cottages, under his business name, was going through. He had been much gratified to find that Glenda had gone and he set to work appointing a roofer to effect repairs on the cottage.

In his own mind, he saw just February and March to get through before the big day when, hopefully, Blayborough House would be his. He had made preliminary enquiries with Paul Winstanley as to how the other two were getting on but Paul would not give anything away. He did mention that James was in the district, a fact that quite surprised Charles. He concluded that he must be lying low, for Bates, in those months that they were on relatively friendly terms, had not mentioned him at all. The conclusion that Charles drew was that James could not possibly be perceived as much of a threat.

Then (and this made him smirk with delight), when he was awarded Blayborough, as he knew that he ought to be, it would be goodbye, Fiona.

After all, he thought, she could not really complain, for what other husband would settle debts that had been caused by his wife's sexual habits?

* * *

Amelia made a conscious decision to avoid Tony for a few weeks, at least until Kirsty was out of hospital. Ralph had been a little cold with her and Amelia did not want him cutting up rough before she had a chance to sort everything out. She planned to leave him the house. It was only right that he should be left that. It had a mortgage on it but, if he got a job, he should be able to pay that – just about, anyway.

Tony was extremely pleased to be nearly getting his hands on the money. He was counting the days until the deal was signed with the major building contractors who were buying the site off Wilkinson's. As January went into February, his attendance at the factory became less frequent. There was very little being produced and the workers were grumbling. They were talking of possible redundancies and Tony did not feel that he could face them and all their problems.

Once all had died down at home and was back onto a relatively even keel, Amelia judged that she could safely return to the arms of Tony. What better time to do that than the day she would hand over the banker's draft for his share?

* * *

Ralph welcomed the brief respite from his wife's lack of interest. He enjoyed the few weeks that she appeared to be her old self again. He watched her carefully, checking her movements, though. He knew that once a person had tasted blood, so to speak, they always wanted more.

It was the evening after she had been to see the firm's new solicitor, the evening that she announced that she was 'just popping to a friend's house, and would only be a couple of hours!'

That was the evening that Ralph hastily arranged a babysitter and 'popped out' too, calling in at the local riding stables on the way.

* * *

"I've missed you," she whispered, "oh, how I've missed you!"

Tony turned to face her. He returned the compliment. It was easy to say words; even easier now that he was clutching a banker's draft.

"Have you got anything fixed up?" she asked, propping herself up on the bed to view him all the better.

"I've had a few things in mind!" He lied so well. "But don't ask any more about it! I want it to be a surprise for you!"

She smiled at him. She was so in love, so deeply infatuated.

"I'll be able to join you in a couple of months. I don't know how I'm going to manage without being near you!"

Tony pulled her towards him and kissed her hard on the lips.

"Then we had better make love again, so that you

have something to remember me by!"

They did not hear the front door of the flat open. Nor did they see Ralph enter the bedroom.

Ralph watched them for a second, writhing on the bed, then he emptied a large bag of horse manure all over them.

"Shit!" he shouted out. "That is just what you both are – lumps of shit!"

* * *

The next morning, Amelia returned to the marital home. She had spent at least half an hour the previous night showering, trying to get all the horse muck out of her hair. Even when she knew that it must have all gone, she stayed under water, quite convinced that she could still smell it! Tony had been strangely silent since Ralph's 'attack'. Amelia had not noticed at first, for she was more concerned with cleaning the mess up. Then, during the early hours, he had snapped out of his mood and was back to his old self again.

"The best thing to have happened," was how he had described it, "it's brought everything out into the open!"

Amelia was overjoyed; so he still thought the world of her, she concluded, in spite of being covered in lumps of horse dung!

"Yes, that's true!" she agreed.

"I do love you so," he said, so convincingly. She believed him, as he knew that she would.

Amelia practically purred with delight and murmured that she just could not wait until they were together properly. "Tell me where you have in mind! Please!"

"No, I said it would be a surprise!" was his answer to her pleadings. Then he adopted a thoughtful look which caused her to ask him what the matter was.

"Well, my love," he began, "if I stay around here much longer, it is going to make life very difficult for you. Ralph will start dragging his heels, refusing to let you go."

"Oh, I don't think so," she replied. "After what he did here, I'm sure he'd be desperate to get rid!"

"No, that's not how I see it – my fear is, you see, that he will do all he can to prevent you from leaving him."

Amelia turned to him, her eyes shining brightly with a brilliant idea. "Then I'll go now! With you!"

Tony was inwardly horrified but tried not to look as though he was. "How I wish you could!" he said, trying to appear tender. "Oh, how I wish you could, but how can you? Our future is only half secure – we need the extra money from the sale of the factory site, then we can live in luxury. I only want you to have the best, you know that!"

Amelia thanked him for thinking so much of her welfare. She reluctantly agreed that perhaps the best thing would be for her to return home and get the site sold to a supermarket giant.

"And if I stay around here, why, it would just be rubbing salt in his wounds," he added. "Before you know where you are, he'll be wanting more than his fair share of all the money as part of the divorce settlement!"

"I hadn't thought of that!" she admitted, "Yes, of course, he'll be entitled to some of the money, perhaps even half!"

"So, darling, get all those legal things tied up in our favour! This is where I'll be staying in France – it is a little guest house near to the property I've picked for us!" He wrote down an address in France and she popped it into her handbag, treasuring it as one might a valuable diamond.

* * *

Just after nine the morning after the dreadful showdown, Amelia returned home to face the music. By half past nine, Tony had gone to the bank with the banker's draft and arranged for the amount to be deposited in his account. It was a lovely large dollop of money! It would look even better, Tony concluded, in American dollars! He checked that all his arrangements were in order. He had his work permit and his visa all fixed up, for he had been preparing for this for a few months. What had caught him on the hop was the incident with Ralph, he now had to bring his plans forward a month.

However, the travel agent was most accommodating and said that if he paid for his tickets now, he could collect them at the BA desk at Heathrow later on in the day.

"So it's a single ticket you're wanting to the States? Not a return?"

Tony smiled at the attractive girl and confirmed that he was not coming back.

* * *

Ralph had been deep in thought ever since he had returned from the little fracas. He had come to only one conclusion, one solution to the problem he was now in.

It was a very neat answer. He spent the hour after dawn congratulating himself on achieving what would turn out to be his pièce de résistance. He shepherded the children off to school in their friend's mother's Volvo and awaited his wife's return.

Oh joy! He heard the key turn in the latch! A sheepish looking Amelia entered the lounge and Ralph went into action with part one of his master plan.

"You look better with clothes on!" he informed her.

What could she say in reply?

Then he sniffed the air (there was no smell but his wife, who felt so self-conscious about it all, was quite convinced that lingering somewhere on her was the contents of a stable) and rolled his eyes.

"That wasn't necessary," she said with reference to the incident the night before.

"Wasn't necessary? In France I'd have shot you both and got away with it!"

The mention of the word France brought the image of Tony to the fore and Amelia straight away decided to tackle the bull by the horns and face Ralph with the truth.

"He's going to live in France…" she began.

"And I suppose that you'll be wanting to join him?" he asked.

Amelia chose not to reply and instead gave him the caring look that he recognised from old. Ralph glared at her for daring to imply that she was needed!

"I think that a divorce is what we both require. Let's not beat around the bush – you will be wanting to join him as soon as you can! I propose to make it a quick settlement, though no doubt the actual mechanics of the whole thing will take ages. I have been thinking and I will be seeing a solicitor today!"

Amelia could hardly believe the speed of it all! In her mind, she was already rid of the factory and taking residence in some chateau.

"What type of settlement?" she inquired, in case the speed of the whole thing involved her losing out somewhere.

"A generous one, I think!" he replied. "I shall give you what is left of my legacy and relinquish my rights to the house. This will enable you to settle all your debts with the factory; naturally I will be severing my links with Wilkinson's and perhaps you'll be able to salvage something out of the wreck!"

Amelia did not mention that she hoped to make a bit of a killing from 'the wreck'. She knew that she had to go to Tony with ample funds – she was not so stupid as not to realise that part of her attraction laid in her access to money! A quick calculation in her mind worked out that she could come out of this most definitely on top. However, speed was of the essence for she did not want Ralph to change his mind.

A thought did occur to her: "What about the children?" she asked.

"I couldn't possibly have the children," he replied, "for you would have the house!"

Oh dear! she thought to herself. I suppose they'll have to come with me!

* * *

Ralph was as good as his word and he disappeared that afternoon to a solicitor to arrange everything. The solicitor wanted to make the whole procedure last many hours of his time. He warned against making generous settlements, especially ones which left the aggrieved party penniless, as this one was doing.

Ralph took no notice and instead insisted on a document being drawn up within the month. He voluntarily left the house and took up residence in a bedsit. A job as a bartender completed the end of stage one of his wonderful plan.

* * *

Amelia had written to the address in France telling Tony about how the plans were going, how Ralph had been so considerate and so on. Days had passed and she had received no reply. She concluded that he must be busy getting things ready for her. Meanwhile, she went ahead with preparations for the divorce, delighted with the generosity of her husband.

In between checking up on the running down of the factory (this was not a hard task for the factory had come to a standstill shortly after Tony had left) and asking how the negotiations were going on for the sale of the site, Amelia and the children were learning French. They had quite taken to the idea of going to live across the Channel. The thought of the impending divorce did not seem to worry them in the slightest. Like all children, they were attracted to staying with the parent that offered them the most. *Pauvre Papa*, as they referred to him now.

Ralph did think that they might have put up a little bit of resistance to going to live with their mother in some foreign country, but she had drawn such a glowing picture of life in France that compared with sharing a cramped bedsit with their father, it seemed somewhat like paradise! They did promise to visit him next Christmas – if he had managed to have bought a house by then!

* * *

Tony penned his old friend James Pearson-Cooper a note, informing him of his address in New England.

'I think that you can safely say that I destroyed him for you! Favour fully returned!' was the final line of the letter.

James smirked with unconcealed delight at the missive he received and announced out loud to his empty cottage: "Goodbye, Ralph, brother dear!" And then he added, "Now, dear Charles, your time is up…"

* * *

James and Fiona had made love many times since they had first met. They had quite surprised each other with their range of skills – she had attributed his to the indulgence he had sought in the bush; he considered that hers had definitely been well taught! To James, the situation had taken a strange turn. He had intended to upset the apple cart by seducing his sister-in-law and then exposing the marriage as a fraud. He never saw himself as a particularly revengeful sort on the whole – apart from, that is, desiring the downfall of his two brothers. He needed to get his own back on Charles for what he had done to his mother all those years ago. However, he had not planned on falling in love with Fiona.

By the time the first day of April had dawned, they

were wondering what to do about the situation.

"Come to Australia with me – I'm sick to death of this country!" he had suggested to her.

"I'd love to but Charles has left me with £10,000 to pay back. I'm supposed to be paying it back bit by bit – I have to get a job to find the money! After all these years, I'm having to take employment!"

"£10,000 isn't much. Charlie boy will soon find that little sum! It's small change for the likes of him!"

Fiona was horrified. The thought of reneging on her debts had not occurred to her honest soul! She lifted herself up on the bed in his rented cottage and told him that she could not possibly do that, "I mean, it would be un-gentlemanly of me!"

"Un-gentlemanly? Well, if that is all that's worrying you then sweat no more! You're not a gentleman, so off to Oz we go! You and me and my £100,000 plus all that lovely interest!"

"You can't go off to Australia with that money! You have to return it."

"Return it? I've no intention of returning it. I'm withdrawing it from the bank in Britain and heading back home with it. What type of fool do you think I am?"

"But you're not supposed to do that!"

"And who do you think is going to stop me? Winstanley? Your husband? Brother Ralph?"

She had to admit that it was highly unlikely that anybody could stop him from doing just what he wanted with the money.

"I mean, you have already intimated that Charles has managed to acquire far more than I have, so he is bound to win. So, why should I stay around to hand back that little fortune to him! In any case, we need the money more than he does!"

Fiona kissed him on the lips and then congratulated him on his excellent idea.

"You know, I never thought about just running off with the money!"

"That's the trouble with you English, you're too damn honest!" he said.

"But you're English too!"

"Ah, but you forget, I was dispatched to Australia for being a naughty boy! Just like the original convicts were!"

* * *

By April, the new bank that had been given the joy of dealing with the Wilkinson Engineering Works and its bank accounts was not very happy about the state of affairs that was developing. They had kept a very close eye on it all, ever since they took the account over on a moment of foolishness based on reading too much into valuation reports and projected figures. They had amalgamated all the various loans and so on into one big loan with themselves, so that they could control the affairs of the company better. When they had taken over the account, they had been told of its prosperous future and the valuable site that the factory was sitting on. The projections based on the orders, they had quickly found out, were dissolving like early morning mists, leaving nothing behind but the dew – each dew-drop being a debt owed. The bank comforted itself with the knowledge that their debt was covered by equity in the house and site. They pressed for details about the possible sale of the site and were fobbed off by Amelia. She told them that negotiations were in hand.

Amelia, for her part, was starting to panic. On the morning that the postman delivered a packet marked from the post office and found it contained the letters she had sent to France, returned as unknown at this address, she received a telephone call.

It was the person who was supposed to be spearheading her campaign to sell the site.

"It's not looking very good, Mrs Pearson-Cooper," he began, "not looking good at all!"

"What do you mean?"

"I mean, well, to be quite frank, I mean…"

"Do spit it out!" she demanded.

"No one is interested in it! Asda have earmarked another site and Sainsbury's have an option on a disused car park…"

"Well, there are more companies than just those two!"

The man went on to explain that if those companies went ahead then the council would not let another firm into the area. "And in any case, there are only so many shoppers!"

Amelia was shocked about this turn of events. "But I was assured by a valuer!"

"I don't know who could have told you that but he was having you on! I'm afraid you will just have to sell your factory site as, well, as a factory site but you won't get much for it. Everybody wants to be on those new sites!"

* * *

Amelia's mind was in a total muddle by the beginning

of April. She had signed the agreement that freed her from Ralph. The divorce proceedings were being helped on their way with generous dollops of legal aid for Ralph (as he was now penniless). As for the situation at the works, well, the new bank representative was just not as approachable as dearest Bernard had been in the past. The bank wanted their security, which was quite understandable as the loan repayments were not being met. So Amelia was bidding goodbye to Wilkinson Engineering Works, settling her debts and sorting out her duties.

Somehow the vision of living in France was fading fast. It had eventually occurred to her, after pondering on the returned letters for a week or so, that she had been well and truly done. There were moments when she had contemplated visiting France for perhaps, she thought, he had given her the wrong address. She even telephoned the hotel and, with her school girl French, had asked to speak to Mr. Tony Driver. Even her faltering knowledge of the language was up to translating the French equivalent of "No, there is no Mr. Driver here."

Suddenly she felt that she was all alone and with no one else to blame but herself. She had gambled everything and lost the lot. Her only lucky break was the fact that she could cover the loans – but only just – with the sale of the empty factory. Therefore she would not be reduced to living in a council house.

* * *

Fiona and James boarded the plane for Perth on April 4th. They had dropped two letters in the postbox, one was addressed to Tony Driver in the States and contained a cheque for services rendered and the other was addressed to Parker, Jones and Winstanley, which would explain everything. They had put a first class stamp on it and were quite confident that it would arrive the next day – the day that the brother who had done the most with his money would stand to collect the keys to his father's mansion.

* * *

Charles had not seen his wife for a couple of days but it did not worry him in the slightest. He did try not to regard her in a permanently bad light but he was distinctly hard pressed to rehabilitate her in his mind as his faithful wife. Sometimes, when he was feeling inclined to be charitable, he did think that perhaps there was not much difference between himself and Glenda and Fiona's relationship with half of the island of Jamaica – sex is sex, after all and, did he not pay for Glenda's cottage and slip her the odd hundred or two?

"What is the difference?" he asked himself. The answer was quite simple, he concluded after a moment's thought: his feelings towards Glenda veered in the direction of love; Page's feelings towards Fiona were based on hate. The fact that Fiona could have allowed herself to be used in such a way meant that she no longer held herself in any regard. It meant that Fiona hated herself also and thought that she had no worth. Charles knew that he could never again love her for she did not value herself; how could he, a true capitalist, love something that was without value? However, the onset of the important day of April 5th 1988 meant that he could put his wife out of his mind, for he had other fish to fry! And what a big fish it was, too! Blayborough House was due to be his, that he was quite sure about. He was glad, in a way, that Fiona had disappeared for he did not want anyone to spoil his moment of triumph.

That morning, he got up early and showered. His family had all been dispatched or had dispatched themselves. Who wants children hanging around on a day like this, even if for the most part they are practically grown-up? he thought. It was a difficult decision to know what to wear. Should he wear a suit, as if it was a formal occasion? Or perhaps a casual pair of trousers and matching jumper? Or a tweed jacket – in preparation for the life of a country gent? He settled on a pair of brown trousers and a toning blazer, it created just the right image, though just who he was trying to impress, he was not quite sure.

He collected together all his documents, which would prove beyond all doubt his chequered attempts to achieve great fortunes with the legacy provided. Even after bailing Fiona out for all she owed, bar a miserable £10,000 or so, it did not look too bad. He did contemplate that if only the date for deciding just who was going to inherit was October 5th 1987, instead of April 5th, he would have been fair skipping to the solicitor's office.

A thought did pass through his mind about just who was going to be there at the offices of Parker, Jones and Winstanley. Would James be sitting smugly, with suitcases full of fivers? What about Ralph, how had he done? He also hoped that John Bates would have had the decency to take the day off today – though he did not relish encountering the husband of Glenda, it did amuse him to think abut the anguish he had put the man through!

When he thought of James, he did think of his mother. It was not often that Charles thought of the woman who had given birth to him but when he did, he instantly dismissed the images that jumped into his brain. "Well, how was I to know that the man…" He never regretted telling his father about the conclusions he had jumped to. He recalled mentioning to his father how strange it was that there was a man in his mother's bedroom when mother was in the bath. His father had shown a great interest in his son's revelations and had rewarded him with a new bike. Naturally enough, Charles was not beyond feeling that here was a source of presents and thus dropped the occasional hint to his father about his mother's whereabouts with a certain man; just a couple of hints, in return for a generous cheque or two. It all culminated in his father asking his son outright: "Have you seen that man again, the one you saw a month or so back?" He had seen the man, so he told his father and got a most fantastic model aeroplane for his troubles. It was a pity at the time that his father had not taken the trouble to ascertain just where his son had spotted the man; but his father was too busy thinking the worst, especially as his wife had told him that she was pregnant with their third child. If he had asked, he would have been told that the man was seen walking down the main street of the nearby town, quite a long way from his alleged mistress. Charles did comfort himself at the time with the fact that he had never lied about the whole thing, for it was not until a few years after that he had found out just who the man was. He was the half-brother of his mother; so it was really quite impossible, or rather just not nice, for his mother to be having a relationship with her brother, half or otherwise.

"How was I to know that she had a half-brother who was the black sheep of the family? How was I to know that he would suddenly arrive on the scene and visit his half-sister? Any normal person would have introduced the man to the rest of the family," he said to himself, "and any normal person would not have a half-brother who was a petty criminal. No wonder she kept him tucked away! No wonder I jumped to the wrong conclusions!"

By the time he had found out the real truth, it was too late for his parents to patch up their differences and re-marry. Too much water had gone under the bridge by then. So, thoughts about his mother were hurriedly dismissed. He knew that his brother James had taken the divorce and eventual death of his mother really badly. Charles knew that there had been some sort of incident at Eton years later, when James was eighteen, but he was not quite sure what lay at the bottom of it. Charles merely put it all down to James flipping his lid.

It would therefore be interesting to meet up with his brothers James and Ralph. He hoped that they would not be too disappointed to lose their inheritance but, as he had always maintained, the rights of the first-born are paramount. Justice in the form of primogeniture would be seen to be done on the morning of April 5th!

* * *

"Don't bother me with the mail this morning, Shelley dear," shouted Paul Winstanley.

"Are you sure, Mr. Winstanley? There is a letter marked urgent, with a London postmark!"

"Junk mail, no doubt! I'll open it later and see what marvellous prize I've won, if only I'll go along to be grilled and buy some timeshare!"

"It doesn't look like…"

"Shelley, forget it! Get the coffee ready for the Pearson-Cooper brothers! This is the most interesting will I've ever handled – mail can be opened anytime of the day, it can wait!"

Shelley reluctantly put the letter to one side but not before wetting her finger and seeing if the ink on the envelope would run. It did, which proved it was not junk mail…

"Shelley, the coffee!" commanded her boss, so she abandoned the letter and went to brew up a pot of hot coffee.

Ten minutes later, Charles bounded up the steps two at a time. He was clutching a number of files that would not fit into his briefcase. He was shepherded into Paul Winstanley's office, where he was surprised to find that he was the first there. "The traffic was really bad this morning – I thought I'd be the last to get here!" he announced.

"Have some coffee, Charles; take a seat."

Charles did as he was told but in reality all he wanted was the keys to the mansion. They made polite conversation about the weather, whiling away the time waiting for the other two to arrive. Charles drank two cups of coffee and still there was no sign of anyone.

"Well, Charles, if they don't arrive in ten minutes then they forfeit the right to the house." Paul looked, for the umpteenth time, at the terms of the will. "Providing, of course, that you have actually done something with your £100,000. I mean, you have, haven't you? Even if it is only interest earned from the bank!"

Charles produced files and passbooks. He placed a pile of contract notes from the stockbroker and share certificates to match them all.

"Goodness me!" was all Paul could say as he saw his desk disappear under an avalanche of paperwork. "You've been very busy!"

It was a very long ten minutes but slowly the clock turned past half nine and Charles let out a loud "Whoopee!"

As the terms of the will insisted, the winner would have to have his claim verified by an accountant, who would examine the situation as it existed on the 5th April 1988. As Charles was the only contender, and a quick glance showed that he had achieved something with the money, Paul Winstanley decided that now would be a good time to visit Blayborough House.

"We can get everything checked later," he said, "let's go and give the place a look-over!" In actual fact, Paul rather fancied a trip out, especially at the client's expense! Charles readily agreed and all the bits and pieces were bundled up together to be sent off to the accountant's office.

"What about the other two?" asked Charles while they were preparing to go. "I mean, shouldn't they be here to return the money?"

This point was something that was causing the solicitor a little bit of concern – just where were they? However, a quick flash of inspiration came into his mind and he replied with total confidence to Charles' questions: "Don't worry – if they don't turn up, we'll take them to court! Could be tricky, but I think in the end, we would win. Nothing is ever a hundred per cent in this world – but I am ninety-nine per cent sure!"

Charles was too excited to take much notice of what Paul Winstanley said, he merely filed it for future reference in case James or Ralph had gone into hiding. They went in their own cars and travelled over to the house in convoy. Paul had various documents with him as well as a number of legal assistants to carry his papers for him. Charles went alone, relishing the journey to his inheritance.

* * *

The building was sensational and perfect. Somehow it was neither ostentatious nor beggarly in its proportions. It had all the beauty of a stately home without being outsize. Charles stood next to Paul and viewed it with wonder.

"Marvellous."

"Exquisite!" agreed Paul. His legal assistants just nodded their heads, unable to surpass the superlatives already used.

"I have the keys!" announced Paul, jangling them in the air. Charles bounded up the front steps which led to the portico.

"Let me open the door!" Charles said and he grabbed the keys from out of the solicitor's hands.

There were many keys on the bunch, as might be expected with a house that size. Some keys were large and old fashioned, others were indicative of the need to keep twentieth century criminals out through the use of a mortise deadlock, unpickable except by an expert! Charles surveyed them all and picked the one most likely to fit. It did not, of course, for the chances of the first key fitting the lock were about fifteen to one! He tried the next and the next, going around the ring until he came to the last one.

"This must be it!" he exclaimed, as the assembled party gathered round. "Wait for it!"

It did not fit either!

"We'll try another door!" suggested Paul and they all trooped off in search of a suitable entrance, dismissing the French windows as somehow not quite grand enough for such a triumphant occasion. They arrived around the back and found the tradesman's entrance, which was deemed better than nothing. Once again, they keys were tried in the lock and once again, they did not fit!

"We should have asked the Grosvenors to be here!" said Paul.

"Who are they – locksmiths?"

"No, they were left in charge of the house while it was empty!"

"Well, let's go and find them!" declared Charles and the five of them went off down the path towards the lodge at the bottom of the drive. It was all rather like something out of an Enid Blyton novel, all that was missing was the lashings of ginger beer.

It was Charles who went up to the door and knocked on it – he considered it his right, for they would ,after all, perhaps be his servants at some date, when he eventually entered the property. The door opened and a bleary-eyed teenage boy stared out at the throng on the doorstep.

"Hello."

"Is Mr. or Mrs. Grosvenor in?

"No, sorry – they're on holiday." And with that, the

boy started to close the door. "And I'm afraid I can't help you," he said through a small clink that was left before he shut it.

"What now?" asked Charles, a little baffled and somewhat annoyed that the moment that he had been working for was turning into a farce.

"Back to the house?" suggested Paul and so they all marched back. It was now starting to rain.

"I really don't understand it," began Paul, "the Grosvenors were supposed to be here, at their house, awaiting instructions. They should not be on holiday, not at all."

"Well, they are," said Charles, "so what are you going to do about it?"

"I don't know, I really don't know."

By now, they were all standing on the croquet lawn at the front, staring up at the house. It was then that one of the assistants thought that she saw someone looking out of the upstairs window. She did not say anything, in case she was mistaken. Then she spotted the face again, and this time she was quite positive about it and felt confident enough to voice her observations.

"Mr. Winstanley?" her voice quivered a little.

"Yes, what is it, Debbie?"

"I think I've seen someone looking out of the window on the first floor." They all turned to face her, then they all, in unison, swivelled the other way and stared up at the windows, of which there were many.

"Thank heavens!" said Charles, grateful for a sign of life. "It must be the Grosvenors. Their boy must have got things mixed up – he didn't look so bright. Now which window?"

"The third one along."

They all peered at the third window on the first floor.

"I can't see anything," Paul said, screwing his eyes up to get a better look. "Do you mean the third from the right or the third from the left?"

"From the right, from the right!" the assistant confirmed.

"Still can't spot someone – are you sure it wasn't just a trick of the light?" Mr. Winstanley turned to give Debbie a hard look which was designed to make her curl up.

"No, I'm sure," she answered quite bravely and then she cried out again, "There! There! He's moved or she's moved! The fourth window, the fourth from the right!"

"Yes. I can see him!" Charles pointed his finger in the direction of the house and the face at the window.

"Oh, yes!" agreed Paul. "There is a face there and it is staring at us!"

The five of them started to wave their arms and hands around like windmills in a row. The face disappeared.

"He's gone to open the door!" announced Charles and they all hurried off back up the steps, under the portico and waited by the front door.

Five minutes later, they were still waiting.

"Surely it doesn't take that long to open a door?" Debbie was getting quite emboldened now.

"Seems strange," Charles said and then he began to walk back towards the croquet lawn. "Let's take another look at the window."

Back on the manicured lawn, they all craned their necks to spot a face peeping at them. It was not long before they were rewarded and once again they waved but not so energetically this time, for they were aware just how foolish they were making themselves look.

A moment later, the window on the second floor opened.

"He's seen us," Debbie cried and they all stared expectantly.

"Can you make out who it is?" asked Charles, feeling that first of all, Paul Winstanley should know what Mr. Grosvenor looked like and secondly, he should take all the blame for the ridiculous situation that they were all in – standing outside in the rain like orphans trying to seek shelter from the storm.

"Mr. Grosvenor had flaming red hair – that chap has dark brown hair."

Charles decided that the best thing to do was to try and make contact with the man.

"Ahoy there!" he shouted as if they were all on the high seas.

The face came forward far enough for them to make out the features quite clearly.

"Good God!" Mr. Winstanley's jaw dropped.

"It's Ralph!" screamed Charles, losing all self control. "What's he doing in my house?"

* * *

Ralph stared down at the ridiculous group on the croquet lawn. He could not help but smile. He nearly laughed but decided that they – down below – might interpret that the wrong way and presume that he had gone mad. It was Charles, usually oh so superior, that gave him his biggest cause to grin. He nearly stamped his feet in a tantrum when he saw just who was in the house. It was a superb moment for Ralph, worth all the few weeks of planning, worth the expense of changing all the locks, worth sending the Grosvenors on holiday.

"I'm Ralph Pearson-Cooper," he had said to them. "You have been absolutely marvellous, taking care of this enormous property after my poor father passed on. It can't have been easy, waiting for the will to be finalised. Please – and I don't want any refusals – accept my offer of a two week holiday in Minorca!"

Off the Grosvenors had gone, leaving the house to Ralph. Of course, they had satisfied themselves about his credentials and asked to see his passport. With them out of the way, it was just a question of waiting for the suckers to roll up!

* * *

"This is a very interesting situation," commented Paul Winstanley.

"Interesting? I'd hardly describe it as that!" replied Charles. He was by now getting rather more than annoyed. As the minutes ticked by, it was apparent to all that Ralph had no intention of letting them in. Various thoughts about the situation were going on inside the assembled throng's heads.

"Well, let's take a look at the position that we are in, at this point in time," began Mr. Winstanley as they settled down on the grass to thrash it out, placing themselves on the travelling rugs that Charles always kept in his car.

"At this point in time, we are sitting outside my houses whilst my brother has taken possession!" said Charles.

"Precisely!" agreed Paul and his legal assistants nodded wisely.

"Precisely what?" asked Charles, feeling ominously like an outsider.

"Precisely that! Ralph has taken possession! He is in the house and we are not! He is squatting!"

Charles was now exasperated with the wise legal councillor. He flashed his eyes at the man, expressing more annoyance that way than any number of words could achieve.

"There is no need to look at me like that!" was the reply that the solicitor gave.

"There is every need! Your firm was supposed to be overseeing all this. I came over here as the rightful owner, only to find out that I have been usurped." Then Charles reached inside his jacket pocket and produced an envelope, and he flourished the contents. "This is your bill that you gave me before we set off on this fiasco. Neatly done, giving me the bill first! How can I pay for services rendered when I cannot even get into the house? And, what's more, why should I pay up when you haven't even done your job properly?"

Paul smiled his smoothest smile and answered: "The bill covers all the work for what was a very complicated will. My legal assistants and I put many hours into overseeing the fair running of the so-called competition, as well as paying the wages of the estate workers, collecting the rents, negotiating new leases, etc. etc. The bill reflects all the work involved up to this point in time, of course. In the circumstances…"

"In the circumstances, the bill will not get paid! You have failed to do what you were required to do – provide vacant tenure!"

"I'm sorry, Mr. Pearson-Cooper," began Paul. Charles knew, as soon as he heard himself being called by his surname, that he was on a losing wicket. "But nowhere in our instructions did we promise vacant tenure, as such."

"But vacant tenure was implied, because the house becomes mine as a result of death."

"But we cannot have been expected to provide for this type of occurrence. Our instructions were quite plain – to oversee the running of the estate until the new owner takes over, to take all reasonable protection against untoward events…"

"Yes – that's it! All reasonable protection – you didn't, did you? You allowed him to squat in my house."

"My dear Mr. Pearson-Cooper," began Mr. Winstanley in his best patronising tone, "I think that you will find that a court of law will state that we did all that we could. No one could be expected to provide total protection – the determined burglar, the arsonist and the ingenious squatter, all these types of people will defeat the best of security systems. There are quite a number of court cases to prove the issue; the police, I am afraid, will probably be the best witnesses… if you wish to take us to court then go ahead! It is a free country!"

Charles put his head into his hands and by doing so, admitted defeat. Paul smirked delightedly. Another satisfied client!

"What is to be done?" asked Charles somewhat woefully.

With an indulgent grin, Paul outlined the position as he saw it. "Basically, it is a question of possession is nine-tenths of the law. Ralph is in possession and he is in the strongest position. We must take him to court."

"Then we will!"

"I was hoping that you would say that," answered Mr. Winstanley quite truthfully. His legal assistant got her notebook out from her bag and started to take notes of the conversation, for future invoicing purposes.

"Right then, let's do it!" encouraged Charles, feeling that his move into Blayborough was only a matter of days away.

"I'm afraid it will not be as easy as that," began Paul dutifully, "you see, it is the question of the will – Ralph will no doubt argue that the house could just as much be his as yours."

"But it isn't his – it's mine!" exclaimed Charles.

"I know that, but will the judge be convinced? He might see Ralph as the victim, the rightful heir. Very difficult – I would have to take council's opinion."

At this, a second legal assistant began to take notes. Charles started to grow aware of what was happening, he almost could see a till emerging in the grass with a bill being rung up.

"Could this be expensive?" was the gentle question that he put.

"Not if you win, of course, for we would push for Ralph to pay your costs."

"But supposing he has no money? Supposing I don't get costs? And what if I don't win?"

"You are ninety-nine per cent sure of winning," said Paul, "and if you win and don't get costs, well, just sell an acre or two! What does land fetch these days? £2500 to £3000 per acre? Well, perhaps you might have to sell more than a couple of acres but you would hardly miss it."

There was a general sniff of money-to-be-had in the air, which encouraged Mr. Winstanley to offer the use of his car phone to find out their position from a barrister he knew.

"From London!" he said. "An expert in squatting laws!"

Charles was feeling somewhat forlorn at all this talk at his expense...

Ralph opened another bottle of port and reflected on his situation. He could not keep holed up in there for ever, he knew that. For one thing, his food supplies would run out, but his drink supplies were well stocked. The electricity and water were both turned on because he had taken the precaution of arranging for the utilities to be billed to him at the house. As long as bills are paid, the companies do not care who the real owner is.

He watched them sitting down – discussing it all, he presumed. He did feel a little bit sorry for Charles, who, after all, had probably more rightful a claim to the house than he did. However, as he had told himself many times in the past month, he was not going to be trodden on again – his wife, his wife's business, his wife's lover, Pat O' Reilly, the bank and so on, had all marched all over him.

Now was the time to fight back and even if, at the end of the day, he had to leave the house, well, he had at least caused the maximum amount of inconvenience to someone.

* * *

Just as Paul Winstanley approached his vehicle, his car phone started to ring.

"Winstanley here," announced Paul down his car phone.

"Oh, Mr.Winstanley! I've been wanting to contact you for over an hour now – you haven't been answering your car phone," exclaimed the secretary at the other end of the line.

"Well that is because I have been sitting on the lawn outside this wretched mansion for over an hour. We've hit a problem: one of the brothers is squatting in the house. I hope you are taking note of the time and date of this call, because there could be a lengthy and expensive court case to come out of all this."

"Yes, I am, I am."

"Well, we need to employ the services of that barrister in London, the Q.C., what is his name?"

"Sir Percy Blythe, do you mean?" asked his secretary in aghast tones.

"That's the fellow – charges double the rest but always, well nearly always, wins. Now what did you want to speak to me about?"

"It is a letter that arrived this morning. Apparently Charles Pearson-Cooper's wife is filing for divorce – she's run off to Australia with James Person-Cooper!"

"Good God!" Paul was getting quiet excited by now. His face was glowing pink and his chest was heaving with the joy of it all. "A divorce case as well! Experts from Australia – perhaps even to be settled in the Australian Courts. I could even combine it all with a trip to watch the Ashes…"

"But Mr. Winstanley," cautioned the secretary, who had a fair amount of nous, "won't all this affect the will? Won't it mean that Charles will have to sell Blayborough House to meet the divorce settlement?"

"Sell the house? He'll probably have to sell it anyway to pay the fees that will come out of getting it back for him! Oh juicy, juicy!" And with tha,t he replaced the telephone and almost skipped back from the car to the waiting throng.

* * *

Ralph watched the scene from a top floor window. He saw his brother storming around in a rage, closely followed by Winstanley and his entourage. Then, after about half an hour had passed, the human contents of the solicitor's office disappeared in their cars, leaving Charles alone on the croquet lawn. Ralph did reflect that he looked a little dejected but then that was part of the fun of taking residence in Blayborough – to make Charles uncomfortable!

Ralph did also consider that now was the time to put his next part of the plan into effect. After all, just having a bit of a laugh at his brother's expense was not enough – he needed a bit of his brother's money too! He heated up his final can of beans and ate them on a porcelain plate in front of the telly.

* * *

Charles sat down in his leather upholstered car, deep in thought. What a day! He had started off the day having won the house and with a wife, of sorts; by the time the sun was setting, he hadn't got his hands on the house and he had no wife! He decided that a review of tactics was needed. He could pursue it all in the courts. "Bad idea," he muttered to himself.

He could pursue Fiona and pluck her from his Barbie-eating, no doubt ex-criminal, surfing-maniac of a brother.

"Do I really want the slut back?"

There was only one answer to the problem and Charles put his Jag into purr mode and drove out of the drive and out of view.

* * *

Ralph pulled his attention away from Corrie and saw headlights coming on and the sleek shape of a car moving seamlessly down the drive. He delved into another mouthful of baked beans and settled down deep into the sofa. It had been an eventful day and as a few hours slipped by in mindless watching, Ralph retired to bed. Nestling down under the duvet, he made a mental note to himself to take a long hard look at his situation in the morning. There was no point in giving himself nightmares by thinking about it now – no house, no wife, no money.

* * *

Charles was, if nothing else, quite artful. There was never a problem which did not present to him a solution to match it. The house was his – the problem lay in the keys, they just did not fit the locks! So, armed with some tape and a hammer purchased from the local DIY store, he returned to attempt a break in. He'd seen it done on the TV so knew just what to do! First of all, lurk in the bushes keeping watch on movements within the house. Charles was not very keen on the lurking bit as the bushes were wet with recent rainfall and the undergrowth was a little bit, well, natural. Charles was never one to lurk where nature lived. He was far too refined for that. He spotted a fox, mouth full of young pheasant and an owl began to hoot in a nearby tree. It was very boring waiting for Ralph to move upstairs. By eleven-thirty, Charles was just about to give it up for the night when he saw movement in the drawing room then lights going off downstairs and on upstairs. He counted the windows and made a mental note.

"Typical Ralph – beds down in the smallest guest room!"

An hour later, when Charles knew that his brother must be in a deep sleep, he made his way to the back of the house.

* * *

Ralph was snuggled deep into the duvet, head resting on feather pillows and mind floating around the pleasurable places of dreamland. He never heard the noise of splintering glass; the slow and careful steps up the stairs and the creak of his bedroom door did not penetrate his slumber at all. It wasn't until the curtains were flung open, moonlight streaming in, and he heard the cry of "Wakey, wakey, you thief of a brother!" that he actually blinked and spotted the menacing figure of Charles.

"Oh, hi," was the best he could manage and then, as he noticed Charles muffled in a scarf with cap pulled down over his eyes, he added, "you're not going to kill me, are you?"

"What and get put inside for fratricide? And then your family would gain the house by default? I hardly think so!"

"What do you want then?" murmured Ralph, rubbing his eyes.

"I want you out of my home! Now, out, now!"

"But I don't have anywhere to go. I'm homeless."

"Not my problem!"

"I've got no wife."

"So?" commented Charles. "Nor have I – but do you see me pinching someone else's home just because she's upped and gone?"

Ralph was by now wide awake and sitting up in bed in his PJs. He could see a chink of light, a glimmer of hope that maybe Charles and he could find a common bond.

"What happened to Fiona then?" he asked in his best brotherly tones.

"Fled to Australia with her brother-in-law – our brother James!" And with that Charles plonked himself on the bed and un-muffled himself. "I ask you, the traitor."

"What a traitor," agreed Ralph, his face, showing concern, was trying to mask the underlying worry about what Charles really wanted. What was his game plan?

"Where's the lovely Amelia then?"

"Gone to live in France and taken the children! Wants to live the good life! Expect she's found a count and a chateau by now…" Ralph added woefully.

"Both our wives have fled the country – ironic, isn't it? Two years ago we were all living happy little lives and then a stupid competition comes along and disrupts it all. Still, I did win and you did lose. Pack your bags, Ralph, it's time to leave!"

Ralph decided to adopt a forlorn look. "Nowhere to go… such a big house for just you… couldn't I just stay in part of it?"

"Why? Why should I let you? Give me one good reason!"

"Because I'm your brother?" It was the only reason that Ralph could think of. "And you have no one else to share it with…"

Charles looked at Ralph and grimaced. It was true, of course, he did have no one and the house was a little on the large size. The whole competition business, the problems with Fiona and Glenda, the sheer hard work of making the most money had all taken a little bit of a toll. He did feel that winning was a hollow victory because he had lost everything that he had gained before. Perhaps he could be generous in victory – and he did need someone to help the Grosvenors with the physical work of maintaining the estate.

"You can have the west wing – that bit there at the end." He pointed to the later addition, which was pleasant enough and quite large by normal housing standards but quite small when contrasted to the rest of Blayborough House.

"Thank you," murmured Ralph.

"But remember this: it's my house, the whole of it, mine, all mine."

"Yes, Charles – I'm grateful."

"And you're only here because I'm a big softie."

Ralph decided to ignore that interpretation of Charles' character. He knew that Charles was only allowing him to stay because it suited him.

* * *

Two days later saw the brothers enjoying a pint at the Nag's Head. They were getting on quite well and

Charles was even allowing Ralph to wander into the main part of the house to watch television – though he was very careful to dispatch him back as soon as News at Ten had finished.

"It was a bit of a rum do that will," began Ralph as he stared at the pint in front of him.

"Well father was a bit odd – but you wouldn't have known that."

"I mean, leaving £100,000 to each of his sons – a test of strength almost."

"Yeah – a test of strength between the three brothers," replied Charles in a smug way that only winners can adopt.

"Except it didn't say three brothers," began Ralph, ignoring the little jibe about him not winning. "The will said £100,000 to be given to each of his sons."

"But there are only three of us…"

The two of them supped on their beer quietly, digesting their thoughts. The barmaid, who looked too old to be a maid, smiled across at them. Her red hair glistened orange under the overhead lights, her bosoms once no doubt large and positioned facing forward, now drooped down to her waist.

"Bet she was a bit of a floozy in her time!" commented Ralph.

Charles broke out into a cold sweat. "Oh, no… no, it can't be… Dad's bit of a floozy. Fiona told me he had a thing going with a barmaid at the Nag's Head – it must be her."

"Surely not!" replied Ralph, eyeing the woman. "She looks, well, she just doesn't, does she? She just isn't a looker!"

"But maybe she was, years ago." Ralph and Charles

both stared at the redhead behind the bar and she grinned back, drying the pint pots at the same time. A moment later, a voice called out from the back.

"Mum, where's my England shirt?"

The two brothers turned towards the back of the bar in horror as a young man emerged.

"I don't know, son!" replied the barmaid.

Transfixed by the scene, Charles' eyes were nearly popping out of his head at the half naked youth who looked every inch the same as he did when he was a twenty year old. Ralph choked on his beer, coughing and spluttering.

Charles spun in his chair to face the choking Ralph and nearly toppled over in his haste. "There's another brother!" he whispered, "Quick, back to the house. It's time to raise the drawbridge!"